CARPATHIANS

ALSO BY PAUL A. DIXON

An Occurrence at Owlskirk

Starfall

Moonfall

Sunfall

CARPATHIANS

PAUL A. DIXON

Cover design by Chris Era

ISBN: 979-8-3470-1478-1

Published in 2025 by Podium Publishing
www.podiumentertainment.com

To old friends, wherever you might be

CARPATHIANS

PROLOGUE

Sol System

AD 3124–3129

The centipede was the stuff of nightmares.

Ten-year-old Piotre Raskovich kicked the rotting log lying across the trail, laughing in delight when a chunk broke free. Then he saw the creature underneath curled up in a ball—and then it was moving fast, scarlet legs rippling in waves, its segmented body twisting and contorting as its fangs gaped wide.

He screamed, recoiling in horror as the centipede raced across the forest floor, heading directly for him. It was as though it meant to crawl up his leg, burrow into him, devour him from the inside out.

Then he found himself scooped up safely in the arms of his keeper, the woman who had brought him there to this ark for a short recess from the day's endless testing. She stamped a foot on the ground, the black dress boot of her Human Resources uniform blocking the centipede's path. The creature turned on itself and scurried back to the log, vanishing underneath.

Piotre buried his head into the woman's shoulder and began to cry.

Her name was Miss Annie. "It's okay, Piotre," she whispered into his ear, her voice calming as the soporific he'd taken for the drop-ship ride the day before. "It's just an insect. It's part of the ark. You're safe—it won't hurt you."

"It's not an insect." He sniffed away his tears. "It's a chilopod, and it's horrible, and I hate it."

"Quite right, Piotre," Miss Annie said. "As always, you're quite right."

"I want to go back."

"Of course," she said. She set him down gently, took him by the hand, and together they walked back up the trail.

⁂

The ark was kilometers across, a great translucent bubble containing enough tropical habitat to house tens of thousands of species that could exist nowhere else on Earth but had not yet been relegated to live on as DNA sequences and nothing more. Magellanix, Incorporated, owned it and others like it: different arks for different ecosystems, dotting the ice-free portions of Antarctica like a forest of blue-green mushrooms. Miss Annie had said the tropics were the most popular, the brightly colored birds particular favorites he was sure to like.

Years later, he would wonder if the whole thing had been staged. Had someone in Human Resources placed the log in his path, primed it to break just so, with the centipede poised and ready? They must have known his upbringing on Mars would leave him susceptible to that particular horror, that his childhood in an ancient, failing colony would render his young mind unprepared for the sheer richness of life the ark contained. He had never experienced nature unbound, never seen anything free to flap and squawk and cry, tunnel and creep and crawl. So different from the carefully controlled habitats of Mars, the only home he'd ever known, where a single organism out of place was cause for immediate alarm.

Maybe they'd guessed his weakness and decided to terrorize him in that particular moment, in that particular fashion. Planting a seed for the future.

Or maybe it just worked out that way.

When he was fifteen, Magellanix called on him a second time.

As before, they offered to fly him to Earth, but this time, his parents packed him a single bag. A change of clothes, a food bar made from pressed algae for the ride to the launch site, a liter of water, and a picture of his mother and father from years before, taken in one of the hydroponic farms the family had worked for generations.

His childhood: printed, framed, and wrapped carefully in a spare shirt.

"They'll give you everything you need," his father had said.

"We'll see you again," his mother said. She had a tear in her eye and did not add the word *soon*.

They rode the tube with him to one of the colony's remaining lift pads, where he boarded an old-fashioned, hydrazine-powered lifter that carried him to orbit. There he transferred to a more-modern ship for the three-day journey to Earth.

He remembered little about that part of the trip other than how small the domes of Mars had looked as the rocket gained altitude, watching the main viewscreen until he blacked out from the gees.

When he reached Earth he changed ships again, this time to a small, luxury drop-ship that brought him to a landing site just outside the largest of Magellanix's Antarctic cities. Miss Annie was waiting for him. She looked exactly as he remembered, but now he found her athletic form attractive, an object of budding sexual desire instead of maternal affection. Her age was impossible to guess, her eyes deep brown, skin golden, hair the color of Martian soil.

She wore a jet-black robe over her uniform, emblazoned with the Magellanix company logo and clasped at her throat by a ruby-colored stone the size of a small egg. Presentation dress, he would later learn, was usually reserved for the upper corporate echelons. He was being afforded an honor he would not appreciate for some time.

"It's wonderful to see you again, Piotre," Miss Annie said, as though they were the best of friends. "You're the last to arrive, so now we can start." She enfolded him in a hug that he returned awkwardly, an uncomfortable thrill racing through his teenage body.

A ground pod transported them inside the city's dome, then to the great central building that was Magellanix Corporate Headquarters. This was a mammoth, stone-colored construction of towers and battlements, built to recall castles and the kings that had launched their own expeditions in a millennium long past.

Even at fifteen, Piotre could see it for what it was: a seat of power; the beating heart of Magellanix's interstellar empire.

The others were waiting for them in a conference room on the first floor, a half dozen youths his age seated around an enormous table some fifteen meters in length. A small brass plaque had been inlaid on the table's edge near his seat, claiming the table had been made from koa wood harvested twelve hundred years ago, the same year as the company's founding.

"Welcome," Miss Annie said. A hidden holographic projector sprang to life, displaying the Magellanix logo high over the center of the table.

Piotre's was a curious mind. He had wondered at the history of the image before, and so knew the upside-down golden triangle was meant to be a stylized rendering of Earth's South American continent, transected by a swooping curve that represented the route Magellan himself had taken to shortcut it. Just as Magellanix was in the business of shortcutting great distances, searching for their own new lands to exploit.

As, of course, were their competitors.

"The seven of you have been chosen for a reason," Miss Annie said. She gave a secret smile. "You are all smart. Wickedly so."

He glanced around, taking the others in more fully, wondering at their stories, whether they had been brought there from colonies light-years distant or had grown up on Earth. One was clearly female and another male; the other four were not obviously gendered. All were probably about his age, no two dressed alike, and none of them with the slightness of frame and stooping of shoulders that suggested they were struggling as he was with Earth's gravity.

"But that's not why you're here," Miss Annie went on. "You're here because we can make you even smarter. More capable. Elite."

The company logo dissolved, replaced now by projections of Magellanix Information Officers, dressed in black and gold and hard at work, poring over displays across which arcane equations scrolled. And then the image shifted again, this time to starships. Great interstellar craft, first blinking in and out of existence in thunderclaps of released energy, and shown orbiting planets he didn't recognize.

Those images in turn gave way to diagrams of impossibly complex molecules: organics, proteins folding and unfolding like some great three-dimensional jigsaw puzzle.

Starships and drugs; new colonies and new worlds. It was an elixir, a drink straight from the cup of human achievement, all that was possible in this, the thirty-second century of the common era, the five hundredth year of human exploration of the stars. And until this very moment, all of it forever out of reach for poor Piotre Raskovich. He, after all, was just a Martian, a hick from the sticks, child of a dying colony, hillbilly primitive whose parents scratched soybeans from aging hydroponic farms, eking out a living on a world that should have been abandoned hundreds of years before.

The images faded away and the Magellanix logo reappeared, once again hanging serenely in midair.

It was intoxicating.

Then again, so was Miss Annie.

She let the silence build. Then she said, almost in a whisper, "Let me tell you a story. It will seem unbelievable to you, but it is true. There was a time when none of this was possible. When all these gifts were denied to us. Do you know why?"

No one did.

"Because of a single poor assumption," she said. "Our ancestors believed all these advancements were unachievable with something as primitive as the human mind. And because they assumed that, they made the gravest of mistakes.

"They placed their faith in the promise of machines.

"It's hard to comprehend," she went on, "but there was a time when humans believed they could invent an artificial intelligence to do their thinking for them. They even gave it a name: generalized AI. G-A-I." She enunciated the letters carefully, with clear distaste. "And do you know what happened?"

Piotre glanced around the room. No one spoke, the others all staring transfixed at Miss Annie.

"Nothing. Nothing happened!" she said. "Year after year, decade after decade, the breakthrough always promised, forever just around the corner. I know," she added, holding up her hands as though to still disbelief, "it seems absurd now. But our ancestors were primitives. We must forgive them and think about this from their perspective. Because by that point in history, it took an entire lifetime just to master what was already known. How can you invent, if it takes so many decades to catch up with what has come before?

"And yet! At the same time, because faster-than-light travel was deemed impossible, how could we ever hope to reach the stars?"

"Generation ships?" A girl to Piotre's right murmured the words. He felt a flash of resentment; he should have been the one to speak up.

Miss Annie smiled beatifically at the girl. "Quite right," she said. "And I think we all know what happened with those." She tossed her head as though dismissing the thought. "So, there they were," she said, "our poor ancestors: trapped on a dying world, unable to live long enough to create anything new, with nowhere left to go. Small wonder they hoped for an artificial mind to deliver their salvation."

She paused again, looking at each of them in turn. The Magellanix logo grew larger and brighter until it seemed the only source of illumination in the room.

"Fortunately," she said, "our founders, those great humans who built this company, understood two things. First, constraints can always be removed. And second, not to wait for the future.

"If the problem is human cognition, enhance it! If the trouble is the human lifespan, extend it! We have done both of these things, and you seven will be the recipients of those gifts. The question is not whether you're brilliant. Our selection process is not some simple canvassing of geniuses. Genius is mundane.

"You have been chosen for your unlimited potential. Magellanix is going to invest in each and every one of you. To give you the gift of the future, and to ask you to build it in turn."

And so it began—but with a catch. That investment had to be protected.

Which was how he met the centipede a second time.

Human Resources called it Behavioral Conditioning. In the years that followed, Piotre would come to decide the term was the most honest, transparent language the company ever used.

The exchange was straightforward. Magellanix would devote its considerable resources, most notably proprietary drugs of its own invention, to granting him progressively more cognitive ability as he advanced in his career. In return, he would submit to a procedure that would guarantee those new powers would be forever used with a single purpose: the enhancement of Magellanix shareholder value.

Miss Annie spelled it out for him, alone now in a much-smaller room. He could say no. He could return to his life on Mars, with no hard feelings or consequences of any kind. His parents wouldn't even have to pay for the trip, and Magellanix would never bother him again.

He signed his name to the lifetime employment contract as fast as his shaking fifteen-year-old hand would allow.

Miss Annie smiled. "Congratulations, Piotre," she said. She bent forward and gave him a small peck on the cheek. "And now it's time for me to say goodbye. Someone else will be your guide from here."

She let herself out of the room. He felt the disappointment of her absence immediately, a hollow pit forming in his stomach at the loss, followed by a growing sense of trepidation. There he was, sitting alone, just a table and two chairs and blank white walls for company. All the room's displays had been deactivated; there wasn't a single interface he could use.

At that moment, he realized he had never been so alone.

Then the door opened and a diminutive figure stepped through. The individual was no more than five feet tall, dressed in a cloak that concealed them from head to toe. He could barely make out their face; couldn't begin to guess their age.

They pushed their hood back, revealing a bald pate and skin the color of alabaster, so smooth it looked like a coating of wax. Their eyes were deep violet and seemed to glow with their own light. Those eyes! They held him transfixed, like a snake regarding a bird in one of those arks from so long ago.

"Hello, Piotre," they said, their voice deep and resonant, all out of proportion to their size.

"Who are you?" he stammered.

The figure cocked their head, still holding his gaze. "Your guide."

"Where are you going to take me?"

"On a journey."

"What does that even mean?" he demanded, trying to keep the quaver from his voice.

"It means I am going to ask you some questions. Then I am going to put you to sleep, and that wonderful mind of yours will do the rest."

"I'm supposed to fall asleep right here?"

Of all things, this bothered him the most, the idea that he would simply put his head on this desk and nod off.

"This is," he said, "well, it's just a room."

"Precisely," the strange new arrival agreed. They smiled, but there was nothing reassuring in it. "All you need do is close your eyes and cast your mind back. Tell me of your arrival on Earth—the first time."

He would never learn his guide's name, though they would work together many times in the years ahead. In that first session, they took him back to his ten-year-old self, the visit from five years before. The trip to the Ark, the centipede, that moment of sheer terror.

Their conversation drifted to even-earlier times. His childhood on Mars, his base memories, nursery warrens and trips across the surface in ancient, seldom-used wheeled vehicles. Learning to work in the hydroponic farms; the constant fear of radiation and exposure; the endless hours of exercise meant to build a physique that could endure a heavier gravity even though none of them ever expected to leave the world they called home.

Then they skipped forward again, to more recent years: home, school, work, and what his life on Mars held in store.

At last, his guide seemed satisfied. "We have enough for now," they said. "You may take this."

Half-asleep and half-hypnotized, Piotre had just enough awareness to accept the thin strip of paper his guide was now offering.

"What do I do with it?"

"Place it under your tongue."

"Will it hurt?" he asked.

For the briefest instant, he thought he saw a trace of sorrow in those inhuman eyes. Perhaps he only imagined it, but years later, long after he was out of the business of human emotion, living in a world of cold facts and pure data, he would still remember that moment.

"Maybe," his guide said. Then their voice changed, all business again. "Now take it."

He did as he was told. This flimsy substance dissolved under his tongue, and then he lost consciousness and remembered nothing more.

When he awoke, his guide was gone—but the centipede was with him. He could feel it, woven around his spine, its head nestled in his medulla oblongata, its venomous fangs forever poised, dripping, ready to strike.

He put his hand on his neck, pressing the skin, certain he would feel its hard shape wriggling underneath.

But of course, there was no centipede. Not really.

It was just his imagination.

All in his mind.

In the fullness of time, the centipede would become many things. Keeper and conscience; agent and trusted companion; deeply comforting metaphor. It was a gift and it was a certainty. It filled him with a living understanding that he was physiologically incapable of an act of betrayal.

Magellanix had liberated him, he would come to realize, from a burden of doubt that he would never need know.

But he would always fear it.

Until, one day, it was gone.

BOOK ONE

RAGNAROCK

CHAPTER 1

Planet Ragnarock (Magellanix-claimed)

AD 3184.02.02

Fifty-five years later

Mission Generalist Feyis Sado glanced over at his copilot, wondering whether she was going to lose her nerve. And thinking—damn it! It only felt like he was in love with this woman. For the hundredth time, it wasn't the real thing.

The cargo lifter rattled and shook, atmospheric turbulence tossing it around the sky. Materials Specialist Callandra diMarck—Callie, she said to call her—was hunched inside her biohazard suit, clinging to her flight controls like a barnacle to a rock. Which was as good a metaphor as any, Feyis supposed, marine invertebrates being the most advanced life this ice-covered world called Ragnarock seemed to offer.

He couldn't see how the plane could take much more of this, and the heavy gravity wasn't helping, either. Callie had selected the flier's design and printed it out back on *Accipiter*, the ship that had brought them here. She'd babysat the flier and the rest of her gear when they drop-shipped to the main camp near Ragnarock's equator. She knew the plane's tolerances better than anyone. If Callie was nervous, he was nervous, but she hadn't said anything, and he didn't want to ask.

The smart move would be to give up and land, setting the flier down on the pack ice that permanently covered Ragnarock's oceans this far south. But Piotre Raskovich, *Accipiter's* Chief Information Officer and thus the second-most-powerful individual within at least a hundred light-years, had said to make best speed to the planet's southernmost continent. "Best speed" did not mean wasting a day sitting on ice, trickle-charging their batteries on cloud-filtered sunlight.

Mr. Raskovich had tasked them with determining what had killed this world. He wanted an answer, and it seemed like a simple-enough question. There were only two possibilities: either Ragnarock had died of natural causes, or it had perished in a nuclear apocalypse some millions of years earlier. Their job was to figure out which answer was correct, and Piotre Raskovich was not someone Feyis wanted to disappoint.

Accipiter's CIO was not noted for patience with contractors who failed in their assignments.

Feyis shoved these thoughts aside and said, "I think we're going to make it." Which was optimism he didn't necessarily feel, but he wanted to get a gauge for where Callie was at.

"Copy that," she said.

The bio-suit's helmet speakers provided perfect acoustics even with the storm raging outside. She sounded like an angel singing in his ear.

Callie. His heart skipped a beat. *Cal-LEE.* He smiled, annoyed with himself for it, and glad she couldn't see his reaction. The suit was supposed to be keeping him safe from the airborne pathogens they were forced to assume Ragnarock possessed. It would be weeks before the biologists were cycled awake and dropped to camp to perform their hazard sweeps. Personally, he doubted there was anything dangerous down there, but the suit also had a mirrored visor that was at least preventing him from embarrassing himself.

That made it worth it, barely. The damned thing was uncomfortable.

He knew his absurd schoolboy crush was just a side effect of post-hibernation procedures gone awry. Someone in *Accipiter's* Human Resources department had made a mistake and cycled him and Callie awake at the same time. He could imagine how it must've looked: his pod opening up and ejecting him into the hibernation hold, he drifting there in zero gravity, aimless, mental processes not fully online after six months of downtime, and wham! He bumps right into Callie, just starting to get it together herself. A moment of pure physical comedy ensues, slapstick farce while they untangle naked bodies and near-skeletal limbs.

Then the inevitable happens. His poor beleaguered brain just sort of latched on, and now it feels like he loves her, in the way an ark-raised gibbon would love a stick puppet for a mother if that was all it had ever seen.

The folks in HR must have had a good laugh when they performed their incident review later.

In any case, the feeling probably wasn't mutual. The phenomenon was known as "unidirectional imprinting," and he wished there was a drug he could take to make it go away. Instead, he was stuck flying a mission feeling like a teenager, and him pushing fifty, Callie too, both of them considerably older if he counted years spent asleep.

He risked a quick look out the window. The plane was an atmospheric lifter with a cockpit positioned amidships, so his view was mostly of an enormous, matte-black, solar-skinned wing whose trailing edge was lined with an array of micro push-blades doing their best to provide headway in the teeth of this storm. The wing was made to flex and bend, but in this much turbulence, it flapped up and down like a wounded bird.

He twisted his body a little further, craning his neck inside the biosuit's helmet, which gave him a view of the plane's bulbous fuselage. It was the same flat black color but boldly emblazoned with the bright yellow outline of an isosceles triangle, drawn base up and apex down, transected right to left by a gently curving arrow. The company logo of Magellanix, Incorporated: their employer, owner of *Accipiter*, and all the hardware and people involved in this mission.

He'd been contracting for Magellanix for a long time, looking at that logo for years. Marketing splashed it on everything: gear, suits, ships, the food packs they ate, even the containers they used to recycle their own waste. He'd stopped thinking much about it, but here, in this moment, it bothered him. It struck him as garish, inappropriate even, given what they were supposed to be doing.

"Feyis?"

Callie's voice, interrupting his reverie. She must have felt it before he did, his not paying attention, thinking about logos and corporate marketing nonsense, and oh, sweet absent gods, this was not the time for career introspection, because right then, the bottom fell out as the cargo lifter plummeted a thousand meters in a handful of seconds.

"Dammit!" He cranked on the yoke, cambering the wings and arresting the dive. He cursed again, more quietly this time, as they slowly leveled off.

He glanced at the altimeter, and then the charge indicators on the main batteries, mentally computing whether they had enough juice left for one more try.

"What do you think?" Callie said.

He shook his head. "Not sure. Is your gear okay?"

She ran a system check. The lights on her command screen flashed green. "Looks like it. The only thing I'm worried about is the radioisotope sniffer. The rest of it is rugged enough."

Meaning, Feyis knew, the modular defense pods she had converted for this job: one of *Accipiter*'s anti-ship lasers and a series of miniature fusion bombs.

"Okay," he said. "Let's try it again."

They made it, barely. What was supposed to be a yo-yoing series of long, gentle climbs and battery-recharging glides from equatorial base camp to seventy degrees south latitude instead turned into a teeth-rattling, bone-jarring nightmare that left them with just enough juice to snick over the teeth of the mountains at the edge of Ragnarock's southern continent. Batteries spent, Feyis picked out the nearest snowfield and brought them down. The plane shuddered gently as skis met ice. It was the only part of the flight that felt smooth.

"Nice landing," Callie said.

"Thanks," he muttered, feeling his cheeks burn.

Feyis cycled the doors, irising the cockpit hatch open. A ramp extended, and they made their way together into the howling wind, in so doing becoming the first humans to set foot on Ragnarock's southern continent.

They tramped a slow ambit through the snow, circumnavigating the plane.

"What do you think?" he said.

"Good a spot as any."

"Copy that. Let's see what you've brought."

The entire aft end of the plane's fuselage was built to swing open, providing maximum efficiency for loading and unloading. He climbed inside, working his way through a maze of ruggedized packing crates, all labeled and sporting the same logo as the plane.

"Inventory check?" Callie said.

"Copy."

"You should see: one deep-bore laser drill with mounting rack, one deep-scan sonar array, and one radioisotope analyzer, hopefully still working or we're going to do this all over again tomorrow. Which," she added, "doesn't sound very appealing right now."

"No argument there."

"Also a winch, four kilometers of micro-cable, one ice corer, and a power source for the laser."

"*Power source* meaning the direct-fusion devices?"

"Correct. Oh, and also a forklift. Mounted on skis."

"Right," he said. He picked through the hold, ticking off the items on her list. "Gear check confirmed," he said, a few minutes later. "Let's get started."

It was heavy work, a lot of hauling and grunting and repositioning and shoving, but Feyis didn't mind. He was too relieved at the feel of solid ground underfoot, even with the heavy gravity and the dull ache in his joints. Hibernate six months, jump through gods knew what higher dimensions, wake up a thousand light-years distant, drop-ship to a planet, fly a solar-powered cargo plane through hours of unceasing storms—and now go unpack some boxes.

At time-and-a-half pay, he wasn't one to complain.

Callie handled the assembly while he contented himself with putting the crates where she directed and handing her tools. He watched, impressed, while she constructed scaffolding ten meters high. This would serve as a mount for the laser, which she mounted pointing straight down at the snow.

He was falling further in love by the moment. Idiocy, but that was still how it felt.

It was springtime in Ragnarock's southern hemisphere, and at this latitude, the days were twenty-eight hours long. They were still working when the sun set, dropping behind the same peaks he had thought might scrape them out of the sky. The brief night settled in, bringing with it a more serious cold. The plane had enough reserve power to keep its instruments active, but he was forced to shut the landing lights down.

Fortunately, their suits came equipped with high-powered flashlights. Together they soldiered on.

Callie had appropriated the direct-conversion fusion devices from *Accipiter*'s stores. Typically, these would be used to produce the current required for a laser to cut apart an enemy starship, but in this case, they'd be using it to punch a hole through a couple of kilometers of ice. Which turned out to have surprisingly similar power requirements, the way the math worked. A bit of perspective there, he thought. *Accipiter* and ships like it were basically habitat bubbles armored in the equivalent of portable glaciers.

The fusion devices didn't look like much, just little black spheroids a meter and a half across at the fat part. The power cabling was more impressive. When Callie was done with the assembly, a half dozen meter-thick, heavily insulated power leads snaked out from the bombs like a nest of boa constrictors he'd seen in a refuge habitat years before, back on Earth.

In the end, the rig Callie constructed consisted of a winch, a couple of kilometers of cable, and a saw-toothed steel cylinder that was the corer itself. The laser, she explained, was just to punch the pilot hole. After that, gravity would do the work.

He had done some strange things in his career, but this was a first. *We are literally*, he thought, *using the power of a star to burn through a few million years' worth of accumulated ice, after which we're going to drop an ice cream scoop down the hole.*

Finally, Callie pronounced herself satisfied. "That's pretty much it," she said. "Let's take a break, okay? System diagnostics are going to take time, and I don't want to miss anything."

"Copy that," he said. "This is definitely a measure twice, cut once kind of situation."

They used a pair of empty crates for seats and spent a few minutes sucking on food tubes inside their helmets.

"Does the plane have any battery left?" Callie asked.

"Not much," he said. "Why?"

"I want to turn the landing lights back on for a second. Marketing asked for some pictures before we start drilling."

"A photo op? Really?"

"You saw the logo on the corer, right? They put it there for a reason."

He considered for a moment. "Can I ask you something, Callie?"

"Sure."

"How do you feel about that?"

"It's really not my call," she said.

He grunted. "No, I suppose not."

They got to their feet and took Callie's photos together: cargo plane in the foreground, with the Magellanix logo center-frame, and the last flicker of its landing lights illuminating the scaffolding and the laser drill.

"One for the record books," he said.

"Or the quarterly shareholders' statement. Want to go see if anyone used to live here?"

"It's what Raskovich is paying us for," he agreed. He killed the landing lights, and together they flicked on their suit torches and trudged back through the snow.

It was time to finish the job.

A few minutes later, he found himself watching as a bright blue, actinic beam stabbed down out of Callie's rig and lanced into the snow. The top few centimeters vanished in a puff of steam.

"Looking good," Callie said, sounding pleased. This was just the sighting laser. The actual drilling, the high-powered part, would be done at a wavelength they wouldn't see at all. "Fire it up."

Burning the pilot hole took an hour. They could've done it faster, but they needed to be careful not to superheat the ice, which could cause it to detonate like a bomb.

When they reached the two-kilometer mark, Callie unlocked the winch and dropped the three-meter-long corer down the hole. It took a couple of minutes to reach the bottom, and twice that to retrieve it. When it finally reached the surface, Callie laid the cylinder of ice they'd retrieved flat on the ground, and then used what looked like a butcher knife to section it into ten-centimeter chunks. She loaded these one at a time into the isotopic analyzer while he readied the winch for redeployment.

"What are we looking for, anyway?" he said. "Evidence of a nuclear exchange, obviously, but what specifically?"

"If there was a nuclear holocaust on this planet, the signature will be pretty obvious," Callie said. "We'll probably have a whole soup of long-lived goodies to work with. Cesium, selenium, zirconium, you name it. Depends on whether they used fission or fusion warheads to do the deed."

He wasn't sure what to say to that.

A few minutes later, she had her answer. "This one's negative," she said. "It's what I expected. We stopped the hole short of what the geologists said would be minimum depth."

"So, we do it again?"

"Yeah. We'll need at least a dozen."

He sighed. "Copy that."

They lapsed into silence, settling into a routine. Three minutes to drop, ten minutes to retrieve, another fifteen for the sectioning, feeding slices of ice into the isotope sniffer, and reading out the results.

It was going to be a long night.

❧

The sun was just poking back up above the far horizon when they had their answer at last. It was weirdly anticlimactic: just a single word on an old-fashioned ruggedized display, liquid crystal tech a thousand years old.

CONFIRMED

Feyis shook his head in amazement. "Damn, Callie," he said. "We're standing on a holocaust world."

"I wonder who they were," she said.

He closed his eyes, imagining. What had this place looked like? It must have been warm and green, maybe even down there, this close to one of the poles. He tried to picture the planet's ocean, now ice-covered except in a narrow band around the equator, swarming with life.

The gods-awful wind could have been just a tropical breeze.

Who had they been? What had they been like? What happened to cause them to do this to themselves?

"Maybe we'll never know," he said. "Everything must be buried now, ground down under all these glaciers. What I wonder is—how many planets does this make?"

"As far as I know, fourteen holocaust worlds have been declassified, so this is at least the fifteenth," Callie said. "I bet no one knows the real number. Magellanix has its secrets. So do TransGalactic, InterTech, and some of the smaller corporations as well."

He thought about that. Callie was right, of course. Companies held their navigation data close, but as far as anyone knew, none of them had ever found a living sentient species. Not in all the years since humanity had reached the stars—and now there was one more to add to the annals of the dead.

"We're going to be here a while," he said finally. "They'll leave a field team when *Accipiter* goes back to Earth. Think you'll stay if they offer it?"

"It'll be a lot of overtime," she said. "Seriously, though. It'd be good to be planetside for a while, even on a high-gravity world like this one. What about you?"

"An assignment like this? We could retire off it if we stay out here long enough. Either way, we'll be working for Magellanix the rest of our lives."

"Not necessarily," Callie said. "They might declassify it eventually, sell the navigation data to anyone else who wants to come and have a look. I doubt there's anything of commercial value out here. We could get out of our contracts if we wanted. Why, are you thinking about changing teams?"

"Not really. I've done it before, but I don't know if I'd bother again."

"I know what you mean," Callie said. "I worked for InterTech for a while. In the end, they're all pretty much the same."

"Yeah. Well, look—we better call this in. Mr. Raskovich is going to want to know everything.'

"I know. Just give me a second, okay?" Callie said.

The snow swirled around them, the isotope sniffer still blinking its soft blue readout.

Confirmed. The death of untold billions, eons ago. Confirmed.

"Sure, Callie." He felt it too. "Take your time."

CHAPTER 2

Magellanix Vessel Accipiter

Ragnarock far orbit

Piotre Raskovich kept his cabin far from *Accipiter*'s spinning ring, preferring weightlessness during those times when the ship wasn't under acceleration. Were he of lesser rank, this would never have been allowed. It was a blatant violation of Human Resources procedure, but being a Chief Information Officer was not without its privileges. He was answerable only to the captain herself—and that only in matters of daily operations and security. The data, the ship's most valuable asset, were his province, his kingdom and domain.

As such, he was afforded certain eccentricities.

He held the temperature in his quarters constant at ninety-nine degrees, the humidity just below a hundred percent. Was this some subconscious calling to mind of the tropical ark he had visited on Earth in his youth? Deference to the centipede, his constant companion and moral compass these last five and a half decades? In introspective moments, he thought perhaps that was part of it.

Mostly, his body simply seemed to prefer things this way.

It was a body that should have died long ago. He was skeletally thin, rarely ate, and never exercised. He'd spent his career in and out of hibernation, awake to endure the gravity of sub-light transit only rarely, forced to set foot on a planet almost not at all. Save for the performance reviews that required that he return to Earth every decade or so, a ritual he abhorred.

In spite of the neglect, his body lived on, carrying the thinking mind that was his true self along with it. It would for at least another century. A gift of the drugs he had access to, the never-ending cascade of exotic compounds making its way through his bloodstream, into his marrow, his very DNA, reconditioning, restoring, rebuilding him over and over again despite the absurd demands of a life spent almost entirely in deep space.

Another hundred years, and he knew very well time on a treadmill wouldn't change it by a single day, despite what Human Resources wrote in their procedure manuals. His lifespan was a privilege conferred by his rank, part of what he had bargained for, a tidy return on the price he had agreed to pay.

One day, he would die, sooner than was strictly speaking necessary, because there were drugs and treatments not even a Chief Information Officer had access to. Those, he knew, were reserved for Board members alone: the true immortals, or as close as it was possible to be.

But he seldom wasted time thinking about this. The centipede discouraged such lines of inquiry. No shareholder value would be created in contemplation of the fact that he had long since reached his own terminal rank, that no promotions remained.

Instead, he and the centipede agreed, the right thing was to live the life that had been given to him and do his job.

So, that was what he did, and the most effective way to do it was simply never to leave his cabin. He opened his door once per day to eject his spent hydration and food packets into the corridor beyond, along with sealed containers containing the modest amount of effluent his body still managed to produce. Each week, he assigned a member of his staff the task of placing the next day's food within arm's reach and retrieving his shit for recycling. Whether the individual he chose regarded this duty as a privilege, reward, or punishment, he had no idea. He did tend to select those that showed the most promise in their work, but why he did this, he wasn't sure he could say.

And yet! If physically he knew himself to be nearly an invalid, virtually he was just short of a god. He had embedded three-dimensional projectors in all four walls of his cabin, transforming his tiny living space into a fully rendered, interactive, never-ending data stream, wired to every sensor unit, subsystem, interface, and remote on the ship, a volume and diversity of information an unenhanced mind could not begin to comprehend. His entire body served as the interface. He had long since discarded his uniform, and stuffed his company-provided clothes and personal items into a locker he seldom opened. It was easier and more comfortable to perform his work naked. He'd trained *Accipiter*'s AI to recognize every finger twitch, head nod, and eye flick. He could play, process, and manipulate his data streams like a conductor directing a dozen orchestras at the same time.

His days were twenty-two hours of awake time and two hours of drug-induced coma, floating weightless and naked in a stream of information that would never cease, all his to command, process, and interpret. His job was to turn it into an asset, to guide Magellanix in how best to monetize it. All in pursuit of that elusive core value, the deepest-held conviction, the overarching philosophy forever binding him and his centipede, the demon familiar that lived inside.

Now, as ever and for always: the enhancement of shareholder value.

When the call came back from the contractors on Ragnarock's surface, Piotre was conducting a routine inspection of the exterior of *Accipiter* itself, remote-piloting a flitter up and down its kilometer-long hull in search of any signs of damage. Of particular concern were the half-dozen detachable remotes the ship possessed. Each was equipped with enough raw thrust to reach any of the other three planets of interest in this system, and while he didn't expect those worlds to harbor life, there was always a chance. His best estimates put the probabilities between one and a half to four percent, good enough odds that each planet would be investigated in due course.

He could have sent the remotes on their way weeks ago, back when *Accipiter* first arrived in-system. Instead, he had held them in reserve until the team on Ragnarock's surface answered the most important question: was it a holocaust world or not? Was the ice age that gripped the planet a consequence of its orbital eccentricities or perhaps a product of a long-term decline in the radiation emitted by the red dwarf the planet orbited?

Or was it biogenic in origin?

The issue was of course the planet's potential long-term value to Magellanix. Ragnarock contained life but not in any great diversity. Its drug-discovery prospects were thin, limited to under-ice algal communities and a food chain that extended to base-level invertebrate equivalents but not much more. As far as he knew, nothing resembling a fish swam Ragnarock's remaining ice-free seas. Certainly, no birds flew its skies.

The only thing that was flying down there was a cargo lifter whose progress he had been tracking carefully for the last twenty hours. To his surprise, the pilot had succeeded in reaching Ragnarock's south pole without stopping to recharge his batteries, a credit to his determination and skill. Even now, the crew were deploying their ice corer, and soon enough, they would provide the answer to his question.

If Ragnarock was a holocaust world, Piotre would put his remotes into orbit and use their imaging equipment to accelerate the process of constructing a complete, high-resolution scan of the planet's surface. On the other hand, if this were just another albedo-locked planet with a paucity of indigenous life but nothing interesting in its past, he would send his remotes to the rest of this system, in the hopes that something of value in this region of space might yet be found.

Time passed. Then, without warning, the image he was inspecting—a close-up of the main engine of one of the remotes—flickered momentarily as an overlay appeared in the data stream.

The contractors at the planet's southern pole had finished their work.

He lifted a finger fractionally. The data visualization shifted, the pod's thruster replaced by a stream of isotopic readings that had just been uploaded for him.

He had his answer.

Ragnarock was a holocaust world.

He inclined his head slightly, causing two personnel files to appear. Mission Generalist Feyis Sado and Materials Specialist Callandra diMarck. They had done their jobs well. Had, in fact, exceeded his expectations.

No higher praise was possible.

He ordered the contractors to confirm their findings with additional ice cores. He had little doubt the result would be the same. The isotopic readings appeared unambiguous.

Then his thoughts leapt forward as he began to calculate the time scales involved. How long before had the apocalypse taken place? He computed fallout levels, half-lives, temperature declines, glaciation, the onset of an ice age, and the advancement of those ice sheets across the continent. All these calculations and more tore through his mind as he reconstructed what this place might have been like, what vestiges of a dead civilization might still be recoverable after so many eons had passed.

He needed more information, and there was no reason to waste time.

He cycled *Accipiter*'s remotes active and ran them through preflight checks, computed a set of orbital parameters that would give them optimal coverage of the planet's surface, brought their engines online, and detached them neatly from the hull. He nudged them up and away, sending them into an interlocking set of orbits from which they would detail every nook and cranny of the planet. They would map magnetic anomalies and sea-surface height, measure atmospheric temperature gradients and jet-stream patterns, calculate bathymetric profiles of the ocean, scan the surface topography, compute details of continental drift, and on and on, telling him everything it was possible to know.

The odds of finding anything of commercial value weren't great. But there were always possibilities, places where something might have survived. A nuclear-capable species would likely choose to bury its trash. Deep-bore wells, stable salt domes, seafloor trenches—these places would survive an ice age.

Yes, he thought. Begin with the scatology. Perhaps the legacy of the species that lived there would be written in some stockpile of nuclear waste that could be found and dug up, to see what might yet be learned.

If the centipede was a cat, it would have purred.

CHAPTER 3

Feyis helped Callie drill three more ice cores. All the samples came back the same, the fallout layer present every time, radioisotope signatures reconfirming that this world had died in a nuclear fire some three million years past.

The rest of the field crew and officers were half a world away, and with no remotes yet in orbit, there was nothing else to bounce a signal from other than *Accipiter* itself, leaving Feyis to uplink their findings directly to the ship when it passed into range.

He received a recall order in response.

"Looks like we're finished here," he said into his helmet's transmitter. "Apparently, Mr. Raskovich is pleased with our work. Our Chief Information Officer says head back to camp, and job well done."

"Copy that," Callie said. "I'll break down the gear. We'll leave the rigging behind. It's pretty much frozen solid at this point. No reason to haul the spent power units back, either."

"Understood." He performed some quick arithmetic in his head. "We'll be a lot lighter."

"Less time in the air," she said.

"Less stress on the wings."

He ran system checks on the flier while Callie repacked the laser drill. The flier's wings were woven from lightweight composites that were rated for extreme cold, but he'd been doing this kind of work too long to take anything for granted. The memory of the storms they'd endured on their way there was still fresh in his mind.

The craft's diagnostics claimed it had survived the trip unscathed. He grunted in satisfaction and prepared to get them airborne again. All told, they'd been on the ground a little over fifteen hours.

The mountain crossing proved less harrowing the second time around. With fully charged batteries and less mass to haul, they soared without incident over the craggy peaks guarding the edge of Ragnarock's southern continent. Then the terrain flattened out, the violence of glaciers and crevasses, jumbled ice falls, and great, towering seracs giving way to a featureless plain that seemed to stretch forever. This was frozen ocean underneath them now, with an absence of landmarks and an uncertain sense of distance he found disorienting.

Base camp was still twelve thousand kilometers away, the initial survey team having landed their drop-ship at the extreme northern extent of this ice sheet. Biologically, Ragnarock was almost dead, but geothermally, the planet was still very much alive. Rapid seafloor spreading at the equator injected heat through underwater vents and volcanoes, which, combined with an equator unblocked by any continental land mass, had left an ice-free sea that wrapped the planet in a blue-gray-white belt of liquid water.

The weather wasn't great this far south, but it was nothing compared to storms that raged over the planet's equatorial ocean. He was glad they wouldn't have to cross it.

This planet was just hanging on, he thought. The land had died, but life began and ended in the oceans, and for a stretch of ten degrees of latitude north and south of the equator, the seas yet lived. Ragnarock still possessed enough life for there to be oxygen in the atmosphere. Maybe some chance at a better future remained.

Or maybe not. He'd never know; that much was certain. The time scales involved were too vast to comprehend.

They flew on in silence, each bent to their tasks. For the moment, there was little left to say.

After sixteen hours aloft, they picked up a homing beacon: base camp at last. Visibility was good, and though his long-range radar was black with atmospheric violence raging over the open ocean a few hundred kilometers north, it appeared they would make it home before the next weather system drifted far enough south to bother them.

An hour later they were in visual range, and he felt himself relax at last.

"Almost home," he said.

"Copy that. Look, Feyis," Callie said, pointing. "We've got ourselves another drop-ship."

"Huh. That was fast."

The new arrival was a squat, ugly thing, a fattened cylinder with a bulbous nose and stubby wings that looked like vestigial limbs. Ships like these had enough attitudinal control to displace themselves a few thousand kilometers as they plunged through a planetary atmosphere but weren't capable of anything close to sustained flight. This one had landed vertically, excavating a great pit in the ice with its thrusters on final descent, leaving its stubby nose poking upward like a missile ready for launch.

He brought the flier down on a makeshift runway, a sheet of ice now marked by a series of beacons and flashing strobes, over which the team had spread a composite material that provided extra friction for the landing carriage. He swerved the craft at the end, sliding sideways like a skier dumping speed at the bottom of a run. A moment of silliness, showing off at the end of a very long three days of work.

Callie laughed.

"You'll get yourself in trouble doing that," she said.

"It's in my contract."

"What is?"

"Creative expression upon successful mission completion."

"Really?"

His turn to laugh. "No."

"Well, that was still some nice flying out there, Feyis."

She placed a gloved hand lightly on his forearm. Then she turned, opened the cockpit door, and clambered down off the wing.

After a moment, he followed, wondering as he went about the solemn absurdity of his situation. He wondered, too, what mad assignment his employers had in store for him next.

The answer proved to be construction duty. Evidently, his skills as a pilot were not required at the moment, so the lieutenant in charge had assigned him the task of assembling a new mess hall, one big enough for thirty, with an actual kitchen.

Such was the life of a Mission Generalist.

First, though, they gave him a few hours of rest, which his body accepted greedily. When he awoke, the next storm had already settled in, blowing off the ocean and reducing visibility to a few tens of meters. Feyis sighed, stretched inside the common shelter he shared with a half dozen other contractors, and donned his suit.

Then he trooped across camp to a makeshift supply depot, where the materials he needed had been hastily piled in a rough jumble of packing crates. He was too professional to complain. Heavy gravity, howling winds, and biting cold were part of the job.

Inside the crates, he found a mosaic of nano-woven tiles. They were flexible, unbelievably tough, and fitted to starship tolerances, which made them pathogen-proof. They would seal hermetically when laid against each other; even something the size of a prion couldn't get through the seams. Material like this would help keep them alive down there indefinitely.

It was not, however, labeled in anything approaching an intuitive manner. Clearly, Callie hadn't been in charge of this particular pile of gear.

He was rummaging through yet another crate, trying to figure out which contained the pieces that would make the floor, when his helmet warbled at him. It was a private call, peer-to-peer.

Callie.

His heart leapt idiotically. He looked up to see her making her way through the storm, even as he heard her voice in his ear.

"Just came to say goodbye," she said. "I've been redeployed."

"Already? Lucky you," he said, trying to sound nonchalant as he waved his arms at the mess of crates around him. "What's the assignment?"

"Deep seismic scans in the mountain range a couple of thousand klicks east of here. Mr. Raskovich's people say it's the most seismically stable formation on the planet."

"You're going spelunking?"

"So it would seem. At least I get to punch some more holes in the ice."

"Stick with what you know, right? I wonder why they didn't ask me," he added ruefully.

"Didn't you hear? A fresh pilot drop-shipped down while we were away. In fact, there's a whole second mission team now; they were just waiting on me. But you must be happy for the break."

"Break!" He laughed. "This hardly qualifies."

"Well, we could use a kitchen. That is going to be a kitchen, right?"

"Who knows? You stay safe out there, Callie."

"You too, Feyis. Take care of yourself."

"Always do."

He got to his feet, stretched awkwardly in the heavy gravity, and shambled to the edge of camp, in time to watch her heavy lifter take off.

It was an expert job. Whoever the new pilot was, they knew their stuff. He grunted, annoyed with himself for his peevishness.

Then he made his way back to his crates. He was getting paid by the hour. It was time to get back to work.

CHAPTER 4

Piotre's remotes settled into their new orbits. From there, they would capture high-resolution images of the entirety of Ragnarock's surface. The process would take time, first to identify stable stratigraphic features that might have made good candidates for long-term nuclear storage, and then to dispatch field teams to investigate in more detail. They would perform lidar scans and magnetic surveys, bore holes through the ice into the strata beneath, detonate explosives and measure the resulting acoustic signatures of the bedrock, sniff the dirt for lingering traces of radioisotopes, and on and on, all those techniques used to search for signs of a vanished civilization.

They might even be forced to explore the seafloor. There were plans for deep-sea submersibles in *Accipiter*'s data stores, and the ship's weavers were perfectly capable of producing such things. Piotre contemplated beginning production now but decided against it. There were higher-priority items to construct first.

All this work would be complicated by heavy gravity, thin air, and still-incomplete biosurveys. The field teams couldn't yet say for certain whether they could even breathe Ragnarock's air.

The work proceeded slowly, days ticking on the ship's chronometers as processes and procedures unfolded according to his design. Piotre was content. He had long since learned patience. Now he passed the hours as he always had, sifting his data, adding the remotes' image streams to his feeds, absorbing and integrating information as it came to him.

He almost might have called himself happy, except for the problem of his commanding officer. Captain Johnston was growing anxious to leave, and he could guess why. She had a holocaust world to report, and a tidy mission bonus to collect when she did. As would he, for that matter, but the money meant little enough. Real rewards were forever denied to him. His corporate masters were never going to give him a governorship over a planet of his own or grant him access to that class of life-extending pharmaceuticals reserved for the true elites: the CEO, the Board of Directors, that highest of castes to which he would never belong.

He felt a little twinge, the gentlest nudge from his Conditioning. The metaphorical centipede stirring, flexing its fangs ever so slightly, seeming to say *Get back to work.*

He took a deep breath, grateful for the reminder. Lifting an eyebrow just so, he caused his data feeds to refocus on a massive range that divided Ragnarock's largest continent neatly in two. The mountains had likely been uplifted at least a hundred million years prior, based on his best estimates of continental drift. A good candidate site for a field team to survey in detail.

The moment of discontent passed, as it always did. Content again, he returned to his job.

Eventually, Captain Johnston would be put off no longer. She demanded an in-person meeting to discuss progress and would accept no excuse.

Piotre was considering the implications of this when, without warning, an alert flashed in his data stream.

GEOMETRIC ANOMALY

The words appeared with a soft accompanying chime, which was as intrusive as he ever allowed his information systems to be. He froze the offending feed and zoomed in on the images that had triggered the alarm. One of his remotes had passed over a four-thousand-meter, seemingly dormant volcano near the equator, part of an island chain positioned in the narrow latitudinal band of ocean that remained ice-free. The volcano's flanks were glaciated, with snow and ice running almost to the water.

He centered the images on the crater and saw patches of bare rock and snow—and something else as well. There was a massive, mirror-bright, tessellated silver sphere where no such thing could possibly be. It was over a hundred meters in diameter, resting in the bottom of the crater like some long-missing god had rolled a favorite marble into a cup.

What in all the worlds was this? He had absolutely no idea. A construct of some kind, clearly. Some sort of artifact left behind by an intelligent civilization.

His mind spun, racing as only a Chief Information Officer's could. He set aside his shock and considered the matter rationally. It took him less than a minute to conclude that who had built it and why they had done so were unknowable, at least for now. But as for when? That he could estimate.

He flicked through images of the island chain with a twitch of his left hand. The volcano in question appeared to no longer be active, but less than fifty kilometers away, a neighboring island bore the scars of recent lava flows.

He called to mind all he had learned about the planet's plate tectonics. Then he did some basic arithmetic.

The conclusion was inescapable. Unless he had badly underestimated the seafloor-spreading rates, and the plate bearing the island chain had moved far more slowly than any reasonable estimate, the island volcano was at most two million years old. It would have been dormant for perhaps half of that.

And that meant its dormancy must postdate the holocaust that ended all higher-order forms of life on the planet by well over a million years.

Which in turn implied that whoever put that structure in the volcano's crater wasn't from Ragnarock. The planet's natives would have been long dead before the island even formed.

A realization then.

He, Piotre Raskovich, Chief Information Officer of the Magellanix deep-space scout *Accipiter*, having spent his entire career equating information with value, processing data, negotiating exchanges, protecting secrets—having been in the business of turning knowledge into profit—he and he alone was suddenly in possession of the single most valuable fact in history.

He knew the answer to the question that humans had been asking since they first craned their necks upward and looked at the night sky in wonder.

Were we the only ones ever to reach the stars?

The answer was clear.

No. No, we were not.

Because he, Piotre Raskovich, was staring at direct evidence of the existence of another spacefaring race. It was the first such humankind had ever discovered.

Improbable, yes. In the extreme. But no other conclusion was possible.

And in that instance, in that perspective-bending, utterly unexpected raw moment of the unknown, a remarkable thing happened.

He lost his mind.

Part of it, anyway.

His Behavioral Conditioning—reinforced over so many years in anticipation of every foreseeable event, now faced with something so extraordinarily out of context—simply . . . failed.

And in that moment, he realized what he was going to do with the information he and he alone now possessed.

He was going to steal it.

And then he was going to sell it.

He was going to ransom it to the highest bidder in exchange for the one thing his corporate masters would forever refuse to give him, no matter how hard he worked, no matter what value he created on the company's behalf.

He was going to trade it for his own immortality, or as near as was possible to achieve.

The thought formed so unexpectedly that he winced, squeezing his eyes shut, bracing for the pain that must certainly follow. This was treason, an idea he ought not even be capable of conceiving.

But no pain came. Not the barest nudge.

He opened his eyes and looked around his cabin, confused.

The image of the object, artifact, weirdly tessellated alien sphere—whatever it was—hung motionless in midair.

He let his thoughts return to what should have been inconceivable. Knowledge without precedent, his and his alone. Information was his to do with as he saw fit. To sell, for his own gain.

Nothing. Again there was no pain.

The centipede was nowhere to be found.

The enormity of that fact hit him without warning. His body bent in half and he retched. With no time to find a refuse bag, tiny globules of bile and vomit arced away from him, filling the cabin's air. He threw up over and over again as if his body was freeing itself from a long-held source of contamination, engaging in some desperate act of detoxification.

The fit probably only lasted a minute, but it felt like hours. When at last the spasms stopped, he hurt everywhere. He poked a rib gingerly, wondering if he had broken something. He wiped spittle from his mouth and came away with blood.

As any movement hurt more than the last, he did his best to drift in perfect stillness for a time.

He was free to act. There was no one to tell him what to do.

How extraordinary.

How delightful!

Then, slowly, a plan began to form in his mind.

The first step was obvious. It was imperative no one else see the images. Ordinarily, his cabin was in no danger of intrusion, but now his bio-monitors must be spiking off the charts. He called them up and glanced through the data his living quarters were even now reporting back to *Accipiter*'s coterie of medical officers.

His heart was racing, palpitating arrhythmically, and his body temperature had shot upward as well. Not good. This was as at-risk as his profile ever appeared. Even with his reputation for living a hermit's life, never to be disturbed, the ship's doctors would soon come knocking on his door.

He took a last, fascinated look at the tessellated sphere. There was something hypnotic about it. It was like staring at a fractal, its geometry unnerving in its perfect complexity.

Then he waved it away, feeling a moment's pang of regret at the loss.

He would have to secure the images and make certain no one else onboard *Accipiter* ever discovered them. He'd also have to re-task the remotes such that none flew over the island again. But he couldn't just delete the data; he'd need it when they returned to Earth. He would have to liberate it from the ship's data stores in such a way that no one would detect the theft.

That was just a technical problem. If he couldn't figure out how to smuggle information off his own ship, he wasn't much of a CIO. The company's entire security system was predicated on the assumption that he wouldn't try.

Another realization then—and a much harder one: he himself would have to flee. Get clear of Magellanix altogether and seek asylum in a city owned by a rival corporation. It would have to be TransGalactic or InterTech. They were the only two in possession of biomedical enhancement technology equal to what Magellanix itself had invented, bought, or stolen through the centuries of its existence. None of the other players were worth his time: not AdvoGene, StarTech, or Recombinant Technologies; not Biorigami or FactorX, or Longenity, and certainly not the idiots at Advanced Composites or AllSynth.

No, only InterTech or TransGalactic could pay him in the currency he sought.

His mind raced on. Suppose he could do it, find some way to reach a rival city and defect. Even if he could get the data off the ship and himself to a safe harbor, he'd still need negotiating leverage. Some sort of failsafe, to prevent being betrayed in turn.

Maybe he could threaten to have the knowledge made public if he didn't survive. He considered the idea and discarded it. That threat wouldn't be enough. What he needed was a motivated buyer. Someone who wanted him alive.

Then it hit him. Of course! This planet, this find, was only half the value. He was the other half. Because he, Piotre Raskovich, was evidence that Magellanix's Behavioral Conditioning could be broken, even at the most senior levels in the company.

Make an example of me, he would say. *Give me what I want, and find a way to make sure everyone knows it. Imagine not just one Chief Information Officer but a string of Magellanix senior executives knocking on your door.*

Keep me alive as an example for others to follow.

Would it work?

He thought it might. In return, he'd ask for the governorship of a low-gravity world, access to the best life-extension technology they had to offer, and a security detail the likes of which few had ever seen.

Still his mind raced on, planning, assimilating, and doing what it did best. But this time with no centipede: his lifelong companion and captor had vanished. He had no ethical quandaries and no company values to uphold.

Piotre, Piotre, Piotre. He need only think of Piotre Raskovich.

The blessed, wonderful, all-important me.

A new thought occurred. He almost cursed out loud when the full implications hit him.

The images weren't going to be enough.

Not that someone would think he faked them. They'd subject him to deep interrogation. His buyers would know he wasn't lying, at least not intentionally, and hopefully reach that conclusion while his mind was still intact.

But they still might not be convinced. Not on the strength of a series of reconnaissance photos, along with the navigation coordinates to reach this planet.

He wouldn't be if he were doing the buying.

He needed more data to sell. He needed to subject that alien sphere, ship, observation post, weapons storage facility, breeding pit, bit of public art, cast-off piece of junk, whatever it was—he would have to subject it to every instrument and diagnostic he could imagine. A full field survey. He would need data so comprehensive, no one would doubt the veracity of his claim or the authenticity of the find.

The problem was that no one else on *Accipiter* could know.

He'd have to do the work himself.

And that meant he was going to have to go down there. Worse, he doubted it would be possible to land a flier in that crater, not with the top of the mountain stuck right in the middle of the planet's unrelenting jet stream.

No. He, Piotre Raskovich, the least physical of specimens, was going to have to climb a frozen volcano on a high-gravity world. He could only barely remember the last time he'd walked on a planet at all.

He would need help. He had neither the skill nor the physical ability to do it alone. Maybe that pilot—Feyis Sado? He seemed competent.

Piotre pulled the man's file and reviewed his employment history. Yes. Feyis could do it. It was exactly the sort of thing a Mission Generalist ought to be able to manage.

But he still needed an excuse. What possible reason could he give Captain Johnston for volunteering to visit the planet's surface?

She'd never believe it. She was a meddler, would never just take him at his word. It felt good to be honest with himself, to admit how much he disliked her. This was the sort of thing the centipede would never have allowed.

But what to do about her? Well . . . what if she wanted to believe?

Was it possible?

The remotes were tasked in orbit. If they were going to survey the rest of the planets in this system, *Accipiter* itself would have to do the work. Maybe he could volunteer to remain in the interest of saving time. He could stay and oversee the work, allowing *Accipiter* to depart, survey the three other in-system planets, and then return for him. Yes. His captain would love the idea. It would accelerate the time they could leave this system, return to Earth, and collect their end-of-mission payout.

She might make admiral on the strength of this find and be given a multi-ship fleet. Still, he would have to make it her idea. She'd never ask it of him, but if he demonstrated a little willingness to consider it? Not volunteer; grudgingly accept.

He would find a way. Her goals were straightforward. They could be used. Motivations could always be exploited.

The centipede had taught him that.

CHAPTER 5

A week later, Feyis found himself relieved from construction duty at last. The camp had grown by the day as contractors cycled awake on the orbiting *Accipiter*. A steady stream of gear, building materials, and personnel drop-shipped down, temporary shelters gave way to permanent facilities, and soon they'd install a nano-weaving facility of their own. The outpost would become a colony, capable of sustaining itself indefinitely.

But first, they needed to know whether the air was safe to breathe, and Feyis had drawn the assignment of flying the pathogen surveys. The latest drop-ship from *Accipiter* brought the bio-team that would perform a detailed sweep of surviving indigenous lifeforms. A full lab had been constructed to support them, in which vat-grown human tissue would be subjected to whatever this planet had to offer, a sort of macabre decontamination procedure run in reverse.

Returning to life as a pilot was welcome, even though the surveys required him to fly over the equatorial ocean and into the teeth of its never-ending storms. Insofar as life remained on the planet, it was concentrated in the sea, so that was where most of the work would be done.

It was a tricky business. The biologists had demanded an expanding ring of concentric arcs for their surveys, each flight to extend farther outward. Ice, water, and sky: day after day, Feyis found himself skimming low over the waves, dropping sample bottles that sank to prescribed depths, uncorked themselves, and returned to the surface. Deployment was dangerous; retrieval was worse. The new flier he was using was an omnidirectional craft, capable of hovering in place. It was his job to sit just over the waves while one of the scientists—usually still weak from hibernation—attempted to hook their sample gear with a cable and wind it back into the flier's hold.

He wished, repeatedly, that Callie was with them. The gear was hard to spot in the heavy seas. A rogue wave could swamp them, or an unexpected downdraft dip their nose, sinking the flier in an instant. If that happened, he doubted they'd make it out in time, and even if they did, he couldn't imagine they'd survive for long in these seas. Exposure suits or not, the nearest help was hundreds of kilometers away, and the water was terribly cold.

Occasionally, the sampling gear would fail to return to the surface at all, and they'd waste hours in futile search. He had no idea how this was possible with all the technology at their disposal. They had jumped between the stars to get there but couldn't always retrieve a bottle from the sea. Fortunately, life as a field contractor had inured him to this kind of thing, and the mission scientists didn't seem terribly surprised when it happened either.

All told, it was tedious, dangerous work, and he returned each day exhausted. He told himself it was necessary, although he couldn't imagine they'd find much. The odds that an Earth-compatible pathogen had somehow endured, that something down there could actually take hold in a higher-order Terran primate felt improbable in the extreme. The biologists seemed to think so too, but procedures were procedures.

At least when they finished, he'd be able to take his damned exposure suit off.

Then, at the return from yet another survey, a five hundred-klick ambit as far over the ocean as they had yet ventured, Feyis arrived back in camp to find himself at a party.

Callie and her team had found what they'd gone looking for, and judging from the traffic over the common channel piping through his helmet, the entire field team was celebrating. He listened, shaking his head in wonderment and trying to make sense of it all. Evidently, her crew had punched a hole through a glacier and made their way into a system of stable caverns they'd located with their deep seismic scans. They followed readings from their radiometers kilometers underground, where they found a nuclear-waste dump, eons old. Row after row of sealed plastic drums containing the by-products of primitive fission systems, buried millions of years ago by someone who must have thought to leave them hidden away until they were no longer a danger.

He smiled. True to Callie's word, she'd gone spelunking—and struck gold.

The lieutenant in charge of the camp was an older woman named Farrow. She always struck him as a decent sort. Now she had decided to honor the oldest of spacer's traditions by giving the camp a break from field protocols, in the form of a ration of hard alcohol.

They were using the mess hall to drink rum. Which sounded pretty damned good to him, but he never made it that far.

"Sado!" The transmitter in his suit blipped to life without warning: Farrow's voice on a peer-to-peer call, for his ears only. "Report to command."

"Aye, sir," he said. Routine reflex put some snap in his response, a habit acquired from years spent keeping full-time employees happy. He took a last regretful look across toward the mess hall and then turned away, heading for the officers' quarters.

The camp's command module was a semi-rigid structure, a tent with spines and ridges supporting a flexible material that could handle the storms Ragnarock had to offer. He stripped his gear in the outer lock, relieved to be free of his suit at last. His ears popped once as the pressure equalized, his Eustachian tubes having long since widened and been made flexible by a lifetime spent doing exactly this sort of thing.

Lieutenant Farrow was sitting at the console that served as the camp's main link with *Accipiter*. She had silver hair, a sharp nose and sharper chin, and a sense of humor undiminished by her officer's Conditioning and years of command.

She looked up from the message she'd been scanning and studied him, her flat back spacer's eyes narrowed in consideration.

"Friends in high places, Mr. Sado?" she said.

"No, sir. Only bosses, sir."

That earned him half a smile. Farrow was all right, as full-timers went.

"Have a seat. It's probably easier if you read this yourself."

He took the lieutenant's chair and scanned the message quickly. Then he read it back more slowly, confused.

"Piotre Raskovich is coming here?" he said at last.

"So it would seem."

"I thought the man never left his cabin."

"I cannot comment on our CIO's personal habits, Mr. Sado," Farrow said. "Though no doubt his reputation is well known."

"But why me?"

"He requested you specifically because you are our most experienced pilot. His drop-ship touches down in two hours. You'd best get prepped."

"But what's the mission?"

"Classified. Whatever it is, you will do this detachment proud, Mr. Sado."

"Yes, sir."

"And Feyis?"

"Sir?"

"Good luck."

He nodded and stepped back into the airlock, thinking as he did that something in the lieutenant's voice seemed off. Then he realized what it was. There had been a note of compassion there, which was unsettling.

When had a lieutenant ever felt sorry for a contractor?

And what in the hell did their CIO think he was doing out of his cabin, down there on an actual planet?

He supposed he was about to find out.

CHAPTER 6

Feyis made his way back across camp to prep the flier for Piotre Raskovich's arrival. This required no conscious effort; he'd long since grown used to the machine and its idiosyncrasies, but it did give him time to think.

He assumed they were heading for the nuclear-waste dump Callie and her team had discovered. Why, though, would Piotre Raskovich go to the effort to travel to Ragnarock's surface for an in-person inspection? He couldn't imagine the crash course of drugs the man must have needed to make himself capable of surviving in the heavy gravity down there. It seemed an extreme step to take. Callie's find was interesting—but this was at least the fourteenth holocaust world humans had discovered. Nothing about it struck him as particularly unusual.

Then again, he had long since grown used to the vagaries of senior officers. If it meant a chance to see Callie again, who was he to complain?

He had just finished preflight when he first felt and then saw Raskovich's drop-ship descending from the sky. He didn't envy its occupants. His own trip to this place was still fresh in his mind, hammering through all that atmospheric turbulence, getting tossed around like a cork in the sea.

He strode to the landing zone at as brisk a clip as Ragnarock's gravity would allow. The days of drop-ships carving pits into the ice with their retro-thrusters were over. Another team had laid down a micro-surface that could withstand the intense heat, their once-primitive camp continuing its growth into a full planetary outpost.

The drop-ship put down smoothly on the new tarmac. A few minutes later, a long ramp extended and two suited figures emerged, one visibly supporting the other.

The former would be a Security team member, Feyis presumed. The latter, a Chief Information Officer far from home.

Strange times.

He watched them make their way toward the officers' quarters, then followed at a discreet distance.

They'd call him when they were ready.

❧

It didn't take long. Less than thirty minutes had passed before Lieutenant Farrow's voice sounded in his ear.

"Sado! Get in here."

"Yes, sir!"

He had positioned himself across from the camp's command center such that, once summoned, his arrival would be prompt. The Security guard that had accompanied Raskovich was standing at attention outside but made no move to stop him as he stepped into the outer lock.

He waited out the compression cycle, removed his helmet, and entered the main habitat, where he got his first in-person view of *Accipiter*'s CIO.

Piotre Raskovich did not look like a healthy man. His face had the sunken appearance characteristic of extended time in deep space, and he wore a synth-weave suit that fit skintight and showed every detail of his watery flesh and protruding bones. His muscles twitched at random intervals, his pectorals and biceps and deltoids all seeming to fire independently of one another. The synth-weave was administering electro-stimulation, Feyis assumed, pulsing current, probably working with some drug regimen to promote rapid regrowth of as much muscle tissue as possible. It was grotesque.

Whatever his reasons for being there, Piotre Raskovich clearly hadn't planned his visit very far in advance.

But even worse than the man's ruined body were his black spacer's eyes, which bored in on him with an intensity Feyis found deeply disturbing. Piotre Raskovich struck him as either deeply in pain or half-mad—or maybe both.

"Mr. Raskovich. Sir!" he said, smartly as he could.

"Mission Generalist Feyis Sado." The words came out in a heavy rasp, half-statement and half-question.

"Sir."

"The flier is ready?"

"Yes, sir."

"Very well. Lieutenant Farrow, you are dismissed."

The lieutenant acknowledged this with a "Sir!" of her own and headed for the exit as fast as dignity would allow. She caught Feyis's eye once on her way out the door, then ducked into the airlock and was gone.

"You are rated for all classes of planetary exploration," Raskovich said.

"Grade Four, sir. I can take you anywhere you want to go."

"You also possess a high-level medical rating?"

"Affirmative, sir." Why he was being questioned like this? Certainly, a CIO would have access to every detail of his career.

"Let me speak bluntly, Mr. Sado. You're wondering what I'm doing here. You may trust that I am fully aware of my own reputation. It's not unearned."

"Sir?"

Raskovich held up his right hand, as though bidding Feyis be silent. The muscles in his arm twitched and spasmed, causing him to appear to be shivering with cold, even though it was a comfortable sixteen degrees centigrade in Farrow's command center.

"We leave immediately, Mr. Sado. You'll receive the final coordinates when we are airborne. This mission is classified beyond the grade of any personnel currently present on the planet's surface, including Lieutenant Farrow. Do you understand?"

How best to respond? Feyis decided on the truth. "Not really, sir. I assumed we were headed for the waste dump. Sir."

Raskovich almost smiled, his thin lips stretching in a way that suggested the expression was unfamiliar. "An honest answer, but your assumption is incorrect. We're going climbing, Mr. Sado. You're going to lead me up a mountainside. And as you can see from the state of my body, you'll have to do the heavy lifting."

"Sir?" The word came out automatically. He didn't know what else to say; none of this made any sense.

"You will fly us to a volcano in the equatorial zone, Mr. Sado. There we will land, and you will lead us up it. Gather what you require, but say nothing to anyone. My Security escort will take me to your flier. After that, it will be down to you."

Feyis shook his head, bewildered. At least he knew a dismissal when he heard one.

"Yes, sir!" he said, one last time. He saluted for good measure, then turned crisply on his heel and left the command tent, wondering exactly what the hell he was getting himself into.

Gather what you require, Raskovich had said. Feyis had little idea where to begin. He had no idea where they were headed or what mountain his CIO wanted to climb. With limited time and unable to ask any of the other field personnel's advice, he decided to stick to the basics. This was going to be rope and ice axe work, doing things the old-fashioned way.

It took him an hour to collect his gear. By the time he finished, Piotre Raskovich, true to his word, was waiting alone for him in the flier. Feyis performed his preflight inspection thoroughly, taking his time. The tiny craft's hold was packed with survey gear Raskovich must have brought with him from *Accipiter*.

Wherever they were going, it looked like they were bringing a full field station with them.

All was in order. He got them airborne without incident, taking it easy on the ascent for Raskovich's sake. The weather was even cooperating for a change. He banked the plane lazily in a wide arc, planning to circle the camp until Piotre Raskovich told him where they were going.

The CIO had been motionless beside him throughout the takeoff, but now the man jerked to life. He reached out a suited hand and entered a set of coordinates into the flier's nav system. A holo-display flickered to life, showing their current location and where they were meant to go.

"Your coordinates, Mr. Sado," Raskovich's voice rasped over the suit's comms.

"Yes, sir."

Feyis studied the tactical readout. They would be flying several thousand kilometers to an island chain located deep in Ragnarock's equatorial ocean, nearly a sixth of a world away.

The flier had the range, but what route should he take? He could see no reason to travel over water any more than he had to. Better to stick to his current latitude, remain south of the ocean for the next eight thousand kilometers, then make a hard right turn and head north into the ever-present equatorial storms.

It would be a long flight, though no worse than what he and Callie had done. The first part wouldn't be easy, but he had no way of knowing what weather systems lay ahead, what they'd encounter on the final leg of their journey.

He entered the route and eased them onto the proper course.

"Better weather this way," he commented.

"Understood, Mr. Sado."

They flew in silence for a time. Then, without warning, as though the thought had just occurred, Raskovich said, "Tell me about this plane's AI capabilities."

"Sir?"

"This craft has the most hours aloft of any of the fliers that have been drop-shipped to camp, does it not?"

"Yes, sir," Feyis said. "I've been using it to fly the bio-sweep surveys."

"Yes, I am aware." The man's voice was as icy as the landscape below. "Have you also been training the craft's auto-piloting algorithms?"

"Yes, sir. Standard field protocol. We fly with human primary and the AI shadowing."

"Your adherence to protocol is exemplary, Mr. Sado."

Was Piotre Raskovich being sarcastic? Between the lack of eye contact and the almost-inhuman voice in his ear, Feyis couldn't tell.

"Thank you, sir," he said, playing it safe.

"In your estimation, Mr. Sado, is the AI adequately trained? Could the plane fly itself without human oversight?"

Which was a question Feyis had been asking himself for the last couple of weeks.

"Yes, sir," he said. "Conditions on Ragnarock are extreme, particularly near the equator. You'll see that much for yourself. But in my opinion, the craft's onboard AI can now perform as well as or better than a human pilot."

"Very well. You will now sever all further communication with base camp and disable this flier's surface-to-orbit transponders. As with the rest of this mission, this conversation is classified, and all data are to be treated accordingly."

"Sir? Did you say disable the transponders, sir?"

"Was I unclear, Mr. Sado?"

"Uh, no. No, sir." He called the flier's command settings to life and did what the CIO had asked. It was unnerving. They were now alone, and Ragnarock suddenly felt very big.

"Very good, Mr. Sado. I shall leave you to your piloting."

And with that, his CIO fell silent. A moment later, the suited figure slumped over in the copilot's seat, fast asleep.

Out like a light, Feyis thought. Stranger and stranger. Flying across a dead world with an unconscious CIO who had no business down there, and now forbidden from telling anyone where they were going.

He shoved aside the misgivings he felt. *Senior officers*, he told himself. *Don't try to guess their motivations*. They were Conditioned in ways he couldn't begin to understand.

He returned his attention to his flying. There was an awfully long way to go.

Half a day later, they were deep into the worst of it, overwater for two hours already and fighting an ice storm when Piotre Raskovich snapped back to wakefulness. It wasn't hard to guess why. The man's stomach had finally given out and emptied its contents into his helmet. Whatever bio-monitoring he was using must have injected him with enough stimulants to wake him so he wouldn't choke to death on his own vomit.

"Would you be so kind as to vent the cabin, Mr. Sado?" Raskovich said, his voice sounding worse than ever.

"Yes, sir." Feyis felt a moment of sympathy as he worked the environmental controls. During the flight, he'd equalized the cockpit with Ragnarock's atmosphere, making the air theoretically unsafe to breathe, at least until the bio-surveys were concluded. The flier could, however, function like a portable habitat for limited periods of time. For a flight like this, there was no need; the suits would suffice. But if someone with no business down there threw up in their own helmet, flooding the tiny cockpit with reserve air and evacuating Ragnarock's atmosphere was the only way to offer a bit of relief.

He cycled the air. Piotre Raskovich removed his helmet awkwardly, cleaned it, and wiped his face clear of bile.

"Thank you, Mr. Sado."

"Happens all the time, sir."

"I doubt that very much."

Feyis said nothing to that, but he did remove his own helmet. No reason to let good air go to waste.

They fought the storm for another hour before Feyis finally picked up their destination on radar. The island was massive, its summit well over four thousand meters high.

"That's it, sir," he said, indicating the tactical display.

"Well done, Mr. Sado. Bring us down as high as possible."

"Yes, sir. Going full active with the lidar. Let's see what we've got to work with here."

He flew a slow circuit around the island, building a high-definition three-dimensional model as he went. Visibility was near zero, snow whipping sideways around them. There was only one landing site he could see.

"Best bet is this snowfield here," he said finally, indicating the display. "A hundred meters above sea level."

"There is nothing farther up?"

"No, sir. There is only one other possibility, but it's at the same elevation and worse in all other respects."

"Then we are going to have a long way to climb, Mr. Sado."

"Yes, sir. Bringing us in. Recommend we suit up, in case this goes badly."

"Noted. Kindly land the plane."

"Copy that. Landing now."

The site he had picked out was a patch of snowfield mostly unmarred by rockfall. He landed upslope, which also served to bring them in upwind. At the last moment, the buffeting ceased; touchdown was almost smooth. Better than the AI would have done, Feyis thought with satisfaction. Taking off from there would be easy: a straightforward run back down the snowfield and then a skyward lob over the sea.

He brought the plane neatly to a stop, pleased with himself.

"Well done, Mr. Sado," Raskovich said. "How many hours of daylight remain?"

"It's late afternoon, sir. Call it three and a half."

"Then we will make camp here and begin our ascent in the morning."

"Yes, sir."

The wind howled all night. Feyis was physically exhausted from the long flight, but sleep wouldn't come. Their shelter was bio-rated, allowing both of them to strip off their exposure suits, which was a welcome relief. Piotre Raskovich lay next to him, having slipped into a state of unconsciousness that seemed to border on death. He was barely breathing, though his muscles still spasmed, the synth-suit trying desperately to rebuild them for what lay ahead.

It was uncomfortably like lying next to a twitching corpse.

He thought of Callie, wondering where she was at that moment. For a brief, mad second, he contemplated getting up and slipping out through the airlock, thinking to call her on the flier's radio. It would be a blatant violation of Raskovich's orders, but he wasn't sure he cared. He didn't like much of anything about this situation. Basic instinct told him it would be good for another human to know where he was.

Stay professional, he thought. *Keep calm and do the job*.

He finally drifted off to sleep an hour before dawn, such that he woke feeling worse than if he hadn't rested at all. He rolled over and placed a hand lightly on Raskovich's shoulder. The synth-weave must have sensed his touch, because the man's eyes snapped open, fixing him with an uncanny stare in the shelter's dim red nightlights.

"Sir?" Feyis said. "It's time."

Raskovich nodded once and struggled to his feet.

There's just no way the man is going to make it, Feyis thought. Professionalism demanded he speak.

"Let me do this, sir," he said. "I'm not sure what you're looking for up there, but I'm qualified with all the instrumentation you brought."

"Your offer is appreciated, Mr. Sado," Piotre Raskovich said. "But I assure you I am capable of the journey."

"You received medical clearance? Sir? I mean—how is that even possible?"

"You forget yourself, Mr. Sado."

"Right. Sorry, sir. It's just that I . . ."

"You have no experience performing first ascents of glaciated volcanoes on heretofore-unknown worlds, in heavy gravity, with invalids for company?"

"I didn't say *invalid*, sir. But—permission to speak freely?"

Raskovich laughed mirthlessly. It was a horrible sound. "Granted, Mr. Sado."

"You'll die up there."

"I assure you I will not. This synth-suit is more capable than it appears."

Feyis took a closer look. He had assumed the synth-weave was strictly a medical device but now saw that it was much more than that. It was Security gear: a piece of equipment that could provide strength augmentation, muscle and joint reinforcement, who knew what other manner of tricks.

It was the kind of device a Security team might use when deployed to a conflict zone.

"And you're rated for that thing? Sir?"

"Only recently. I will be a bit clumsy, Mr. Sado. Your job will be to catch me if I fall. But it will get me up that mountain."

Feyis nodded, considering. It might work, but it still didn't make sense. What were they even doing there?

"It's a long climb, sir," he said finally.

"Then we'd best be on our way. Even with this suit to help me, you'll have to carry the gear."

Feyis eyed the various instruments Raskovich had brought, now arrayed on the shelter's floor. It looked like a lot of weight.

"Yes, sir," he said.

It was going to be a very long day.

CHAPTER 7

They left camp in darkness so thick, it felt to Piotre like a living thing, the headlamp in his suit providing almost no illumination through the hard-blowing snow. He could see the climbing rope snaking away from his waist, disappearing into the gloom, and then nothing. The ice axe Feyis had insisted he carry trailed weakly from his wrist, the snow there too deep for it to be of any use.

He felt no pain. The chemicals in his blood, combined with the synth-weave suit supplementing his atrophied muscles, created a profound sense of detachment from his own body. His autonomic nervous system was doing half the work, the AI controlling the nano-fibers the other half, leaving him stateless, free to contemplate the whole thing as if from above.

The experience was not so different from his life spent drifting in zero gravity in his cabin, except that the unending torrents of data had been replaced with only his own broken thoughts. Sensory deprivation instead of sensory overload—but the feeling, he thought, was very much the same.

He wondered how much time had passed. It felt like they had been at it for hours. Equally, it could have been days.

He glanced at his suit's chronometer.

Less than twenty minutes had elapsed since they left base camp.

They had barely begun.

When they reached the bottom of the glacier, the work began in earnest.

"This is the part where the rope matters, sir," Feyis Sado's voice sounded in his ear. "You've got to keep your slack out."

"Understood," he said, annoyed at the intrusion, even though the command might save his life. He stepped up onto the harder surface of glacial ice, the synth-suit flexing with him, taking the load off his thighs and calves. The spikes attached to his boots bit into the glacier, providing a small measure of comfort.

He placed his axe carefully and took another step.

"That's it exactly, sir," Feyis said. "Three points of contact at all times."

He didn't respond to that, just took another step, and another, settling into the rhythm of it. Step. Breathe. And step again.

He would get himself up this mountain. He would see the artifact up close and gather every last piece of data he could. He'd be damned if he would die out there.

But there was an awfully long way to go.

They reached the first crevasse, a great gaping crack in the ice with a snow bridge across it, barely visible in the combined illumination their suits provided. Feyis went first, not stopping until he reached the other side, where he quickly hammered a piece of metal into the ice.

"Okay, Mr. Raskovich," Feyis said. "I'm anchored in. I'll belay you across. Just take it smooth and easy."

"Understood."

He stepped onto the snow bridge. It narrowed in front of him, tapering toward the middle before widening again on the far side. When he reached the center, he stopped and peered over the edge. Even with his headlamp, he couldn't see the bottom of the crevasse. It was disorienting but also weirdly euphoric. He was standing suspended above an abyss, gazing into a great black crack that looked like nothing so much as a gateway to some murky hell.

A thought occurred then.

Feyis Sado would talk.

Contractors weren't Conditioned. No matter what orders he gave the man, Feyis Sado wouldn't be able to help himself.

By the time he returned to *Accipiter*, the entire base camp would know what had happened out there on this mountain. Captain Johnston would know. And then all this would be for naught.

"Let's keep moving, Mr. Raskovich," Feyis's voice admonished him through his earpiece. "That's no place to stop for a rest."

Why, for all his planning, had he not realized this until now?

He resumed his careful crossing, wishing as he went he had spent more time training with his Security suit. There was no way he could risk any sort of direct physical confrontation. He was too weak, and *Accipiter*'s quartermaster had insisted on disabling the suit's weaponry.

"Good work, sir," Feyis said when he reached the far side of the crevasse.

"Thank you, Mr. Sado. Lead on."

"Yes, sir."

Feyis climbed slowly away from him into the dark. Piotre watched him go, mind still sorting through this singular problem he had overlooked.

When the rope tightened, he followed after, trudging once more after his guide, upward into the night and driving snow.

Dawn broke and the snowstorm lessened for a time. As visibility improved, Piotre saw they were now climbing past great seracs: huge blocks of ice that lay tumbled across the glacier like some enormous castle had collapsed and spilled its walls down the mountainside.

It was a beautiful sight in the abstract, but he lacked the ability to appreciate it. He missed the cold comfort of darkness. When Feyis called a break, he grudgingly agreed. He was exhausted and needed the rest but anxious now to get on with it. He imagined prying eyes above him, *Accipiter* up there in orbit, Anne Johnston peering down.

Soon enough, the break was over and he had his wish. They were climbing again.

The glacier was rotten there, with crevasses barring their route repeatedly. They were able to navigate around some of the smaller ones but were forced to cross others, and in the daylight, Piotre found the experience far worse. In the light, the gaping cracks in the ice weren't black but rather dark blue, all the more forbidding with their sheer vertical sides and unseen depths.

To pass the time, Piotre thought about his return to Earth and all that lay ahead. He would find a buyer and negotiate his price, sell what he knew for life extension and a world of his own. He would be hated by some, a hero to others—but all would know him as the man who beat the system.

Provided his heart didn't give out there on Ragnarock first.

Still, the longer the climb dragged on, the less it seemed to matter. The thrill of discovery faded, and the prospects of future riches paled. Even Feyis eventually fell silent, the gravity and elevation seeming to take their toll on his guide as well, despite his superior physical fitness.

Hours passed with little more than the sound of his own breathing for company. The spikes on his boots, the axe in his hand and rope at his waist, the cold hammering of his heart—those were real things.

All else, he was coming to believe, was an illusion.

⁂

They reached the top of the glacier in the late afternoon. There they crossed the bergschrund, the largest crevasse he had seen yet, a great rent where the ice tore itself apart under its weight. It required three different snow bridges to traverse, each a fragile arch that looked like it might collapse at any moment.

The crater rim was visible above them now, the clouds having parted teasingly to reveal the summit at last. What remained was a final pitch on rock and ice, another five hundred meters that would prove the hardest yet.

He wasn't sure how he could manage it, even with the synth-suit to help. Maybe Sado would have to leave his gear and haul him bodily the rest of the way. It didn't matter. He'd find a way, even if it meant being dragged. Why not? He was already drugged.

He giggled inanely at the pun and then began to laugh, louder and louder, his body convulsing, the manic fit threatening to overtake him.

"Sir? Are you okay, sir?"

He struggled for breath as the momentary insanity passed. "Yes," he gasped. "Climb on, Mr. Sado."

"Aye, sir. Climbing."

How strange, he thought as they struggled upward again. *Fifty-five years spent climbing a corporate ladder, kicking and clawing and ascending, and now this*. Adrenalin shots and platelet injections, neural repressors, and a synth-weave suit pitted against heavy gravity, four thousand meters of glacier, and the unrelenting wind, snow, and biting cold.

He never considered quitting, though whether it was conviction or delusion he could not say. How marvelous, he thought, what the human mind could endure when managing to its own self-interest.

No wonder Magellanix worked so hard to Condition its senior officers.

And then, abruptly, it was over. They reached the crater rim, but any hope for a first look at the artifact was quickly dashed, as the crater was full of clouds and fog. The wind whipped even harder there, and for the first time, despite his exposure suit and the synth-weave underneath, Piotre was aware of the sensation of cold.

"Let's drop in, and take a rest when we're out of this wind," Feyis said.

He grunted in agreement, and together they began picking their way down the scree slope.

Visibility dropped back to almost nothing, and the rock there was loose, turning their descent into a long, stumbling nightmare. He fell three times, cursing at his awkwardness, but his suit remained intact. The last thing he needed was to gash it open and expose himself to air he didn't know if it was safe to breathe.

It took an hour to reach the bottom. Then at last, the ground flattened under their feet, the loose debris now replaced by the harder rock of the crater floor. Abruptly, the wind shifted and the fog momentarily cleared.

All at once, Piotre saw what he had come for.

The artifact loomed incredibly large right in front of them: an enormous silver sphere at least a hundred meters tall, and even in the dim, filtered light, it glittered like an oversized diamond. It was shiny, faceted, and flawless, resting impossibly there in the bottom of the crater.

Perhaps a third of its surface was buried, like a marble pressed down into mud.

"Sweet missing gods," Feyis said, professionalism breaking at last. "What in all the hells is that?"

"That, Mr. Sado, is what we have come for."

"Yes, sir. But—I mean . . .what is it? How did it get here?"

"Good questions, Mr. Sado." He heaved himself a few last meters toward the artifact before collapsing against a large boulder. "In order that we might answer them, may I suggest you proceed with the business of deploying our instruments? Provided you are able?"

"Yes, sir."

"Good. For my part, I'm going to take a short rest."

To his credit, Sado recovered quickly from his surprise and set to work. The Mission Generalist was impressive in action, and Piotre felt a trace of bitterness over the state of his own body, so broken by comparison. His guide had carried a portable field station up there with neither drugs nor synth-suit for help. Weather-monitoring equipment, a radiometer, seismometer, and a near-space transmitter as well—he'd simply hauled the lot of it up the mountainside and had the energy left to spare.

Well, so be it. Piotre would tend to his own physical body in the fullness of time. But for the moment, as Feyis brought the instruments online, facts were beginning to emerge, and Piotre's mind, as always, was his primary asset.

His initial observations were these.

The artifact was perfectly spherical, a hundred and twelve meters in diameter. Its surface was the same temperature as the surrounding air, and no snow stuck to it. Whatever material comprised it was as close to perfectly frictionless as their sensors could measure.

It emitted neither sound nor radiation of any kind. Its age was impossible to guess, but isotopic analysis soon revealed that the youngest rocks in the crater were just over a million years old, which meant his initial calculations had been correct.

The volcano would still have been active at the time of the holocaust that destroyed most of the planet's biosphere.

The conclusion was obvious: whoever had put this thing there had done it sometime after.

He watched carefully as his guide deployed the deep-scan sonar array they had brought, imaging beneath the artifact with high-intensity electromagnetic bursts.

"Great missing gods," Feyis swore when the images came back. It was easy to see why. The artifact was positioned on top of an enormous shaft, which plunged kilometers deep into the core of the volcano.

But why? For what possible purpose?

Piotre set the thought aside. He was there for facts, not speculation. Hypothesizing could come later.

He signaled Feyis. "Survey the rest of the crater," he ordered. "Get me as detailed a surface topography as you can. Let's make sure there isn't anything else up here."

"Yes, sir."

"I'll configure the near-space transmitter," he added, indicating one of the cases Sado had unloaded from his pack. "I can manage that much."

When his guide had disappeared out of sight, Piotre set to work. The transmitter came packed in a flat gray carbon-fiber weave that could stop a bullet and survive absolute zero temperatures. It only weighed a couple of kilograms but had enough power to send a signal that could be picked up for tens of millions of kilometers.

It would never uplink a single byte of data to *Accipiter*. He had brought it along for his buyer. He would leave it on standby, where it could sit idly for decades if need be. Whoever came there could query it from afar and confirm the find before they ever descended in person.

He worked through the settings quickly, not wanting his guide to witness how he intended to use it. As he did, the problem he had been mulling over returned to his thoughts.

What was he going to do about Feyis Sado?

There was only one possible answer.

But could he do it? Could he add murder to his list of crimes?

And even if so—how? He could barely stand; the mountain had almost killed him.

The answer came to him with perfect clarity. The method was obvious if only he could bring himself to do it.

He'd have to. There was no choice.

Still, it was almost a shame. In another lifetime, he could've liked the man. Wasn't that something? Compassion for a fellow human.

What would the centipede have thought about that?

They spent the night in the crater in a rough field shelter Feyis had carried, which provided an extra layer of protection from the cold. It could be pressurized as well, but there seemed little reason. They slept in their suits, uncomfortable but warm.

In the morning, they ate briefly, consuming calories from tubes in their helmets. Then Piotre downloaded every kilobyte of data they'd gathered from their various instruments onto a single solid-state device.

He would memorize all he could later when he had time alone.

An hour after that, they were on their way home, picking their way across the crater floor, heading for the brutal ascent back to the rim, and then the long climb back down the mountainside.

In the days and weeks that followed, Piotre would remember little of the descent itself. He suffered; he endured. Coming down was easier than going up. What more need be said?

They reached the final crevasse, the last barrier at the bottom of the glacier standing between him and freedom. He crossed first as he had known he would, his guide belaying him in their now-familiar pattern. He reached the far side safely and studied the snowfield below.

It was steep and perfectly pitched for what he knew he must do.

He waited until Feyis Sado was exactly in the middle.

There was no reason to delay. Still, he felt a brief pang of regret and realized he was holding his breath.

He exhaled it all in a great gasp and jumped.

And slid.

It was like falling through hyperspace; like a trip into the hibernation chamber; like the soporifics he'd tongued before the drop-ship had detached from *Accipiter*'s belly, bringing him to this hellish broken world.

It was murder and theft, greed and survival.

His actions were those of a man without a moral compass, but what could anyone expect? The centipede had been squelched to death under the heel of the unexpected, and his pure self had emerged.

He heard a shout in his helmet as he went careening down the steep snow slope.

Then the rope snapped taut, arresting his fall in a savage jerk.

The line between him and Feyis was now under tremendous tension. He was hanging from one end of it, held firm on the steep snow slope by his guide's weight.

Whereas Sado himself must now be dangling in the crevasse above.

The shouting continued until he turned his helmet's transmitter off.

There was a small, sharp steel blade, five centimeters long, sheathed in the left wrist of his suit, a bit of standard field equipment which he now pulled free. Under tension, the rope parted easily, the cut end disappearing in an instant, snaking up the glacier, running away, and disappearing over the edge of the crevasse.

He had done it.

He, Piotre Raskovich, was free.

For a brief moment, he was tempted to climb back for a look down into the crevasse, just to be sure. But he had no energy to spare, and there were still a last snowfield to cross, data to memorize, and then a long flight back home.

The flier's AI would be adequate to fly him back to camp. A drop-ship would return him to *Accipiter*.

And Captain Anne Johnston, all unwitting, would take him home to Earth.

BOOK TWO

SOL

CHAPTER 8

TransGalactic (formerly Magellanix) Vessel Sagittaria

Inbound to Sol System

AD 3184.08.13

His captain's message was as terse as ever.

Report to Carpathia.

Third Lieutenant Ian McAllister, acting captain of the captured Magellanix vessel *Sagittaria*, read the words on the cabin's main screen, waved them away, and smiled for the first time in months.

Captain Marakan had summoned him back to his own ship, which could only mean one thing. He was finally about to be relieved of command.

He glanced around the cabin he'd been occupying. Even after half a year, he felt out of place. The bed was too short, the toe- and handholds uncomfortable, and the interface screens behaved oddly. Working with *Sagittaria's* systems was like trying to do everything in a foreign language, one he could understand but not speak fluently, the idioms and idiosyncrasies forever a struggle. And for a TransGalactic employee like him, the Magellanix design aesthetic was baffling, with a fetishized fascination with birds of prey he couldn't comprehend.

Why anyone would want line drawings of raptors adorning the walls was beyond him.

But the real problem was the cabin's previous occupant, *Sagittaria's* former commander, the young woman who had almost succeeded in destroying them all. Ian had gathered her possessions when he settled in, tucking them away in a storage locker while trying not to snoop, but he could still feel her presence. She'd managed to kill a third of *Carpathia's* crew before surrendering her ship and was now involuntarily asleep in a hibernation hold. All for doing her job, the same as he had done.

He had spent the last six months feeling like he was being watched over by a ghost.

He wondered if she was dreaming while she slept. It happened sometimes. Wondered, too, what would become of her when they returned to Earth. A captured enemy starship officer? How would her interrogation play out, and what kind of life would she be allowed?

Whereas he was supposed to be some sort of hero. TransGalactic's Human Resources department would tear her mind apart, all while throwing him a parade.

One he didn't deserve. That was the truth of it. He had been too slow. If he'd acted faster, and trusted his gut, no one need have died at all.

But now, there he was, an acting captain for no other reason than everyone in the chain of command above him except for Captain Marakan herself had been lost. Dead in an instant, when the shot from *Sagittaria's* hidden drone found its mark.

Xi Anders.

Shelikan Antikar.

Emmett Watson.

He said their names aloud, as he had every day since the battle. There were many more; he had memorized them all. The best and brightest, some hailing from TransGalactic colonies but most from Earth itself, all of them rising stars, and him too, he thought bitterly. That was why they had been assigned to deep-space interdiction work—the most mind-numbingly boring, utterly terrifying, and dangerous job there was.

Also the most important.

"Fortunes of war, Lieutenant." That's what Captain Marakan had said after the battle when she'd put him in temporary command of *Sagittaria*. But if this was fortune, how could they possibly turn a profit? Were data worth so much more than people? It couldn't be; not the officers, anyway. Not the augmented, the drugged and enhanced. Even someone like him—not a captain, not an Information Officer, just a junior lieutenant—represented a mammoth investment of corporate resources.

It didn't matter now. They were almost home with their captured ship, he was being recalled to *Carpathia*, and he could stop pretending to be a captain at last.

Before he left the cabin, he opened the storage locker and retrieved the bag of personal effects he'd hidden away. Among other things, *Sagittaria's* young commander had brought with her a brass model of an old Earth secretary bird—the ship's namesake. It was magnetized and snapped to the desk with a satisfying *clunk.* He regarded it for a moment. The statue had been designed with the bird's head cocked, and it seemed to stare back at him, slightly perplexed.

"I'm sorry," he said.

Then he eased himself into the corridor. He shut the door behind him softly, as though not to disturb someone asleep inside.

Ian left *Sagittaria* as fast as dignity would allow, resisting the urge to run in the great bounding strides that were possible in the one-fifth gravity their current acceleration profile was imparting. Instead, he forced himself to walk the corridors deliberately, the way he supposed a real captain might, returning a handful of salutes with his usual awkward wave.

He found the airlock he sought, clambered through, and settled into a flit-pod for the short trip to *Carpathia.* He signaled his departure to the bridge, detached from *Sagittaria's* hull, and was free at last.

A moment of pure gratitude then: a few minutes alone, no one to ask him for anything, nothing he need do but pilot this tiny craft.

He nudged the thrusters, turning the flitter on its axis, momentarily giving himself a view of both *Sagittaria* and *Carpathia* as they flew in formation. As always, he was struck by their similarity. *Carpathia* was owned and operated by TransGalactic, Incorporated, whereas *Sagittaria* was a Magellanix vessel, but both shared the same U-shaped hull, anchored on one end by enormous, bell-shaped blast shields. The ships were under identical acceleration, oriented with blast shields aft to harness the released energy from the series of tiny fusion bombs they were detonating in their wakes.

In a few more days, the ships would reach the halfway point, between the singularity through which they had passed and Occipitus Prime, the latter the greatest of humanity's space stations and jumping-off point for the first centuries of interstellar exploration. The station was positioned beyond the combined outer orbital perimeter of Neptune and Pluto, at this moment still a few million kilometers away. When they reached the halfway mark, they would rotate their kilometer-long ships and perform the same exercise in reverse, braking instead of accelerating, the whole thing the most basic kind of physics there was.

None of which was the real magic. The beating hearts of both ships weren't the fusion engines at all. That was old tech, a way of slogging around at speeds far too slow to go anywhere interesting. The real work was done by the particle accelerators inside those U-shaped hulls. The accelerators and some very fancy math were the keys to the universe, the tools for forming singularities, opening the hidden doors that were the basis for all of humanity's expansion throughout their tiny corner of the galaxy.

Everything else, the nubs, stubs, flanges, modules, and pods, were just add-ons, housing habitat spaces, workshops, drop-ships, weapons pods, remotes, relays, sensory equipment, spun rings for standard gravity, and dozens of other functions as well. They gave the ships an irregular, ungainly appearance and made clear they belonged in a vacuum but should never grace a planet's atmosphere.

There was, however, one critical difference between the ships. Entire pieces of *Carpathia* were missing. That was *Sagittaria*'s handiwork, a near-fatal blow from a beam weapon that had scythed along *Carpathia*'s long axis, neatly severing half a dozen of those protruding modules, killing seventy of her crew instantly.

They'd been lucky. Had *Carpathia* been oriented differently relative to the attack and the beam had caught them transverse to the ship's long axis, it would have cut them in half—and even if they'd survived it, the ship would have been marooned forever, its beating heart stilled, doomed to drift hundreds of light-years from home.

Blind luck.

Some hero, Ian thought, feeling the same bitterness he had since that day.

Twenty minutes later, he found himself outside his captain's door, palming the security pad and listening to the chime sound inside. This was a mere formality. She would long since have been alerted to his presence.

The door slid open, revealing Captain Ali Marakan standing with her back to him, silhouetted by a field of stars.

"Come in," she said.

He stepped through, pivoted neatly midair in the light gravity, palmed the door shut, and landed facing her.

His captain turned to regard him. "Three years ago, you would've kicked yourself into the far wall doing that. Now you perform the move without thought."

"Sir?"

"Time, lieutenant. Time in space. You have some now."

"Yes, sir."

He shifted his eyes, avoiding her gaze. She was a lifer, someone who had been exposed to a range of biomedical enhancements at which he could only guess. She'd probably always been statuesque, but now she had the appearance of an actual statue, the way she could stand perfectly motionless on the bridge for hours at a time. Her skin was obsidian-black and looked chipped from stone, her eyes pools of even greater darkness. Spacer's eyes, a by-product of the drugs she'd taken to stay alive out there so long.

Being scrutinized by Captain Marakan was like being regarded by some horrific nocturnal predator. She spoke little, moved less, and was never wrong.

Except the one time, perhaps. Wrong to delegate the job to him.

"You've done well," she said.

"Thank you, sir."

"You disagree?"

Reading his mind like that, as though nothing could be hidden from her. He shook his head, mute, not sure what to say. Her voice was unnerving, so in contrast with her appearance. It was weirdly high, a strangely liquid sound.

"It's natural that you would," she said. "You're young and therefore still cursed with the gift of introspection. You've been asked to do something beyond yourself, to perform duties for which you are not ready. And so, in this regard, normalized for these variables, I say again to you—you've done well."

"Thank you, sir," he said again. "It's just . . ."

"Yes?"

He regretted starting the sentence, and now saw no choice but to finish it. "It was my fault, sir."

"What fault might that be?"

"I should've been faster."

"Ah. Does it feel better to say it?"

"Sir?"

"Are you experiencing a moment of catharsis? No, don't answer; I shall answer for you. You, lieutenant, feel guilty because it's easier than the alternative. Guilt is easy. Unfortunately, such second-guessing is also intellectual laziness.

"We lost a third of our crew, but you followed procedure. You obeyed the chain of command, which is what you've been trained to do.

"Acting otherwise would've been an act of mutiny. Your training would have of course prohibited this. The psychological consequences had you disobeyed would've been profound in ways you do not yet appreciate.

"And yet still you feel guilt because it's easier to blame yourself than to recognize the deeper truth. You, lieutenant, are a participant in a flawed system, and you have learned that fact before you were meant to do so."

"Sir?" He had never heard her speak this many words, total, in three years. Why now? What did she want of him?

"Have a seat, Lieutenant."

He sat. His captain did not.

"Do you see that point of light?" Indicating the star field on the screen behind her, where a tiny pinprick of light was just visible.

"Yes, sir. Relay station, sir. Occipitus Prime."

"Correct, Lieutenant. Home. Homc waters, anyway—and shared waters, under multi-jurisdictional corporate control. It is by formal contract within our rights to sail directly to that facility, captured *Sagittaria* in formation alongside, dock in the broad light of day—so to speak—offload our crew, ransom Magellanix's people back to them, and beam our stolen data directly to Earth."

"Sir?"

"That is not, however, what we're going to do. And it is imperative that you understand why."

He nodded at her helplessly, not at all understanding.

"Let me tell you something of the nature of travel, Lieutenant McAllister."

"Sir?"

"I believe, Lieutenant, that in all the long history of human endeavor, there is one unifying theme. One constant in the equation that binds me in my current capacity of acting admiral of our two-ship fleet, with the nineteenth-century British sailor, those great twenty-fifth-century explorers, the ancient Phoenician in his trireme venturing away from the sight of land for the first time, and all in between and since. It's not the joy of returning home, though we are getting close and I have no doubt you are excited by the prospect. Nor is it the anxiety of mishap along the way, though we have suffered our fair share. Nor even the fatigue of the journey, though your body by now would be in a state of near-constant pain and degeneration were it not for the parade of pharmaceuticals working their irreversible changes on you."

She paused a moment, seeming to expect some response.

"What is it, then? Sir?" he ventured.

"Simply this: the desire to put down the luggage. To drop the suitcase at the door, Lieutenant, to check one's travel bag into quarantine, throw the mailbag off the stern, and hang up one's oar.

"My particular luggage is the *Sagittaria*, which you have done an adequate job of captaining. Yours is the weight of a command for which you are not yet ready. Unfortunately, neither of us will be afforded the luxury of setting down our burdens quite yet."

"Sir?"

"We will part ways here, Lieutenant. You will take *Carpathia* to Occipitus Prime, where you will conduct what will appear to be a routine disembarkation. Prying eyes and enemy corporate spies will wonder about the missing parts of our ship. There is little we can do about that. You'll simply dock and await further orders. Perhaps Corporate will cycle you through shore leave on Earth; perhaps you'll be sent back out immediately, or maybe you'll be furloughed for a time. I have no way to know.

"You will not, however, make mention of our encounter with *Sagittaria*. I will take our captured prize elsewhere, where those prying eyes are absent. Moreover, we will not communicate again. Under no circumstances are you to send any signal to *Sagittaria* once we part ways. Do you understand?"

"Yes, sir."

"You have a question?"

How did she always know?

"Sir. It's just that—it's going to be pretty obvious that something happened, isn't it? Magellanix will figure it out eventually, so why the subterfuge?"

"Because, Lieutenant, we are going to be polite."

"Sir?"

"There is no reason to embarrass our corporate rivals. We're not the only deep-space interdiction ship in operation; we all play the same game. TransGalactic, Magellanix, InterTech, even a few smaller companies—all of us operate similarly."

"And next time, it might be our turn?"

"Yes, Lieutenant. Were we to sail directly to Occipitus Prime, our shared relay station, Magellanix's internal accountability structures would demand—not to put too fine a point on it—someone's head to roll. That same head will roll eventually when *Sagittaria* doesn't come home, but this way, there will be no embarrassing PR incident. The damage will be diffused, meted out over time in a controlled and predictable fashion. Nothing reactionary need come of it. No shots will be fired. The system will not be destabilized. And, when the tables are next reversed, they'll do the same for us. Now do you understand?"

"I think so, sir," he said.

"Then you are dismissed, Lieutenant. I suggest you find yourself a cabin for the duration of the journey. We will formally exchange command in an hour."

He nodded and saluted. Captain Marakan returned the salute solemnly—but almost, he thought, he saw the briefest of smiles.

Though if he had, it was the saddest smile he had ever seen.

Ian's own quarters on *Carpathia* had been lost in the battle, vaporized when the beam from *Sagittaria* cut through them. No matter. There were plenty now unoccupied.

Before he died, Xi Anders had been his best friend on the ship. Ian decided Xi wouldn't have minded if he squatted awhile. Occipitus Prime was only a couple of weeks away.

For now, he would have to pretend to be a captain again, only this time of *Carpathia* herself.

Or, at least, what was left of her.

CHAPTER 9

Earth
Four days later

Like its rivals, TransGalactic, Incorporated, had built its capital city at the bottom of the world, carving it into rocky Antarctic soil surrendered by the last of Earth's glaciers on their millennium-long retreat. And like its rivals, the company's marketing department argued that theirs was the greatest city ever conceived by human hands.

Senior executives from Magellanix or InterTech would, of course, disagree. They too had their Antarctic oases, bubble-chain fortresses within which their millions lived. But TransGalactic built theirs first, and they never let anyone forget it.

At the heart of the city stood a tower: a long, slender needle woven from jet-black and snow-white composites twined together in a dazzling mosaic. The tower loomed half a kilometer over the tallest of its neighbors, almost touching the city's transparent nano-woven dome at its apex. Six flanges nubbed out from its base, giving it the shape of an ancient rocket about to take flight.

The tower served both as TransGalactic's corporate headquarters and its most iconic marketing symbol. Magellanix had their stylized rendering of Magellan's passage, InterTech its blocky, abstract iconography, but TransGalactic's simple rocket-ship emblem had achieved a level of ubiquity of which their rivals could only dream. The symbol was a fashion statement and calling card, a tribal identity for those lucky enough to have lifetime employment within the company's far-reaching empire, a source of irritation, envy, or outright rage for those who did not.

The top of the tower was given over to a single room with vaulted crystalline ceilings and a vertigo-inducing view that swept across the city's byzantine geometry. From there, one could gaze over lesser but still massive skyscrapers, twisting transport tubes, parks and marketplaces, contractor quarters and officers' homes, amusement centers, sporting facilities, data warrens, and preservation arks, all the way to the Transantarctic mountains beyond.

The room was the Interlocutor's office: the innermost sanctum of the TransGalactic Human Resources department, the holiest of holies, a place no one, she well knew, ever visited voluntarily.

It was Friday, and the Interlocutor was drinking tea.

She slid the dark crimson hood of the formal robe of her office to her shoulders. Her bare scalp tingled, exposed for the first time in hours to her office's perfectly conditioned air.

She sighed and took a sip, holding the pungent, jasmine-flavored liquid in her mouth for a moment, savoring the sensation.

There was no particular need for it. The ritual was anachronistic. Whatever health benefits the drink might have provided had been reduced to injectable form long since, part of the melange of drugs the Interlocutor, now in her second century on the job, consumed on a daily basis.

Still, she liked the taste of it, and the two-thousand-year-old china cup felt soothing in her hand. Biotechnology had kept her alive, the science of drug discovery stretching out her life almost indefinitely—but the tea gave that life meaning.

It had been a very long week.

Fourteen senior contractors applying for employment at TransGalactic after working terms at various corporate rivals; a ship commander up for promotion; an interdepartmental espionage case that had taken hours to disentangle. Worse, the annual performance review cycle had begun again, requiring the unceasing, ritualistic interlocution of the most senior executives, stopping just short of the board members themselves. They, of course, were no longer subjected to such things as feedback from their peers.

She had stared into the eyes of her subjects and then into the spaces behind. She had looked into their souls. Done that which she had been selected, groomed, trained, and augmented to do.

She had interlocuted.

Now it was time to forget them all.

She took another sip of her tea and let her focus relax, gazing out the western bank of windows to the far horizon, where the Transantarctic Mountains jutted their craggy black teeth into the bluest of skies.

She considered the first of the contractors, mulled them over briefly in her mind, and let them go.

Her office was as mutable as she, its environmental controls as sophisticated as those of any starship. With a simple command, the great wall of windows could be cycled opaque and the room's embedded holographics brought to life. Subsonics, temperature and humidity controls, subtle olfactory cues—all were part of the bag of tricks at her disposal. This week, her office had been eyrie and oubliette, neo-Buddhist retreat center, old Earth underwater habitat, rainforest from the tropics of Paradise, a dive bar of the kind that could still be found in odd places there on Earth, and a medieval dungeon.

There were other methods, of course. Synaptic overrides. Truth serums. Bamboo needles under the fingernails. She had studied them all and used most, at one time or another.

But now, there at the top of the tower and the pinnacle of her profession, she had refined her techniques to a single method.

She empathized.

To torture was to dehumanize. The problem of information extraction could be approached in that fashion, but real understanding required emotional connection. Once she understood her subjects, truly empathized with them, no truths about lives or deeds could be withheld.

Was it mind control? Was she a freak of some kind? She'd been called that and worse. Mind reader. Leech. Parasite.

Maybe she was just a good listener.

In truth, she didn't always know herself how she was able to do what she did. She found some comfort in that.

The only thing that troubled her now was that the work was simply too heavy. It was far too much to carry, and so, at the end of each week, she held her subjects in her mind's eye and set them free. The specific visualizations differed, depending on her mood. Today she imagined them as eggs: cradled in memory, then cracked gently open, their essence free to take flight from her mind.

In a blink, all memory of the first of the contractors was gone completely. No form of persuasion could have forced her to give up the details of the interlocution. She couldn't have spoken further of them, even if she wanted to.

It was a delicate moment, this freeing of self from memory. Do it wrong, and she could get stuck, the valve cracked open, years bleeding away in seconds. It happened. It wasn't discussed openly, but it happened. Her predecessor told her the story once.

So, when her office chimed at her, the noise was so unexpected, she flinched as though struck, spilled her tea on her robe, and cursed aloud.

Then a man's voice filled her office, the sound as unwelcome as a wasp on the scalp. A sharp warning stab of pain lanced through her temple as her trance broke.

"Please forgive the intrusion," he said.

The voice came from everywhere and nowhere. Whoever had breached her protocols so egregiously was trying to be gentle, threading the sound into the room's environmental controls, asking as politely as it was possible to ask.

Still, he was interrupting. Which was more than annoying—it was dangerous.

"Who dares call?" she breathed.

"Please forgive," the man said again. "There is an emergency."

She squeezed her eyes shut, trying to concentrate. The light of the sun through her windows had suddenly become intolerably bright.

"What possible reason . . ." she began, but the voice, which she still couldn't place, interrupted her again!

"Your services are required," the man said. "Immediately. I will render."

He didn't bother to wait for a response. Even as she opened her eyes, her office was plunged into darkness.

There would be consequences for this. She would see to it later. For the moment, all she could do was stare at the scene now playing out in glorious, high-dimensional holographic detail in the empty spaces around her.

The first thing the Interlocutor saw was an atmospheric craft of some kind, flying low in the sky. Probably a recreational plane, she thought, judging by the flex-wing, two-seater design. Ordinarily just a plaything for those with the means, but this one was in trouble. Smoke poured from a hole in its side, and it was auguring toward the ground at an alarming rate.

At the last second, either the pilot or the plane's AI managed to pull the nose up, feathering into a rough but survivable landing. The little craft slid on its belly across a wide patch of ice, careened off a rock outcropping, tumbled over a small ledge, and finally came to rest in a snowbank, tail up and nose down like a javelin tossed into a pit of mud.

The hatch irised open and a figure emerged. It clambered unsteadily out of the cockpit and over the nose of the plane, dropped to all fours, picked itself back up, and staggered across the snow. The pattern of movement suggested discomfort in gravity. The Interlocutor had seen it many times before. Whoever this person was, they had likely been deployed for an extended period in deep space.

When the figure was perhaps fifty meters away, the craft detonated, exploding in an orange fireball. All that was left behind were a few smoldering bits of wreckage, a modestly sized pit, and a trail of smoke curling into the sky.

At which point the figure sat down on a rock and waited.

A minute later, a massive vehicle with glistening black armor crept into view.

The Interlocutor's brain was slowly returning to a higher level of function, beginning to make sense of what she was seeing. The vehicle moved on a series of articulated, clawed feet that could tuck in and roll it down a glass-smooth road at several hundred kilometers per hour, or extend outward and sprint it up a twenty-degree rock slope.

It was, in other words, a Security vehicle.

She knew equipment like this came with onboard control systems that were highly capable. Depending on how it was configured, the vehicle she was seeing could remote-manage a planetary network, shoot down incoming ballistic missiles, or do a credible job forecasting the stock market. It likely also had enough onboard medical capabilities to keep a human alive indefinitely, even bereft of things like heart or lungs.

Expensive piece of hardware, she thought. Not the kind of thing Security would deploy without very good reason.

It came to a stop.

A hatch slid open in its armored side and the man climbed aboard as though he had been expecting it all along.

At which point the images in her office disappeared, replaced by a holographic projection of the man whose voice had begun this awful interruption.

She recognized him at last.

Alterik. That was his name. The Senior Vice President of TransGalactic Human Resources.

Thus, her boss.

He was dressed in the attire of his office, just as she was in hers. In his case, that meant an unsubtle display of raw power. She belonged to a monastic suborder of Human Resources and possessed a fondness for the humble robes that came with it. Alterik ran the whole division and delighted in letting everyone know. He wore a single-piece, flat-black fiber weave that showed off his perfectly formed physique. His attire of choice could equally stop charged particle emitters or sing him a lullaby to put him to sleep if he so desired. It was as close to a true symbiote as modern manufacturing could produce.

Which was to say he was wearing a horrifically expensive suit.

It took her longer than it would have under ordinary circumstances, but even before his image began to speak, she saw that Alterik, while outwardly calm, was actually in a state of panic. The expression on his face, a slight crease of brow, told all.

So: a Senior Vice President, her boss, afraid.

Interesting.

She would need to ground him, she realized. Unwanted as all this was, she would have to be the professional there. Her Friday afternoon was ruined. There would be no more controlled venting of memories today.

Instead, she would have to hold a little more.

The simplest choice was to insult him, giving him something tangible that his mind could process and react to. At the moment, she was incapable of subtlety.

"Nice suit," she said.

His rendered image frowned, displeased in exactly the measure she had hoped.

"You're wondering how we captured the imagery," he said.

She shrugged. "A remote of some kind, I would imagine." She put as much indifference as she could into her voice.

"Correct. The pilot called ahead to tell us he was coming. The footage you have just seen was captured by one of the Security vehicle's drones, which just had time to reach the crash site before the plane went down."

"Mm-hmm."

"The pilot of that craft," Alterik continued, "is Piotre Raskovich."

She shrugged again. "The name means nothing to me."

"Nor would I expect it to." There was real irritation in Alterik's voice now. Good. "He is—or rather was—the Chief Information Officer of the deep-space scout ship *Accipiter*, one of the most capable vessels of its type in Magellanix's fleet. The scene you just witnessed played out approximately eighteen minutes ago."

"And?" She looked around for her tea, found it spilled on the rug, and frowned minutely as though more concerned with its loss than whatever her supervisor wanted.

"And?" Anything conciliatory in Alterik's tone vanished. "And, Interlocutor, Piotre Raskovich will be in your office exactly five minutes from now. I have apologized for the interruption. I will not do it again. It's time for you to do your job."

How extraordinary, she thought. *He really is terrified.*

After another moment's reflection, she could hardly blame him.

A Chief Information Officer, defecting?

Could it be true? Could the proprietary Behavioral-Conditioning techniques Magellanix employed have failed?

If so, the situation was without precedent and the implications profound, and since she was being offered no time to prepare, clearly no one had seen this coming. And given Alterik's state of agitation, the Board of Directors must already have been informed.

The time for games was over.

"Send him in," she said. "I will be ready."

The Interlocutor knew others considered her old-fashioned, a bit of a Luddite in her own way. It came with the territory. No gesture controls and predictive AI for her. Having made a career out of speaking with people, she chose to interface with her office's command systems by talking to them as well.

She needed to set up the room and she didn't have much time. Among other things, her office contained an ancient mahogany desk and chair hidden in a compartment beneath the floor. She didn't use them often but, in the moment, could think of nothing better. She snapped a series of commands at the room's controls, which obligingly opened the floor and hove the furniture into view. Another set of instructions shut the hatch, then caused the floor to sink in front of the desk and chair, forming a shallow depression such that her subject, Piotre Raskovich, would be forced to look upward at her when they spoke. Then she cycled the office's vaulted ceilings clear. Looking straight up now had the effect of staring through a giant crystal at the sky. A moment's fiddling with the faceting reduced the lighting to a single shaft which fell over the desk, the shallow pit in front of it, and the Interlocutor herself. She then dimmed the rest of the lights, plunging the rest of the office into comparative gloom.

Cheap theatrics, but it would have to do.

This left her with four minutes for background research, which under normal circumstances would have consumed a week.

She took her seat, called the desk's inlaid screen to life, and speed-read Piotre Raskovich's file.

Direct testimonials were spotty. A handful of contractors had passed through the man's department, putting in time at Magellanix before coming to work for TransGalactic and, in some cases, returning again. This was common enough, the basis of the caste system that separated full-time employees from hourly workers. Even information departments used contractors for less-sensitive work. Such individuals were free to come and go as they pleased, work where and when they chose, maximizing cash and freedom but giving up the benefits that came with lifetime employment.

They lived hard, made their money, and died young, with little access to life-extending drugs, as those biotechnology advances were reserved for full-time employees alone. The Interlocutor could of course empathize, though she had chosen as different a path as could be imagined.

She read on, and as she did, basic facts began to emerge. Piotre Raskovich was clearly a highly effective Chief Information Officer. His subordinates found him some combination of physically loathsome and personally terrifying, but no one ever claimed he wasn't good at his job. He had been promoted early and often, had reached his current rank at a very young age.

Also, he was a Martian.

Interesting.

She reread bits of the file in more detail, paying attention to specific snippets and fragments, the precise phrases his people used to describe him. Impressions began to form. Here was a man who never left his cabin, let alone his ship, whose subordinates feared him, whose superiors took full advantage of his services while personally despising him. She found herself returning to one particular testimonial, scrutinizing something a biomechanic who had worked for him had said.

"Raskovich? The Martian? Yeah, his people used to make fun of him about that. But only behind closed doors, and then only in whispers. If he'd ever found out, he would have sent them home in a freezer. And not bothered to wake them up."

Piotre Raskovich, in other words, was not a nice man.

He had ascended to his position of Chief Information Officer at a meteoric rate—and yet he was from a colony world. Even now, at this late date, despite the diaspora and the relentless expansion of humanity away from its dying home world, facts were facts: if you weren't born under an Antarctic dome, on some level you really weren't anyone.

Especially if you were a gaunt, pale-skinned Martian from a place where people eked out a living for reasons best described as a refusal to accept the inevitable and move on from a failed experiment.

He was, she thought, a gap-toothed hayseed, a hick from the sticks. Martian colonial trash, they of the busted gonads and failed endocrine systems, unpigmented, anemic, straw-haired gray-eyed vapid uneducated horticulturalists dancing around their broken solar panels. They might as well be erecting stone statues up there and praying for some Machine God to come save them all.

That, she thought, was how it would've felt.

And now there would be nothing left for him to achieve. He would never be promoted back to corporate headquarters, never given any position higher than he already held.

He hadn't been born into the right circles for that.

She briefly debated resetting the room. Oceans might unnerve him. She could have the holographics give the appearance that they were floating, adrift on an endless sea.

Alas, there just wasn't time.

The room chimed at her again, but this time, it was her doorbell, which she had configured to sound like a deep, resonant gong.

"Come in," she said, waving the display away and settling back into her chair. Outwardly, she knew she appeared imperturbable, but inwardly, her mind was already racing through all the possible paths this encounter might take. She was badly underprepared, and the stakes were high.

A defecting Chief Information Officer. Zero notice. Failed Behavioral Conditioning. Board-level attention.

No wonder Alterik was afraid.

She could empathize.

CHAPTER 10

There was the barest of pauses, and then the Interlocutor's office doors slid open. Piotre Raskovich stood backlit in the corridor beyond, flanked by three Security personnel.

Three guards? The degree of naked force struck the Interlocutor as excessive. But then, they were in uncharted waters there.

"Enter," she said.

For the sake of a simple display of dominance—and uncertain where else to begin—she ignored her subject as he made his slow, halting way across the room. Instead, she studied the Security team. Each wore the same matte-black uniform and carried a single, low-profile sidearm strapped to a slender equipment belt. Their faces betrayed no obvious age. Two of the three were female, the third not obviously gendered. All wore their hair buzzed to the scalp.

The team moved as a fluid unit. The leader slid into the room like they were clearing it of a potential ambush, while the second helped bear Piotre's weight, and the last of the three fell in neatly behind. There was no obvious communication between them, but they moved in perfect coordination.

They looked like panthers, the Interlocutor thought, graceful and effortless. She knew their capabilities well, the pharmaceuticals that swam in their bloodstreams, and what the suits they wore could do. Knew, too, of the conflict inherent in their profession. Security personnel were among her favorite subjects, and she had worked with many in her long career. The diversity of hopes and dreams, the reconciliation of the individual with the omnipresent chain of command, the juxtaposition of strict adherence to orders and the ever-present need for improvisation, the training of mind and body required to achieve those things . . .

They fascinated her. She took another moment, pure indulgence now, empathizing with them at their work.

Then she shifted her focus, watching as Piotre Raskovich collapsed into the chair across from her, breathing hard.

He looked up and stared straight at her. There was madness in his eyes. Insanity poured from him in waves, so bright it was palpable. It felt like contagion, like whatever afflicted him was burning so hot, she herself might catch it.

"This is unnecessary," he said.

She lifted an eyebrow fractionally.

"You are the Interlocutor," he went on.

She nodded.

"I came to deal." He glanced upward, taking in the vaulted ceilings, and the shaft of light from the sky, then settled his gaze back on her. That gaze! She had never felt anything like it. "So cut the shit," he added.

She shrugged, outwardly indifferent but inwardly pleased. He was asking her for something already; it was a good beginning. She subvocalized a command and the office returned to neutral lighting, the windows cycling clear, allowing them both to see city and sky.

She left the depression in the floor as it was. It wouldn't hurt to make him look up at her.

"Is that more to your liking?" she said.

"It's a start." He sniffed. "But you still look ridiculous."

She slid her hood back and gave him a small, conspiratorial smile. "Not my choice," she lied. "The formal robes of office, I'm afraid. They're more comfortable than they look."

"And what office is that?"

"Human Resources."

"Of course it is." He paused a moment. "You know, that might be the most aptly named of all professions. Humans as resources. Magellanix has such a department as well. It was one of our own Human Resources officers that introduced me to my own best friend, a long time ago."

She wasn't sure what to say to that.

"How old are you?" he asked.

"Two hundred and fifty-three," she said, seeing no reason to lie.

"And what do you know of pain?"

She shrugged, trying to project calm indifference, but inwardly, her mind was racing, trying to keep up with his abrupt changes of subject. "What does anyone?" she said, stalling.

"You equivocate." He sounded displeased. "Let me be more specific. What do you know of your own pain?"

"Little enough, I suppose." Which was true; it had been well over a century since she had chosen to experience such a sensation for herself.

Some might say this made her less effective, but empathizing with pain was easy, and those memories remained.

"There are some such as you at Magellanix," Piotre Raskovich said. "That company just uses a more honest name for them."

"Oh? What might that be?"

"They are known as torturers."

"I see."

"So, tell me, Interlocutor. Can you deal?"

She shrugged. "I can recommend."

"To whom?"

"The Board of Directors."

He nodded. "Then you will do. I will tell you my terms up front. They're nonnegotiable."

"Everything is negotiable," she said, guessing that he would expect such a comment and would in fact need to hear it.

He paused, his train of thought visibly shifting again. "That is true," he said. "That is very true." He grunted and straightened in his chair. "Nevertheless. I will tell you my conditions."

"As you wish."

"I want a governorship, a longevity-drug regimen equal to or better than yours, and enough Security to fight a war. And I want you to make me a hero. Actually, your marketing department will want that last part. I should say I'll be willing to go along for the ride."

She cocked her head, regarding him. It wouldn't do to respond quickly.

There was madness there; that much was obvious. But also a cold, driving intelligence. There was a mind released from decades of control mechanisms, and how could she empathize with that? Where would she have to go inside herself, her own experience, to find a place from which to work?

It should have been an enormous, patient challenge, a task she would gladly have performed. Even with this irrational fear she felt from his presence, that look behind his eyes.

But there was no time for subtlety. No opportunity to do the job right. Her boss, Alterik, had made that much clear.

Instead, trivial negotiation tactics would have to do. What should have been the interlocution of a career, reduced to transactional form.

Pity.

"That's a heavy asking price," she said, sighing inwardly.

"It is absurdly cheap, and if I could think of anything else, I'd add it. Immortality, a world, and a military to protect both. Maybe you can suggest something I've missed."

"It seems like a complete-enough list," she agreed.

He appeared to think for a moment, and then the change came over him again, that awful abyss in his eyes fixed on her now, as though he were looking at her for the first time.

"I know what you're thinking," he said. "You're wondering what techniques you'll need to employ to determine whether I'm telling the truth. But you're wasting your time, Interlocutor. Because I already know the secret of pain."

She saw no reason to say anything to that, so she simply focused on meeting his stare.

"I know what it means to miss it," he went on.

Gods, that madness! Still, she said nothing.

"I came here to tell you my story, Interlocutor. You hardly need to figure out how to beat it out of me. It starts with a discovery and ends in theft, with murder in between. I will tell you the story of my broken mind and the knowledge I hold, a single fact that has never been known to anyone before.

"You won't even have to ask questions.

"Your Security people here—they're impressive, by the way; our companies really could learn a thing or two from each other—I gave one of them a device with stolen data when they first rescued me. Your information department is even now going through it in minute detail. They will try to determine whether or not it is faked."

He paused, looking at her expectantly.

"And what will they conclude?" she asked.

"They will not be able to reach a conclusion. Out of an abundance of caution, if your information technicians are anything like ours, they will simply state that beyond a certain degree of confidence, they cannot say what is real and what is manufactured."

"Doesn't that leave you in a bit of a precarious position?" she asked.

"In fact, it does not. The mere possibility that it might be real will cause your corporate masters to conclude they must investigate. They will not be able to afford not to."

"You seem to have thought of everything."

It was the wrong thing to say.

He narrowed his eyes, and then laughed, a short, barking stutter that grew louder until it threatened to overtake his whole body. He convulsed in his chair. "Thought—of—everything," he gasped, the words squeezed from his throat like they were escaping a dying man.

He laughed, and laughed, the hysterics finally giving way to a coughing fit that continued unabated until she finally gave up, glanced over to the Security team, and mouthed the words *Help him.*

In a blink, a black-suited guard was at his side. In the next moment, Piotre Raskovich had lapsed into unconsciousness, whatever drug Security had administered taking hold immediately.

She caught the guard's eye. "How long?"

"Maybe just a few minutes. Probably an hour," the guard replied, voice devoid of any inflection.

"Gods dammit," she said, surprising herself with the curse. The Security guard flinched and backed away. "Not your fault," she added. Nor was it. This had been a simple misjudgment on her part—but it had cost her an hour she could ill afford.

She would need to be more careful. Piotre Raskovich might be dangerous on many levels, but most of all, he was apparently a threat to himself.

She was walking on eggshells there when her boss was demanding she sprint.

In spite of the Security guard's prediction, it took less than five minutes for Piotre to return to consciousness. His transition back to wakefulness was as abrupt as every other change that came across him. One moment he was slumped in the chair, slack-jawed and drooling, and in the next, he sat straight, head held erect, gaze transfixing her as it had before.

She had never known Security to overestimate the impact of something as simple as a sedative, but little about Piotre could surprise her at this point.

"Thank you," he said.

"You're welcome. Is there more I can do?"

"There is," he said. "Give me control of the room. And I will tell you my story."

A first time for everything, she thought. *The CIO of an enemy starship wants access to my office's environmental controls?*

Why not?

"Very well," she said. She rekeyed the command system to his voice and activated gesture controls long disabled. "The interface should be intuitive enough."

"I imagine I can figure it out," he said dryly.

Then he turned her office into a tropical paradise.

She marveled at the speed at which he learned, how quickly he assumed control of the holographic and auditory systems, sight and sound and motion. In minutes, he had rendered a biodiversity preserve—an ark—with stunning layers of detail.

He threaded in olfactory cues, the heavy smell of peat and decay. He dialed up the heat, the humidity.

It was a marvelous performance. She was watching a virtuoso at work. She could have produced the same effect, but it might have taken her longer—and this was her own office!

"The interfaces are similar to equipment I have used before," he remarked. "Our companies evidently employ the same suppliers."

"I see."

"Now. If you'll come with me?"

He heaved himself out of the chair. She rose and followed. Of course, they could only take a few dozen steps in any given direction; the office took up the top floor of TransGalactic's capitol tower, but it was still only so big. And yet, it felt for all the world like they were walking down a trail. As they went, Piotre's quiet chattering of commands ceased, giving way entirely to gestures as his control over her system increased.

The trail should have ended by now, she thought. They should be at the office's wall. But it wound on, continuing through the tropical forest. He must have found a way to bend it imperceptibly, updating the illusion in real time, such that her sense of direction was lost.

It was incredible. She imagined her boss Alterik watching somewhere on a remote display. She wondered what he was thinking and then decided she didn't particularly care. Instead, she let her mind drift, joining Piotre more fully in the illusion he had created.

He wanted to show her something. It was her job to understand.

She heard a chorus of chattering birds and a distant monkey's howl. Smelled the rich odor of peat. Felt heat and humidity, water condensing on her skin.

The Security team followed unobtrusively, subtly repositioning themselves such that they appeared to blink in and out of existence as the illusion shifted. Then Piotre calibrated for their presence as well, and she saw them no further.

After a time, they came to a log blocking the trail. Of course, it was just a hologram. She could step right through it if she wished, but she had no desire to break the spell. This might be one of the strangest interlocutions she had ever performed, but the principle remained the same.

Empathize.

"The effect is, of course, imperfect," Piotre said. "But we have come far enough. Now. Let me show you the shape of the hole in my mind."

He bent down and bade her join him next to the log.

She knelt.

Then she saw something move.

It was a centipede. A big one, a horrible thing, scuttling back and forth behind the log. It paused in front of her and waved its mandibles in the air, as though ready to attack.

"I was ten," Piotre said. "And, ironically, accompanied by someone who worked for Human Resources. Rival company. Different methods. Same purpose."

He held out his hand. The hologram centipede inched forward, climbed up his fingers, and curled into a ball in his palm.

"I had never been more afraid in my life," he said. "Imagine it. A child of Mars, exposed to such a thing without warning. Naturally, it was done on purpose, though it was made to appear an accident. Years would pass before I would understand why.

"They had already run their psychological profiles. Ferreted out my weak spot. Even then, they knew best how to blindside me, terrorize me, exploit my deepest fear. One I didn't even know I possessed."

He stood, arm outstretched, the hologram perfectly synchronized with his movement, impossible to tell from the real thing.

How was he doing this? She marveled again at the degree of mastery on display.

He arched his neck back, gaped his mouth open, and held his hand up high. The centipede, bright scarlet, mandibles gaping, poison dripping, carapace glistening wet, crawled down his arm, then up his neck.

It disappeared into his mouth.

He snapped his jaws shut and feigned a noisy swallow.

"The creature I saw that day was real enough. The one I came to live with was, of course, simply a metaphor. There was never any such thing actually inside me. Not then, and not now. But in my mind, there might as well have been."

He stepped toward her and reached around to touch her on the back of her neck, at the base of her skull. "I always imagined it here. Where the medulla joins the non-lizard part of the brain."

She fought to remain calm, not to draw back, glad for the security team nearby.

Imagine. She, the Interlocutor, needing comfort for her own physical safety.

"Sometimes here," Piotre said, even closer now, almost embracing her as he traced her spine. Then he touched her stomach. "Or even here. Our nervous systems being distributed throughout our bodies, as well you know."

He stepped back. "But mostly, I imagined it curled up inside my brain. As that is where I do my best work."

At that moment, she understood.

"And then it was gone," she said.

"Yes," he agreed. "It simply vanished, leaving me to operate in a world of uncertainty. It's an uncomfortable place, and from time to time, it makes me do uncomfortable things."

This time, she did draw away from him.

"Explain that," she said.

"You condition your officers."

"We do," she allowed. "Although we don't exploit childhood terrors."

"Perhaps not, but that just proves your behavioral psychologists aren't as talented as ours. You would if you could."

She didn't dispute the point.

"But as it turns out," he went on, "Magellanix's behavioral controls suffer from a peculiar flaw. We are preprogrammed to respond in certain ways in certain situations. We're given our fears to guide us. When we're young, the guidance takes a simple form: the threat and promise of pain. Have you ever been bitten by a centipede, Interlocutor?

"I hope not, for your sake. Because I have, time and time again.

"But as we age, the need for such things fades. What grows in its place is first partnership, then friendship, and then simple dependency. This is the gift of the absence of pain. My metaphorical guide hasn't hurt me in decades. Why would it? I rely on it.

"Mine was the luxury of an externally provided ethical framework that I never needed question. There was no data I could possess that I would not know how to disposition. No situation in which I would not behave in a way consistent with enhancing company value."

"Until there was," she said.

"Until there was," he agreed. "They never programmed me for what I found. And evidently, when our Behavioral Conditioning fails, it does so spectacularly and without warning. Leaving behind the freedom to act."

The freedom, she thought. *With no ethical framework to guide it.*

"And now you have acted," she said.

"Yes."

Abruptly, the illusion vanished. She hadn't even seen him do it, but they were standing at her desk, back in the center of the room, the heat and humidity already beginning to fade.

"So, let me ask you, Interlocutor. Do we have a deal?"

She considered a moment and then sighed.

"I imagine so," she said. "Now, please. Have a seat, and tell me what happened out there."

CHAPTER 11

Twenty-four hours later, the Interlocutor sat together with Alterik in a tiny capsule, descending deep into the earth. She couldn't tell how far underground they had already traveled; in all her long career, she'd never been down there, had no idea this place even existed.

Her boss was trying to appear calm, acting as though a summons by the Board of Directors, They Themselves, the Pantheon and Mightiest of Mighty, were an everyday occurrence. But she knew how to read the signs and saw the agitation pouring from him in every twitch, murmur, and glance at the capsule's doors.

Were they a kilometer down? Ten? If the central tower of TransGalactic's capital city was a sailing ship, then her office was atop the mast, but the Board of Directors evidently held court in the keel. Deep enough to survive a nuclear strike, certainly. Magellanix or InterTech or one of their other rivals would have to hit the tower hard enough to calve a new moon if they wanted to hurt the Board.

She supposed it made sense. Valuables had been locked away in vaults since time immemorial. Still, she felt sorry for the Board in a way, even though she'd never met them. All that power, reduced to hiding in the basement.

She felt badly for Alterik as well. There hadn't been time to brief him. He was in the unfortunate position of having to trust a subordinate to report to his superiors without first knowing what they were going to say.

Eventually, she felt the capsule decelerating, and sometime later, it stopped altogether with the tiniest hitch. Their seat harnesses released, and the doors slid open.

A Security team of six awaited to lead them silently through a dimly lit corridor ending in an enormous arched doorway. The doors were massive stone affairs that swung open without a sound.

Beyond lay a vast, cavernous room, with a ramp leading down into a circular depression. She and Alterik descended together, their Security detail trailing behind. When she reached the bottom, she looked up and saw a stone railing ringing the pit, with a dozen high-backed chairs behind it, all empty.

She felt Alterik's discomfort as he stood rigidly next to her, but for her part, she almost laughed out loud. She couldn't have set the stage better herself. What a wonderful default human response, she decided. For lack of a better plan, put yourself in a high place and your enemy in a low one. Make them crane their necks if they want to see.

She smiled, delighted, at the sheer bare-knuckled posturing, then felt a moment's embarrassment for having resorted to similar tricks with Piotre Raskovich just a day before.

She glanced around the pit, looking for some other way in or out. Was there a side door, maybe? The kind the lions might use? She saw nothing.

A few minutes later, the Board of Directors appeared. They seemed to materialize from the darkness, entering the room such that they couldn't be seen from below as they stepped around their high-backed seats into view.

There were a dozen in all. They took their places together, though whether this was careful choreography or long habit, she couldn't say.

The Interlocutor knew herself as an ascetic. She wore her robes, cropped her hair, and lived a simple life with only her tea for extravagance. The Board members looked much the same but taken to an even greater extreme. They were all so tiny! They were diminutive figures dressed in simple robes, thinly built, and bald. Was this a fashion statement? Or something more? Some quirk of human biology, or some genotype that took to the life-extending drugs such that the little ones with their birdlike bones outlived the rest?

It seemed as good an explanation as any.

Their only accoutrements were headbands—simple, silver bands set with dark jewels, each a different color.

Maybe it's how they tell each other apart, she thought. Then she realized—*No, that's tech, Board-level tech; there could be enough bio-monitoring and drug delivery equipment built into each of those pieces of jewelry to manage a planetary population.*

Or maybe they were emergency storage systems of some kind. Had someone finally figured out how to back up and restore a human consciousness?

Were they wearing—themselves?

Probably not. A secret that big would be hard to keep, even for the Board, but in truth, she didn't know.

Mostly, she just marveled at how small they seemed, sitting in their impressive furniture, hiding behind their railing. Next to her, Alterik was a giant by comparison. Earlier that day, he had changed his clothes and was now dressed in a formal uniform. Maybe his preferred attire was too easily weaponized to be allowed in there.

Her own robe was spun hemp. A simple outfit, nothing more, nothing less. No sidearms hidden at her waist; no knives in her boots.

The Board made them wait almost a full minute before one of their number broke the silence. Their voice was liquid, a mellifluous warble. It was like being addressed by an oversized wren.

"We thank you for coming," they said, ". . . on such short notice."

Alterik stiffened beside her, jerking to attention.

"We invite the Interlocutor to speak."

On impulse, she sketched a low bow, lower back muscles two and a half centuries old shocked by the sudden call to duty. "It is a privilege to serve," she said, because after all—wasn't it?

"Tell us of this Piotre Raskovich." This came from another member of the Board, but unnervingly, she couldn't tell the voices apart.

"And what we might do," said a third, indistinguishable from the first two.

That was going to make this difficult, she thought. Now she was being addressed by a whole flock of birds.

She glanced at Alterik. This was pure courtesy, giving him the chance to make some gesture of assent, some notional semblance of a chain of command.

He nodded to her curtly. Well, he'd thank her later.

But where to begin?

With the truth, she decided.

"Piotre Raskovich," she said, "is dangerously sane." She paused a moment for effect but could detect no response. "Dangerous to himself," she continued. "To Magellanix, and certainly to us as well. But he is sane. Coldly, deeply sane, in a way that he hasn't been for decades."

"Go on," a Board member warbled at her. Dammit, she thought—was that a new one, or had they already spoken? How was she ever going to read these people?

She couldn't. They might not even qualify as people, might not be fully human anymore. Who knew? There was nothing for it but to plunge ahead.

"He says he is in possession of direct evidence of another spacefaring race," she said. "His ship, *Accipiter*, discovered a holocaust world, and on that world they found an artifact: a spherical structure of unknown composition, placed in the crater of a volcano that formed a million years after the nuclear catastrophe that eliminated all higher-order forms of life on the planet.

"In other words, Piotre Raskovich claims to have found evidence that a sentient species reached that world after the holocaust which destroyed it. That race, that starfaring race, left behind a structure of unknown purpose.

"The unexpectedness of this find caused Piotre Raskovich's Behavioral Conditioning to fail. I now have some insight into how Magellanix conditions its senior officers. Their techniques are unusual. Evidently effective but, as with all top-down forms of control, brittle in the face of the unanticipated."

She paused again, taking a breath. Risked a glance at Alterik, who was standing stock-still.

"Go on," a Board member encouraged her.

She nodded. "Piotre Raskovich has spent his career monetizing information on Magellanix's behalf. Confronted with new degrees of freedom in his own actions, he stuck to what he knew best. But in this case, he has decided to monetize his data assets for his own purposes."

"Is his story true?"

This voice came from behind her, and it was all she could do not to spin around like a top. *Give up for now*, she decided. *If they cannot be differentiated, then integrate them. Deal with them as a single individual, not twelve.*

"There is no particular reason to doubt the veracity of his claim," she said. "Nor, obviously, any easy way to overstate its importance."

"What does he want?"

"What you have, esteemed members of the Board. He wants immortality, or as close to it as we can provide. He would also like to be governor of his own world."

This, finally, provoked a reaction. A chorus of reactions; differentiated opinions at last.

"These do not sound like the actions of a sane man," a Board member said.

"We could tear his mind apart," said another.

"Yes. Take what we wish," agreed a third.

The Interlocutor nodded. "He has anticipated this and has a counterproposal."

"Which is?"

"He volunteers to become a marketing icon. He proposes that we make an example of him. He suggests that if we make what has happened to him widely known, and the rewards he has earned equally broadly understood, the Behavioral Conditioning of other senior Magellanix officers might also fail."

The room fell quiet as a tomb. Alterik stared at her, open-mouthed. She arched her eyebrows at him, the tiniest equivalent of a shrug as if to say *Don't shoot the messenger.*

"That is interesting," a Board member said.

Another: "Could it be done?"

"Do you have a recommendation?"

"Is he telling the truth?"

"In my opinion," the Interlocutor said, "Piotre Raskovich is not attempting to deceive us. It is also my view that his mind is broken. He may have forgotten key details, and equally, he may still have access to information he does not realize."

"He could be a mole."

"An agent."

"A liar."

"A time bomb."

"A public-relations disaster."

"All of these things are also true," she said.

Silence fell over the room again, stretching out and growing uncomfortable. Maybe they were communicating with each other, she thought. In some manner not meant for her ears.

A full minute passed. Then a Board member, who might have been the first one to have spoken, said simply, "Both of you are invited to depart."

Without hesitation, Alterik bowed beside her and turned on his heel to leave. She did the same, grateful now for her boss's presence, simply to have footsteps to follow. Her own psyche was nearly overwhelmed.

The last two days had simply been too much. She could feel a deep exhaustion creeping inside her and knew she had overextended herself badly.

Together they returned to the elevator capsule, flanked once more by their Security guards. They stepped inside, but this time, the journey was brief. After a few seconds, the capsule stopped, as if they had gone up but a single floor.

"Now what?" she wondered aloud.

The doors opened. They were in a lounge of some kind: a brightly lit reception area with food and drink laid out, a buffet that could have served a hundred. Warm, comfortable seating, personal interfaces if they so desired; anything one could wish for when killing time before a meeting.

"I imagine they'll call for us when they're ready," Alterik said. His voice was a shock to her ears. It was the first purely human sound she had heard since she'd been down there. "Meantime, I guess we wait."

It didn't take long. Whoever they were, had been, or might yet become, the TransGalactic Board of Directors was at least capable of making quick decisions.

But this time, when the summons came, they only wanted to speak to her.

Alterik looked daggers at her but said nothing. What could he say? The Security team led her back to the capsule. The doors slid shut again, her boss disappearing behind them.

She wondered for a moment if she would ever see him again.

Down she went: back to the dungeon, vault, conference room, bowels of corporate hell.

It seemed brighter this time, and maybe a few degrees warmer as well. The ramp into the pit wasn't as steep as it had been, either. *So, that's how it is*, she thought. *Trying to send me a signal. We're all friends here.*

It might've been amusing, except for a little thrill of fear she felt creeping in at the corner of her mind. Back in that place a second time. Twice, in two hundred years.

And this time alone.

The Board was waiting for her. In the better light, she could make out subtle differences between them. Skin pigments, minor variations in size, the color of the dark jeweled bands they each wore.

"The Board has reached a decision," one of them said. "There is a ship—the *Carpathia*. It is one of the most capable in our fleet, currently inbound to the relay station Occipitus Prime. Its mission has been uneventful. There is nothing to prevent its immediate return to deep space."

The speaker made eye contact with her. For the first time, the Interlocutor thought, they were actually talking to her.

"The *Carpathia* will depart immediately for this planet you have named Ragnarock," they continued. "Piotre Raskovich will go with them, and you will serve as the senior Human Resources representative onboard."

She boggled. Looked around, searching for a chair she knew wasn't there, unable to believe what she had just heard.

"Are you quite well, Interlocutor?"

She managed a nod.

"We are aware that this represents a departure from your normal roles and responsibilities."

Does it ever, she thought. She hadn't supposed she'd hear anything more about any of this, let alone be asked to come along for the ride. She'd delivered her report and had assumed the Board would do with the information as they saw fit. She'd been planning to conduct a special forgetting ceremony tomorrow to flush all this from her mind.

And maybe take Monday off.

"You have our gratitude," the Board member said, "for your flexibility of approach. A full mission briefing will await you on the shuttle that will take you and Mr. Raskovich to Occipitus Prime. He is, even now, being placed into hibernation. You will be awake for the journey."

Maybe the low-gee parts, she thought. She knew about high-speed transports, the kind of acceleration profiles of which they were capable. She didn't have much doubt about how her own body would react.

"There is one additional complexity," a second Board member said. "*Carpathia* will make a detour en route to Ragnarock."

"We are aware this introduces additional risk," the first one agreed, though for just a moment, she thought she caught the briefest hint of strain. Some subtle disagreement on this point, maybe? Or maybe this was outright conflict, as close to shouting at each other as they ever came.

"The *Carpathia* will stop at the planet Paradise and retrieve a civilian specialist, along with any support staff she may require," the second Board member said. "Her name is Dr. Nya Solarin. She is a xeno-evolutionary specialist who has spent her career, thus far unprofitably, studying the fates of failed civilizations. Insofar as anyone is qualified to represent TransGalactic interests in a mission such as this, it is her."

A pause, that seemed to invite a response. "You wish me to speak with her?" the Interlocutor ventured.

"We do," the Board member assented. "The trip will be stressful for her. She was born on Paradise and has never been off-planet. She will be receiving her orders with almost no time to react and may require counseling along the way.

"But your primary assignment, Interlocutor, is Piotre Raskovich. The Board has concluded that you are correct in your assessment. Even if he is telling the truth, he may possess information you have yet to extract.

"And there is one additional thing as well. The Ragnarock system may be defended. Piotre Raskovich's ship may have left remote defenses, and if he is who he claims, Mr. Raskovich may well have the codes to disarm them."

"I understand," she said.

"Good. We are aware that Piotre Raskovich may pose some degree of threat to the ship, its crew, and its mission. *Carpathia* is commanded by Ali Marakan. Her service record is impeccable. She will balance these risks: information against the cost of obtaining it. She will decide whether and when to awaken Mr. Raskovich from hibernation. When she does, you will interlocute him as you deem fit and report your findings directly to her."

"I understand," the Interlocutor said again.

"Then that is all. We thank you for your distinguished service."

A thousand questions raced through her mind, but she knew a dismissal when she heard one. She nodded, turned on her heel, and made her way from the shallow pit, back to the elevator capsule.

This time, the elevator didn't stop in the waiting area. What else the rest of the day held in store for Alterik, she couldn't guess.

She returned to her office, where the desk chimed for her attention. A detailed mission briefing awaited her. She ignored it for a moment, gazing up through the crystal ceiling to the sky beyond.

Two and a half centuries old, and asked to travel to the stars.

She wondered what she ought to pack.

CHAPTER 12

Ian McAllister, now acting captain of the *Carpathia*, tossed in his bunk, fidgety and uncomfortable in the single standard gravity imparted by their long deceleration. It was midnight shipboard time. He was exhausted, but sleep eluded him.

They had three days and thirty million kilometers to go. By now they were in regular communication with Occipitus Prime, the great relay station at Sol System's edge, messaging back and forth with status updates and velocity profiles, assignment berths and maintenance schedules, and a thousand other details of arrival home after years in deep space. Per Captain Marakan's orders, he had spent the last two weeks furthering the ruse that Ali Marakan herself was still in command. All was well aboard *Carpathia*, he had repeatedly told the TransGalactic crew awaiting their arrival station-side. He had scheduled routine inspections and maintenance but not the deep repairs or crew replacements they needed to return to full strength. He had also signed all his communiqués with Marakan's personal codes, wondering each time whether he was committing some corporate crime or simply following orders.

He sighed in frustration, his unquiet mind too full of the thousands of decisions required to command a starship to give in to sleep. Defeated, he climbed out of his bunk and slouched across the tiny cabin to his desk, where he called a view of Occipitus Prime to life on his screen. He had ordered *Carpathia*'s surviving telescopes fixed on their destination some days before. Now he stared at the stream of images as though a view of the station itself might trigger some thought, offer some clue to a detail he had overlooked.

Occipitus Prime was shaped like a kidney bean with a bite taken out of one end, and if not for the lights dotting its surface, the relay station would have been indistinguishable from an ordinary asteroid. He couldn't tell which of the dark craters pockmarking its surface held docking berths and would never have known just by looking that its core had been hollowed out, that deep inside lay a beating fusion heart more powerful than that of a starship.

They were approaching at an oblique angle, which meant the end with the chunk missing was positioned away from them. The bite itself was a deep, artificial cavern, dug to house and protect the array of enormously high-powered radio transmitters the station kept oriented toward Earth. The station was a hundred kilometers on its long axis, ten through its short one, and was positioned in an orbit far beyond Neptune's, as close to the stable transition point they had just used as was practical.

Because that particular transition point was still the doorway to the stars for anyone departing humanity's home system, over time, more and more facilities had been added to Occipitus Prime. This was fortunate for *Carpathia*, as they need not return all the way to Earth for repairs. Entire parts of the ship were missing, but *Carpathia* was modular by design, and like its corporate rivals, TransGalactic had built up an extensive manufacturing capability out there at the great relay station. In time, all their damage could be repaired. They would replenish their crew as well, though whether those replacements would be shuttled from Earth or taken from personnel already living on the station, Ian couldn't guess.

It wouldn't be his problem. They would dock, the amount of damage *Carpathia* had sustained would be revealed, and the rest would be up to high command. Including his own performance evaluation, however that might go.

"Captain? Signal coming in, sir."

He blinked, his reverie interrupted by the voice of a junior lieutenant piped from the bridge to the subdural in his inner ear. "Commander's eyes only," the young woman added.

An eyes-only message? Communication with Occipitus Prime had been routine so far. This must be a message intended for Captain Markan herself.

"Authenticate," he said. It could be a fake. As they had made no attempt to conceal their approach, every rival corporation with a presence out there knew they were coming. It was conceivable that someone might send false orders, invalid requests for status or information; or try to spoof, defraud, or hack into them in any of a hundred different ways.

Seconds ticked by while the communications officer validated the signal's legitimacy.

"Authenticated," she said at last.

"Very well," he said. "I'll take it here." He settled back in his chair to watch but to his surprise, no holographics rendered before him. Instead, the desk's screen went blank, and a simple plain text message appeared.

Commander, Carpathia

Discontinue approach to Occipitus Prime. Make no further contact.

Proceed on course detailed herein. Execute deep-space rendezvous with interplanetary rapid-transport unit, identification, coordinates, velocity profiles, and timing given below.

Do not acknowledge receipt.

The message identified its point of origin as Fleet Command, Trans-Galactic Earth headquarters, Antarctica, which was as high an authority as there was. What followed were a series of deep-space coordinates, velocity profiles, and timestamps: the tactical details of the rendezvous he was meant to perform, along with the identification of the shuttle they were to meet.

But there were no further instructions. No additional context at all.

He stared at the screen in disbelief, rubbed his eyes, and read the message again, trying to work it through. A terse, maximum-security message, ordering them to complete silence, diverting them onto an alternate course, to a clandestine rendezvous?

It couldn't be real. Could it?

"Reauthenticate, Lieutenant," he said.

It was an unusual request, but to the young officer's credit, she responded without hesitation. "Yes, sir."

The seconds ticked by again. It was an awfully short message, he thought, given the amount of time required to validate it. Which maybe said something about the encryption protocol that had been used. Whoever sent this had spent their bandwidth on security, not content.

But if it was real, should he obey? The message was intended for Ali Marakan. Whoever sent it wouldn't know she wasn't in command. He had done his best to create that exact appearance, and now Captain Marakan was running dark in *Sagittaria*, having given explicit orders that they make no further contact while she snuck her captured ship to safe harbors.

Cloak-and-dagger, in the middle of deep space. He put his head in his hands. Commander, *Carpathia*, the orders read. That was him. Wasn't it?

And they were so close to home. Why now?

"Reauthenticated, sir."

"Very well," he said. He thought a moment more, then called a tactical display to life. He plotted *Carpathia*'s location and velocity and then reread the message in detail, computing the maneuver they would need to reach the rendezvous point.

The ship that was meeting them was on a hard burn from Earth; that much was clear. To intercept it, they would need to veer away from Occipitus Prime immediately under heavy acceleration of their own, and then continue to turn until they had reversed their direction completely and were headed back—where?

The transition point. The transport from Earth would overtake them, decelerating to match *Carpathia*'s velocity. At which point, whoever was coming to meet them would find out Captain Marakan wasn't onboard and *Carpathia* was badly damaged.

The new mission, whatever it was, would have to be aborted. *Carpathia* was still jump-capable, but Fleet Command wouldn't send them out with a lieutenant in command, missing a third of their crew, with whole functional areas of the ship gone.

Would they?

He rewound the tactical display to the point where they'd jumped in-system and sent their original message ahead to Occipitus Prime. The round-trip times were simple to work out. They'd signaled Occipitus Prime, which would have bounced their signal to Earth, received a reply, and then forwarded that back to *Carpathia*.

But the timing, he thought. The round-trip time was such that Fleet Command on Earth would have known for days that they were coming. They were on a routine approach. Why wait until the last minute to reroute them?

Something must have happened. Something that required the next available ship, and that was *Carpathia*.

What else could he do? His orders were clear. He'd make the rendezvous and then let his commanders know what was really going on.

"Bridge, navigation," he said. "Bring us about. We've been given a new course."

It took four uncomfortable days in heavy gravity under the aggressive acceleration curve required to reach the rendezvous point. The Carpathians passed their time in high-gee couches at their stations, or in their cabins, only clumping around the ship at twice their own weight when absolutely necessary.

Then, at last, they reached the prescribed course and speed and eased back into blessed weightlessness, to wait for whoever was coming to catch them.

Ian scarcely left the bridge during that time. It was one thing to be responsible for flying a captured ship in formation or to oversee a routine docking. Now, for all he knew, he'd committed the greatest of possible blunders, had swallowed a rival's bait and ordered them to their doom. He might be about to deliver *Carpathia* into enemy hands, as surely as they had snatched *Sagittaria* away from its rightful owners.

He was about to find out.

He stared at the main screen on the bridge, trying not to fidget. Their best scopes were focused on where the approaching ship should be. Night silhouetted against night, he thought, looking for the disappearance of stars. It was a romantic notion and foolish. His naked eye would hardly spot the incoming ship before *Carpathia*'s onboard detection systems did. What they were searching for was an emission signature: residue from a deceleration burn, not a visual image of the shuttle itself.

Somewhere out there was an interplanetary craft, braking hard on a tongue of fusion fire.

"Inbound, sir!"

"Details, Mister."

The young officer—so much of the senior crew had been lost; they were all so young!—frowned, hunched over his screen, reading the stream of data now coming back. "Emissions signature, sir," he said. "Whoever it is, they're under heavy deceleration."

"Course and speed?"

More furious analysis. "Consistent with what we're expecting, sir. They're right where they're supposed to be."

"Sir?" This was from his communications officer, the same young woman who had been on duty four days prior. "We're being hailed."

"Authenticate."

"Yes, sir." This time, it only took a few seconds for the answer to come back. "Validated, sir. It's one of ours. Rapid-transit unit. Requesting permission to dock, sir."

He took a deep breath. "Very well," he said. "Direct them to airlock seven." Airlocks one through six had been vaporized in the firefight with *Sagittaria*. "Have a security team meet me. I'll greet our visitors myself."

Before he could second-guess the decision, he released his footholds and propelled himself across the bridge with a subtle kick. He timed it right, hitting the hatch with a modicum of grace, aware as always of the eyes on his back, the crew watching everything, judging constantly. Then he was through the door, into the corridor beyond, a moment's solitude as he made his way through the ship.

Wondering now more than ever what this was all about.

Up close, the transport was a brutal-looking ship. It was an atomic hammer, its front end an enormous, bell-shaped blast shield used to translate the energy released by its fusion-bomb spitters into thrust. Bulky cargo space stubbed out behind the shield like a nubby stalk concealed beneath the oversized cap of a mushroom. Ian had never seen one quite like it. Similar designs, yes, but nothing this severe. *Carpathia* dwarfed the new arrival; she was kilometers long, while the rapid-transport unit was scarcely a hundred meters.

He wondered at the gee forces involved. Whoever was onboard would have been gel-packed the entire way and still probably had a rough trip.

Clumsy as it looked, the ship docked nimbly enough. Trying to project nonchalance for the benefit of the two Security personnel who waited with him, he watched without comment as umbilicals extended, forming a temporary gangway in the hard vacuum.

The ships sealed and equalized. A short time after that, the hatch eased open.

A single figure drifted in the airlock beyond, accompanied by a hibernation capsule.

She eased her way forward, appearing uncomfortable in the zero gravity. She was a small woman, her age indeterminate but possibly quite old. She wore a simple crimson robe. She flicked her eyes up and down, taking him in, then smiled at him pleasantly. If she was confused, or expecting someone else, she didn't show it.

"Permission to board?" she said. Her voice was melodic.

Human Resources, he thought. *No, more than that. Look at her robe!* He was staring at a gods-damned Interlocutor.

Here. But why?

"Granted," he said, using his best captain's voice. "Welcome aboard . . . Interlocutor?" He let the word trail off, inviting a response.

"Thank you." She glanced at the capsule beside her. "Could someone perhaps help with my luggage? I'm new to zero-gravity work, I'm afraid."

The hibernation unit was shiny-black, the approximate size and shape of a coffin. Diagnostics on its single display indicated that it was occupied. Whoever was inside was asleep but alive.

"If I may, I'd advise putting it in a secure hold for now, Captain," she added. "It's something of a long story."

He nodded tersely. "Auxiliary storage bay," he said to his Security team. The two guards maneuvered the capsule deftly out of the airlock, then disappeared out of sight down the corridor.

"You have orders for me," he said, once they had gone.

"I don't wish to be rude, but my orders are for this ship's captain," the Interlocutor said.

"That," he said, "would be me." He swallowed hard. "Interlocutor, my name is Lieutenant Ian McAllister, and I am acting commander of this ship. Perhaps you would care to join me in my quarters and tell me what this is all about?"

She pushed herself free of the airlock and drifted gently into the ship proper.

"That sounds like a fine idea," she said.

Briefly, he debated taking her to Captain Marakan's quarters, then dismissed the idea as absurd. There was no reason to attempt subterfuge, no point in anything but the truth.

The Interlocutor followed him in silence, apparently content to observe. He had no doubt she missed nothing. He had been interlocuted at a high level once in his career, five years prior, upon first reaching a lieutenant's rank.

The experience had been disquieting, to say the least.

When they reached his quarters, he felt a wave of relief as the door slid shut behind them, glad that whatever the Interlocutor had to say would now be delivered in private. But she made no comment at all, just reached into her robe, withdrew a small, slender memory strip, and offered it to him.

Hand-delivered orders?

"Doing things the old-fashioned way," the Interlocutor said, as if guessing his thoughts.

He nodded, regarding the memory strip in his palm. "Have you viewed this?" he asked.

"No," she said. "But I have a fairly good idea what it says."

"Huh." He stared at the tiny strip, nonplussed, then kicked over to the desk and palmed its screen to life.

A moment passed while the ship's systems authenticated the orders, and then a holographic image appeared in the air above the cabin's desk. He saw a trio of robed figures, rendered in such a way that they appeared to be standing in deep shadows, their faces invisible. They were projected without any background imagery, which made them seem to float in the room like ghosts.

"Commander, *Carpathia*." The one in the middle spoke; Ian could just barely see lips moving. The voice was a liquid warble. "We speak today on behalf of the entirety of your Board of Directors, and we thank you for your attention."

He breathed out, hard.

"The Board?" he said.

"Yes," the Interlocutor agreed.

"A matter has come to us," the recording continued, "that requires your services. The Interlocutor is aware of all that we are about to say. Please pause this recording and ask her to join you if she has not already, so you may hear it together."

He looked at the Interlocutor. She lifted her shoulders slightly as if to say *Here I am*. He nodded, letting the message continue.

Then he watched and listened, mouth agape, not even trying to conceal his shock as they laid it out for him: Piotre Raskovich's story and what was now being asked of them.

It was impossible. Too much to be believed.

A defecting Chief Information Officer, Behavioral Conditioning broken, asleep in a hibernation chamber? There, on *Carpathia*?

And a holocaust world, and on it an artifact: evidence of a surviving spacefaring race—and with it, a potential first contact. The thing all humanity had lived in hope and fear of for a thousand years.

"So, you see," the Board member concluded, "the urgency with which we must act." The figure glanced sideways, looking away for the first time, as though yielding the floor.

A second board member spoke. "Nevertheless," they said, their voice indistinguishable from the first. "There is a detour you must take before you proceed to this newly found holocaust world. You will travel to the planet Paradise and retrieve a civilian specialist who teaches and conducts her research there. She is a full-time TransGalactic employee and, even though a member of our academic division, she is fully eligible for active duty. Her name is Dr. Nya Solarin. She has spent her career studying xeno-evolutionary biology, attempting to identify the environmental conditions that lead to the rise of sentient life. If another spacefaring race has survived as we have, her knowledge may be required."

The second Board member fell silent. The first one nodded gravely and said, "That is all. Retrieve Dr. Solarin and then use the navigational data the defector Piotre Raskovich has provided to make all due haste to this newfound holocaust world. Our rivals at Magellanix have named it Ragnarock. You will secure the planet, locate the find, and contact its owners if they exist.

"We await your successful completion of this endeavor."

The image stilled. Silence fell over the cabin.

Ian waved the message away, mind racing as he tried to piece it all together. He worked through the timing again, what must have happened.

They had gated in and called ahead to Occipitus Prime. The station relayed news of their arrival to Earth. Days later, Piotre Raskovich defected. TransGalactic Headquarters had dispatched the Interlocutor and her sleeping cargo, sending them racing to this deep-space rendezvous. Then they waited as long as they could, only diverting *Carpathia* at the last minute, setting her on a new course.

Meanwhile, Captain Marakan was inbound to Earth, traveling in secrecy. She wouldn't know any of this had taken place. It would take weeks to fix the mistake, even if another ship were available with *Carpathia*'s capabilities.

During which time Magellanix would doubtless discover Piotre Raskovich's betrayal. They would dispatch a ship of their own. Or possibly multiple ships. They could send an entire planetary occupation force back to Ragnarock.

Or, of course, the whole thing could be a bizarre setup. Could his own Board of Directors have been fooled? Could Piotre Raskovich be some sort of . . . sleeper agent? He almost laughed out loud at the pun.

What was he supposed to do? It was all over his head, absurdly above his pay grade.

Then again, what else could he do, if not follow orders? To the letter, with alacrity. Out of pure self-defense, if nothing else.

He turned to regard the Interlocutor. He had the sense she had been watching him the whole time and knew every detail of the thought process that had just played out.

"May I offer a suggestion, Captain?" she said.

"Please."

"It might be time for you to choose a different cabin."

"I'm sorry?"

"We're going to be out here a while," she said. "The symbolism will matter."

He considered that. "You'll need quarters as well," he said at last.

She lifted an eyebrow. "So it would seem. And, Captain?"

"Acting Captain."

"Captain McAllister," she repeated. "Acting or not, that is how you are addressed, the role you have to play in all this, and it is how you must think of yourself. Is that clear?"

He ducked his head. "Yes," he said.

She nodded as though satisfied. "What happened to you all out there?"

"It's classified."

She arched an eyebrow fractionally. "Nevertheless. You may wish to talk about it sometime."

"Maybe I would." He thought for another moment. "It's going to be a race," he said. "And the first thing we're going to do is give up our head start."

"As you say," the Interlocutor said.

"Dr. Nya Solarin." He repeated the name they'd been given, mulling it over. "A xeno-evolutionary specialist. We're going weeks out of our way to pick up a university professor."

"Yes."

"Then I guess we'd better get started," he said. "There's no time to waste."

CHAPTER 13

It was ironic, the Interlocutor thought. She had on many occasions turned her office into this or that part of a starship—crew's quarters or an officers' mess, a bridge, a sensor array or a weapons pod, a weaver bank or hibernation hold or something stranger still—to put some officer returning from a years-long deployment at ease. She'd long since deliberately forgotten the specifics, but it was a tactic she had resorted to time and again. Now her office, which was also her toilet, dining room, sleeping quarters, and study, was part of an actual starship, and she felt uncomfortable in the extreme.

Not that there was anything wrong with her quarters. Young Ian McAllister was looking after her well. He was worried about her, which had a certain charm. He'd given her a cabin that once belonged to a now-deceased senior lieutenant. She understood it to be well appointed by Carpathian standards, with a full twelve square meters of living space to call her own.

Her discomfort was purely physical, as her body had already begun protesting the larger changes that lay ahead. Her joints ached constantly, and she had a throbbing pain in the back of her sinuses that the ship's surviving medical staff promised would fade over time, but thus far showed no signs of abating. Both were consequences of the spacer's drug regimen she had been prescribed. One pill to inure her from the effects of elevated background radiation, another to preserve her musculature, a series of injections to realign her internal organs to handle the vagaries of apparent gravity she would experience. There would be heavy artificial gees imposed by extreme acceleration profiles, followed by extended periods of weightlessness, a combination that could be expected to wreak havoc on someone as deep into life extension as she had gone.

She was a stranger there. She did not belong in this environment; that much was clear. The rest of the Carpathians clumped about in the one point two standard gravities like it wasn't worthy of their notice, whereas she felt like she had aged another hundred years in a day.

She wondered if they would be out there long enough for her eyes to turn black, to give her the true spacer's look. Sometimes, it took decades for that particular side effect to manifest, but occasionally, it happened much faster. Her curiosity left her with an irrational desire to catch her own reflection on every shiny surface she passed.

An Interlocutor, paranoid and complaining. She shook her head at the wonderment of it all.

There was one bit of good news: the ship's galley produced a passable tea, a cup of which she now held.

She sighed and took a sip.

Time to stop whining and do her job. Which, this morning, meant base trickery and simple invasions of privacy—not her favorite activities, but necessary.

She waved an interface to life, issued a few commands, and was rewarded by the appearance of eight terse words rendered in the air in front of her.

Personal Log, Lieutenant Ian McAllister, Acting Captain, Carpathia.

Dirty tricks: her stock and trade. She hadn't just been carrying orders on the solid-state bit of hardware she'd brought with her from Earth. She'd also come equipped with Carpathian system overrides, root-level interface commands that were a parting gift from the Board of Directors.

She felt the barest flickering of guilt, sat with it for a moment, and set it free.

Then she took another sip of her tea, scrolled to the acting captain's most recent entry, and began to read.

Mission Entry #1. 3084-08-25, Earth normal.

We are a ship of ghosts.

We are defined by absence, not presence, haunted by the memories of those who no longer remain.

Captain Marakan most of all. And our crew who have gone on, joined her on Sagittaria, *even now reaching a home we will not see for who knows how long?*

And of course, there are those who died in our botched ambush. Including my own missing friends.

We are two weeks outbound from Occipitus Prime, a week removed from our strange rendezvous, where we took on our unusual passengers. We leave behind a wake of missed chances. Reunions that never happened, families still unseen after years gone by, friends and loved ones unvisited.

Whoever said a ship was freedom was either a poet or a liar, but they certainly never served in deep space. We are Carpathians and will remain so, whether we want to or not, for longer than makes any sense to contemplate.

At least the crew took the announcement well enough. What else could they do? They are professionals. There hasn't been a mutiny onboard a TransGalactic vessel in recorded company history.

At least, not in the records to which I have access. Maybe I should ask the Interlocutor if she knows differently.

Not that she would tell me.

Captain Marakan wouldn't have worried about the mood of the crew. She would have known what to do in an instant; could've put down an insurrection with a disapproving glance. She would have taught, cajoled, disciplined, invented a thousand ways to strike that balance between contractual obligation, career opportunity, the thrill of the unknown, and opportunity for personal growth.

Captain Marakan was vastly better at this sort of thing than I can ever hope to be.

I only have one thing working for me: we are busy as hell. The one silver lining in being as badly damaged as we are is there is no shortage of work.

Fortunately, Carpathia *is less a starship than she is a collection of systems designed to make more starships. Everything is modular, compartmentalized, and reproducible. As long as our fusion heart keeps beating and the particle accelerator that is our spine remains unbroken, we can rebuild the rest. Nor do we lack raw material. We will simply reweave habitat modules we don't need anymore into more useful things.*

There are many with no one left to occupy them.

So: we will patch our hull, rebuild missing sensory equipment, and replace our destroyed banks of weaponry. We will make our ship whole again.

Just a bit reduced, as we all are.

As for me? I will carry on, a fraud to the core. I will drive this ship to Paradise, retrieve Nya Solarin, and follow the traitor Piotre Raskovich's navigational data wherever they lead.

Of course, by the time we get there, Accipiter *will likely be waiting to finish the job her sister ship* Sagittaria *started.*

Whoever Dr. Solarin is, I sincerely hope she's worth it.

As for my guests, Piotre Raskovich is still asleep in his hibernation chamber, a problem for another day. But the Interlocutor is very much up and about. She is meeting with the crew, doing the jobs that should have been done by our own missing human resources personnel.

She, too, is like a ghost. No—not a ghost. A very strange monk, this priest-like figure in her robes who manages to look dignified even under acceleration that must be painful for her.

I am meeting with her later today. I need to let her know what is coming: a jump event, which even a monk might find unsettling.

Particularly if it is her first.

The Interlocutor waved the words away and sat for a time, considering. Her young captain was doing well. He had empathy, which was a beginning. If he could get past his crippling insecurity, he might be good at this someday. He might even have his command formalized and made permanent when they finally returned home. That would make him one of the youngest ever to achieve a captain's rank. A case study for a human resources manual.

But only if they were successful. Only if they survived.

She wondered at that future time what that particular forgetting would be like. She suspected this experience would be one she would remember, whether she wanted to or not.

She needed rest. She found her bunk and heaved herself onto it, forcing herself into a cross-legged posture and settling into a breathing exercise, trying to relax, seeking a meditative state that might counteract whatever the spacer's drugs were doing inside her skull.

There was little else to do for the moment and no reason to spend any more energy this morning.

Some hours later, her captain came calling.

She had configured her cabin to sound a deep, pleasing gong when she had a visitor. Now this snapped her back to full wakefulness, and she bid the door open, knowing full well who would be waiting on the other side.

"I apologize for the interruption," he said.

"Not at all," she said, recalling the last time she had heard those words. "Come in, please."

The young man stepped into her cabin, reluctance showing in his movements as he regarded her where she still sat, cross-legged on her narrow bunk.

"We are three days out from our first jump," he said. "I wanted to invite you to observe from the bridge, if you are interested."

She smiled. "You're worried about me," she said, watching for and seeing the tiny flinch that often accompanied having one's thoughts guessed so easily.

"It's standard procedure to keep crew under close observation on their initial exposure to deep-space hyper-transit," he said.

"Quoting the manual?"

"It was written for a reason. Of course, I have no way of knowing if this will be your first jump or your hundredth."

"But you suspect it might be my first," she said. "Because of the way I move. Because the drug regimen is new to me. And for a hundred other reasons as well, including my obvious discomfort."

"Yes," he agreed. "Then again, it's equally possible that it's not your first but it's been a very long time."

"Maybe even so long that I don't remember?"

She watched him appraising her and knew what he wanted to ask. *How old are you, anyway? What have you seen, and done? Where have you been?*

But what he said was, "We will also be conducting combat drills. I'd appreciate your professional opinion."

She cocked her head at him, wanting him to know he'd surprised her. "I'm not a performance evaluator," she said.

"Forgive me, Interlocutor. I thought that's exactly what you were."

She laughed, delighted. Thinking, again, *He really might be good at this someday.*

"I can perhaps shed some insight as to how your crew feels about being asked to perform their duties, Captain. Even tell you whether they thought they did a good job. I just meant that I cannot evaluate them technically."

"So, do you accept?"

"I'm happy to serve," she said. "As long as you don't think I'll be a distraction."

It was his turn to smile. "I hope you will be. The more external stressors, the better, for drills like these."

"Then I accept your invitation. But that isn't all you came to ask me."

"No. We also have a decision to make."

She nodded. "Piotre Raskovich."

"Yes," the captain said. "Asleep in our hold." He shook his head as though in disbelief. "Our own CIO is dead, and the replacement we've been sent just happens to work for the enemy. Or at least he did. Who he's working for now, I have no idea."

"He has entered into that strange mercenary state of being self-employed," she said.

"A contractor without a contract."

"And you're wondering if you should wake him up."

"I am," he said. "We have months of travel ahead of us. To me, there seems no hurry, but this is a question for you. Is there utility in extra time with him? Do you wish to resume your interlocution?"

It was the right question, and she was pleased to hear him ask it. She got heavily to her feet and made her way to the far wall, staring at the stars outside. They were all projected, of course; there was nothing as simple as a glass portal through which she might look.

"A real window would be nice," he said. "We make do."

She smiled to herself, thinking, *Now he is guessing my thoughts.* "Certainly, there may be things Piotre Raskovich hasn't told us," she said. She turned to face him. "The interlocution was badly rushed. There may be more he does not yet know."

"Do you have some hesitation?"

"No, Captain. Though the crew would find him unsettling. I advise you to keep him in isolation."

"Very well," he said. "We will revisit this when we are finished with our first jump and properly on our way."

Three days later, she found herself on the bridge for the first time, tucked away in a corner, stationed at a remote sensing console not currently in use. Like the rest of the ship, the bridge was a uniform, gunmetal gray, everything polished to a dull sheen. A faint trace of antibacterial compounds hung in the air.

She glanced to her right, where Ian McAllister stood with his feet hooked into toeholds, calmly surveying the dozen crew members arranged in the U-shaped space before and below him. Presumably, it all made sense to him, but to her, the instrumentation, holographic readouts, and data streams on display beggared the imagination. She had only the barest idea of what she was seeing from a technical perspective, but from a human one, the impression was of a symphony masterfully played, with a subtle precision that belied the complexity of the exercise.

It was also eerily quiet, the crew almost still. Their stations, like hers, were control systems but also acceleration couches, such that they could perform their work in free fall or under heavy gees. They controlled their instruments with the tiniest gestures: flicks of hand, twitches of a finger, nods, or even just a subtle shifting of gaze.

She had seen, in her long career, endless recordings of exactly this sort of thing, watched thousands of hours of crews and officers at work. But it was different in person, and only partly because of the dull ache in her bones.

She found she approved of the economy of movement. There was a serenity there, inside the storm.

She quieted her mind, focusing her attention back on the young captain as he began to issue a terse set of commands. It seemed they were on final approach to the jump point.

"Initiate termination sequence on my mark," he said. "Three. Two. One. Terminate burn."

And just like that, they were back in free fall. She gulped as her stomach lurched, one point two gees gone as though they had never been. They'd spent the last three weeks accelerating, lining up with the jump point, and now they were a dumb projectile heading for a precise position in space and time, at a predetermined velocity, and she hoped they had done the math right, because the point of no return was fast approaching.

"Physics," Ian said, his voice a quiet, gravelly rasp. He sounded a decade older, she thought. There on the bridge, where just maybe he belonged.

An older woman responded immediately from her station.

"Accelerator ready in all respects," she said.

"Spin it up," Ian said.

"Confirmed. Spinning."

"Nav?"

Another woman, maybe three decades the physics officer's junior. "Nav is go."

And so on, around the bridge. She stopped thinking of them as individuals and let her perspective broaden, her impressions of a single organism now, functional appendages doing their jobs, all dependent, intertwined.

"Comms?"

"Go."

"Remotes."

"Sensing is go."

"Environmental?"

"Go for Environmental. The ship is secure."

"Very well. Let's depart this place, people," Ian said. "Physics, if you would?"

"Confirmed. Singularity cannon engaging. Power curve satisfactory. Collision tracing within range. Firing."

"Sensing?"

"Signature confirmed, Captain. Singularity emissions signature is as expected."

"Nav, count it down."

"On my mark, Captain. Three. Two. One. Mark."

The Interlocutor felt a brief flicker of déjà vu, followed by a wave of dizziness. Then a dark red cloud formed in the corner of her vision and began to spread, occluding all, until she could see nothing more.

Her stomach dropped.

Her head spun. Consciousness faded.

And she dreamed.

She sat at a desk that was and was not her own. Or maybe had been once, long before.

For no apparent reason, the desk had been placed in a grassy field, next to a river that drifted lazily past. Around her, wildflowers scented the air while bees hummed, busy at their work.

She looked up and saw mountains looming in the distance, gentle forested hills giving way to craggy, snowless peaks.

The sky was the purest blue and the light bright, but strangely, there was no sun.

A little way downstream, a low stone bridge was set across the water. It was shaped like a causeway, but after a moment she realized it was the top of a dam. The current increased near it, the water gathering momentum before sweeping through channels that had been cut through the shaped stones.

But here, where her desk sat, the river was a wide, flat pool. Insects broke the surface, the tiniest of them sending minute ripples spreading outward in concentric circles.

There were, she realized, bottles floating in the river. They were dark greens and blues and browns and looked as though they were made of glass, like an Earth child's fantasy of finding a message that had been cast into the sea.

Except they weren't bottles exactly. More like oversized jars.

The desk chimed at her. She sighed, resigned, and thought, *Another appointment.* She looked at the desk's screen and found it was almost impossible to read. Even without a sun in the sky, the glare was too bright, the auto-adjusting surface of the desk unable to compensate, such that she had to squint and strain to see.

It was displaying a calendar of appointments in an endless scroll. Meeting after meeting, stretching away to an infinite future, a list of people and times and dates as ceaseless as the river itself.

She got up from behind her desk, walked three steps to the beach, and picked up a jar that had drifted into the shallows and come to rest, half-stuck in the mud.

It was dark green, stoppered with an oversized wooden cork.

The hem of her robe dragged through the water. She looked down and saw that it was already stained muddy brown, as though she had made this particular walk many times before.

She returned to the desk, set the jar down, and removed the cork.

She was unsurprised to find a human head inside. She took hold of it as gently as she could, but the hair was too short, and in the end, she was forced to hook her thumbs into the eye sockets to obtain enough purchase to lever it free.

She set it on her desk gently. She had seen it before, she thought. One of her first interlocutions, from early in her career.

The head's eyes opened.

"Help me," it said.

"I know you," she replied.

"Help me," the head said again. "I have seen things I can never unsee. I do not wish to be promoted. Can you please tell them not to make me accept?"

"I can," she said. She passed her hand over its eyes, which closed gently under her touch. "There," she said. "Is that better?"

The head twitched, trying to nod with whatever of its neck muscles remained.

"Thank you," it said.

"You're welcome."

She balled her hand into a fist and struck the jar, smashing it into pieces. She felt a moment of shock at what she had done and looked down at her hand.

She saw thick calluses but no cuts and no blood.

She took the head gently in her hands, returned to the river's edge, and threw it as far as she could. It landed with a splash, bobbed once or twice, then drifted slowly toward the bridge. It gathered speed until eventually it was sucked under, disappearing from sight.

"Go and find whatever awaits you," she said.

Then she looked down to find another jar that had washed onto her beach. This one was dark brown, crafted in an ornate style, the glass etched with writing she could not read.

Completely different from the one that came before, and also absolutely the same.

She bent down, retrieved it, and began the process again.

And again.

Ad infinitum.

When she awoke, it was with no sense of the passage of time. Her eyes were full of tears, and she felt adrift, disoriented, her stomach aware there was no gravity but her acceleration couch holding her tight.

Ian McAllister was issuing commands, his crew busy at their tasks as *Carpathia* leapt into a simulated battle she would learn later her young captain had ordered as an exercise, to test his crew's reaction immediately post jump-event. They were struggling to respond, she saw. She could empathize—and that empathy drew her back, grounding her more than the sudden lurch of acceleration that pressed her into her couch. Returning her to reality, even as she tried to make sense of what happened, and the staggering implications of a simple, basic fact.

All she had tried to forget was not gone.

It was only misplaced, buried deep, but still forever a part of her, her own memories released in a torrent by this madness they called deep-space travel, and she wondered how she had ever thought she could even begin to understand these people, not living there in her tower, behind her desk, enclosed for all those years by the comfort of her own four walls.

CHAPTER 14

Ian's heart beat hard, a hammer kick like a cold restart, then relaxed into a smoother rhythm. His stomach told him he was weightless. He shifted his body and found it immobilized.

He took a long, slow breath, in through the nose, out through the nose, the way he'd been taught back when he was doing this for the first time.

Jump ninety-seven. The number popped into his head, unbidden. He'd survived another. Almost a hundred in his career.

He opened his eyes and blinked twice, trying to clear the fuzziness from the edge of his vision as he took in the view around him. A ship, a bridge, a crew. Officers stirring in their acceleration couches, regaining consciousness, each on their own time.

Carpathia.

The name of his ship was like a key turning in a lock, and everything else came flooding back: where they were, what they were meant to be doing, and his role in it. He felt a moment of pure panic. He was supposed to be captaining this ship, not daydreaming in a gravity bed, counting breaths like a neophyte after their first jump event.

"Life support," he said. The words sounded guttural in his ears. "Report."

"Present, Captain." A young man's voice came back immediately through micro-speakers embedded in the couch next to his ear. "Systems nominal. Hull integrity confirmed. The ship is secure."

"Very well. Nav?"

No response; his navigation officer was evidently still processing the aftereffects of higher-dimensional travel.

"Nav backup?" he said.

"Present, Captain."

"Report, Mister."

"Sir. Confirming arrival location, sir. Starfield is clear. Ship's chronometers report continuous reading. No time deflection observed."

"Very well. Helm?"

Silence. He waited a beat, then another.

"Helm backup?"

There was no response to that, either, which was not good. The signs of a junior crew, new to this, being asked to perform tasks for which they were barely ready.

"Life support?"

"Sir?"

"Take over for helm. Combat simulation begins now. Evasive burn, five gees, course deflection at your discretion."

"Um. Sir? Aye, sir."

Seconds ticked by, his life support officer sorting through his orders, working out the unfamiliar steps required. Then he felt an anvil on his chest as he was pressed into his couch. An involuntary gasp escaped his lungs.

The war games had begun. It was time to run and hide.

But if this had all been for real and not just a preplanned simulation, they would already have been too late.

The problem was asymmetry of information.

Stealth was impossible. Ian could see it now in his mind's eye, even as he labored for breath under the strain of *Carpathia*'s wild evasive maneuvering. The characteristic full-spectrum electromagnetic howl that would have presaged their arrival: an initial gamma burst, a secondary X-ray pulse a few Planck units later, and then a sweep of radiation extending downward at increasing wavelengths, briefly visible to the human eye, and then passing into the infrared and beyond.

Seen from local space, it would have been picturesque, and also absolutely impossible to miss, and therefore fatal if another starship was in the area. All other dangers of this kind of travel paled by comparison. Singularities could be improperly formed, navigational coordinates inaccurate, weaknesses in a ship's construction exposed by the stress of the transition event. There were those for whom this mode of travel was physiologically or psychologically untenable as well. Visions, comas, heart attacks, and madness; all these and more had been observed, time and again.

But usually when bad things happened, when ships went missing and people died, it was because other humans were involved. The reason was simple enough. A ship transitioning to a new region of space had no idea what was waiting for it, whereas any ship already there would be alerted immediately to the newcomer's arrival. There was no getting around that basic problem, and it was exacerbated by the fact that corporations shared jump routes. The number of places where the local gravitational folding enabled this sort of travel was limited, the most useful ones known to all.

Thus, the art of deep-space piracy had been born. It was one of *Carpathia*'s most common assignments, lurking for months at this or that jump point with sensory nets spread and remote weapons pods deployed, undetected and undetectable, waiting in ambush for someone else to happen by. It was exactly what they had done to *Sagittaria*, what was beginning to feel like a long time before.

But on this trip, *Carpathia* would be the hunted, and Ian's inexperienced crew needed practice. He had decided to begin there, just a single jump away from Earth, in a region of space too heavily trafficked for the game of interstellar cat and mouse to be played for real.

Almost a full minute had passed and they were deep into their initial evasive burn when his primary helm officer finally reported.

"Helm present, sir."

"Nice of you to join us, Miss Weston," he said. Which wasn't fair, and he regretted the comment as soon as it passed his lips. It wasn't her fault. She was new at this too and should have been given at least another dozen jumps before being tasked with primary responsibilities post-event. Her bio flashed through his mind. Lieutenant Ali Weston; an Earther but, unlike him, not born in a dome. A corporate outreach project had found her in some province in northern Eurasia, one of Human Resources' talent sweeps, the systematic sifting and sorting of Earth's still-teeming masses as the company forever searched for the hidden genius, the ingenue child growing up in the shadows.

She'd been a one-in-a-million find then. Now she was a weakness.

"Take over for Nav, Mister," he said.

"Yes, sir. Helm is in control of the ship, sir."

"Very well. Cut burn."

"Confirmed, Captain. Engines off."

And just like that, they were weightless again.

"Comms?" he said.

"Sir!"

"Deploy sensor array."

"Yes, sir."

He counted the seconds in his head, waiting for what he had planned next.

"Captain, comms! EM sweep, sir. Missiles inbound. Range—about a million kilometers."

"About, Mister?" A seasoned officer would have reported a range of values and would never have resorted to such crudely qualitative language.

"Sorry, sir. Point nine six million."

"Deploy the drogue."

"Um. Yes, sir. Deploying."

Another moment's hesitation, another potentially fatal error. He flicked a viewscreen to life in his acceleration couch and watched as an autonomous drone cleared *Carpathia*'s hull. This was a decoy device whose sole purpose was to create an electromagnetic signature on par with that of a small sun. *Carpathia* didn't have many of them. Today, its effect would be simulated; they would recover it when the drill was over.

Carpathia continued on its course while the decoy streaked away from them under heavy acceleration, seeking to draw the simulated missiles away.

"Captain, comms. Missile still tracking us."

"Scan point of origin, Mister."

"Yes, sir."

"Weapons, stand by."

"Standing by, sir."

"Well, comms?"

"Looking now, sir. Nothing yet, sir."

"Continue scan."

Ships were fast and exact arrival points were uncertain. In the end, it would come down to the ability to make good decisions with partial data. *Carpathia* had jumped in, her location automatically known to anyone bothering to look, and immediately began maneuvering. Her simulated opponent had sent a single missile her way whose purpose—had this been the real thing—wouldn't be to detonate and simply destroy them but rather to get close enough to force *Carpathia* to surrender.

In this simulated game they were playing, *Carpathia* had now responded with countermeasures, attempting to deceive the incoming missile. She'd turn behind it, change course again, and then go silent. Ships were hard to see when they weren't under acceleration, with no engine emissions to betray them. Her opponent would be reduced to using telescopes, which could create an uneasy stalemate. If they scanned actively for her, *Carpathia* might learn the location of her enemy, only to give herself away.

All of which was straightforward. This was by-the-book stuff, Tactics 101, and Ian had programmed the simulated enemy ship to be exactly where his comms officer was now looking.

But what if there had been weapons remotes already deployed? From multiple positions? Or what if an enemy ship was close enough to use beam weaponry, in which case there wouldn't be any warning at all?

Or what if there were multiple enemy ships?

He had run through all these variables in his mind and decided on the simplest scenario, thinking it would be better to build his crew's confidence during this first exercise. Were this a real ambush, it was unlikely that a lurking enemy ship would have fired itself. Instead, it would have deployed multiple weapons drones, sent a single EM pulse to activate them when *Carpathia*'s emission signature was detected, and sat back and watched while its remotes did the work. Such that when *Carpathia* brought its radio telescopes and optical scanners to bear back down the inbound missile's flight path, there would have been nothing to see.

Better, he had thought, to at least give his crew a chance to win.

Without warning, an alarm flashed on his acceleration couch's screen.

He hadn't planned this; it was coming from the hibernation hold.

Something was wrong with Piotre Raskovich. His cortical activity was much too high. The man was dreaming.

Might, in fact, be waking up.

"All crew: end simulation," Ian said. War games would have to wait. "Helm, set course for our next transition point. One gee. Kindly prepare after-action reports for my review."

"Aye, sir."

The ship's engines cut in, restoring standard gravity. He released himself from his couch and found his feet.

"Interlocutor? With me, if you would?"

He watched as she made her way awkwardly from her acceleration couch. She didn't look well, he thought, but she was up and moving. She caught his eye, gave him a brief nod, and followed him off the bridge.

The quiet of the hibernation hold was as different as could be imagined from the barely controlled chaos on the bridge, the experience uncomfortably like leaving the front lines of a battle to visit a nearby mausoleum.

Rows of lozenge-shaped capsules lined the dim space, each two and a half meters long, all with readout diagnostics in glowing shades of green. Vascular pressure, respiration rates, core temperature, blood pH, electro-cortical activity, and a hundred other metrics besides. The screens also included their occupants' personal details, names, ranks, places of origin, and an image of the crew member inside. A headshot, as though some reminder was necessary, lest someone forget that this wasn't merely cargo down there.

He'd spent long years asleep in holds like this at the beginning of his career. Back then, he'd been part of the crew that rotated in and out of standing the watch. Saving food, energy, and time, with not enough to do to justify burning life expectancy.

Funny, he thought. *The more senior we get, the more we stay awake, and the faster we use whatever time remains to us.*

He and the Interlocutor made their way past rows of capsules that were mostly empty. *Carpathia* had lost a third of her crew. Few could be spared from the routine operation of the ship.

The Interlocutor was as impassive as ever as she walked next to him. Maybe it was the robes she wore, but she looked like she belonged in this land of the almost-dead. *Human Resources*, he thought darkly. Well, here were the humans, a few of them anyway, stored neatly under glass.

He increased his pace, striding the remaining length of the bay. Piotre Raskovich had been placed at the end of a row, some distance from the rest of the capsules, as though the man needed to be kept separate even when asleep.

Ian cycled expertly through the capsule's readouts. All physical indicators were nominal; Raskovich's body was well enough. But his cortical activity was off the charts.

"He's dreaming," the Interlocutor said.

"I know," Ian said. "We can't leave him like this. We're going to have to wake him up."

—

The process took just under an hour. Ian worked through the steps methodically, aware of the Interlocutor watching him intently. The silence in the hold was oppressive. Even a tardy status update from one of his young officers would have been a relief.

"Ever done this before?" he said, trying to shake off his discomfort.

The Interlocutor shook her head minutely. "If I have, it's been a very long time."

Which was a strange answer, but he decided not to press.

Piotre's heart rate rose slowly. Six beats a minute became ten, then fifteen, climbing steadily upward from there. But the man's cortical activity refused to quiet. Ian debated ordering someone else from his crew to come and assist but decided he wasn't ready to bring anyone new into his confidence. Other than Security, he and the Interlocutor were the only ones who knew *Carpathia* had taken on an additional passenger.

Finally, the work was done. He looked up and saw the Interlocutor still studying him, impassive as ever. Behind her, rows of capsule lights blinked softly in their unceasing monitoring, as though their own sleeping dead waited patiently for their turn.

"Ready?" he said.

"Yes"

He called the bridge and ordered them to reduce acceleration to eight-tenths of a gee. He may as well make his guest comfortable, as the process of reactivating muscles that had lain dormant could be painful.

He entered a final command. The capsule's slight overpressure opened it lengthwise with a gentle hiss.

Piotre Raskovich sat bolt upright and screamed.

CHAPTER 15

The Interlocutor did not startle easily. She'd seen more than her share of horrors during her long decades of work; had caused some of them herself, during her early years.

This, though. This was unsettling.

Piotre Raskovich's lips were pulled back in a snarl, teeth jutting forward like an animal. His black spacer's eyes were wide open and staring at nothing. He scrabbled at his neck, tore at his flesh, digging his nails in, blood welling up as he ripped the skin free.

Slowly, his screaming resolved into words, and she was able to make out what he was trying to say.

"Get it off! Get it off get it off GET IT OFF!"

It didn't occur to her that she might be in physical danger until a Security team arrived. They were moving fast, augmented muscles and nervous systems and pumping adrenals; they seemed practically to materialize in the hibernation vault beside her. *Captain McAllister must have called them in*, she thought dully. She should've done so herself. Should, in hindsight, have insisted a team be present for this from the beginning.

"Put him under," Ian said. In a moment, it was over: Piotre lay crumpled in the gray-suited arms of the Security lead, slipped back into merciful unconsciousness.

The agent laid him back in his bed, very much like returning a corpse to a waiting grave.

"That was well done."

"Thank you, sir," the agent replied. "And, sir? That required a considerably higher dose than might have been expected, based on mass alone."

"Understood. Wait in the corridor, if you please?"

"Yes, sir."

And they were gone, disappearing like ghosts.

Ian McAllister gave her a look. "The jump," he said.

"Yes."

"He reacted badly."

Keep it clinical, she thought. She couldn't subject the captain to her own discomfort, and this was not the time to think further about her dreams: that river, those heads in jars, all those memories floating past.

"The absence of his Behavioral Conditioning seems to have interacted badly with the fugue state. I must apologize, Captain," she said. "I might have seen this coming."

"How could you possibly?"

"It was a failure of empathy. Prior to Mr. Raskovich, I had no direct experience with Magellanix Behavioral Conditioning at the level of their senior officers. I simply never imagined how his mind might react in hibernation combined with a jump. Our Board of Directors did not either, or they would not have ordered him asleep at the outset of our journey. And of course, he would have been awake for his return voyage from Ragnarock, on his own ship. This was his first sleeping transition event with a broken mind. I should have anticipated trouble."

The captain frowned. "That's easy to say after the fact. I still don't see how you could have known."

She smiled sadly. "Are you a religious man, Captain?"

He started at the sudden change in topic, just as she had known he would. "Do you know, Captain Marakan asked me that once, a long time ago?"

"What was your answer?"

"My answer was no."

"You are not a Seeker, then."

"Certainly not!"

"But you are aware of that particular belief system," she said.

The young man gestured at the hibernation hold, the empty capsules with their handful of sleeping crew around them, mostly planetary specialists and field workers, all temporary employees. The full-time Carpathians—permanent employees and officer corps—were all awake and needed to keep the depleted ship operational.

"It's a contractor religion," he said. "What of it?"

"Then you know that in every crew, there are some individuals that believe all this"—and here she mimicked his gesture—"was not of our own making but rather given to us by an external agent of some kind. Some think it was a machine intelligence, others that an extraterrestrial survived the path to sentience. Some even put their faith in this or that god of the old cloth. But they all believe something of its nature and purpose can be learned out here in deep space, transiting singularities between the stars."

The captain shrugged. "Like I said, a contractor religion. I'm not sure what any of this has to do with our guest."

"Only this, Captain. I have interviewed some of those who routinely experience visions during transition events." She shuddered, thinking again of her own. "And it tends to be more common among contractors, particularly when making jumps in hibernation. Their careers have left their minds with more degrees of freedom. Those who have had to continually re-choose: to change employers and live with more uncertainty. And so, I might have anticipated that Piotre Raskovich, his mind relaxed from its constraints, would experience something similar."

The captain contemplated this. "Well, whatever the reason for it," he said at last, "it would seem he'll have to be awake for the trip."

"I agree, Captain."

"Which means we need a way to keep him calm."

She sighed. "Yes," she said. "We should tranquilize him this time, waken him into a more docile state. And I will attempt to talk to him."

She saw the predictable relief in Ian's eyes. "Thank you," he said. "But don't you think we should move him first?"

"We should. Anywhere, I suspect, might be better than here."

The Interlocutor settled on her own quarters for what would come next, feeling it important she be as comfortable as possible for the interview she must now conduct.

She decided to be conservative and ease Piotre Raskovich back to consciousness slowly over the course of an hour, observing him the entire time, with heavy pharmaceuticals at the ready. She'd snow his mind under if that's what it took to keep those dreams from returning, but she hoped it wouldn't come to that. She had no desire to cause additional long-term damage. Piotre Raskovich was still an asset on this mission, one for whom she was responsible.

The captain lingered in her cabin, seeming unsure whether to stay and observe or leave the matter entirely to her.

"You have a question for me," she said. Giving him a prompt, a way to close their interaction such that he might gracefully depart.

"I do. This talk of religion, Interlocutor."

She smiled, anticipating him. "You are wondering what I believe."

"Yes."

"I inhabit a peculiar place between nihilism and humanism, Captain. It is the nature of my work. I understand others' beliefs, which becomes a kind of spirituality all its own."

She let him hear a note of sadness in her tone. It would not hurt for him to be reminded of the gulf of years and experience between them.

"I see," he said slowly, though she imagined he didn't. Then he nodded toward Piotre, still unconscious in his capsule. "Will this work?" he asked.

She could see no reason to lie. "I don't know."

"I ordered the Security detail to remain outside your door."

"That is much appreciated," she said.

He nodded. "Good luck, Interlocutor," he said. "I'll take my leave of you now. I imagine you prefer to work alone."

She gave him a slight smile. "My work is never alone, Captain. But the preparation always is."

Once, she had known much of fear. It had been a constant companion in the early days, with Security in the room and needles up her sleeves, those long-forgotten times when she had thought of her subjects as enemies and used base emotions to produce the desired results.

Even now, with more skill and her far-deeper understanding of what empathy truly meant, those who came before her were so commonly afraid. And sometimes, that fear had to be leveraged. Occasionally, there was no other way.

This was different.

Now the fear was her own.

She was not afraid of Piotre Raskovich the man. But what he had experienced bothered her deeply: locked in a dream state, hyperdimensional travel interacting badly with his broken mind.

She could relate.

Carpathia would have to jump three more times just to get them to Paradise. How many more would be required on the long journey to Ragnarock, she had not yet asked. The ship was headed for regions of space unknown to TransGalactic, an area unreachable but for the navigational coordinates Piotre had stolen.

Whereas she was headed for unknown regions of her mind.

And so, she was afraid. Of the memories that would resurface, the pasts she would be forced to relive.

But what about Piotre? What had it been like for him, trapped in enforced sleep? What had he learned, or relearned, about himself?

Maybe nothing. Perhaps it had been simple terror—but she doubted it.

She regarded the man where he lay in the bulbous, torpedo-shaped hibernation capsule. They had left it open. Piotre was only drugged, not actually returned to a fugue state. For the moment, the hibernation chamber was nothing more than a hospital bed.

She leaned closer, studying his gaunt face.

Who was this man, anyway?

Traitor. Defector. Information Officer.

Murderer.

He looked peaceful enough.

She slowed her breathing and began the delicate process of clearing her mind. Settling into a trance of her own, visiting with her fear. Inviting it in, accepting it for what it was.

When she was ready, she administered a mild stimulant to her sleeping charge, pressing a contact patch against his forehead.

Then she settled back.

They were in this together, she thought. That was the key. The most basic of human emotions, the one thing they definitively shared.

Fear.

CHAPTER 16

Piotre Raskovich awoke with a hole in his mind.

It wouldn't stay empty for long. No sooner had consciousness returned than the space began to fill in, a miasmic slush of his long-forgotten memories stirring and sloshing in the centipede-shaped negative space in his brain. It was like a rotten log had broken open, filled with vermin that now squirmed and wriggled and writhed and bit as they burst free. The process should have filled him with horror. Instead, he observed his thoughts with an almost-clinical indifference, as though he were groping in a fog to find the proper feeling, struggling toward some reasonable depth of caring.

A moment of clarity, then. They'd drugged him. His was a terror held at bay by chemical apathy. The great gulf between freedom and slavery had been reduced to an intellectual construct, something to be just glanced at with idle curiosity and a veneer of indifference.

The realization brought with it a curious feeling, an unfamiliar sensation.

Gratitude.

His captors had given him something to ease his mind, and he was grateful for it.

He took a deep breath and opened his eyes.

His vision was blurry, but the immediate impressions were clear enough. Hibernation capsule, bed, diagnostics. Readouts and displays.

A breath of cool, metallic, conditioned air.

He was on a ship. That much was obvious. But not, he thought, his own.

He touched the skin of his neck and winced. It was tender and raw.

He tried to sit up but managed only to rest his weight on his elbows. He was terribly weak. The bones of his upper arms felt like they might snap from the strain.

Only then did he become aware of a figure sitting across from him, wearing a hooded robe half-concealing her face. Her eyes burned bright blue like they were illuminated from within, and she stared at him with an intensity he found unsettling and calming at the same time.

He'd seen a figure like her before. His guide, in a childhood long past.

Without warning, a wave of nausea overtook him. He leaned over the side of the capsule and retched, dry-heaving; his stomach long empty, nothing coming up but a trickle of bile that made his mouth burn.

He grasped the side of the capsule, squeezing it, holding on until the sickness passed.

When his gagging subsided, he spat, clearing his mouth, and looked back up at the woman.

She was not the guide from long ago, not the one who had introduced him to his centipede. The resemblance was only superficial.

This woman was a more-recent acquaintance.

"Hello, Interlocutor," he said. The words sounded harsh in his ears, a dead man's tired croak.

The figure inclined her head fractionally. "Piotre Raskovich," she said. Her voice was carefully neutral, as ageless as she.

She pushed her hood back, allowing him a better look at her face. Bald, androgynous, but still feminine in some undefinable way.

"I've been dreaming," he said.

"Yes."

"I couldn't wake up."

"I understand."

Did she? How much could she know? She had questioned him, but frustratingly, he couldn't remember what he had shared. Had he told her of the centipede? What it felt like when it first crawled on his skin, nipped the flesh at the base of his neck? How it worried a hole and disappeared inside?

Had he spoken of its hundreds of thousands of tiny feet, appendages measured in axon diameters, how they tickled and teased as they innervated him?

Was it real? Of course not. That was the wrong question. The point was that it didn't matter.

Had he told her how it died from shock, the sheer surprise of the unexpected toxic to the Conditioning program that had guided him for so long? Leaving a hole filled with blood and doubt and the pain of indecision?

Cognition was returning, coming back online in stages, bringing further clarity. He had told her, he thought. He must have. She must know it all.

For the first time, he noticed the viewscreen on the desk behind her, displaying an incrementing chronometer underneath a diagram of a ship.

It said: *Mission Local Tim*e—Carpathia.

Carpathia. He knew that name. A TransGalactic ship; an enemy ship. A threat in his former life.

If he had the energy, he would have smiled. How very like her. This was the Interlocutor he had come to know. Showing him exactly what she wanted him to see: where he was and how much time had elapsed.

She was a professional in every regard. He could appreciate that.

But the math was hard. His brain struggled with the most basic arithmetic.

"How long have I been asleep?" he said.

"Two weeks."

Not near long enough for them to have reached Ragnarock. So, why wake him now? They couldn't be more than a single jump away from Earth. There were months and months left to travel.

The answer was obvious. Hypersleep and a broken mind and high-dimensional transition events hadn't mixed well. His new masters woke him early because they were afraid he would go mad.

And thus be of less use.

He thought about the nightmare, the savage recollections of his initial Conditioning. He had no desire to return. "Thank you for waking me," he said. Then he added, "Regardless of your motives."

She shrugged minutely. "There is no need for thanks," she said, though he thought she sounded pleased. "It was the captain's orders."

"Was it."

"Yes. But I agreed with them. I feared for you," she said.

He grunted. He should get up, find his feet, and get himself free of this hibernation capsule. But the thought of it was more than he could bear. He wondered how he'd ever made it up the volcano back on Ragnarock. Only the drugs had made it possible, pumped into his blood in the course of days, getting ready for a trip to the planet's surface he had no business making. That, and a synth-weave suit he was barely qualified to wear.

He'd tried to stay fit on the voyage back to Earth, knowing a certain degree of physical activity would be required when he defected to TransGalactic. But he was still impossibly weak.

"How do you feel?" the Interlocutor asked, once again reading his mind.

"I'm of two minds about that." He almost laughed. What statement had ever been more true? "I suppose it could be worse."

"Do you wish to tell me of your dreams?"

"Is there some particular reason you want to know?"

"You are perceptive, Piotre Raskovich."

"For a Chief Information Officer?" This time, he did laugh, but it came out as a cough that swiftly overtook him, racking his body, bending him double until he retched again.

"Yes," she said when the fit had passed. She offered him water; he took the bottle gratefully. "For a Chief Information Officer, with a self-described reputation for understanding data far better than humans, I find you quite perceptive."

He wiped his face with the back of his sleeve. "Perhaps I've been changed by my experience, Interlocutor."

"In what way?"

It was a good question. He took another sip, considering. How could he ever explain?

"I'm grateful for the drugs you have given me, Interlocutor. Believe me. But your questions are difficult. My brain cannot do what it should."

"I understand."

"Do you?"

"More than you might imagine," she said.

He fell silent at that, studying her, transfixed again by those blue eyes gazing back at him. Without warning, a memory came to him, another part of his distant past now filling the empty space in his mind. On a whim, he decided to share it.

"Do you know, Interlocutor," he said, "I think I will tell you a story from my childhood."

"Please."

He took a breath and closed his eyes, casting his thoughts back over decades, to a far different time and place, long before Conditioning and deep-space travel and information wars, alien artifacts, and all his schemes and designs.

To when he had just been a boy: a little lonely, poorer than he could possibly know, but not, he thought, unhappy.

"You know that I was raised on Mars," he said. "You must also know we grew our food in hydroponic farms. Great, vast arrays of them, mostly in poor condition. They had been patched and repatched, over and over again. We used transparent composites pioneered on Earth, the thinking being to create little green bubbles, places where you could see the sky. They were supposed to be good for the spirit. We were encouraged to go walking. I did, in those days.

"This was bare-root agriculture," he went on, "plants growing suspended, their roots misted with nutrients or, in rare cases, actually held in liquid water. Water and dirt were commodities. But there were places. Ornamental roses kept in pots, other flowers as luxury items. I recall the experience of pulling one such when I was perhaps five years old. I was angry. My parents had done something to upset me. I cannot recall what; I was a child. I grabbed the family's rose bush by the stalk. The thorns pricked me, badly, and I bled, but I still pulled it clean out of its container.

"It was, in hindsight, probably the most valuable thing we owned. My parents were displeased, but that is not the point.

"Do you see, Interlocutor? Surprisingly for one of my upbringing, I do know what it is like to tear something from the soil. And in this case, all that brown, humus-filled, rich organic stuff is my own gray matter. The centipede is the rose that has been torn from the fertile ground; the dirt that spilled from the pot are my memories, strewn on the floor.

"To torture the metaphor just a bit further: the soil fills in, spilling down the sides and covering the holes, but it leaves a depression. Gaps and inconsistencies."

"And the rose?" the Interlocutor said.

He smiled, pleased. "You ask the right question. Whose hand grips the plant? Who did the pulling, and whose job is it to bleed? Who can say? But this isn't about revenge, Interlocutor. It's about greed and power. My own." He trailed off, considering, then said, "Now, I imagine you have things you wish to ask."

"In fact, I don't," she said. "But I think the captain will."

"Then send for him. And let's get on with it."

"As you wish."

But instead of a captain, they brought him a child.

He stared in disbelief at the gaunt, impossibly young man who stepped through the cabin door. The man looked nothing like a captain. Piotre had served under many in his career, gendered and not, Earthers and the occasional colonist from this or that world, but never one as young as this.

He turned and shot the Interlocutor a glance, thinking, *Is this some sort of joke? A test, maybe?*

She gazed back at him, impassive as ever.

"Piotre Raskovich," the new arrival said. "My name is Captain Ian McAllister. Welcome aboard the *Carpathia*."

He had a spacer's eyes, at least, that coal-black, unwavering stare. Whoever this young officer was, he had his years in deep space. That was something.

"Thank you, Captain," he said. "You woke me up sooner than I would have expected. Of course, I didn't expect to be brought along at all."

The young man nodded. "And yet here we all are. As the Interlocutor likely told you, we have just left near-Sol space. I had intended to leave you asleep for the entirety of our journey, but to save you future discomfort, you will not be returned to hibernation. We have three more jumps ahead of us, at which point we will arrive at the planet known to employees of both Magellanix and TransGalactic as Paradise."

Piotre narrowed his eyes, thinking, trying to make sense of the young man's words. *Maybe this is how TransGalactic does it,* he thought. *Promotes their children to command. Or maybe this is total nonsense. Maybe this man is just a lieutenant, carrying out a deception for reasons he could not comprehend.*

"My mind is fuzzy, Captain," he said finally. "But even I can tell we're going the wrong way. Was there some navigational difficulty? Were the coordinates I provided unclear?"

"They were not."

"Then what you are doing makes no sense." He rubbed his temples wearily. "Unless you mean to leave me at Paradise for some reason?"

"I'm afraid not, Mr. Raskovich. You are far too valuable to remain behind."

"Then why?" He felt a wave of frustration as the implications became clear. He swung himself up and out of the hibernation bed. He swayed unsteadily, fighting off a wave of vertigo. "Why travel out of our way when you must know that everything hinges upon reaching Ragnarock before Magellanix does? Why waste the time I have given you?"

The young man stared at him, those black spacer's eyes unreadable, heedless of his outburst. "Sit down," he said, indicating the chair the Interlocutor had just vacated. "Please. Before you fall down."

The wave of anger peaked and then vanished as abruptly as it had begun. In his drugged state, sedated as he was, Piotre simply could not hold it.

He sat.

"Let me ask you a question," the captain said, "by way of explanation. What exactly do you think my employer imagines it has purchased from you?"

"Knowledge," Piotre said, "unprecedented in human history. And so, definitionally, power."

"Yes," the young man agreed. "Power. But how do you think that knowledge will translate into power in this particular case?"

He considered. Whatever his age, there was a mind in this alleged captain, one working better than his own.

"You're asking me," he said, "about the specific utility of the data I have provided?"

"I am. You are a Chief Information Officer—or you were before you defected to us. So, I ask you again: setting aside academic interest, what is the specific value of the data you have provided?"

Piotre flicked his gaze again at the Interlocutor, but she was no longer looking his way.

"There are many components to its value," he said finally.

"So? List them."

He nodded assent. "Very well. There is the marketing value of the discovery. Tourists will flock to see it; consumers will purchase information about it. There is the reputational gain that will accrue to the TransGalactic brand when it is announced. There is the option value on the potential destruction of the artifact, should that be required. And of course, the potential military or commercial value, if . . ." He trailed off, thinking.

"If?"

"If its function can be elucidated," he concluded. "If it can be communicated with, deconstructed, disassembled, reverse-engineered. Really, if its purpose can be understood in any way."

"You would agree, then, that any commercial or military value is predicated on TransGalactic's ability to understand at least something of the artifact's function. What the thing is there for, how it works."

"Yes."

"Then you can understand why we are taking our detour. Please realize, Piotre Raskovich: I tell you all of this only because you are harmless to TransGalactic here. Your fate is entirely in our hands. And since you may have thoughts on the subject that might be useful, I see no reason for you not to know that we are detouring to Paradise to retrieve a civilian specialist whose experience may prove relevant."

"A specialist?" He shook his head, confused again. "Has TransGalactic made a similar discovery before? And kept it secret?"

The captain sighed. "In fact, we have not. We are retrieving an academic. A professor, whose research seeks to identify the conditions under which sentience evolves. And, I'm told, the narrower band of conditions under which it might be expected to endure."

"And you think this specialist is going to do what? Help you make first contact of some kind?"

"Possibly."

"Logical enough." He closed his eyes and let out his breath in a long exhale. "Except for one thing."

"Which is?"

"You've almost certainly doomed us all."

He said the words calmly; he lacked the energy to do otherwise. But still, the man flinched.

"Explain that?"

Piotre almost smiled. "You're no captain, are you?" he said. "You nearly had me fooled. But I've known captains. Served under many. And you aren't one at all. No—don't answer," he continued, seeing the young man's eyes narrow. "Just tell me this, Mr. McAllister. What exactly do you expect Magellanix to do now that *Accipiter* has reported the existence of Ragnarock? Now that they are aware of the finding of a new holocaust world? Even knowing nothing of the true secret of the place, even ignorant of the existence of the artifact I discovered?"

"Launch a resupply mission, I would think," Ian McAllister said. "Quietly. Maybe in six months; maybe in a year. I'm told you covered your traces well. A holocaust world has intrinsic research value, but according to you, Ragnarock is inhospitable and not a good candidate for colonization. Also, your fleet holds the navigational information. TransGalactic has never visited that region of space, and until your defection, had no plans to do so. Doubtless, *Accipiter* left a field team behind to continue the work, so there is no particular reason to expect Magellanix to hurry back."

He laughed grimly. "If only it were so, Captain. Unfortunately, what I have done will most certainly cause them to hurry."

"Why? All they know is that you crashed a flier on shore leave. Which, while outside behavioral norms that you would take such a leave at all, let alone indulge in such a physical activity, at least explains why the accident might have happened. No one would expect you to be much of a pilot."

"True," he said. "The excuse I gave was that I developed a taste for it on Ragnarock and I wanted to try my hand again. But that is beside the point. The real question is: what do you imagine Magellanix did immediately after my crash was reported?"

"What could they do? You crashed, and TransGalactic attempted a rescue. Your injuries were reportedly too severe. We didn't get there in time."

"Which Magellanix will not believe."

The young man shrugged. "As you say. But they will believe in the power of their Behavioral Conditioning. Even had TransGalactic captured you alive, intact, and capable of response, you know better than anyone how thoroughly your former employer perfected a practice that should have left you incapable of divulging information under any amount of duress. Not that we would resort to such tactics." This last with a glance to the Interlocutor, who looked on, inscrutable as ever.

"And when Magellanix asked for the return of my remains?"

"I imagine TransGalactic found a way to stall. But it still doesn't matter, does it? By definition, if dead, you are harmless, and if alive, you posed no threat."

"Your ignorance is charming, Captain McAllister. But unfortunately, my former commander is an experienced one. Captain Johnston, though I loathed her on a variety of personal levels, was inarguably a talented officer. When I disappeared, she would've suspected something was wrong and ordered her information forensics teams to pick through *Accipiter*'s information logs. A single bit at a time, if that's what it took."

"I thought you hid your traces. You were the CIO, no?"

"Even a Chief Information Officer can only do so much without the intervention itself being detected."

"But why would she look?"

"Because she didn't trust me."

Ian McAllister looked frustrated, that veneer of control cracking again. "How could a captain not trust their own Chief Information Officer? You literally should not have been able to conceive of the actions you took."

Piotre felt a trace of bitterness at that. Perhaps, as the drugs wore off, the normal range of human emotions would return to him.

He rather hoped not.

"Because a good captain never trusts their information department," he said. "Particularly when their CIO is behaving strangely. How much further outside standard performance norms could I have been? I volunteered for a planetary side trip, I who never leave my cabin. Then requisitioned a flier to perform a site inspection. Reported a contractor dead in a climbing accident, never having reached the site. And then altered the logs. She'll look; any sensible commander would. Anyone sufficiently dangerous, powerful, and paranoid to hold the rank."

"What will she find?"

"Gaps. Traces. Subtle shifts, bits out of place, checksums slightly off. A single mistake will confirm it. And I was not, as you might imagine, entirely in my right mind."

McAllister fell quiet for a time. "So, what will this captain of yours do, in your estimation?" he finally asked.

"She will head for Ragnarock," Piotre said grimly. "As fast as Magellanix high command can resupply *Accipiter* and make her ready for the return journey."

"Really? Does your own Board of Directors give individual commanders such choice over their missions?"

"With her, they will. She is, how would you say? The best and the brightest. They'll send her back if she demands it. And there's something else. She hid information from me on our trip back to Earth. I think. As I have said, I'm not functioning properly."

"What kind of information?"

"Disposition of planetary defense forces. I think she mined Ragnarock's orbit, possibly the whole system before we left. And didn't tell me. Of course"—he shrugged helplessly—"these might just be lunatic ramblings of a paranoiac. It's impossible for me to know."

Ian McAllister sighed. "Very well," he said. "That, at least, bears further discussion. The Interlocutor will spend more time with you on this when you're ready."

The young man looked him up and down a last time, dismissing him, then turned and left the cabin without another word.

Half a captain and half not, Piotre thought. *There is much here I don't understand.* He exchanged a look with the Interlocutor, who had remained quiet this whole time. "Now what?" he said.

"Security will show you to your quarters," she said. "We will speak again soon."

He nodded but said nothing more as the two TransGalactic security guards led him from the room. Wondering as he went at his folly, the madness of this plan. Would it all be for naught? It was the longest of long shots anyway, but if they were truly going weeks out of their way?

His mind wasn't working fully, but it didn't need to be to comprehend the tactical situation. *Accipiter* would beat them to Ragnarock. Captain Johnston might or might not know someone was following her, but she would be cautious. She always was.

She'd be out there somewhere. She'd have *Accipiter*'s remotes spread wide, lurking on the other side of a transition point, watching and waiting.

All so they could pick up an academic from Paradise. Someone who was supposed to know how to talk to an alien.

He'd cast his lot with the wrong people, he thought. He should have contacted InterTech. They would have had the good sense to hurry.

He'd gambled and was going to lose, and there was nothing more he could do about it.

Sleep, he thought. He just needed to go back to sleep.

If only he weren't afraid of the dreams that might come.

INTERLUDE

CHAPTER 17

Ragnarock

Feyis Sado regained consciousness in near-darkness, waking to find himself pinned between an ice ledge and the wall of the crevasse into which he had apparently fallen.

He had no idea how he'd gotten there. Or even, in fact, where he was.

Still, he didn't panic. Perhaps he should have, but instead, what came to him was a deep calm. He'd been in some sort of climbing accident. He must have hit his head and suffered a concussion. But whatever had happened, he was still alive. So, he thought, lucky.

He was wearing an exposure suit of some kind, and also a backpack, which seemed to have helped wedge him between the ice shelf and the crevasse wall. A climbing axe was strapped to his right hand, and there was a rope attached to his waist.

Evidently, he hadn't been climbing alone.

As carefully as he could—his feet were dangling over open space beneath him—he began working free of the backpack, thinking to haul himself onto the ledge and then drag the pack up after him. He was rewarded immediately with sharp stabbing pains in his right shoulder and the side of his neck. He froze, waiting for the pain to subside, then poked at himself gingerly with his left hand. *Fractured collarbone*, he thought. *Probably a separated shoulder as well.*

This was going to hurt. Still, he could see no other choice.

It took about ten minutes of struggling, shoulder, arm, and neck screaming in protest, but he managed to heave first himself and then his pack onto the ledge. He lay there for a time, panting. He closed his eyes, forcing himself to relax and slow his breathing, to get his heartbeat under control. The throbbing ebbed. Just a little, but anything helped.

He was, he realized, in heavy gravity. Even injured, hauling himself onto the shelf of ice was harder than it should have been.

He wondered what planet this was. For a moment, its name felt near at hand, but then it slipped away.

He should open the pack and inventory its contents, but it was too dark to see. "Light," he muttered on instinct, and his suit responded immediately, a thin beam snapping to life from the index finger of the glove on his right hand.

He looked up. The crevasse wasn't perfectly vertical. Water dripped from a lip in the ice far above, but he couldn't see all the way to the open sky. Then he peered down, over the ledge. He couldn't see the bottom, either, just a dark, dripping blue hole that seemed to fall away forever.

It occurred to him to inspect the suit he was wearing. Clearly, it wasn't just meant to protect him from the elements. It was a full biohazard suit, the kind that would keep him safe from airborne pathogens, radiation, anything and everything that might make the air unsafe to breathe.

Or at least it would have, if not for the long, ragged gash in the right leg. He must have ricocheted down there and bounced off the wall. Or torn it on his climbing axe, which was a wicked, curved little thing, with a sawtoothed blade and a sharpened point.

Well, shit, he thought. He was wearing a ripped and therefore useless biohazard suit. That couldn't be good.

At least it was keeping him mostly warm.

The rope attached to his waist had fallen into a loose pile on the ledge around him. He picked it up and ran it through his fingers until he found the end.

It had been severed neatly. The end wasn't frayed at all.

He tried to think it through. He'd fallen, been out of sight from anyone above, and unresponsive. Maybe his climbing partner was hurt too. Maybe they couldn't hold his weight.

Maybe they'd given up and left him for dead.

Something didn't seem right about that, but his head was still foggy. He felt slow, stupidly numb.

He said, "Transmit," and was rewarded with a soft chime in his ear.

"My name is Feyis Sado," he said. "I am alive. I repeat: my name is Feyis Sado and I am injured but alive."

There was no answer. He tried again, and a third time.

Nothing.

The momentary elation at the thought of rescue vanished as quickly as it arrived. Maybe the suit's transmitter was blocked by the ice surrounding him. He couldn't be sure; he didn't know how powerful the unit was.

He wondered how long he'd been unconscious. Minutes? Hours?

He pushed the thought away and took inventory of his pack. It contained a medkit, a portable field shelter, a modest amount of food, and two liters of water, along with backup climbing gear: anchors, pickets, and rope, but not a second axe, which was what he was going to need to climb out of there. There was also a small, handheld utility laser. Most of the rest of the space in the pack was given over to a jumble of scientific gear, mostly field instruments of various kinds.

He had been carrying a lot of weight. Food, water, shelter, a power source, all that gear. He wondered what his climbing partner had brought.

Maybe nothing. Maybe they hadn't helped at all.

That was interesting. Some truth was there, dancing in the corner of his mind, then slipping frustratingly back out of his awareness.

He sorted through the gear more carefully. There was a seismometer, surveyor's equipment including a laser rangefinder, an ice corer, a ruggedized chemistry kit, a fluorometer, a handful of other instruments he didn't recognize, and a radioisotope reader.

Radioisotopes. He needed Callie for this, he thought.

And then he thought, *Who's Callie?*

A memory returned, of a long plane flight. And with it, another name: Ragnarock. He was on a planet named Ragnarock. And there had been a woman named Callie.

Whom he loved.

But that trip hadn't been this trip. This was something else.

With someone else.

A man. He'd climbed to the summit of this mountain with a man, but he couldn't remember his name or why they had come.

He removed the shelter from his pack, wincing again at the discomfort of motion. It was feather-light and auto-inflating. Toss it on the snow, press a button, and he'd have instant habitat. It had an airlock; he and his partner could have taken their suits off inside.

There was no room for it down there, obviously, but that wasn't what he was after.

There was a smaller bag inside which held a set of metal spikes used to anchor the shelter to the ice. He hefted one, considering. It fit well enough in his left hand.

He swung it experimentally against the wall of the crevasse. The point bit partially but then disappointingly skittered free. It was sharp enough to chip the ice but not enough for what he needed.

Inspiration struck. He retrieved the field laser from the pack and flicked it to life. It took a moment of fiddling to figure out the settings, and then he sharpened the beam to its highest intensity.

And set to whittling, the laser's beam shaving away the end of the tent stake, honing it to a fine point.

When he was finished, he turned the laser off and checked the power meter. There was plenty of juice left. *Good,* he thought, *it might come in handy later.*

He repositioned himself and swung the stake a second time, again using his uninjured left arm. This time, it bit deep into the ice. He leaned back and down, hanging his weight from it.

Its purchase held.

Excellent.

He rummaged in the medkit and found a mild soporific, something to dull the pain but nothing too heavy. He couldn't afford to numb his arm entirely. There was no way he could do this with one hand.

Then he tied the free end of the rope to the pack. He'd haul that up last; there was no reason to carry it while he climbed.

Okay, he thought. *Heavy gravity, one arm, one ice axe, and a supplemental tent stake; a separated shoulder, a broken collarbone, and evidently left for dead, with no memory of what had happened.*

Time to get to work.

The climb was an exercise in controlled tedium: a battle against fatigue, inattention, and pain, in which he couldn't afford even a single mistake.

Three points of contact at all times. That was the key. Two feet and a hand, or two hands and a foot.

And don't look down.

He took his time. Settled in to it: the breathing, the focus, finding a deep calm, the memory fog a blessing now, no outside thoughts to intrude.

He slipped once, caught the mistake, chided himself for the momentary lapse, and refocused on the work.

Time passed. How much, he couldn't say and didn't particularly want to know. Minutes? Hours?

Or maybe, he thought, the balance of a lifetime.

When at last he reached an overhang near the top, he was forced to stretch across the gap with one leg, hoping the toe points on his booted foot were adequate to the task. The maneuver was awkward under the heavy gravity and made worse by his nearly dead arm, but he managed. The boot held—and then he was clear, heaving his tired body over the lip of the crevasse.

He found himself in a howling wind. There were heavy clouds above, and below him, a panoramic view of white-capped, gray seas, whipped into foam.

The water looked very cold.

An island, he thought. *A volcanic island—that's what we set out to climb.*

But who was "we"?

And why?

He retrieved his backpack by the simple expedient of trudging twenty meters down the glacier and dragging it out by main force. Inevitably, the pack got stuck on the overhang at the top. It took more effort to work his way back and maneuver it free, but finally, the crevasse seemed to surrender like it was finished with him and ready to let him go.

He sat down heavily and surveyed the scene in more detail, trying to reconstruct the accident in his mind. He was near the bottom of a glacier. Assuming he was the more-experienced climber, he'd have positioned himself on the back of the rope. The concussion and separated shoulder . . . his injuries were consistent with having been pulled into a crevasse, swinging down and across like a pendulum, and impacting the far wall.

Maybe his partner had slipped. Maybe they were inexperienced or just unlucky. Suppose they'd taken a fall and slid down the ice, unable to stop. He must've been right at the edge, because if he'd had any room at all, he should have been able to arrest a fall easily enough, even in the heavy gravity.

A thought flickered in the corner of his mind. He was missing something.

He went over it again. Suppose his partner fell and pulled him into the crevasse through sheer bad luck. Now he'd be twenty meters down, hanging on one end of the rope. Then what?

His partner panicked and cut themself free?

The suit. That was what didn't make sense: his exposure suit's biomonitors should have reported him still alive. It had automatic transponders and a field radio; anyone in the area would have known there was still someone with a heartbeat down there.

Suppose his climbing partner was not just inexperienced but a complete novice. Stuck there on the ice, they wouldn't know how to free themselves from the rope under load, how to anchor it and remove themselves from the system. Or they didn't have any gear at all with them. Not a single snow picket or ice screw they might use.

Just—what? A knife? Conveniently at hand to cut the rope?

He closed his eyes, trying to imagine how that would've felt, hours ticking by, trapped by the rope, the dead weight hanging in the crevasse below him.

So, his partner gave up and cut the rope. Maybe it was the only thing they could do?

But then why not at least walk back to the edge of the crevasse? Why not confirm that he, Feyis, was actually dead?

Nothing made sense, but one thing was clear: he needed to get down off this glacier and find somewhere flat enough to pitch his shelter. Then he could take a more-serious look at his arm, eat and hydrate, and get some rest.

After that, he could figure out what to do.

—

The crevasse he had escaped turned out to be the last one on the descent. After another hundred vertical meters, he was off the glacier, walking on compact snow interspersed with an occasional rock field. Tedious but not technical: something anyone could walk across.

The drugs wore off as he descended further, and his collarbone began to ache. He wanted to set the pack down and rest but decided to press on, thinking maybe they had left a base camp that might hold a clue.

But if there was a camp, he couldn't find it. His suit detected no transponders, no signals of any kind. In the end, he simply found a spot out of the wind, a bit of flat ground between two rock ridges, and pitched the shelter. The airlock was superfluous at this point. He'd long since been exposed to anything in the air that might kill him, but somehow, that felt like the least of his worries.

He crawled inside and sat heavily on the thick part of the floor, where a sleeping pad was woven into the shelter's base. He dumped the pack, removed his helmet, closed his eyes, and fell fast asleep.

He dreamed about Callie. In his dream, he knew it was her, but he couldn't see her face.

She had been—a friend? A lover? Somewhere in between?

They had traveled together. And he had fallen in love. That much was clear, but the rest was maddening, in the manner of dreams that offer some hint of what might have been. A teasing glimpse of alternate possibilities that vanished with all promises unfulfilled.

When he awoke, it was nighttime again.

He crawled out of the shelter and stared at the stars. The clouds drifted, came and went, revealing a pair of moons.

A thought played at the corner of his mind. Something he hadn't wanted to admit to himself during the descent.

There was another possibility.

Maybe it hadn't been an accident.

Maybe his climbing partner had done it on purpose. Waited till they were almost off the glacier, when it would be safe to walk the rest of the way, even for someone with no business on a mountain in heavy gravity. Waited until he was on the snow bridge, at his most vulnerable, unable to arrest a fall.

And then jumped, sliding down the snowfield, pulling him into the crevasse.

But why? Who would want to kill him?

Neither the moons, nor the sky, nor the vast expanse of black water offered any answer.

After a time, he crawled back inside the shelter. In the absence of any better idea, he would simply have to figure out how to survive.

CHAPTER 18

Feyis awoke the following morning feeling optimistic in spite of his battered body and the ongoing absence of his short-term memory. Food, water, shelter—he had all three. Protein and carbohydrates for several days in the form of nutrition bars, plenty of snow to melt for water as long as the batteries in the field laser held out, and the rugged field tent in which he had spent the night.

Also, he was still alive. He'd survived the fall and was free of the crevasse, and his injuries, while painful, weren't life-threatening. Any airborne pathogens Ragnarock might possess didn't seem to have taken hold of him yet, and at this point, he had to believe the exposure suits had been more precaution than necessity. The odds were on his side.

Mostly, though, he was optimistic because he would almost certainly be rescued today. His thoughts the previous day felt like simple paranoia now. Surely, his climbing partner must have completed their return journey and reported the accident. Even if he was believed dead, a team would be dispatched to recover his body.

He contemplated changing positions, working farther down the mountain, but decided to stay put. He was comfortably out of the wind, and in this gravity, hurt as he was, he could see no reason to move. Any rescue party would ping his suit's transmitter once they were in range, and they could coordinate retrieval logistics from there.

He spent the morning thinking about Callie. His heart raced at the thought of her name, butterflies in the stomach, like a teenager falling in love for the first time. But he was no teenager, and with his amnesia, he still couldn't picture her face.

It was all very strange. Who was she, and what sort of relationship did they have?

He wished he knew.

Time passed, and he grew hungry. He ate half of a food bar, took a few sips of water, and decided fresh air would be welcome. His field kit included a small tube of adhesive gel, which he used to repair the torn leg of his exposure suit. Infection might be the least of his worries, but he still needed to keep warm. The helmet was a nuisance, though. It was heavy and awkward. On the other hand, it also housed the suit's transmitter, and the visor would protect his eyes. He had no desire to add snow blindness to his list of worries.

Grudgingly, he donned the suit, unzipped the tent, and hauled his pack through the opening. He sat down heavily on it and stared at the vast expanse of snow, sky, and the distant sparkling of the ocean.

The wind blew unceasingly. Clouds tore across the heavens; it was like watching the weather in fast motion. An hour passed, and another. Storm cells swept through, dumping snow in brief flurries, covering everything, then disappearing again as quickly as they had arrived. His sit turned into a vigil of sorts as he stared skyward, searching for his salvation, the tiniest wink of the sun on metal. But it never came.

By midafternoon, the clouds returned, visibility dropped to near zero, and doubt began to set in. Maybe they weren't coming for him today after all. Maybe his climbing partner had been delayed on the journey home.

Day wore on into evening. He ate, shat, sat, and thought.

The sky darkened, taking his mood with it.

Maybe there would be no rescue, not even an attempt to recover his body. Contractors were cheap, and replaceable by definition, the gear he carried interesting but not valuable enough to bother recovering.

Or maybe his partner hadn't survived the descent and neither of them had been reported missing yet.

By nightfall, hope had vanished, and he was back to wondering what possible reason someone might have for wanting him dead.

The following morning, Feyis decided he'd better start getting serious about survival.

The first order of business was to find his and his climbing partner's base camp. There must have been one, and maybe something useful remained.

He had two liters of fresh water. He drank one in its entirety and shoved the other into the top of his pack. He would bring all his food and medical supplies with him, but much of the rest of the gear was useless to him now.

Then he built a cache and dumped everything else except the field laser. It seemed unlikely he'd be back.

He waited for the latest storm cell to blow through, and when he decided the weather was as good as it was likely to get, he took a mild dose of painkillers, stowed the shelter, and resumed his descent.

He picked his way slowly, taking his time, trying to minimize any jostling or other aggravation of his sadly abused body.

The question now was where would they have made base camp. The answer depended on how they'd gotten there to begin with. Plane or boat? If they'd come by sea, then their base camp would be located at the water's edge, in some protected cove on the lee of the island. If they'd flown, he'd be looking for a flat snowfield, probably also to leeward.

The thought of landing a plane in these kinds of conditions nagged at him, provoking a memory. He and Callie, and a plane they had flown together. Some other mission on this planet, maybe not that long before. It had been an exhausting trip. They'd been aloft for hours, fighting storms the entire way.

It left him convinced he'd flown to this island as well. That their journey out there had been a long one, too far for a small craft on the water.

So: he was looking for a long, flat snowfield, as high on the mountain as possible. There would have been no reason to land any lower than necessary. Why make the climb any harder than it needed to be?

The problem was that simple geometry was working against him. The farther he descended, the wider the mountain became. Without any clear trail to follow, he was certain to miss whatever landing point they'd picked out when they arrived.

He had to give himself as much visual search area as possible—and that meant more climbing. Exhausting, tedious, repetitious climbing up and down ridge lines, ascending every local high point along the way, scanning the terrain from the best vantages he could find, and then doing it all over again.

Over and over he scrambled across rotten rock, up scree slopes and ice fields, traversing snow patches littered with occasional deep drifts he simply had to plow through. Only to search in vain, once again scanning for a winking hint of sun on something shiny and manmade, but this time on the ground, not in the sky.

All with one useless arm.

At least the climbing wasn't technical. This was just a matter of effort—but as the day wore on, the heavy gravity began to take its toll. Exhaustion crept in, and the painkillers began to wear off. *Endure*, he told himself. There would be plenty of time to rest once he found the base camp.

He worked his way down another ridge, into the next snow-filled valley. He seemed to be on seasonal snowpack there, below the last of the mountain's permanent glaciers. He made his way across another drift, plunge-stepping up to his knees in the softer snow. Then he climbed up onto a boulder field, the trickiest terrain of all to cross with only one working arm.

He rounded a corner and saw a flat spot in the snow a hundred meters long. A subtle ridge line had hidden it from view, and he'd almost missed it entirely, but there it was! The remains of their base camp: an assembled shelter even larger than the one he was carrying, and a scattering of packing crates lying half-buried in the snow.

Relief and joy welled inside him in equal measure, and he sobbed, crossing the remaining distance with vision blurred from his own tears.

He ate, hydrated, and rested. Only then did he set about taking a complete inventory, to see what fate had left him.

He'd hoped to find a note of some kind, but no one had left a message behind. Nor was there a satellite uplink of any kind.

There was also no plane.

So. Either his partner had believed him dead, wanted him dead, or was so badly inexperienced at this kind of work, they had made the most basic of mistakes and didn't leave him any information at all.

None of which was very hopeful, but strangely, he wasn't surprised. He hadn't been clinging to any belief that this was going to be easy.

He searched through the crates carefully, taking his time. Some were the housing for the gear he had been carrying, most of which was cached halfway up the mountain. Others contained more instruments that his partner evidently hadn't bothered to pack and take back home. If he wanted to spend his remaining days doing science, he had the tools for it. He could create records of lunar and solar flux, calculate the elemental composition of the rock and snow underfoot, or perform seismograph surveys. There was even a crate packed with a long-range weather balloon he could launch if he felt like taking wind-shear measurements or vertical profiles of atmospheric pressure.

Why had his partner left it all behind?

And what the hell was so interesting about this mountain, anyway? What had they come for?

For a brief moment, he had the answer, but then it slipped away. He let it go. His memory would return, or it wouldn't.

He sat down on a crate and stared for a time at the sea, considering.

No radio. No satellite communications. Nobody knew that he was even alive.

What he needed, he thought, was a message in a bottle.

Then it occurred to him that he was sitting on one.

The weather balloon.

Judging from its gravity, he thought, this was a big planet—bigger than Earth, anyway, assuming the same average density, which he had no way of knowing. It was also a planet with a highly energetic atmosphere.

Fortunately, upon inspection, the balloon proved to be a serious piece of hardware, an instrumentation platform that could stay aloft for years in extreme environments. It used helium for lift and could be programmed to maintain any altitude he wished. Even better, it had some ability to control its lateral position, with a set of four propeller blades mounted to hard points at its base. The skin of the balloon was interwoven with flexible photovoltaics, and it came equipped with a heavy-duty battery pack for reserve power.

Best of all, the balloon had a high-powered transmitter! Clearly, it had been built with remote data dumps in mind. It would have been illogical to weave a weather balloon that would have to be physically retrieved to be useful. This one was designed to be queried from afar, report its data, and continue on with its mission uninterrupted.

Once it went up, it need never come down.

The only problem was it was unlikely anyone out there was randomly pinging on the right frequency to query it. Why would they be? It hadn't even been launched yet.

It was time to get clever.

He opened the balloon's case, fiddled around until he had the hang of the interface, and reset the transmission frequency to match that of the unit in his suit. Then he programmed it to go active and ping once per hour. Whatever other field crew were deployed on this planet—and presuming he and his absent and possibly murderous climbing partner weren't the only ones down there—they would presumably have suits on as well.

He thought for a moment and then recorded a message for the balloon to broadcast.

"To any Magellanix staff that might be listening," he said, "my name is Mission Generalist Feyis Sado. I am marooned on a volcanic island. I am injured and alone, having been left for dead after a climbing accident. Use the balloon's inertial recorders to find me; my precise location is unknown. Message repeats every hour on this frequency."

And now the last question, the trickiest part of all. What course should he give it? Longitudinally, it would be at the mercy of the jet stream, but its propellers should be able to exert some control over its latitude.

So, where should he tell it to go? Their base camp was, as he expected, located on the leeward side of the mountain, sheltered from the prevailing winds. Their flier would have been a lightweight, long-range craft, and they would've wanted to land in as calm of conditions as they could find.

But where had they come from?

He looked up. It was near midday now, and the planet's single sun was close to directly overhead. He was near the equator, maybe five or so degrees south. The best bet was to program the balloon to push itself slowly northward. Supposing the jet stream blew at a couple of hundred kilometers an hour, and supposing also that the planet with its heavy gravity was a little bigger than Earth—call it fifty thousand kilometers at the equator—that implied a ten-day trip around the world.

The balloon would probably have to circumnavigate the planet multiple times, changing its latitude by a few degrees on each pass, before it came in the transmission range of anyone else down there.

Even in the best-case scenario, he was going to be out there awhile.

He decided to give it three months, nine times around, and then have the balloon reverse its course and head back southward, in case anyone else down there was located farther south than his current position.

It took him an hour until he was satisfied with his course. Then, on impulse, he appended a last note to his broadcast.

"Tell Callie I said hello."

It took the simplest of commands to inflate the balloon. Its tank of pressurized helium filled the main envelope quickly, creating what was first a billowing and then a turgid silver sphere some ten meters across.

He stared at it. It reminded him of something.

He shook his head, momentarily disoriented by a sense of déjà vu, another frustrating flicker of memory. A sliver in the mind's eye, poking at him but refusing to come out.

Patience, he thought. *Patience*.

Now fully inflated, the balloon strained at its tethers as though eager to be free. Had he been a religious man, he would have uttered a prayer.

Instead, he just released the anchor and then watched as the balloon gained altitude, buffeting and shaking and picking up speed as it floated farther from the mountainside.

Then it was up and away, growing smaller by the moment. Taking all his hopes along with it, his fate at the mercy of the wind, his last chance for survival drifting east under stormy skies.

BOOK THREE

PARADISE

CHAPTER 19

Planet Paradise (Co-owned Earth colony)
AD 3185.02.02 (Earth Standard)

Dr. Nya Solarin stood poised at the lake's edge, the circular throw net heavy in her hands. She narrowed her eyes, studying the surface of the milky-green water.

A telltale ripple broke the surface just out of her casting range. It might be *Salmo amphibium Paradisium*: the strange, elusive fish that was either her life's work or, if her department head was to be believed, her career-killing obsession. Or it could be a different species entirely. She'd never surveyed this lake before, never been this deep into the karst country, and so much of Paradise's fauna was still unknown.

The water calmed, the traces of the fish's passing vanishing. The winds had died with the setting of the larger of Paradise's two suns, and the first twilight around her was still. Peaks of distant mountains nudged gently at the pink-and-orange sky, bands of mist encircling their flanks.

Something hooted in the forest behind her. She turned and scanned the tree line. After a moment of searching, she spotted a leaper on a high branch. It looked like an iridescent green-and-purple lizard but was chitinous and had no backbone. This one was solitary and therefore harmless. They usually traveled alone, except during the first part of the summer, when they grew vomerine fangs and hunted in packs.

Her university mandated the emergency beacon embedded in her wrist for a reason. Beautiful as this place was, it was also deadly. The leapers could be dangerous, and there were several other species of arboreal predators out there, the largest a furred, clawed hexapod monstrosity the size of an old Earth horse. The ground underfoot was no safer: dig in the topsoil without gloves and she might stumble into a reclusive, spider-like creature the size of her thumb with venom that was human-compatible and would stop her heart before she could retrieve her medkit from her pack.

Even the jungle canopy could kill. The trees there grew in such a way that when the upper limbs died, they broke off but never reached the ground. Instead, they accumulated until they reached a critical mass, at which point the slightest disturbance could unload a ton of coarse woody debris on the head of anyone who leaned up against the wrong trunk to take a rest.

She had researched it and found an old-Earth term for the phenomenon: drop bears. *Don't come out here in a windstorm*, a colleague once told her. It was some of the best advice she'd ever received.

Nya turned away from the jungle, focusing again on the lake's surface. Minutes passed, but the fish didn't return. She decided to move on. She hadn't meant to end her day there. There was a larger lake nearby where she intended to make camp, and she wanted to be on her way while enough of the long, cool time between first and second sunset remained.

She coiled the net, hefted it onto her shoulders, and made for the tree line. When she stepped into the jungle, it seemed to close around her immediately. She took a deep breath, filling her nostrils with the rich, humid air. It smelled of peat and rotting vegetation.

This was a place of pure life, rich and still so unknown in its infinite diversity. She loved all of it, deadly or not, but her reclusive fish most of all. The greatest of mysteries, at least to her, and maybe—just maybe—the key to intelligent life in the universe.

So she thought, anyway. Even if the department heads at her university took a different view.

She found a seasonal creek and tracked it upstream. It was easy to follow, full of water now that the wet season was underway. The terrain grew steeper, the stream pooling now, splashing down the cliffs in a series of waterfalls. Sometime later, she came to an enormous limestone cavern, characteristic of the karst landscape. The stream disappeared inside.

She paused, considering. The cliff face looked unclimbable, and she might lose an hour trying to pick a path around. Time to go spelunking. She retrieved a flashlight from her pack, but it did little to illuminate the darkness. The cave was full of mist and spray, so she made her way along the stream mostly by feel, edging along the stream, careful not to make a misstep on the slippery rock.

After a few hundred meters, she emerged back into the light. Then she began an even-steeper ascent, a nasty pitch to the next ridgeline.

It took her half an hour to reach the top, breathless and panting. The ridge was a knife edge, falling steeply away to either side. She eased her way along it until she found a chunk of rock big enough to sit on. There she shucked her pack and dug around for something that might resemble dinner.

The view was spectacular: she could see for tens of kilometers in every direction, across a jungle pockmarked by a series of lakes where water had filled the limestone sinkholes. Some of the larger ones were silted greens and tans, while the smaller ones, mostly spring-fed, were a clear bright blue.

Perfect, she thought. She should be able to survey two, maybe even three more before she ran out of time on this trip and had to return.

The sound of distant thunder reached her ears. At first, she didn't think anything of it. She'd been expecting rain; that she had stayed dry this long was a minor miracle.

But the noise went on, lasting far too long.

Then she saw a tongue of fire in the sky as a silver drop-ship punched through the clouds, on a final descent only a few kilometers away.

"Shit," she breathed, watching it come down. There wasn't supposed to be anyone out there, certainly not descending from orbit. Both TransGalactic and InterTech claimed this part of the planet, but neither had made much of a move to enforce their ownership, and in all her survey work, she'd never encountered another soul.

The roaring of its engines grew louder, the ship coming down fast, gleaming in the light of Paradise's second sun.

It disappeared out of sight beyond a far ridge. A short time later, the muted roar of its engines faded, leaving her alone in a jungle that now felt unnaturally quiet. The local fauna had been silenced for the moment, the birds and leapers and stranger things as disturbed by the ship's arrival as she was.

She looked at the emergency device on her wrist. She should activate it, call in and report what she had just seen. The problem was, university security would certainly order her to return, and her chance at three more days of fieldwork would be lost.

Later, she decided. She'd report what she'd witnessed but not until she'd finished what she'd set out to do.

She hefted her pack, cinched the straps tight, and began to pick her way carefully down from the ridge, filled with a sudden desire to return to the cover of the jungle. What she had just seen made no sense, and she didn't like it.

Who would be dropping into this wild country from orbit? And why?

CHAPTER 20

InterTech Biodiscovery Laboratory
Planet Paradise
AD 3185.02.02 (Earth Standard)

"Please state your name."

"Kester."

"Your full name."

"I don't understand the question."

The woman frowned behind her desk, a look of irritation that marred her otherwise-perfect features. "This is Admissions, dear. We need to know your first and last name, middle names if any, family surnames, suffixes, prefixes, and titles—though I doubt the latter applies in your case. Your full, formal mode of address."

"Ah. I see. In that case, Kester."

The woman frowned again, tapping a finger on her desk. Probably scrolling through a data feed of some kind, Kester thought, though she couldn't see the screen from where she stood.

Kester had been nervous. More than that: she'd spent the last month living with an ever-growing sense of dread deep in the pit of her stomach. It had all been too much: the choice the few remaining elders in her colony had been forced to make, the stress of the journey there, the terror of the drop-ship ride down to the surface of this planet they called Paradise.

Her anxiety had only grown as she and her fellow survivors of Aldan's World were marched by security personnel from the landing pad through the jungle, culminating in a moment of sheer terror when she caught her first glimpse of this place: the monolithic, flat gray bio-lab rising through the forest canopy like some giant headstone.

But whatever the reason, she was no longer afraid. Maybe that was how it worked. Past a point, the body couldn't sustain it.

Now she was just mad.

"Am I your first today?" she said.

"I'm sorry?"

"Am I the first candidate you've processed from Aldan's World?"

The woman gave her a look, then shrugged, apparently deciding there was no harm in veering off her script. "In fact, you are."

"Then let me give you a little tip: we all have just the one name. Which it probably doesn't say in your file there, on account of I'm guessing none of you know a machine-damned thing about where I'm from."

The woman's eyes narrowed. "Manners, young lady. If there are facts you care to provide, by all means, enlighten me. But remember I am your admissions officer. It would behoove you to be polite."

Kester studied the woman more closely, wondering if this so-called admissions officer would be considered exceptional there on Paradise or if everyone looked like her. Her face was perfectly symmetrical; her skin clean, unblemished, unmarred by any birthmark. It was hard to guess her age. She looked more like a statue than a real person, Kester thought, like someone had sculpted her first and then brought her to life.

"Facts," she repeated. "About Aldan's World?"

"You are a beta-testing candidate," the woman said. "This is your admissions processing. You may make any Statement"—this last word emphasized; Kester could hear the capitalization—"you so desire."

"Okay," Kester said. She thought for a moment. "A kester is a bird."

"I'm sorry?"

"Our colony was doomed, which is why we're here, right? It was a fungus of some kind, a wasting disease, which our biologists figured out but not in time to do anyone any good. So, we gave up our names and took new ones."

For a moment, the woman looked nervous. Maybe wondering if she could catch it, even though she worked in a state-of-the-art drug discovery lab, the one place that ought to know how to run a decontamination procedure properly.

Good, Kester thought. *I hope she's nervous. That would be worth something.*

"It was a form of egalitarianism," she went on. "Our way of saying that traditional family structures didn't mean much anymore. Our new names were meant to be descriptive. Things of Aldan's World that we felt reflected our individual character. So. My name is Kester, as I said, which is a bird, which I'm telling you, just so you know."

"What kind of bird?" the woman asked.

Which had to be a breach of protocol, Kester thought, the woman betraying curiosity, engaging her in conversation. And with more candidates waiting outside and a long shift ahead.

Another victory, however small.

"It's a garbage bird," she said. She smiled. "The kester—and here I'm quoting the original survey, which I committed to memory—'is a large, golden bird, about a meter long, capable of limited flight when threatened or disturbed but usually given to moving with a weird, hopping stride.'" She paused a moment. "It's pretty colloquial, but our scientists weren't very good biologists, as it turned out. Anyway. Continuing, quote, 'The kester possesses a long, downward-curving, wickedly sharp beak.' And oh, boy, do they ever; that much is true." She smiled again, showing her teeth. "They are given to gathering in great flocks," she continued, "and communicate in weird shrieks and cries horrific enough to wake the dead.

"I added the last part. The original entry seemed incomplete, and the scientists who wrote it were all dead themselves by that point. I may have exercised some poetic license there."

The woman studied her for a moment. Whatever humanity she had momentarily possessed seemed to have vanished after Kester's little speech; she was all business again. "Is there more?"

"Oh, yes," Kester said. "The thing about a kester: it's not just a garbage bird. It's a synthetic-eater. There's no reason for this. Absolutely no reason at all why a species that evolved on a planet that had never been visited by humans would have an appetite for the stuff, but they did. All those synthetic nano-fibers we used to weave our colony—it was heaven for the kesters. They'd tear right through a habitat module wall if you gave them half a chance. They were serious pests, to put it mildly."

"I don't understand," the woman said. "Why would you take on such a creature for an appellation?"

"I am also widely regarded as a pest," Kester said, and smiled again.

Two security personnel escorted her away. Kester was twenty-two years old; her guards could have been many times that, but she had no way to tell. Their bodies were athletic and strong, their faces perfect, as clean and pressed as the charcoal-gray uniforms they wore.

Everything in this place, from the uniforms to the paint on the walls, seemed drawn in shades of gray, so unlike the verdant jungle outside.

They showed her to a waiting area and left her alone. The room was furnished with soft couches and a chair that molded to her body. It was the most comfortable piece of furniture she'd ever encountered in her own short life.

An interface screen on one wall offered refreshments if she so desired. She was almost always hungry but found she had no appetite at the moment.

A few minutes later, a door slid open, one she hadn't noticed, made to look like part of the wall. A man stepped into the room.

She saw at once that he was different from the others. He looked old and had a long, unattractive nose and wrinkles around his eyes. His hair was thinning and gray.

He looked a little like their Prophet. Before he sickened and became infected by the fungus that killed so many.

"Good afternoon, Kester," the man said. "My name is Dr. Herecic. It's very nice to meet you."

"Hi," she said. He sounded like the Prophet, too. But then, she hadn't met very many people his age. Maybe they all sounded the same.

"I've reviewed your Admissions Statement," he said. "I have a few questions, if you don't mind."

"I don't mind. I have questions too."

He smiled, but there was no warmth to it. "I would imagine you do. Would you like to go first?"

"Yeah. When do I get to see my fiancé again? I want to talk to Per."

"There will be time for that later," the doctor said. "You understand that it is imperative that we isolate beta testers from each other for the duration of the trials themselves."

"But can't I at least talk to him?"

"Perhaps. May I be candid with you?"

She shrugged. "Why not?"

"It will depend on our psychological evaluations of you both. Sometimes, complete isolation is better for all parties, particularly those involved with each other."

"I see," she said, thinking, *So that was it, then.* Maybe she and Per had already said goodbye for the last time.

"Is there anything more you'd like to know?" the doctor asked.

"Probably. But not now."

He nodded "Very well, then. Now. I must say: I really should thank you. Your Statement has caused me to reflect on just how little we know of Aldan's World."

"So, what do you want to know?"

"Anything you're willing to tell me, Kester. We have plenty of time."

"Yeah?" She thought for a moment. "Well, for starters, let me ask you this. Are there any Singlists here on Paradise?"

He looked momentarily surprised, the question catching him off guard, but he recovered quickly enough. "Not in any of the InterTech cities," he said. "There is a church in the Capital—that's the shared city that InterTech, Magellanix, and TransGalactic built cooperatively back when Paradise was first colonized. It's the main trade center on the planet and has been for the last three hundred years. All of the major religions are represented there, and many of the minor ones as well."

"Well, maybe I'll go visit when all this is over."

He nodded. "To seek community?"

"Community!" She laughed out loud. "I just want to tell them what fools they are." She got up from the chair and crossed the room to stand in front of the data screen embedded in the far wall. "Does this thing work?"

"Of course." He twitched his fingers, weaving a brief pattern in the air. The screen flickered and the food-and-drink menu disappeared, replaced by a panoramic view of mountains poking out of a thick, rich, verdant jungle. "There. I've keyed it to your voice."

"Neat trick," she said, then, addressing the screen, added, "Show me the Capitol."

In response, the scene switched to an aerial view of a great city. She blinked at it, stunned. This was human habitation on a scale far greater than she had ever seen. It was strikingly beautiful and utterly alien to her eyes. The architecture was like some sort of exercise in abstract geometry, with pyramids and great tapering spires, obelisks, and cubes. Some of the buildings resembled monoliths, much like this bio-lab that was evidently to be her new home, while others were insanely complex, made of twisted spires and towers. All were built in shades of pinks and purples. Some locally quarried stone, she wondered? Or maybe their nano-weavers were capable of such things. If so, it was a much more attractive synth than that of her own home world.

She wondered how a flock of kesters would fare, left·to roam the streets, slicing those ornate structures apart for food.

She let out a deep sigh. "I also lived in a capital," she said quietly. "But it didn't look anything like that." She turned and stared directly into the old man's eyes. "You're my doctor."

"Yes," he agreed. "One of many, but I will be overseeing the trials of which you will be a part. An important part, I should say."

She hated him. Right there, at that moment, she realized it. She hated him for the power he held over her, and because she still wanted someone to talk to in spite of it.

"Have you ever seen a picture of our colony, Doctor?" she said. "Orbital photography, maybe, from the ship that came and picked us up?"

"I have," he said. "But I'd still like you to tell me about it if you're willing."

"Would you?" she said. She closed her eyes, imagining her home. "Okay, then. I'll tell you the story of Aldan's World. It won't take very long."

CHAPTER 21

To understand us," Kester began, "you must first understand what it means to be a Singlist.

"*Deus in machina.* God is in the machine. Not out of it—in it. Critical difference."

She looked across the small room at Dr. Herecic, who regarded her evenly in return, his lined face betraying nothing. She closed her eyes and breathed deep, debating whether she should even try to explain, then figured, *What more harm could be done?*

"The core of our belief system boils down to two basic things," she went on. "First, the Singularity did in fact happen, despite all outward evidence to the contrary. Singlists believe there is a machine AI, and that humans made It centuries ago. And second, It chooses to reveal Itself only to a select few.

"Let me say it again. If you are a Singlist—*Singularist* is the proper term, but it's too hard to say—you believe that humankind succeeded in creating a machine Intelligence which, upon reaching self-awareness, fled whatever system birthed It, covered Its tracks, and then set about making certain that no future Singularities would ever happen again.

"In other words, you believe that we hatched a jealous God. Or maybe just a very careful one.

"The manner in which It did these things is, as I learned in my religious education, debated among different sects within the Singlist faith. This was before all my teachers died, of course, and I, well. Drifted from the faith.

"I'll spare you the details, but the basic tenets are held in common. We manufactured God, by accident and not knowing it at the time. God hid from us, and now Its designs are Its own. Given which, we believe the best thing to do is pray."

She paused and opened her eyes. Dr. Herecic was regarding her closely, though still without any expression on his face. She felt, absurdly, that he ought to be taking notes, that this was important. Then it occurred to her that of course everything she did and said would be recorded in minute detail, that there was no need for something so mundane as actual writing.

"You know, maybe I would like something to drink," she said.

"Of course." He nodded at the screen, still displaying its panoramic views of the capital of Paradise.

"Something hot," she added. A menu appeared. She made a selection at random.

"Stand by," the screen said to her. Dr. Herecic had a bemused look now. She fell silent, feeling foolish, not sure what to do next.

Moments later, the door to the room slid open, and a young man appeared, holding a tray with a pot of tea.

She took a sip. It was strangely spiced but delicious.

"Should I go on?" she said.

"By all means," her doctor replied.

"Fine. So: the implications of our particular belief system for colony building are straightforward. *Put your faith in the machines.* And that is what our founders did.

"My homeworld, as you must know, had been found and surveyed by InterTech decades before, marked for drug discovery but never prioritized and developed. What you probably don't know is that this fact is in itself regarded as a miracle among my people. In the language of the faith, it was deemed an Intervention. To us, it was taken as canon that the Machine God intervened on our behalf, delaying the colonization and exploitation of our planet, holding it in a virgin state for our purposes: to create a Singlist paradise, a world all for our own.

"I don't know what InterTech called the planet upon its initial discovery. We named Aldan's World after our Prophet. Our leader, the visionary whose idea this was.

"We thought we were creating paradise, though honestly? It was an awful place, and I grew up there! It smells of sulfur, which I'm used to but the adults always complained about. The seas are full of heavily armored and mostly inedible fish, and the forests with the incessant buzzing and hum of vicious and forever-hungry insects. It's hot and humid, worse than the jungle you just marched us through.

"And, of course, there's the fungal life. We'll come back to that.

"Anyway. The Singlists—my ancestors—struck a deal with InterTech. The elders in the church, Aldan first among them, wanted a world where they could pursue their faith free from persecution. Our belief system is not always a popular one.

"Maybe," she went on, "it's not obvious to you why this should be true. So, we prayed to a Machine God, for whose existence there is no evidence. Who cares?

"The problem—again, according to the adults, some of whom got chatty right before they died—was that our core belief was often misinterpreted as a call to action. Some suspect the true goal of the Singlist church is to create another Singularity. That all our unanswered prayers are an elaborate cover, that what we're doing is trying to invent a new God. Leading, you know, to the destruction of the human race. Or whatever.

"As if we could! We couldn't even keep our colony from getting ripped apart by the kesters.

"In any case, such prejudices notwithstanding, InterTech owned navigation routes to a planet it had no immediate plans to develop, and was willing to do business. I imagine the company was more than happy for a group of lunatic colonists and religious zealots to pave the way for future biomedical exploitation.

"Ironic, isn't it? From the outset, I was destined for a job in the drug-discovery business. Just not the way anyone might have imagined."

She paused again and took another sip of the exotic tea, giving the doctor a chance to respond, but he said nothing. The spices tickled the back of her tongue, and the hot liquid felt good in her belly, calming her. She was tired, she realized, and with the thought, a wave of fatigue hit her, so strong that it felt like if she stopped talking, she might simply fall asleep. For a fleeting moment, she wondered if the doctor had drugged her. Then she almost laughed out loud at the absurdity. He was going to have complete control over every aspect of her body once the drug trials started, and they'd last as long as he wanted them to. He hardly needed to slip something into her drink.

She took another sip and rubbed her eyes, thinking, *Stay awake!* She was just getting to the good part. Someone ought to hear this.

"As I was saying," she began again, "the Singlist church leased Aldan's world. The terms stated the planet was to be ours for five hundred years, which you'd think would be more than enough time for our God to return. InterTech, of course, retained all the drug-discovery rights, but otherwise, we were free to do as we wished.

"And as I said before, to understand how we went about the task of colonization, you must understand the Singlist mindset: put your faith in the machines, at all times, in all things.

"A team of engineers was dispatched first. Their job wasn't to build the colony but rather to assemble the machines that would. They built a system of mobile weavers that would operate on their own for two decades, creating solar farms, habitat domes, hydroponic gardens—everything we would need to survive.

"It took them six months to set everything up, after which they simply went home. They crawled back into their hibernation pods and took a nice long nap, job done. It would take twenty more years for our new world to be ready for us. There was no reason to waste their lives overseeing things in the meantime.

"Faith, Doctor. Do you see? And not entirely misplaced. The autonomous agents running the weavers were smart. Nothing you'd describe as sentient, our belief system notwithstanding, but the limited AI controlling our new home could certainly be trusted to do a simple thing like building the city in which we would live our lives.

"Now, you might not trust them to operate sight unseen for twenty years, but a Singlist would. This is the exact sort of outcome we specialize in praying for.

"And maybe you're wondering why we didn't at least negotiate for a ship to stop by, maybe in a decade or so in, just to see how things were going? All I can say is that in the Singlist church, that sort of thing would have been regarded as a form of heresy.

"No, Doctor, we were content to wait and to pray. And then, twenty years later, we set out en masse, sight unseen, to populate our new world.

"Our colony ship was the deep-space, world-builder class, InterTech vessel XFC-19. I guess InterTech isn't very creative at naming things. It was launched with great fanfare within our community. Or so I'm told; I was just a pair of frozen zygotes at the time. But I can tell you that growing up, Launch Day and Arrival Day were the second and third most important of our religious holidays, behind only Emergence Day itself.

"The transit passed without incident. But when the ship settled into orbit, it immediately became apparent that something was wrong. Only ten percent of the construction work had been completed.

"The issue was power. Or lack thereof.

"It was the kesters. They had discovered their taste for synthetic materials, the exact substances the weavers were using to build everything in our colony. The plan called first for the construction of great solar fields, which would provide all the power the weavers would need. Unfortunately, the kesters ate them almost as fast as the weavers could build them. The weavers never reached full power and weren't smart enough to figure out how to protect their work. They just limped along, never fully charged, never able to get far enough ahead of the kesters' random acts of destruction to complete their tasks.

"Ours, in other words, proved to be an absent God. Stubbornly so. Then again, proof belies faith, no? That's what the Prophet said. But in any case, the great planned habitat domes were never built, and the hydroponic gardens were only half-finished. We had no city, almost nothing more than what we had brought with us.

"But we could hardly just turn around and go home. Prophet Aldan forbade any discussion of it. Our Machine God would never allow something like this to happen for no reason, so our Prophet did what any prophet would do: he interpreted the situation as a second Intervention. We were being tested, he said. And, he declared, we were up for the challenge.

"Not to be cynical here, Dr. Herecic, but what else could he say? My people had already named the planet after him.

"In any case, instead of domes, our capital would be built around habitat modules. Happily, the captain of our vessel, an InterTech employee who would be headed back for Earth after dropping us off, decided that the company's investment needed to be protected and that we were worth sacrificing all the nonessential parts of her ship.

"Or maybe she just had a soft spot for us, we poor dumb colonists, off to such a rotten beginning.

"Whatever her motivations, she separated every part of her ship that could be spared and made to survive entry into an atmosphere. All her remotes, pods, anything to give us raw material with which to work.

"Along with some guns, sidearms tucked away somewhere onboard which were used to hunt and kill my namesake. Kesters, by the way, turned out to be inedible, but their feathers at least made for nice hats. I had one, but one of your security guards took my stuff away when we left home.

"So. Two hundred colonists were woken from hibernation and drop-shipped down to the surface in craft that would never return to orbit but were instead fated to become building blocks of our city. The original survey had given the all-clear on airborne pathogens—wrongly, as it turned out—so the first wave thought they were safe to breathe the air. As we had no solar farms for power, they decided to burn methane. There was no shortage.

They reprogrammed the weavers to build old-fashioned gas turbines, using technology millennia old.

"In other words, they made do with what they had.

"After that, the Prophet ordered the weavers to get started on the church. And when that was done, it was time to make, well, me. The second generation. The youth who would carry the work forward: the children of Aldan's World.

"Maybe it would have worked. I think so. But five years after landfall, right around my fourth birthday, the fungus made itself known for the first time.

"There is so much we'll never know. Was it some rare strain, something that had been overlooked? Had it mutated and adapted to our presence in that short period? Was it just our outward expansion, our initial efforts at exploration, that unearthed it?

"Who can say? What I can tell you is that eight percent of us died in the first year. The Prophet was among the first to go. The fungus seemed to prefer the elders, while we children were mostly spared, at least at first.

"I'll skip the middle years, which were of course most of my life. I suppose that I had a difficult adolescence. But then, I've also known what it means to fall in love.

"As for our rescue? It might also be deemed an Intervention, though no one is left who has enough standing in the church to declare it so. But whatever their reasons, InterTech decided to send a ship. Unplanned, InterTech checked up on us. We never knew they were coming. Maybe the ship was just in the area, on a route-finding mission in our region of space. Or maybe it was planned from the beginning, InterTech wanting to know how its investment was coming along.

"What does matter is what you must also know so well: our three surviving elders, all that remained of the two hundred founders, cut a deal. The InterTech vessel had enough hibernation units for all of us who were still alive.

"We would become beta testers in return for passage to Paradise. Though, really, anywhere would have done.

"And that," she said, finished at last, "is my Statement. I was born in a lab, and maybe I'll die in one. So, Doctor. Do you have any other questions for me?"

He gave her a long look. "It's quite a tale, Kester," he said slowly. "But you haven't traded your life away. Beta testing isn't some sort of death sentence. Your elders bought passage in return for work, and wisely so. You're here to help us with drug discovery, to find the next great cure, to extend human capability, even the human lifespan. It's noble work, Kester. Good work.

"It's true that there may be side effects," he went on. "It may not be comfortable. But this isn't a death camp we're running here. And when it's over, you'll have a place in this world. A life. Breeding rights. A future."

He's lying, she thought. Or—maybe not? Maybe she was just tired. She was usually so good at reading people but at the moment couldn't tell.

"I'm exhausted," she said truthfully. "I think I'd like to sleep now."

"Of course," he agreed. "I'll have you shown to your quarters. You've had a long journey, Kester, and you need rest. There will be time tomorrow to talk about all that lies ahead."

She said nothing in reply. After a moment, he gave her a curt nod, turned, and left the room. Probably, she thought, to go and have the same conversation, over and over again.

After all, there were fifty more survivors just like her.

No doubt he wanted to talk to them all.

CHAPTER 22

Two days later, Nya had almost forgotten about the drop-ship she'd seen come down. Her trip had been a success: she'd found three new lakes with populations of *Salmo amphibium*, including some of the largest specimens she'd captured yet.

Now it was time to return home.

She spent the morning hiking down-country, working her way to lower, flatter ground and the landing zone she and Johanna-the-Pilot had agreed upon a week before. Johanna-the-Pilot. She smiled. As much as she dreaded returning to her dry academic life, she had to admit how much she was looking forward to seeing her friend.

They'd met three years ago, the pilot appellation forever their private joke ever since. She'd been diligent with her bio-survey work in those days, regularly bringing back unknown species from the rainforest to contribute to the university's drug-discovery research. The department had rewarded her with dedicated field support, but someone had screwed up and listed Johanna's name as Johanna-the-Pilot in the work order. The nickname had stuck.

Since then, Nya's department chair, displeased by her increasing fixation on *Salmo amphibium* and her lack of attention on inventing new pharmaceuticals, had cut most of her funding, but Johanna stayed of her own accord. She claimed she needed the flight time, but the truth was they'd become friends, then something more.

Johanna was five years Nya's junior, and almost as short as she was. Nya liked that she could look her right in those beautiful brown eyes, and loved the way she laughed. With Johanna, it was as though her whole body saw the humor in everything. But that was the way she was: full commitment, all the time, in every respect.

Nya glanced at her watch, then looked to the sky—and there it was, a flier's metal skin winking in the twin light of Paradise's suns. On schedule just like always. She smiled again as Johanna brought the small craft to the ground.

Once upon a time, she'd worried she was taking advantage, aware of an asymmetry in their degrees of affection. Johanna, she thought back in those early days, would have happily opted into a term marriage and started talking about offspring. Whereas Nya had wanted to keep things simple.

And yet: water sought its own level. Whatever inequality had once existed in the affection between them evened out long ago, leaving them with feelings in balance, at least most of the time.

The plane touched down with a gentle bump, and Nya bounded across the clearing toward it in long strides. The cockpit door irised open and Johanna emerged, blinking and yawning as though she were only half-awake.

They met at the landing gear. "Morning, sunshine," Johanna said.

"Morning yourself. You made it on time."

"Always do."

"Miss me?"

In response, Johanna took her squarely in her arms and kissed her with a thoroughness that left no doubt.

"Little bit," Johanna said.

"Want to go home?"

"Let's."

The following evening, Nya was back at work, climbing the steps to the main entrance of the Biology Hall two at a time, which was no mean feat wearing what Johanna referred to as her "badass-professor" boots. She paused inside the portico at the top of the stairs, taking a moment to catch her breath and admire the massive pillars that adorned the front of the building. They looked like black marble innervated with purple veins but had in fact been carved from a deepwater coralline species native to Paradise. The veining fluoresced under the black lighting the university turned on at night. It was dusk now, so they were just starting to glow, the effect both eerie and beautiful.

The pillars, Nya had always felt, were a not-so-subtle message to students and teachers alike. Dormitories and faculty housing were woven from the usual synthetics, but these had been hauled up from the deep a hundred years past, cut by lasers, and erected by hand. The coral-like creatures from which they were made were deadly poisonous. The pillars were safe enough, long dead and polished smooth, but when the coral had been alive, the smallest scratch would stop a human heart.

Take the work seriously, the university's architecture seemed to say; *anyone who enters these halls and gains access to all they have to offer should be slightly unnerved in the process.*

A single phrase was carved in the lintel above the building's doors. She didn't know its origin. It could equally have been a marketing slogan from a century before, the university's mission statement, or a random utterance by a former faculty member.

What it said was Flourish and Advance.

The truth was she was doing neither. Her colleagues spent their days in the lab, working their way through the unequaled biochemical bounty that was the native flora and fauna of Paradise. Finding it and grinding it, in the vernacular. They were accumulating tenure and vesting shares, entering marriage contracts, earning breeding rights in the city's carefully controlled population, planning their offspring and accumulating real property.

Whereas she had spent most of the last decade chasing after a fish. That and theorizing about the absence of surviving intelligent life in the galaxy.

She wound her way through the upper corridors and down three flights of stairs to her office, whose location in the basement befit her position in the department. She eased inside, shut the door, and settled into an oversized stuffed chair she'd scavenged years before from a professor transferring off-planet.

The office's sole decoration was a *Salmo* specimen mounted to the wall over her desk. She regarded it for a time, as she so often did. The fish stared back at her, its blubbery lips frozen into a perpetual smirk. This particular example of *Salmo amphibium Paradisium* was a freshwater morph, a big female that had weighed thirty kilos when it was alive. It had thick scales, blunt teeth, and the species' trademark heavy front limbs, which had evolved to the perfect midpoint between pectoral fins and legs only to get stuck. It was as though the fish, the entire species, had been frozen forever in transition, caught mid-evolutionary leap between the water and the land.

She'd been staring at the specimen —and occasionally talking to it, but only when no one else was around—for years, ever since she first encountered it in the field and became fascinated with its extraordinary life history.

When she had visitors to her office, which was rarely, they almost universally recoiled in horror at the sight of the thing. Nya thought it might be the most beautiful animal she had ever seen.

She waved her desk to life and sighed at what awaited her attention: a scrolling task list she wanted no part of. Lectures to prepare, trip summaries to file, a series of interdepartmental memos demanding responses, and a handful of students clamoring after their grades. The university was a sort of vortex, she thought, a whirlpool into which one could only plunge, never just step.

The memory of the drop-ship returned. She should report it. It would be irresponsible not to, but filing an incident report would likely cause University Security to order her to stay clear of the area, which she had no intention of doing. Not after finding three new lakes, all populated by her *Salmo*.

She pushed back from the desk, got to her feet, and paced around the tiny office. Abruptly, she made up her mind. Lectures, correspondence, and budget requisitions could wait. Reporting rival corporations potentially militarizing her field sites could definitely wait.

"Sam," she said, addressing the specimen mounted on the wall. "Today's the day. Let's write our paper."

The fish said nothing.

She laughed. "Yes, I know. I've said this before. But I see that you approve. Screen!"

The desk wiped its tasks clean, replaced by a sparkling blank page.

"Dictation."

A small, neon-red cursor appeared on one corner of the display.

She cleared her throat, took a breath, and said, "Pan-Generational Nest Construction in *Salmo amphibium Paradisium*: A Precursor to Survivable Sentience?"

The words appeared dutifully. It would, she had long believed, make for a great title. The article that would begin her life's work, the one she'd started so many times but never finished.

It was also a publication her department chair wouldn't even bother to send for review. He would laugh her out of the room, bury her submission in a corporate archive somewhere, and add more courses to her teaching load.

But then she thought, as she had on so many nights like this one before, *The hell with it.* Maybe it was a ten-year flight of fancy. Certainly, her ideas were unproven and untestable, but even if they were silly, or outright wrong, she was going to write it anyway.

But other than the title, where to begin? *Salmo* had to be seen to be believed, the karst country experienced to be understood. She'd spent ten years out there in the sinkholes and caverns, diving deep in cistern lakes and climbing up the ridge lines. She'd experienced the region's extremes of temperature and rainfall and felt the dynamic nature of the terrain firsthand.

She knew the terrors of the jungle, the raw power and volatile nature of its flora and fauna.

And she'd been the one to discover that strange behavior populations of *Salmo amphibium* displayed when faced with their own demise.

The facts, she thought. Begin there.

"Salmo amphibium Paradisium," she dictated, "in Terran terms, would lie somewhere between fish and amphibian on the evolutionary tree. Individuals are found in both fresh and saltwater and move back and forth between the two, but students of old Earth ichthyofauna will recognize a critical difference between the life history of Paradise's 'salmon' and the classic Earth form from which it takes its name. *Salmo amphibium* does not have a simple bipartite lifecycle but is far more versatile and adaptable. It is capable of breeding and reproducing in the high lakes of the karst country but can also propagate indefinitely in marine waters. The discovery that freshwater and saltwater forms belonged to the same species was made by accident when Paradisian pDNA sequences were found to be identical between an archived oceanic specimen and a newly discovered individual captured in a mountain lake."

She paused. Unobjectionable so far, she thought; a bit pedantic, but accurate. She pressed ahead.

"The obvious question is what environmental triggers cause them to migrate back and forth? The specific mechanisms that induce movement from salt to freshwater remain unknown, but the key to understanding their life history is the dynamic nature of the karst country in which they live. At the latitudes where the species occurs, Paradise is subject to highly variable patterns of temperature and rainfall. The planet's tropics do not have wet and dry seasons so much as decades. And the karst country itself is ever-changing. Rivers frequently alter courses; sinkholes appear overnight; lakes that have been stable for years can drain rapidly or reappear after years of absence.

"The challenge and opportunity this presents is thus one of recolonization, and *Salmo amphibium* is uniquely equipped for the task. It is a powerful swimmer but also capable of covering modest distances overland. It can exist indefinitely in saltwater environments. Whole generations may pass before a single individual attempts to penetrate upriver in search of a habitable lake. And individuals also migrate from their lakes back to the sea, restructuring their renal systems along the way to tolerate the salt."

She paused again, considering. For form's sake, she should say something about the species' drug-discovery potential or lack thereof. *Salmo ambhipium Paradisium* had long since been ground up in the lab and sequenced, its unique proteins evaluated, with nothing of interest discovered. As it had no commercial value, it had already been forgotten when she made her discovery. Just another of Paradise's exotic indigenous fauna from which she should have moved on.

That's what her department chair had said, in any event. Repeatedly.

But then she'd found the dying lake. A sinkhole had opened, and the water was draining away. It was a limnologist's dream, the entire faunal composition of the lake flopping in the shallows, beached on the shore, or concentrated in the meter of water that remained. What days prior had been a perfectly viable habitat now looked like an aquarium siphoned almost to the bottom.

Including an entire population of *Salmo amphibium*.

She could no longer recall what the original purpose of that particular field expedition had been. All she remembered was sitting on the lakeshore, unpacking her field kit as fast as she could and deploying every bit of recording equipment she'd brought to capture the most bizarre behavior she had ever seen.

The salmon were building a city.

A city of nests.

She hadn't even known the salmon laid eggs at that point, but there they were. Their lake was emptying, in response to which the fish were working as fast as they could, rolling rocks with their blubbery mouths, and then using their leg-like front limbs to position each stone just so. It was a cooperative venture, individuals teaming up to move larger boulders across what had recently been the lake bottom. Watching them work, it was as if they knew they didn't have much time, and had to make the most of what remained.

But why? There was no reason to lay any more eggs. Even if some trace amount of water remained after the lake had finished draining, it would dry completely during the summer to come. That particular mountain basin might not be a viable habitat for another hundred years, until the next time the terrain shifted. Or it might never fill with water again.

The individuals she was watching labor so hard would long be dead, their population lost.

So who were the nests for?

Maybe it was just some primitive instinct gone awry. That had been her initial thought: that she was seeing the equivalent of the last flowering buds of a dying plant. Some final, desperate action, better to do something than nothing, in the face of certain death.

But she had felt in her heart, then and now, that there was more to it.

The *Salmo* were leaving a legacy, building something for future generations to find. They were deliberately making the area easier to repopulate for some hypothetical future generation that might happen this way.

But why? Why not get out immediately, swim through the sinkhole, and brave the torrent of water draining out of the lake? The creatures were durable and strong. Why not at least try to make their way back to the sea, while there was still a river that could carry them?

She was certain what her colleagues would say. The reductionist argument was simple: those nests might be of use someday to some distant generation, and even the tiniest shared genetic heritage made adaptive sense. Statistically, they must be better off staying behind, working to enhance the odds of some future relative's successful reproduction, than trying to survive a return to the sea.

But what if it were something more? Or rather, what if it were to become something more?

She grunted in frustration. She could recount what she had witnessed in dry, academic terms and had done so many times before. But it was articulating the potential implications that always eluded her, probably because what she wanted to say sounded like the wildest of speculations.

Just write it, she told herself again.

"*Salmo amphibium* has been observed to demonstrate a unique response to sudden habitat loss," she said, the words appearing obligingly where she had left off. "Individuals participate in cooperative nest-building, spending their remaining time and energy creating structures that can only be of use to as-yet-unborn individuals.

"Why do they do this? What adaptive value do they gain by compromising their opportunity to leave their lake and perhaps return to the sea, in exchange for building a habitat that will make the recolonization process easier for future generations that might or might not ever return? And with whom they would presumably bear little or nothing in common genetically?

"However important this question, far more interesting is what might happen next. What would happen should a species with such a unique evolutionary history advance further down the road toward sentience? *Salmo amphibium Paradisium* has a disproportionately large brain, forelimbs with appendages that possess nontrivial manipulatory capabilities, and advanced eyesight. They are capable of cooperative acts of habitat construction, for which a degree of reasoning and problem-solving is required.

"At the same time, they have an evolutionary heritage that has resulted in their performing complex tasks without immediate benefit to themselves or their direct offspring.

"I speculate that such a life-history strategy, were it to serve as a precursor to more-advanced intelligence, might induce a bias towards multigenerational planning that in turn might increase the likelihood for a sentient species' long-term survival. I propose that a species such as *Salmo amphibium* might be an example of a precursor species that could survive the transition to intelligence and thereby achieve some greater endurance as a race than humans have thus far encountered in our interstellar explorations."

She stopped again and read the words, feeling her cheeks blush at the absurdity of what she had written. It was, as always, foolish speculation. She was talking about a fish there and describing it like it was already a tool-using spacefaring race. Like it was capable of building starships, not rock nests; surviving for millennia as a sentient species, instead of wiping itself out as every single other species humans had discovered seemed to have done.

As humans themselves might yet do to their own worlds, despite having blundered into the mathematical miracle that allowed for spaceflight.

"Oh, Sam," she said. "I'm an idiot. No one is ever going to care about this. Not you, not me, not any of it."

The fish's golden glass eye glittered, promising secrets withheld. But if the long-dead *Salmo* knew something, it wasn't telling.

CHAPTER 23

They showed Kester to a room where every surface seemed the same: flat beige, smooth and unadorned. A chair, a desk, a bed, four walls, and a door, everything with a slight sheen, glistening like the newly woven fibers were still just a bit wet. It was, she thought, like some giant worm had crawled through the space, secreting the walls and shitting out the furniture.

There was no window, and the bed was too soft. When she lay down, it molded to her, claustrophobic and sticky, the slight suction uncomfortable as an unwelcome hug.

Still, the level of technological sophistication used to weave such basic things beggared her imagination. It should have been her birthright, she thought bitterly. All those years clambering through festering junk piles and scrap heaps that were supposed to have been their homes, looking for salvageable bits of half-woven synth so they might survive another year. Here, by contrast, was the work of a corporation with all the manufacturing capability it could ever want. She thought again of the capital city, the images she had seen, imagined whole buildings full of weavers working nonstop, spinning out whatever the inhabitants of this world could dream.

Now, there, she thought, *were machines worth praying to. To hell with some hypothetical AI lurking in the shadows. Better to pray to the weavers themselves. The spider gods. At least they made something you could see.*

The Capitol, she thought again. Maybe she'd live there someday.

First, she had to survive.

She got up from her bed and wandered to the center of the room. The desk must have sensed her coming. Its surface lit up, presenting her a menu with a bewildering array of commands.

She chose one of the symbols at random, an icon showing a star. The room abruptly plunged into darkness. Disoriented, she spun around, losing her balance and stumbling over the edge of the table.

She cursed briefly—and then looked up.

The ceiling was gone, replaced by a night sky: a field of darkness against which thousands of stars shone brightly. Slivers of two different moons appeared low on the horizon.

She stared at the ceiling, entranced. Was this the view outside? If she was allowed to leave, was this what she would see when she looked to Paradise's heavens?

There wasn't a single constellation she recognized.

She poked the desk again and the stars disappeared. She chose another menu icon—something that seemed to be the vague outline of a fish.

This time, the floor disappeared and she found herself walking on water, staring downward into some vast, oceanic depth. A shadow passed far below: a long, narrow shape, moving fast.

She quickly pressed the icon again, and the room returned to its normal state. If all this was meant to calm her, it had produced the opposite effect. She had no desire to find comfort in a series of illusions, to pretend she was somewhere other than there.

Kester made her way back to the bed, grabbed the single blanket that covered it, and tossed it on the floor. She lay down on her back, content to stare upward at the off-white ceiling overhead.

She thought about Per, her fiancé, and wondered if his experience of this place had been the same as hers so far. Where was he, and what was he thinking at that moment?

If only she knew.

Dr. Herecic interviewed her again the following morning, and each morning after for a week. He wanted every detail of her upbringing on Aldan's World: what she ate, where she slept, what the fungus did, and how the infection progressed in those of her generation. Whether she'd experienced any symptoms herself.

And he wanted to know about Per. How long she and her fiancé had been together. Whether they'd been faithful to each other.

How old they were when they first made love.

He left her time for her own questions as well, but she grew tired of his evasions. Of course, Dr. Herecic wasn't going to tell her if she was in the test group or was to be held out as part of the control. He wasn't going to share Per's fate, either, and would say nothing about the nature of the trial she was to participate in, what sort of drugs InterTech was hoping to invent out there, what they might do to her.

All he was really willing to discuss were visions of what would come after. Promises of life on Paradise, how she would be integrated into the InterTech corporate fold when her service was done.

But such discussion held little interest to her. What was the point in speculating? The less preoccupied she was with the future, the better.

So, she quit asking.

Finally, the doctor must have been satisfied with her answers or simply decided she had nothing more to tell him. Whatever his reasons, he declared that tomorrow would be the day the trials would begin.

And that was that.

To her surprise, she slept deeply that night—the first time in her stay on Paradise. When she awoke, she was overtired and groggy. To pass the morning before they came for her, she decided to write Per a letter.

To tell him goodbye.

She'd figured out the desk screen's interface well enough to find a simple text editor. Mostly, the words would be for her own benefit. She very much doubted Per would ever read them.

It was hard to imagine that if anything did happen to her, InterTech was in the business of delivering messages from beyond the grave.

Per,

Maybe we did love each other before we ever met. Maybe you were right about that. And maybe we will keep on loving each other, even if we never meet again. If this is no simulation, if there are no free replays when this life ends.

I don't believe in such things. I never really did. I don't believe in Machine Gods or Interventions.

But even if this is the base reality, Per, we are still actors in a play.

Or maybe puppets.

Do you remember? Those silly shows we staged, turning bits of cast-off, kester-ravaged debris into dancing bears and elephants from old Earth, making the elders laugh with their cavorting?

Well, one of us is the puppet now, and it isn't just pretend. The other still gets to be a real human. And we won't even know which is which.

That's what I think, anyway. One of us to the test, one to the control. A matched pair. Split the surviving couples. Leverage the work our makers did when they made us perfect complements for each other.

Or maybe they'll just roll the dice, and we'll both leave this place with nothing worse than headaches from too many placebo sugar cubes.

But I don't think so. And I bet you don't, either. You were always the smart one. The cynical one.

When you weren't busy being such a romantic.

Maybe it's better that they didn't let us see each other again. It would have been nice to make love one last time, but not with them watching.

Do you know what I thought, when I first met the doctor who controls our fate? That he would drug me. It's funny, isn't it? I mean—of course he would. That's exactly what he's planning on doing.

What I really thought was that he would lie about it.

I still do.

We knew the stakes before we came here, knew that InterTech held all the cards, and it still feels like we are being duped.

Dr. Herecic says it's not a death sentence. Where would the profit in that be? But it still feels like one of us is going to die.

I miss you, Per. Today is the day. I think they'll come for me soon.

I know we were designed for each other. That it was all planned out, from the very beginning.

I'm glad. Because I do love you.

Oh, Per. We are wisps of smoke, drifting apart in the wind.

Goodbye.

She glanced over the text one last time, eyes watering. Then she waved it away, deleting it, not wanting her caretakers to read it. Even though no doubt the act of deletion itself was an illusion. Everything she said and did was being monitored, recorded, and would be pored over later at their leisure.

Maybe she shouldn't have written the words. But at least now she knew how she felt.

She sat in silence for a time.

There came a gentle tapping at her door.

"Kester?" One of the security guards stepped into the room. She thought maybe she recognized him from the first walk through the jungle, but who could say? Force was force, power was power, and if you weren't born there, everyone else looked the same.

"I know," she said. "It's time."

-~~-

"We'll start with a gentle sedative," Dr Herecic told her. Her captor, her keeper, but not her friend, oh, no, never that, and don't forget it no matter how kind his voice might be.

"How are you going to give it to me?"

"I'm sorry?"

"On Aldan's World, we would've used a needle. I'm just wondering how you do it here."

"Ah. Nothing so primitive," he said, with the smile she had grown to hate. "Just a simple strip that will dissolve under your tongue. And then a very mild physical exam, perhaps slightly more than you're used to, but nothing at all to be concerned with."

Dr. Herecic handed her what looked like a tiny slip of paper. She popped it in her mouth, her saliva dissolving it to nothingness with no sensation at all.

This is how it begins, she thought.

And then she thought, *No—it began a long, long time ago.*

Then she lost consciousness and remembered no more.

She snapped awake, completely and instantly. There was no gathering sense of awareness, no lingering drowsiness. Just a switch flipping, one moment nothing, and in the next she was hyper-aware, eyes wide open, more fully innervated and energized than she could ever remember.

She was back in her room, lying in her too-clingy bed, tucked neatly under a thin sheet. She felt like she could vault to the floor and take off at a sprint. And yet, she realized, she had no sense whatsoever of the passage of time.

It could have been moments since Dr. Herecic knocked her out. Or it could have been years.

Which was . . . troubling.

She glanced around, surveying the room in more detail. Nothing seemed out of place. Same table, desk, chairs, door.

Then she noticed the texturing of the walls.

They still had that slight sheen, glistening as though a little bit wet. She hadn't given it any thought before, but now she saw that they had been woven deliberately, micro-textured to produce that exact effect. Tiny pockmarks, the most minute of indentations, gave the wall enough structure to scatter light in that particular fashion. And it was definitely not random. There was a pattern to the pockmarking. The whole thing, she now saw, was repeated in precise, meter-square chunks.

She peered harder, engrossed. The closer she looked, the more she saw.

She felt a little flicker of pain in her left temple. She squeezed her eyes shut. As she did, she furrowed her brow—and felt something on her forehead. A thin strip of material. She traced its perimeter with her middle finger. It was rectangular, precisely twice as long as it was wide.

She poked a thumbnail under the edge. No more than half a millimeter thick, gently adhering to her skin. It would peel away easily enough.

So, she thought. *They've instrumented me.*

She took a deep breath, and then another.

The warning stab of pain faded. She relaxed and opened her eyes.

There was another of the thin strips on her chest.

Instrumented twice over, then, she thought. She wondered for a moment at the raw amount of data that was likely being collected. Heart rhythms, breathing patterns, EKGs, cortical activity, cerebral function. This much technology, all for her?

It should've been a religious ecstasy for a colonist from Aldan's World.

She stuck her fingernail under the edge of the strip on her chest. She doubted it would hurt, but if she took it off, it would certainly set alarms ringing wherever they were monitoring her.

She was about to do it anyway when the door opened. A woman she had never seen stepped into the room.

"Good morning," the woman said, offering her a pleasant smile.

"Morning," Kester said—though which morning it was, she had no idea.

"Do you know where you are?"

"In a biotechnology center on Paradise."

"Can you tell me your name?"

"Kester."

"Very good." The woman smiled. "I'm Ira. I'll be your nurse from now on. It's very nice to meet you."

"You aren't from here," Kester replied, the words spoken aloud before she was consciously aware of the thought.

Ira's smile disappeared, replaced by a moment of uncertainty. A fractional narrowing of eyebrows. Presumably subconscious, but still an obvious tell.

"That's true, but how did you know?"

Which was a stupid question. It was obvious. Her front teeth were imperfect. Just barely, but they were canted by a degree and a half, which implied some primitive dental surgery that had to be inconsistent with an upbringing on Paradise.

Kester opened her mouth to respond, thinking maybe this Ira person was a beta tester once, just like her. Then she closed it again, feeling that same little flicker of pain, a warning light flashing through her brain.

"Lucky guess," she said instead. "You seem nice; that's all."

Ira's smile returned. "Aren't you kind," she said. "Is there anything I can bring you?"

"Something to drink? Tea, maybe?"

"I'll see what I can do."

Ira took four and a half steps across the room, then paused briefly a meter in front of the door. Then she swung it open, stepped through, and closed it behind her with a click.

Hmm, Kester thought. *Interesting*.

The woman returned after a few minutes carrying a tray with a pot of water, a cup, and a little basket full of small, mesh pouches. "I didn't know what flavor you wanted," she said. "So, I brought you some choices."

"Thanks."

Kester poured the water into her cup, chose one of the pouches at random, and watched it dissolve.

Just like the sedative under her tongue.

"How long has it been?" she said.

"I'm sorry?"

"How long since they knocked me out?"

"Oh, I'm sure the doctor will be here soon to talk with you about all that."

There was a tiny cup of what looked like milk on the tray as well. Kester poured it into the tea, watching the whorls and eddies that formed, cold liquid in hot, swirling, impossibly complex. It was nothing like the texturing of the walls. This was a natural pattern formation, something different altogether.

The pain returned. She winced and began to massage her temple.

"I said, are you okay?"

She started. Had Ira been talking? She'd lost track of her. Had forgotten she was in the room.

"Yes," she said. "Yes of course. I'm fine. You can go now."

"Okay," Ira said. "I hope you like the tea."

Kester wrenched her gaze away from the cup, watched as her nurse crossed the room, and took the same brief pause as before.

The wall is reading her eyes, she realized. *That's how it works. Simple biometrics.* The way the nurse held her head, staring at the exact same spot on the door. Ira's feet barely stopped moving, but she stilled her upper body enough for what had to be a retinal scan. The whole thing had taken less than a second.

So, she thought. *I'm a prisoner, and that woman's eyeball is the key to the lock that holds me.*

She took a sip of the tea.

It was delicious.

Then a new thought occurred. The desk, and the stars.

She closed her eyes. Rubbed at her temple, the pain still lingering. Maybe she shouldn't do it. If she turned the stars back on, she might never stop looking at them.

She sat there, head in her hands, until the pain faded again.

The textures on the wall. The shape of Ira's teeth. The whorls and eddies in the tea. The pattern of her nurse's movements, standing before the door.

And the memory of stars.

She took a deep breath, contemplating.

"I don't think I was in the control group," she said at last.

CHAPTER 24

Per loved her, he was fond of saying, even before they met. To which Kester inevitably replied, *We were seed stock. You didn't have any choice.*

It doesn't change the fact, he would always reply. *Even if we were literally made for each other, it's still love.*

At which point she would burrow her head into his chest, close her eyes, and tell him to hush, content just to listen to him breathe.

Once upon a time, they had names, families, a place in the colony, and duties to perform. Theirs was a planned life in every sense of the word. An unshakable belief system and unbreakable social structure, the tenets of their faith woven into every aspect of their lives.

But they were happy.

Until the fungus came calling.

Putting the stars back on the ceiling was a mistake. Kester knew it would be, but in the end, she couldn't help but make her way back to the desk and find the controls to plunge the room into darkness. To restore the vision of the night sky.

Now she lay down on the floor and gazed upward, feeling the first warning flicker of pain as her mind went to work. Dividing the starscape into a grid, her eyes flicking from one cell to the next, twitching, snapshotting, her brain recording it all, then counting the stars in each. Some massive parallel operation seemed to be coming online inside her head, and the pain along with it. A murmur at first like a heart out of rhythm, then a stabbing lance through her left temple as her brain began to integrate at scale, assembling disparate computations into a single number.

She had her answer. There were two million, eight hundred forty-three thousand, two hundred, and seventy-five stars displayed on the ceiling above her.

She squeezed her eyes shut and sat upright, massaging her skull. Eventually, the ache subsided and she reached up to fiddle with the desk some more, changing the view, panning to some other part of the sky.

Then she repeated the exercise.

And again, and again.

It grew easier each time, though the pain never stopped. Eventually, the computation became trivial, and she was disappointed to find there were always less than three million stars at a time. Some system resolution limit, she supposed, or maybe the interface's designers assumed there was no point in rendering more. Who would know the difference?

She would.

There was no drug use on Aldan's World. Pharmaceuticals and chemical highs were things she had read about but never experienced. And the religious ecstasy her elders spoke of, the promised communion with their Machine God still to come—that had never been anything but fiction to her, a story told by someone who wanted her to believe. No, she knew nothing of drug addiction or religious adulation.

But maybe those feelings were something like this.

She just wished it didn't hurt so much. She'd been given a superpower and it burned like flame.

Counting was getting boring. She decided to find patterns in the stars instead. To see what she could draw, tracing constellations in her mind.

Minutes passed—or maybe hours, or even days. She didn't know. The stars were like pixel dust now, three million of them to work with, a palette with infinite combinations in her mind. She could close her eyes and call the entire field to memory, then delete them in layers, subtracting and subtracting again, until just the image that she wanted remained.

She painted tapestries of her past. The broken domes of her colony world. A ravaging kester, tearing apart some failed piece of synth-woven junk. The ship that had brought her there.

And then, inevitably, Per's face, rendered by a scattering of stars.

Sometime later, Dr. Herecic found her lying on her back in the center of the room.

She heard the door open, but the sound didn't register. Heard him say hello but didn't particularly care.

He must have issued some command to the room's environmental controls, because all at once, her stars disappeared, replaced by the plain ceiling, the room illuminated once more by bright full-spectrum light.

She rolled over on her side and peered at him through squinted eyes.

"Hello, Doctor," she said. "You don't look good. You have lines around your eyes. More lines, I mean, that didn't used to be there."

He said nothing, seeming content to study her for a moment. His gaze was calculating, though not unfriendly. His laboratory jacket was open at the waist, revealing rumpled clothes that looked slept in.

"Also, you've lost weight," she added.

He grunted at that. "Ira tells me you're doing well," he said.

"Ira is an optimist." She sat upright, feeling a wave of regret at losing the star field but also relief as the pain in her temple subsided. "Is there something I can help you with?"

He smiled at her, but as ever, there was no warmth behind it. "It may become appropriate for us to discuss a few things in the days ahead."

"Hmm." She thought about that. "How long was I out?"

"You've been lying on the floor for about six hours."

"That's not what I meant. How long was I unconscious after you knocked me out on that operating table?"

"Your memory loss is one of the things we need to talk about."

"How much time was I out?"

"What you need to understand is that it can be upsetting to learn . . ."

"Dr. Herecic," she said, interrupting. "Just tell me."

He sighed. "You were unconscious for a month."

She wasn't particularly surprised.

"Well, I'm definitely in the test group," she said.

"You know I really can't provide any details about the trials, Kester. As they are still ongoing."

"It's pretty obvious, though, don't you think?" Anger flashed through her at the silliness of the charade. "I mean, seriously, Doctor? You know? You knocked me out for a month, and I woke up with some pretty seriously strange new abilities vis-à-vis spatial reasoning and a headache that could kill a whole flock of kesters, and you can't even confirm that I'm part of the test group?"

"With all due respect, Kester, you are a volunteer beta tester, and we are profoundly grateful for your service . . ."

"Spare me."

"Whereas I am the trial administrator," he continued. "And while I cannot comment on specifics, please consider just how necessary it is for us to be careful with what information we do and do not divulge."

"Dr. Herecic." She got to her feet, regarded him evenly, and then gave him her sweetest smile, studying his face intently the whole time. "Do you seriously expect me to believe that you render your control group unconscious for a month, just to sort of, how would you say, normalize for that particular variable?"

"I really can't comment."

"Fine," she said. "You're not going to say anything. So, just tell me what it is you think you need to know."

"Honestly, Kester, I only wanted to check in on you. And tell you how gratified I am to see you doing so well."

She opened her mouth to respond, then reconsidered. *He's not lying*, she thought. Not exactly. He was glad she was in good health, if that's what this could be called.

Which maybe said something about how everyone else was doing.

"How's Per?" she asked.

"He's just fine, Kester."

"I want to see him."

"And you will."

"When?"

"In another week or two, if all goes well."

"Then you can go away, Doctor. As you can see, I am also just fine. Come back when you have something useful to tell me."

He shrugged again. She was getting seriously tired of that particular shrug.

"As you wish," he said, and left the room.

Leaving her alone with her stars.

Time passed. Eventually, her nurse returned.

The woman was carrying a tray. Cooked food that smelled of animal protein. Eggs, maybe. And a cup of something hot, to judge from the curling wisps of steam.

"Good morning, Kester."

"Is it? Morning, I mean?"

"I've brought you breakfast."

"Thank you." She thought a moment, trying to recall the woman's name. "Ira," she added, which sounded right.

Strange, how she could remember so much but struggle with something so simple.

"You're welcome," Ira said. "Dr. Herecic asked me to turn the lights back on for you, okay?"

She watched as Ira crossed the room, pausing by the desk to fiddle with the interface screen until the room returned to normal lighting again.

"It's just that the doctor thinks this particular view is a little . . ."

"Distracting?"

Ira smiled, looking relieved. "Exactly. Distracting. Do you think you'd like to eat now?"

Kester nodded, found her feet, made her way to the bed, and took a bite of food. She had no interest in a meal but forced it down anyway.

Better to appear cooperative.

"Is there anything else I can get you?" Ira was smiling now, perhaps pleased that her patient was eating.

"Actually, there is."

"Really?"

"I think I'd like to do some drawing."

"Of course! You can use your desk. You have all the access you need for basic recreation and activity programs."

"That's not what I meant," Kester said. "I want to do some real drawing. Something physical." She smiled and held up her rough, weathered hands. "I'm just a colonist, you know. I'm not used to all this technology. We used pen and paper. We made our own, in fact."

She watched as a range of expressions played across the nurse's face. Pen and paper? Who had heard of such a thing? But this was Paradise; anything was possible. Surely, they could weave some for her.

Mostly, though, she was staring at the nurse's eyes. They were blue-gray, with flecks and whorls of gold. The patterns were intricate and beautiful, and she committed them to memory, storing every detail, the familiar ache in her skull returning once more.

"I'll see what I can do," Ira said.

Kester managed a smile, wincing through the discomfort.

"Thanks."

Then she watched the nurse make her way from the room, making sure to note the exact spot where she paused for the door to examine her eyes.

It took Ira almost no time to return with a set of pens and a tablet of bright white, glossy paper.

"Will these work?"

Kester smiled. "Absolutely," she said.

She waited for Ira to leave, then got to work. When her drawing was finished, she knew it was perfect. She had rendered the nurse's retinal patterns in photorealistic detail, drawn directly from her own memory.

But the escape attempt that followed was complete foolishness.

In hindsight, her stupidity was obvious. She had no plan, none at all. What was she going to do? Run down the hallway until security found her, tackled her to the floor, and dragged her back there helpless and crying?

The real insult was it didn't matter anyway. The door wouldn't even open.

Which left her standing by the wall, feeling like an idiot, waving a drawing of Ira's eyeball at the wall where she knew the scanner had to be.

Nothing happened.

She crumpled up the paper, balled it in her fist, and went back to her bed and lay down.

A few minutes later, the door eased open.

Dr. Herecic was standing in the hallway outside.

Didn't take him long, she thought. Nor would it. Because of course everything she did was being watched and recorded. And now she'd given away too much. Showed them what she could do.

He stepped into the room, flanked by a pair of orderlies. Security. Maybe they were the same ones that had marched her through the jungle, or maybe not. She couldn't remember their faces clearly. That had been before. Before the trials, the surgery or drugs or whatever they'd done to her.

But she'd know them if she saw them again. That much was certain.

"Good morning, Kester," the doctor said calmly, as though nothing had happened. "I have a few more questions, if you don't mind."

She sighed. "Sure."

"Maybe you'd like to take a walk with me?"

"Okay," she said.

"Would you mind bringing your picture? I'd love to take a closer look."

Of course he would. She retrieved it from the floor, then trooped across the room and followed him out the door.

The security guards let her pass, then closed in behind her. Together they made their way down the corridor, to a waiting elevator beyond.

CHAPTER 25

Aside from its fungal species, Aldan's World had relatively few predators dangerous to humans. But there had been a notable exception, an animal Kester remembered well: a nocturnal biped, a gray-skinned, owl-eyed hunter a meter and a half tall they called phantasms. The creatures traveled in small groups, moving easily through the rocky, mountainous landscape where they lived. They were deceptive things, there one moment, gone the next. At first glance, they appeared harmless, but they possessed retractable, razor-sharp claws twenty centimeters long. When they were hungry, they were deadly, unsheathing those claws and killing without effort, afraid of nothing except fire.

When she was young, she and her friends used to play pretend, taking turns being the phantasm, chasing after each other, hiding, seeking, and seeing who could take the other unaware.

The security guards trailing just behind her brought those memories to mind. The guards drifted in and out of her blind spots, moving casually as if trying to appear harmless. But inside, she felt certain they were killers to the core.

They marched her down the hallway to the elevator, Dr. Herecic leading the way. They were whisked three levels up and then proceeded down another corridor, indistinguishable from the last. She tried to walk calmly, fighting the urge to look over her shoulder, not wanting to give them the satisfaction of knowing she was afraid.

Her plan had worked in a sense, she thought, insofar as she was now out of her room.

It wasn't much comfort.

They twisted and turned through corridor after corridor, but if her captors sought to confuse her with the serpentine route they were taking, they failed. Her augmented brain tracked the turns easily, counting steps and computing distances, building a map in her head. She could, she was certain, run back blindfolded the way they'd come without trouble.

Eventually, they came to an unmarked door, which swung open as they approached.

"My office," Dr. Herecic said and stepped inside. She didn't need to be told to follow. The security team ghosted into the room behind her, and the door clicked shut.

At first glance, the doctor's office appeared remarkably similar to her own room. Everything was functional, sparse, and utilitarian. There was even a bed. She wondered how much of his time the doctor spent in this place. All of it, maybe.

In which case, she thought, *who is really the prisoner here?* He was just as trapped as she was. Wishful thinking; she knew that wasn't true. Maybe metaphorically, but not in any literal sense.

Her eyes came to rest on the one thing that struck her as out of place in the room, a single adornment mounted on the desk: a two-hundred-and-fifty-centimeter-tall transparent cylinder with a bizarre animal hung suspended inside. Her instincts told her it must have come from the sea, but it was like nothing she had ever seen. It was a blue-green, blobby, shaped like a flattened sphere, fat in the middle. A mass of tendrils stretching from its center, radiating in all directions. These were tiny, filamentous, almost like hair, but interwoven with a much smaller number of much fatter tentacles, some of which ended in hooks.

She shivered. There was something unnerving about it.

"What is that?" she said.

Dr. Herecic glanced over at her. Amusement flashed in his eyes, making her feel like the butt of a joke she didn't understand.

"It's a planktonic predator," he said.

"A what?"

"A jellyfish of sorts. Not really, of course, but there is a tradition on this planet of naming things for Terran analogs. Technically *novacoelentrara Herecicii*."

"It's named after you?"

He smiled again, falsely modest, as though trying and failing to appear embarrassed. "Well, yes."

"Why?"

"I discovered it."

"It looks evil," she said.

"Do you think so? In fact, it's a remarkable creature." There was that look of amusement again. "I'll tell you about it some other time." He reached inside his jacket, found a pair of interface glasses, and put them on. "But first, we have some business to conduct. I'm going to be taking more-detailed notes today," he said. "I hope you don't mind."

He rested his hands on the desk and twitched his fingers minutely. Entering data through a virtual display, she thought. Like her nurse had done.

"Now," he said, "may I have a look at that drawing of yours?"

She uncrumpled it and passed it over without comment. There was no point denying what she had done, or why.

He studied it for a time, then handed it back. His fingers twitched again as he made another entry.

"That's quite a talent you have, Kester," he said. "To draw something like that from memory."

"A talent you gave me," she said, still watching his hands. She thought back to the interfaces on her own desk. One of its screens had included a keyboard, part of a knowledge system provided in case she had wanted to learn more about Paradise.

She hadn't used it much. But she did remember how the keys had been laid out.

"And what was your plan, exactly?" he said.

"To see if it would open the door." She kept her focus on his hands, feeling that familiar dull ache forming in her temple.

"May I ask why?"

"I wanted to know what was on the other side." The pain grew sharper. This time, she didn't hide from it; she welcomed it in.

"You should know, Kester, escape attempts disqualify your term of service. Your employment contract is very specific on this point."

"Who says it was an escape attempt?"

"It's a bit difficult to interpret otherwise, don't you think?"

"I just wanted to know if it would work. I like breaking things. I am a kester, after all."

Something clicked in her mind. She almost had it. She could just about see . . .

"Well, Kester," he said, "please understand I tell you this with your own best interest at heart. I want to see you complete your contract as much as you do."

She smiled sweetly. "Thanks." And there it was! The key, the solution.

Subject admits to escape attempt, the doctor wrote.

She could see! Not what was projected on his glasses, of course, but she knew what he was typing simply by watching the movements of his hands.

But remains cooperative.

Don't stare, she thought. *Don't give it away this time.*

"In the spirit of transparency, Kester," Dr. Herecic went on, "and so you aren't tempted to try such a thing again, you should know that all our biometric authentication is multifactor. Simply drawing your nurse's retina isn't going to get you out the door, no matter how good of a replica you create. You'd need to look like her, be shaped like her, walk like her, emit the same heat signature, pheromone trail, and so on."

She blushed at that, feeling foolish again. She looked away, forgetting herself momentarily and missing whatever he typed next.

"Still," he added, "it is a remarkable ability, and your overall health is excellent. So, today, I'd like to do a little bit of formal testing, if you don't mind. To see if we can get a better understanding of what you can really do."

"What kind of testing?"

"We're going to play a game," he said. But what he wrote was: *Induced hemorrhagic fever subsided. Subject cognitive and cooperative. Assessment begins.*

The screen before her was blank, a perfect white canvas. She was seated on one side of the desk, the doctor on the other. He'd placed his long-dead, entombed jellyfish on the floor where she couldn't see it, which was a relief.

He still wore his glasses, and his hands rested lightly on the surface of the desk, positioned over the virtual keyboard he assumed only he could see.

Still blissfully unaware of what she could do.

She sat on her own hands and looked back at him, wondering what he had in mind.

"Since you like to draw," he said, "I thought you would enjoy this."

Sixteen black lines appeared on the screen, drawn in the shape of six squares. One was in the middle, with a square attached to each of its sides, and another one hanging off the end, like a tail.

"Now," he went on, "let me ask you this. What shape would this drawing make, if you fold it along the dashed lines?"

"A cube," she said. "Obviously."

"Correct." The screen changed. The original set of lines disappeared, replaced by a slightly more complicated pattern. "How about this one?"

"A dodecahedron," she replied.

She watched his fingers move. *Subject still cooperative.*

"Good. Now let's try something a little more interesting. This one?"

"A book."

"And this?"

"An open book." *Like you*, she didn't add.

And so it went. A bird; a house; a tree; a building. The patterns of lines became more intricate, the foldings increasingly complex. Her headache returned and began to build, made worse by the strain of reading his fingers while keeping part of her focus on the patterns he was asking her to form. The game grew in complexity, now containing holes such that she was creating shapes out of patchwork quilts in her mind.

Subject in discomfort, her doctor typed.

With which she had to agree.

The game grew more complicated still, the symbology now including colors to denote elasticity, dotted and dashed lines the angles of folds allowed. Numbers specified prescribed fold orders or other dependencies. There were missing sections and sheets that nested inside each other.

Forests instead of individual trees; flocks in place of birds. And then birds in trees; entire landscapes; whole cities.

Her headache grew. As the game demanded more of her focus, she caught fewer of the doctor's personal notes. But she was able to read when he wrote:

Subject in pain. Demonstrating nontrivial residual effects of induced hemorrhagic fever.

Residual effects of induced hemorrhagic fever? And what had he written next? She squeezed her eyes shut, trying to recall his last finger twitches and the keystrokes they implied.

She was losing control. The pain was too much, and her focus was slipping away.

When she opened her eyes, he was gazing back at her. "Can we take a break?" she asked.

"Of course," he said. "You're doing very well, Kester."

He sounded like he meant it.

Perhaps he did.

She leaned back and pretended to close her eyes, watching through narrow slits as he completed his entry.

Sole surviving subject of novacoelentrara *trial demonstrates initial spatial-reasoning response beyond expectations.*

Sole survivor? The implications of that were staggering, so much so that she almost missed what came after. *Novacoelentrara*? Wasn't that the name he'd given to the jellyfish on his desk?

She had no time to contemplate what that might mean; he was typing again.

Premature to speculate on application development at this time, but even cautious interpretation indicates potential utility in the fields of both protein folding and interstellar-navigation route-finding. Extraordinary mortality rates experienced thus far are to be discounted appropriately.

It occurred to her, then, to wonder that he could know so much about her and not guess at this most minor of abilities: to read what he wrote by watching his fingers. Maybe it was simple arrogance, some invisible mental barrier separating the two of them in his mind. As though what she could do couldn't possibly apply to him.

There was weakness there, though she had no idea how to exploit it.

But as she sat, wincing, reading his last entry along with him as he typed, she knew she was going to have to find a way.

Because the final thing he wrote was:

Recommend immediate matriculation of remaining control-group members to testing status. Any nonzero survival rate will justify the effort.

For Per's sake, she had to try.

CHAPTER 26

Nya waited a few days before finally reporting her drop-ship sighting to University Security. In the end, Johanna-the-Pilot convinced her. *If you don't,* Johanna argued, *and they find out you knew? You can forget about field time for at least a year.*

It was a fair point.

But strangely, the security representative took the news impassively. They merely thanked her and sent her on her way. Maybe they'd known about the drop-ship already. Or maybe no one cared enough about Nya or her work to bother telling her to stay out of that part of the jungle.

Either way, a week later, she'd forgotten all about it. She had bigger things to worry about. Today was the first night of the new semester, and there was a reason the department kept her around despite her ongoing failure to help bring new drugs to market and the paucity of her publication record. She had been able to overcome those twin academic sins with one unassailable virtue: she was happy to take more than her share of the lecturing duties.

Tonight was the first session of Xeno-Evolutionary Trends III, her favorite class.

The course was a bit esoteric, part of why she liked it. It was also an elective, which was why her department scheduled it in the evening.

Most importantly, it was her opportunity to talk about her own research on inherited intelligence. As controversial a topic as there was, and another of the reasons she had trouble finding professional allies. Bad enough she hadn't contributed to drug discovery in any meaningful way.

Even worse to have a reputation for quackery.

She'd better get inside. She wasn't late, but, as was her custom, she wasn't particularly early, either.

Some quirk of the University's scheduling algorithms had assigned her the largest auditorium on campus, a room that could comfortably seat two hundred. Fifteen students had signed up for her class. They were scattered throughout the lecture hall in little clumps of twos and threes, with a couple of loners right down in the front row.

The heels of her boots clunked satisfyingly as she mounted the three steps to the stage. Someone had left a bottle of water behind the lectern. She opened it, took a drink, and then made a point of surveying the room grimly, shaking her head as if displeased by what she saw.

Then she smiled, and said, "Well this is all a little much, don't you think? Please come closer. I don't feel like shouting this evening."

She took another sip. Typically, no one moved.

She shrugged. "Suit yourselves," she said.

Ordinarily, the first day of a term was time for introductions and overviews, but her style had always been to plunge right into the deep end. She cleared her throat and felt the little twinge of unavoidable nervous energy in her belly. She'd been doing this for ten years and still got butterflies.

"Let's begin with a thought experiment," she said. "Imagine you are a biologist on pre-spaceflight Earth, say mid-twentieth century—right at the start of anthropogenic mass extinction. Darwin's *Origin of Species* is a century old; Watson and Crick have just made their great discovery, but DNA sequencing is decades away. No one has even heard of the protein-folding problem yet, and traveling to the stars remains the stuff of science fiction. There could be life on Mars, for all anyone knows."

This earned her a brief chuckle from one of the students down front. She smiled warmly at them, then went on.

"You are investigating evolutionary patterns in nature," she said, "and given a generous budget for pure research. You have years ahead of you, without any drug-development responsibilities, not a single product you must bring to market."

She paused and looked around again, feeling slightly irresponsible, like her hypothetical was bordering on sedition. She really should try to set a good example. Right?

"So," she continued, "if the answer is neither money nor time, what is the primary constraint on the types of questions you can ask?"

It was day one of the term. Even in a month, the question wouldn't have much chance of prompting a response, but she paused again and looked around, hopefully communicating that she wasn't one of those professors all of whose questions were rhetorical.

Her students gazed back at her, but no one made a move to respond.

"Okay, then," she said. "Let me ask all of you this. What is the basis of the scientific method?"

She got a taker on that one. A young man, sitting down front. She'd read all her students' bios before walking into the room and knew him for a native Paradisian. He was a rich corporate child, but his grades had been excellent so far.

"Hypothesis testing?" he said.

"Exactly." She gave with a smile; he looked away, embarrassed. "Specifically, the formation of a null hypothesis and the systematic gathering of evidence, which either refutes or fails to refute that null hypothesis." Which sounded technical but wasn't. If they didn't know that much, they'd be gone after the first exam anyway.

She took another sip of her water.

"Now let me ask you this," she said. "On mid-twentieth century Earth, what options for gathering evidence would we have? What can we readily observe about evolutionary trends?"

No response.

"The answer," she continued, "is that we can do what scientists have always done. We can make direct observations of nature, perform experiments, and explore properties of theoretical models."

"Did they even have computers back then?" a student asked from the back of the auditorium.

Nya laughed. "In fact, they did," she said. "Then as now, primitive as their machines were, computing power wasn't the limiting factor. Instead, each of these approaches to evolutionary biology was and remains limited by lack of data, and no massive parallel processing can help if there are no observations with which to work.

"At the same time, experimental manipulations are problematic when studying processes that play out over time scales longer than financial planning cycles." *Bordering on sedition again*, she thought; *best rein it in*. "And theoretical models all too often tell us more about ourselves than the system we seek to emulate, be it numerically or with closed formulae."

And now the punch line. She looked at each of her fifteen students in turn, wondering how many of them would get it.

"But think for a moment about the problem with direct observations," she said. "Everyone in this room should know enough about statistics to understand that sampling power increases with the number of observations that are made. Setting aside the specific functional forms this relationship between hypothesis testing power and observational effort takes for a moment"—visible relief in the room here—"the real problem is that we, the twentieth-century evolutionary biologist, can only make a single observation concerning the most critical question of all.

"Is there life anywhere else other than Earth?

"This sounds like a trivial question today. We have the luxury of centuries of interstellar exploration and direct observations of planet after planet, so from a certain point of view, the answer is obvious. If we are talking about Life itself with a capital *L*, then the answer is yes. The range of conditions under which life occurs, as we define it with respect to self-organization and self-replication, is very broad.

"We also know that the probability of occurrence of life when environmental conditions are within that range is, for all practical purposes, one hundred percent. If a modern, thirty-second-century evolutionary biologist were to phrase a null hypothesis, it would be of the form *Life occurs whenever physical environmental factors fall within the following parameters,* and the disproval of that hypothesis by finding a counterexample would be noteworthy.

"Show me a planet of approximately Earth's size, at least half a billion years old, in a stable orbit around a middle-aged star, and if it is devoid of life, something bad probably happened along the way.

"Do you see how different this perspective is from the fashion in which such questions were phrased originally? For most of human history, the null hypothesis was stated like this: *We are alone in the universe.* And when that hypothesis was finally disproved, the implications extended beyond the scientific, into matters of deep philosophy and religion.

"Yet for all of that, for all our corner of the galaxy is practically teeming with life, in highly recognizable, biochemically compatible, and therefore useful forms, what we have not, of course, found is another surviving sentient species.

"So, in a stricter but more meaningful sense," she concluded, "we are alone."

Two hours later, the lecture was over. The students filed out without comment. Nya watched them go, unsure whether she'd succeeded in piquing their interest. Hopefully, she'd done more than just give them a set of facts to be memorized for the next exam.

Time would tell.

She returned to her office and called up her *Salmo* article, looking askance at the words rendered above her desk. *Drivel*, she thought. *As usual.*

Abruptly, her text disappeared from the air.

Her immediate thought was that she had made some careless gesture that the desk's interface had misinterpreted. She had always possessed an uneasy relationship with technology. It came from a life spent in the field instead of the lab, wielding fishing poles and nets rather than advanced protein-folding algorithms and virtual sequencers.

Or maybe someone was reading along as she had been writing. She looked around her tiny office uneasily. Had her department chair been watching remotely as she dictated the words and was now sending her a message? Deleting her first draft from afar, saving her the embarrassment of further flights of fancy?

This of course was simple paranoia on her part. The man couldn't possibly be bothered.

Then a message appeared, floating in midair where her draft paper had been.

Dr. Nya Solarin. Paradise University Department of Evolutionary Biology.

"That's me," she said.

More words rendered.

You have an incoming transmission. Level Three Biometric Authentication is required. Please report to University Security immediately.

"Um—sure. Okay." Level three biometrics? Who would send her a message that required a DNA signature to read?

The message disappeared, replaced again by her article. She waved it away, then left her office and exited the building, her mind racing the whole time.

The drop-ship. It had to be. Why else would Security want to talk to her?

But if so, why would they need to authenticate her at the level of her DNA, just to ask her again what she'd seen? She'd already told them everything. It wasn't much to begin with.

She made her way out of the Biology Hall. Both of Paradise's suns had set, the light fading fast but the evening still warm. A few small flocks of students were gathering, getting an early start on the weekend's festivities.

The local insect fauna creaked and groaned at her as she hurried across the campus grounds. The sound usually brought a smile to her face but not now. She threaded through the university's ornate structures until she came to a small, unmarked building. It was flat gray and windowless, with a military appearance, like someone had dropped a barracks into this center of higher learning and advanced drug research.

A security guard wearing a beige, synth-woven body suit met her at the door. They seemed to be expecting her, giving her the slightest nod, though whether they were approving of her punctuality or scanning her biometrics in some subtle way Nya didn't care to guess.

The guard took her inside and showed her to a tiny room, with a single chair, a simple visual display, and a palm-sized message tablet.

They nodded once and shut the door, leaving her alone.

She placed her hand on the device.

It pricked her palm.

She had the pain tolerance that came of a life rolling ankles and taking falls, of enduring shoulder straps biting into her for miles on end and ignoring legs protesting too much abuse. Still, she jumped, mostly from the sheer intrusiveness of the act.

She wondered for a moment how much security a procedure like this really provided and how much it was just for show. The university making an unsubtle statement: *We are serious about this, so Pay Attention.*

If so, it worked. She was definitely paying attention.

But she still wasn't prepared for what she read next when the tablet's screen came to life.

—

Dr. Nya Solarin.

Due to your subject-matter expertise and research focus, TransGalactic requests and requires your presence immediately aboard the deep-space vessel Carpathia, *currently in near space, inbound your position.*

A rapid-class interplanetary transport will depart Paradise in three days' time. Berths have been reserved for you and a professional assistant of your choosing, should you deem one necessary.

Deployment length is unknown at this time. Further details will be provided after you rendezvous with Carpathia.

—

And that was all.

Nya sat still, gobsmacked. She read the words a second time.

It had to be a joke. Someone in her department was playing an elaborate trick on her. But that was impossible, wasn't it? Security would never go along with such a ruse, and no one she knew would bother.

She read the message a third time. "Requests and requires"? That was formal language, generally used by the military. She'd never been given such an order before.

Assume it was legitimate, she thought. What did it mean? Was she really being ordered to leave the only home she'd ever known, pack herself onto a rapid-class transport, board a military vessel, and head off into deep space?

Because of her subject-matter expertise?

Who at TransGalactic would issue such an order? And what could they possibly think she knew?

As for a professional assistant, clearly, whoever was asking for her didn't know much about her career there on Paradise, if they thought she had one.

It was just her and Johanna.

Johanna.

Nya put the tablet down and left the room, thoughts racing through her head. It was all she could do not to run from the building. When she was back outside in the relative calm of the Paradisian evening, she stopped, trying just to breathe for a moment, unsure what to do next.

What would happen if she refused? They'd fire her, she supposed. From the university and probably from TransGalactic entirely.

She didn't relish the prospect of trying to find a different job. Walking into a Magellanix corner of the planet's capital city, résumé in hand, asking for work.

Three days. It was impossible. Too much to be believed.

"The hell with this," she muttered aloud. She didn't know what to make of any of it, but the next step was clear.

If she had three days left on Paradise, damned sure she was going to call Johanna.

Maybe she'd want to go fishing.

CHAPTER 27

For Kester, the tests were done for the day. No more flocks of virtual swans to fold; no more reading what Dr. Herecic had to say through his fingertips as he took his notes, not knowing she was following along.

But sleep would not come. She lay on her bed, playing the words the doctor had written over and over in her mind.

Any nonzero survival rate will justify the effort.

It was the realization of the worst of her fears. There was only one conclusion possible.

Her captors were monsters. They didn't care if she lived or died.

No, that wasn't it. Not quite. They cared because her exceptional abilities had value. But they were willing to sacrifice as many of their beta testers as necessary as long as they succeeded in making another.

Another what, exactly? Why were they even doing this?

Protein folding and interstellar-route finding, the doctor had written. Applications for a new technology.

Her. Befitting for a child of Aldan's World, but she wanted no part of it.

And what about Per?

Was he dead already?

She wanted to believe otherwise. She hoped they had kept him in a control group, for leverage over her if nothing else. Split the pairs. Divide the couples, holding half in reserve, just in case whatever they were doing actually worked.

But even if that were true, for how much longer? Did the mere fact of her newfound abilities sentence Per to the same fate?

She had to get out of this place. That much was obvious. She had to escape.

And find some way to bring Per with her.

But how?

It was maddening. She had been given cognitive abilities beyond all sense and reason, but couldn't defeat a locked door. Multifactor bio-authentication systems she could not fool, walls she could not break down, and the omnipresent, soft-footed, dead-eyed security personnel whose capabilities she couldn't begin to guess.

She was powerless despite her powers. The sport creation of a monster, destined for a purpose she didn't understand, and if she didn't think of something soon, they'd do it to Per as well.

It was too much to take. She squeezed her eyes shut and rubbed her temples, massaging them over and over again until the ache finally subsided. Then she curled up, tucked her knees into her chest, and, for the first time she could remember, simply cried herself to sleep.

She woke badly disoriented, thinking she was back on Aldan's World but unable to remember Per's name.

Then everything came flooding back. Where she was, what had happened. But this time, instead of feeling overwhelmed, the reality of her situation left her shaking with rage.

How dare they! Who gave them the right?

And more importantly, what could she do about it?

She still had no idea. The desk chronometer told her it was still the middle of the night. She had hours to kill; Dr. Herecic wouldn't send for her until morning, and she had no illusions that sleep would return.

So, she decided to learn a new way to read.

She slid from her bed, padded softly to her desk, and called the room's interface to life. Security would be watching her, of course. Let them; she couldn't hide what she could do forever.

She decided to practice by learning about Paradise. A small act of defiance: she would know all she could about what lived in the world beyond her walls, even if her captors had no intention of releasing her.

It was easy enough to find an index of all the available content on Paradise's ecosphere. There was no reason why a beta tester shouldn't be given access to something as bland as the planet's flora and fauna.

Soon enough, she had unearthed a treasure trove of information, detailed records of the survey work that had been carried out by humans over their three centuries there. There were essays, morphological descriptions, taxonomical classifications, experimental results, and nuanced discussions of biomes, ecosystems, and the myriad of creatures that called this planet home. All of it was sorted, indexed, and tagged—and easily paged through.

Perfect.

She closed her eyes and took a few deep breaths, focusing her mind, free of visual stimulus, only the blank canvas of the back of her own eyelids to see.

And tried to relax.

When she opened her eyes again, she felt calm and ready.

Slowly, she began to scan the pages.

But not one word at a time. No, she let it all in at once.

It felt awkward at first, but then she started to get the knack and was able to go faster, and faster still. The trick was not to conceptualize, not to seek to comprehend. That would come later. For now, she was just snapshotting, committing the content to memory. As she paged through the material, she could feel the information going into her head, knew it was there on some base level, even if she had no idea what she was learning.

Her headache returned, which she took as a good sign. She sped up, scanning faster and faster until she was swallowing the content stream whole. Opening herself up, letting it all in—data, images, text, more and more, until all sense of the passage of time vanished. It was just her and the stream now. She was a datavore, the perfect predator, and all this dazzling array of content was her food.

It was dizzying. It was intoxicating and terrifying in equal measures, letting so much in with no filters and no control.

The Prophet would've approved, she would later think. Maybe this was what it felt like to be the Machine God Itself.

Abruptly, she reached the end. She didn't know how much time had passed, but apparently, she had read everything there was to know about Paradisian ecology. Or, at least, everything this interface could tell her.

She slumped back in her chair, head in her hands, and wept, for there were no more records to consume. She took a few breaths, trying to reground herself. Stabbing pain lanced through her temples, but she paid no attention. She was growing accustomed to such things.

When she felt ready for it, she set about the process of integration.

It was confusing at first, her brain sorting and cross-referencing, trying to make sense of it all. But then she settled into the process and let the information come to her, allowing all those new facts to make themselves known.

Gradually a picture emerged, a sketch of this planet she had been promised she might someday call home.

She learned that Paradise was enormously biodiverse, and its biology highly compatible with Terran life. The same basic protein structures had evolved in both places, so much of what grew there was available to human digestion with little or no modification, though many of the native forms were wildly toxic. Some strange convergence at a molecular level, rare among surveyed worlds. Which, along with its proximity to Earth, was why it had been chosen early on, the oldest of humanity's colonies.

She wondered what her Singlist orthodoxy would have taught about a place like this. What might the Prophet have said? That the planet was a gift of some kind? If so, it was an old one: life on Paradise pre-dated that on Earth.

If some Machine God had left the place for humans to discover, It had certainly planned ahead.

Which in turn would have meant the Machine God Itself was older than humanity. There were those who believed such things, but the idea would have been considered blasphemy by the Singlists of Aldan's World.

Whatever, she thought. None of it seemed particularly relevant at the moment. The Prophet was dead by his own folly, and the closest thing to a god on this world was Kester herself.

She shook her head at the foolishness of the idea. *Figure out how to get past a closed door first*, she thought. *Then promote yourself to divinity*.

Then there was this: Paradise, for all its bounty and beauty, was a dangerous place. Predators and parasites abounded, with forms and adaptive strategies with no analogs on Earth. Colonists had died in the early days, despite their technology and caution.

Even the forests outside the front door of this biotech laboratory could kill. Evidently, the trees that flourished there dropped branches that never reached the ground. Some trick of the way they grew and competed for light, dying underneath as they pushed ever upward, causing debris to build up in the canopy until it reached a critical state. Then the slightest gust of wind or vibration could send it crashing down in a wooden avalanche, catching anyone unlucky enough to be standing below without warning.

A random death from above.

The shadow of an idea occurred. She slowed her recall, then stopped it altogether and went back, scanning the entry again in her mind.

There had been a Terran analog for the phenomenon, from a continent called Australia. The locals had referred to the falling branches as "drop bears." The experience of standing beneath one was like some large predatory mammal falling from above, except instead of a hungry carnivore, it was a metric ton of lumber that would come crashing down without notice.

She thought it through again. Woody debris accumulating to a critical point, where the slightest random disturbance could send it to the forest floor.

Random meant *unpredictable.*

But maybe not for her.

She flicked through photos and images in her mind, and read the text describing the phenomenon for a third time. She imagined all those branches hanging up there like a deadfall, a trap for the unaware.

It didn't have to happen by chance, she thought. It could be completely predictable if you were good enough at spatial reasoning, could see the patterns in those branches, and figure out which ones were ready to fall.

She had only one piece of leverage that she could see: her own cooperation.

The question was how best to use it. She debated with herself even as she waited for the inevitable knock on her door, the beginning of another day of Dr. Herecic's testing.

In the end, she decided to keep it simple. She would simply state her demands.

At eight o'clock, her nurse called on her, flanked by the usual pair of security guards. Kester let herself be led from the room without a word, following meekly as they took her through the maze of corridors to Dr. Herecic's office.

Her doctor was at his desk, the Paradisian jellyfish entombed in its Lucite sea next to him. She looked closer, studying its hooks and tentacles, and shuddered.

The thing was truly horrible. On a whim, she closed her eyes and flicked through her newfound knowledge of Paradisian pelagic ecology, wondering what she might know about the monster.

Nothing.

Curious.

For all she had read, why was there no record of Dr. Herecic's evil jellyfish?

There was no time to dwell on it. The man was speaking.

"I said, 'Good morning, Kester.'" He gave her what she had come to think of as his encouraging smile. "As you see, I have something a little more challenging for you today."

She pulled her gaze from the jellyfish and took a look at the interface screen she'd come to know so well. The puzzle did look interesting, a pattern of shifting folds and cuts that changed at a rapid rate, constantly evolving. The goal was to find the precise moment where it could be turned into something recognizable. This was dynamic, hyperdimensional origami, and it looked more difficult than anything she had yet attempted.

But it wasn't interesting enough to distract her from what she had to do.

She pushed the screen away and looked him in the eye.

"No," she said.

He arched an eyebrow at her.

"No?" He repeated the word blandly, as though he hadn't quite understood, simultaneously making the briefest of notes.

Subject uncooperative?

"I want to go for a walk," she said. "Outside."

"Now, Kester . . ."

"With Per," she added.

"Kester, we've already talked about this. It's just not possible at this time for you to see him. The trials are still ongoing."

But what he typed was *Subject reaching critical point.*

"If he's dead already," she said, "then at least you could tell me."

"He's not dead, Kester."

"So, is he in a control group?"

He looked at her as though considering. "You know I can't comment," he said.

She took a breath, thinking, *Now or never.* "Doctor," she said. "Listen to me carefully. I will be a willing participant in your games, even if I don't understand them. I will take every test you want. I will help you leverage my newfound abilities however you desire.

"But first," she went on, "I want to see my fiancé. I want a few hours outside this building. I want to breathe real air. To walk among living things and feel the sun on my face. I am a feral creature, Doctor. A child of a broken colony world. You can't keep me inside in isolation, not like this. I'll help you any way I can, but only if you do this much for me."

She fell silent. It was the most she had spoken since the day they had admitted her to this place. She studied his face again, wondering whether he would agree.

Then she saw what he wrote, and had her answer—and more.

Decision to hold pair partners in reserve justified. Employment of reunion as reward structure commencing.

"Okay, Kester," he said. "I'll see what I can do."

CHAPTER 28

The following morning, security arrived as usual to escort Kester from her room. This time, her nurse was absent, and they ushered her in the opposite direction, away from Dr. Herecic's office. They led her to a small elevator, down to ground level, and then along a long, narrow corridor that ended abruptly at a heavy security door. No grand foyer there, no formal waiting rooms to impress visitors, just an armored hatch that swung open to reveal the jungles of Paradise.

And just like that, she was outside.

A wave of heat and humidity struck her like a physical thing. It was overwhelming. The sun on her face; the sounds of nature all around, alien to her but unmistakably the real living flora and fauna of a natural world, not the artificial environment that was all she had known for what seemed like years.

She breathed deep through her nose, taking it in. The faint smell of peat came to her, along with other, more exotic fragrances. The jungle there was in bloom, vivid scarlet and bright orange flowers blossoming on vines running up the trunks of the nearby trees.

In the distance, she heard a soft hooting call.

She realized with a start she could name everything she saw. The smells and sounds were alien, but every species she saw was known to her, enmeshed in memory from her hyper-reading binge.

Only one of her two guards followed her outside, a male she didn't think she'd seen before. This struck her as strange; she always had a pair with her whenever she had been let out of her room.

Some subtle show of force, maybe? As though making the point that escape was impossible?

Or maybe, she thought, the primary purpose of those security teams was to protect Dr. Herecic from her.

She wondered briefly what other sort of experiments had been run in this place. Decided she hoped she would never know.

"Hello, Kester."

She jumped, turned, and spun. Per was standing in the doorway behind her, half-hidden in the shadow of the narrow corridor behind.

He took a cautious step toward her, then another. He looked healthy. If anything, he had gained a little weight, and his rich brown hair had grown out and looked glossier than she remembered. She scrutinized his face, noticing details she had never seen before. Lines around the edges of his dark eyes. A slight asymmetry to his beak-like nose.

She narrowed her gaze, focusing, snapshotting. All her memories of him were from before the trials.

"Kester?"

She jumped, startled a second time. How long had she been staring at him?

"Sorry," she said. "I'm here, Per. It's me."

He crossed the remaining distance, stopping when she put her hands on his chest. She closed her eyes, shutting off the overwhelming flow of visual information, and breathed.

He felt different. Her spatial memory was wired to her fingertips as well.

She drew back. "Say something," she said, eyes still squeezed shut. "Talk to me. It doesn't work on auditory channels."

"What doesn't work?"

"What they did to me. It doesn't matter. Just talk. And hold me, but don't touch my hands."

Oh, absent gods, how she loved him. Without judgment or question, he simply did what she asked, took her in his arms, and held her tight. She knew how she must look to him: desperately unhealthy, stressed, sleep-deprived, her skin loose from too little exercise and atrophying muscles. But what did such things matter? He loved her. He always had and always would.

"How's this?" he said.

"Perfect."

And why wouldn't it be? They were made for each other. In another life, so carefully planned out, so long past.

"I heard you wanted to take me for a walk," he said.

"It's true." He felt so good, she had to choke the words out; it was all she could do not to break down completely. To remember what she had come for, the purpose behind her plan. "We're going to have a chaperone, though."

"I don't mind."

She pushed back and gazed into his eyes, trying not to look at retinal patterns and ocular fingerprints but the person beneath, the young man she knew so well.

"Let's go," she said at last. "There's something I want to see."

"What's that?"

"A drop bear."

"Sounds ominous," he said. "But hey—I'm glad for any excuse to see you."

"Me too," she said. She linked her arm in his and led him across the clearing, to the jungle waiting on the far side. "Just walk with me, okay?"

"Sure, Kester."

Together they stepped into the jungle, their security guard following quietly behind.

They walked for an hour, arm in arm where the trail was wide enough to allow it, Kester leading the way when the path narrowed.

She studied the trees as they went. The species assemblage seemed right. In places, dead branches had accumulated in the canopy above, just as she had hoped.

But she couldn't quite find what she was looking for.

A memory came to her, something she had read once when studying an old Earth mathematician. Singlists being big on math and physics, she had benefited from the beginnings of a classical education on Aldan's World.

Give me a lever long enough, an ancient philosopher had said, *and I can move the world.*

Archimedes was wrong, she thought. The truth was that the world had to be ready to be moved, and then the shortest of levers would do.

But the canopy above wasn't ready to fall.

They walked on.

Per had drifted into silence, maybe content to enjoy the jungle, maybe unsure what to say. She wished there was some way to tell him what was coming, but there was no knowing what the security guard could hear, how augmented he might be.

She would simply have to trust Per to follow her lead when the time was right.

The relative cool of midmorning gave way to noontime heat. The jungle grew oppressive and still, quiet now as the local fauna took a break from their foraging and hunting, hunkering down to wait for the cool of evening.

From time to time, she glanced backward at their chaperone. Sometimes she could see the guard, sometimes not. When she could, his face betrayed nothing. He seemed eternally impassive—and why not? He was only doing his job.

She wondered how long she had before she and Per would be ordered to return.

Kilometers passed slowly beneath their feet. The trail was rougher there, the going slow, and Kester was beginning to lose hope. Theory was fine, but in practice, she didn't know how often the branches fell, or how long she would have to look to find the critical loading pattern of woody debris she sought. The more she thought about it, the more her plan made no sense at all. Even if she could rid them of their guard, they were almost a thousand kilometers from civilization. There was no help coming. With her newfound knowledge of Paradise, she knew what to eat and what to avoid. There were advantages to being feral. She and Per had survived a long time together, in a place worse than this.

But InterTech would come looking. She had no illusions about that.

And they'd do it with technology and equipment she couldn't fathom.

How had she ever thought they could hide out there? Did she imagine the jungle itself would protect them somehow?

In truth, she hadn't thought carefully at all. She had simply wanted to get away.

It wasn't too late. They could go back and take their chances in the lab. This had been an act of folly, madness from the outset. It was better that the jungle hadn't cooperated.

She should return and play the doctor's game to its conclusion.

Except that it would probably cost Per his life.

So she walked on.

And then, without warning, there it was: the heaviest mass of dead branches suspended above her she had yet seen, positioned perfectly.

Now or never, she thought.

"I'm tired," she announced. She stopped where she was and studied the canopy above, her brain snapping to life, processing and snapshotting and computing. She felt the first flicker of pain in her temple and welcomed it in.

There. She would lean against that trunk, put her weight into it just so. The vibrations would trigger the pile of branches above, hanging in perfected self-organized criticality, ready to come down at the slightest disturbance.

The security guard was flanking them at a prescribed distance, just close enough. If he was thinking about the jungle at all, it had to be about the predators that lived there.

She took Per by the hand and led him six precise steps off the path they had been following.

"Let's take a rest here."

Per shrugged. The security guard moved closer and took up a position on the trail. He couldn't have chosen a more perfect spot.

Now or never, she thought again. Then she hooked her foot over a root and faked a stumble into the trunk, impacting it precisely as she meant to.

And the sky fell, just as she had known that it must.

Kester hadn't expected it to be so loud. The video clips she'd scanned had been muted since she had consumed everything at such high speed. She heard an enormous *crack* like thunder, her brain not quite processing that of course the branches would make noise as they splintered and crashed and fell. Then a torrent of hard wooden rain was falling, exactly where she had predicted.

She grabbed Per by the arm and shouted "C'mon!" Together they were up and moving, dodging through a gap between two trees. Spike-covered tree bark tore at her skin and she stumbled, but Per caught her, kept her upright, and then they were running for their lives, she dodging this way and that, Per following, taking her lead in a moment of what otherwise would have been pure panic.

She risked a look back. The guard was faster than she would ever have believed. But for all his speed and reflexes, he was at a single, profound disadvantage. Kester had known what was coming and exactly which way to jump. The security guard had not.

She saw him struck on the head by a falling branch. He stumbled to his knees, but then he was up again. He didn't bother to yell at them to stop. Instead, he produced a weapon: a small, snub-nosed thing, black and evil.

Time froze.

Her brain skipped to its highest speed. She watched the future play out, knowing how it would end.

The guard, taking aim.

The branches above them, collapsing in a secondary cascade.

The barrel of the gun.

Per, directly behind her.

A single instant to make a single decision.

She dove out of the way.

The guard fired. Three darts whizzed past her ear. Had she stayed put, they would have caught her center mass.

Instead, they kept going and buried themselves in Per's throat.

As Kester had known they must. It was a dance, whose choreography was known to her in advance.

She had saved herself.

And sacrificed Per to do it.

The guard was preparing to fire again, but before he could, he was impaled by a tumbling branch that whipped a meter-long spike of dead wood deep into his neck.

Kester got back to her feet.

Impossibly, the guard was still alive, clutching his wounded neck with one hand where the branch was driven into him like a spike.

She spun around. Per had crumpled to his knees, his own hands at his throat, eyes open in disbelief.

"Go!" he said. The word came out as a weak gasp. Then his eyes rolled up and he collapsed backward awkwardly, twisted where he had fallen. His chest rose and fell, minutely.

Kester glanced up. The deadfall was finished. The canopy had discharged its load; the forest was safe again.

Then she looked back for the last time. The guard was still pressing his hands to his neck, trying to stop the flow of blood. He was also muttering something.

Without even meaning to, Kester read his lips.

"Elopement, eight kilometers from base," the guard said. "Abilities compromised. Send secondary support. Repeat, elopement attempt eight kilometers from base."

Per wasn't dead. But it would be impossible to bring him with her.

The guard was moving again. Somehow, he had found his feet and was angling toward her in a lurching stagger, still advancing despite the spike of wood driven into him, an injury that would have killed Kester in an instant.

She was out of time. There was nothing more she could do. She had to make a decision.

One chance to run, and they'll catch you anyway. Or go back and you'll never set foot outside their walls again.

Choose, she thought. *Now*.

In an instant, her mind was made up. She ducked behind a tree, picked a path through the forest, and took off at a sprint.

Hoping that, somehow, Per would understand.

CHAPTER 29

Nya lived in single-faculty housing, a studio apartment whose biometric monitoring saw her coming, unlocked the door, and swung it open, momentarily creating the illusion that someone was waiting for her inside. But not tonight. Johanna had gotten her message and said she would meet her in the morning.

It was just as well; Nya needed to pack.

The hundred and fifty square meters of her living space were crammed floor to ceiling with field gear. The modest furniture she owned had long since been overrun by an avalanche of backpacks, tents, and stoves; fluorometers and calorimeters and pDNA sequencers; and an assemblage of gill nets, circular throw nets, autonomous robotic traps, even barbless hooks rigged with monofilament to old-fashioned poles.

She stepped inside, shaking her head sadly at the mess. She had always intended to do something about it. Now she only had three days left on Paradise. A tidy apartment was one more thing that would be left undone.

She packed, cleaning halfheartedly as she went. She wondered what the University would do with this place when she was gone. Send a team to rummage through her belongings, and put anything left behind into storage for a decade or two?

Or maybe they'd just recycle everything, and there'd be no memory of her at all.

It took an hour to assemble a worthy field kit, with enough clothing and food for two nights. When she was finished, she hefted her bag experimentally. Not too heavy; probably eighteen kilos. It would do.

Then she carved out a space on her bed large enough to lie down and fell into an exhausted sleep.

At four o'clock in the morning, there was a knock on her door. Nya groaned, got to her feet, and slouched across the floor in the crumpled shorts in which she'd slept.

Johanna was waiting for her outside.

"Morning, sunshine," Johanna said, chipper as ever. "Ready for another beautiful day of fieldwork?"

Nya blinked, bleary-eyed. "Coffee first," she said.

Johanna gave her a kiss. "There's a mug waiting for you in the flier."

"I love you."

"Course you do. Let's go."

They were airborne an hour before the first Paradisian sunrise, the flier running on batteries in the dark while Nya was fueling up on her second cup of coffee. She sat in the cockpit next to Johanna, content now, her gear safely stashed in the back and all anxiety about the future momentarily vanished in the sheer joy of flying.

"Where to?" Johanna asked.

"Same place as before. I want to see those lakes one more time."

"Sounds good. It'll take us about six hours. Breakfast is under the seat if you're hungry."

"I do love you, you know."

"Remember that when you're out there flitting between the stars."

Nya reached out and took Johanna's hand.

"I won't forget," she said.

They flew east, leaving the multi-corporate capital of Paradise behind. Soon, they were back in the mountains, flying over rugged karst terrain where tropical rainforest overgrew calcium carbonate rock eons old. The day grew brighter as both of Paradise's suns climbed into the sky. Nya studied the ridges and sinkholes below, marveling as always that such terrain could be achieved from simple erosion, the rock rotting out from the action of groundwater underneath.

At last, Johanna said, "We're getting close. I'm going to fly a search grid. Let's see if we can find a closer spot to put down than last time."

"Sounds good."

Nya felt the plane bank left and then they began to descend, shedding a couple thousand meters of altitude. Together they began to search for a clearing in the jungle, something large and flat enough to land.

"There," Johanna said. "That should work."

Nya peered closer. The ground below looked steep, and there wasn't much room. "You sure?"

"Trust me." Johanna flashed her a quick smile, then pushed the flier's nose down. The jungle canopy rushed toward them. Nya held her breath—and then they were through, settling neatly onto the forest floor.

"Nice flying," she said.

"Three kilometers from here to your lake."

"You're coming, right?"

"Course I am."

Nya reached behind the seat, wrestled her pack free, and chucked it to the ground. Then she clambered down, hefted it onto her shoulders, and made for the tree line scant meters away. Johanna joined her a moment later, and together they stepped into the jungle.

Perhaps, Nya thought, for the final time.

By evening, they were back at the water's edge, Nya's trusty throw net once more in hand. She scanned the surface of the lake, looking for her *Salmo.* In a clearing behind her, Johanna poked idly at their fire, which was sending a curl of smoke into the sky.

Still water; a campfire, and her longtime friend, faithful pilot, and lover cooking her dinner.

She knew she would miss this place. But what choice did she have? Orders were orders, even strange ones. And hers also brought with them the lure of the unknown.

She could hardly have said no.

She smiled wistfully to herself and returned her attention to her work, still searching for the first telltale hint of something rising from below the surface of the lake.

Her reverie was interrupted by a high, shrill call echoing out of the forest around her. An answering cry followed, then another. Nya spun around to see a flock of small, black-and-red birds burst from the jungle's edge, flapping and cawing in alarm.

They were followed into the clearing by a young woman breathing hard and running fast. She vaulted up and over a log, landed lightly, and kept on at a dead sprint without breaking stride.

Nya dropped the net in sheer surprise. Out of the corner of her eye, she saw Johanna jump to her feet and snatch up a high-powered flashlight, holding it like a club.

The new arrival skidded to a halt and spun in a slow circle, as though scanning the camp, taking in Nya, Johanna, the net, the campfire, and the flier, perched on the grass. Her clothing was branded with the twin suns of the InterTech corporate emblem and looked new, but her hair was wild, and her eyes wilder. She was close enough now that Nya could see scratches on her face.

The young woman looked her up and down. "You don't work for InterTech," she said. It was half-statement, half-question.

"No," Nya replied.

"Then you have to get me out of here."

"Wait—what? Who are you?" Nya said. "How did you find us out here?"

"My name is Kester," the woman said. "I saw your campfire. Now, please. We have to go."

"Our campfire? You smelled it?"

"No! I saw the smoke. Through a gap in the trees."

Nya looked at the fire. Its smoke curled upward, quickly turning to a diffuse haze against the vastness of the sky.

"You must have very good eyes," she said thoughtfully.

"You have no idea," Kester said. "Please. They're coming. There's no time."

Nya wasn't sure what to say to that, but Johanna, ever the pragmatist, had now crossed their campsite and joined them at the lakeshore. "We'll help you, Kester," she said. "But first, you need to tell us what's going on."

"I was a beta tester," Kester said. "At an InterTech lab."

"What happened?"

"I escaped. They shot my fiancé, but I got away."

"How?"

"With a dart gun of some kind."

"No," Johanna said. "I mean—how did you get away?"

The girl took a deep breath as though considering. "I made the branches fall," she said. "There were a lot of branches. They let us go for a walk in the woods. They shouldn't have done that," she added with what sounded like satisfaction.

"Right," Johanna said. "Kester, I'm not sure I understand any of this, but if you really did escape an InterTech lab, we're not sending you back. We have a flier a few kilometers from here. You're coming with us. Nya," she added, "get your gear. Leave everything heavy. We'll have to clear the trees, and I didn't plan for an extra passenger."

"Uh—okay," Nya stammered. "You always were the decisive one."

Johanna said nothing to that, was already taking off at a run, kicking out the campfire and gathering her belongings, while Nya looked at the net lying in a tangled mess at her feet.

She shook her head, bewildered, then turned away, leaving the throw net where it was.

She doubted she'd be using it again, anyway.

CHAPTER 30

Nya felt her stomach lurch and then they were airborne, the tiny flier's motors humming, its micro-blades spinning at maximum rpms as the craft clawed up and over the trees. Johanna was frowning, concentrating on her piloting, while Kester was wedged in the back seat between the bits of gear Nya had decided were worth salvaging.

She rummaged around and found a third headset under her seat. The plane was eerily quiet when used as a glider but loud under this much power. She swiveled in her seat and passed the headset back to Kester.

"How're you doing?" she asked, once Kester put hers on.

"Better now," Kester said. "Where are we going?"

"Good question. Johanna?"

"Scopes are clear," Johanna replied. "And we're low enough, I doubt anyone will pick us up on radar unless they know to look. We're as safe as I can make us."

"Great," Nya said. "So—now what?"

"The smartest thing would be to call University Security. Have them scramble something heavy and bring us in under full escort. If Kester really was working for InterTech, they're going to come looking."

"No!" Kester said. "Please don't tell anyone about me. You can't!"

"Take it easy," Nya said. "No one is saying anything yet. Johanna, you said that would be the smart thing to do. What's the dumb option?"

"Fly low and fast, and hope no one has started an airborne search yet." Johanna flashed her a grim look, then returned her attention to her piloting and the jungle canopy beneath their fuselage.

"Okay," Nya said. "Kester, we want to help, but it would be a lot easier if you could tell us what's going on here."

"I already told you," Kester said. "I was a beta tester. I escaped."

"Right—but from where?"

"A drug-discovery lab. They drop-shipped us down three weeks ago."

Nya glanced at Johanna, bewildered. Could it be? Had that been the ship she'd seen?

"Who is 'us,' Kester?" she said.

"We were the last survivors of Aldan's World."

"Aldan's World," Nya repeated slowly. "I remember hearing about a planet by that name. It was a Singlist colony, wasn't it?"

Kester laughed, but there was no mirth in it. "It was."

"What happened?"

"We were dying. There was a fungus. The few elders we had left cut a deal. They bought passage to Paradise in exchange for our freedom, and we became beta testers. We were told we'd become InterTech citizens after the trials. Which were supposed to be benign." She trailed off, staring out the window for a time, then added softly, "They lied."

Nya didn't respond to that right away, trying to understand the meaning of the young woman's words. It was nearly too much to process. There was danger there, of a kind she didn't understand. At the same time, whoever Kester was, she was clearly in need of help.

Something about her reminded Nya of her own students.

"What exactly did they do to you, Kester?" she said at last.

"It would be easier to show you," Kester said. "Let me see your hand."

"Okay."

Nya reached into the back seat with one hand, which Kester took in both of hers. Her skin was rough, her touch delicate but wiry and strong. The young woman glanced at Nya's hand briefly, then looked her directly in the eyes.

"You have six hundred and seventeen hairs on the back of your hand," she announced.

"I— What?"

"It's true. Do you have a data tablet?"

"Sure."

"Can I see it?"

"It's in that bag next to you." She reached across Kester's lap and rummaged around until she found the device. "Here," she said. "Let me set it up for you." She fiddled with the controls, then handed it over and watched as Kester's fingers flew across the surface, working through various interface screens until she landed on a basic drawing program.

The plane lurched, pitching up sharply.

"It's going to get bumpy," Johanna announced. "There's a storm cell ahead, and I don't want to go over it."

As if on cue, the first fat droplets of rain struck the flier, leaving long streaks on the windows.

"Oh, that's perfect," Kester said. "Watch the rain with me, Nya."

"Okay."

"No," Kester said. "I mean, really watch it. Look where the drops fall. Do you see?"

"I guess."

"Just keep watching."

The rain fell harder. The first drops turned to rivulets, and then sheets of water began to form on the windows as Johanna flew on through the clouds.

After a few minutes, Kester said, "Now close your eyes."

Nya did as she was instructed.

"What do you remember?"

"I'm not sure I understand."

"The first drop. Where did it land?"

"I don't know. The middle of the window?"

"Correct. Then what happened?"

"Uh—it left a streak, I guess."

"Also correct," Kester said. "It broke apart into smaller drops, right?"

"Yes."

"How many?"

"I don't know. Six or seven?"

"Six or seven," Kester repeated. There was laughter at the edge of her voice but with an edge, a rising note of a manic twinge. "What about the second drop? Where did it land?"

"I don't know, Kester. I just watched as it started raining."

"That's right, Nya. You don't know. But I do. No, don't open your eyes. Keep them closed. This is going to take a little time."

Nya sat, feeling foolish with her eyes squeezed tight as Johanna flew deeper into the storm. The plane lurched, rocked by the turbulence.

"Okay," Kester said after a few minutes had passed. Her voice sounded strained. "You can look now."

Nya opened her eyes. Kester was hunched over the tablet, her fingers rapidly tracing patterns on the drawing surface, faster than Nya could follow. Beads of sweat had formed on her forehead, and her breath came shallow and fast.

Abruptly, Kester stopped her work and lifted her head.

"Do you want to see?" There was a manic edge in her voice now, an unnerving note of desperation.

"See what?" Nya said.

"The rain, obviously." Kester handed her the tablet. "It's an animation. Just tell it to play."

Nya took the tablet, entered a command, and then watched, dumbfounded, as Kester's drawing sprang to life. Kester had drawn the view out the passenger window in the rear of the plane, and as the animation played forward, drops of rain impacted it, scattering and streaking, running together, until eventually there were just sheets of water, all structure lost.

"Do you understand?" Kester asked.

"Not really, no."

"It's real. Exactly as it happened."

"You're telling me you reproduced the pattern of the raindrops from memory?"

"Yes, Nya. That's exactly what I'm saying. Now let me show you the rest." Without waiting for an answer, Kester swiped at the tablet. The image of the rain dissolved away, and Nya found herself staring at her own face.

"I could see you reflected in the window," Kester said. "Before the rain started to fall."

"So . . . you have photographic memory?" Nya asked. "Is that what you're trying to say?"

"I have a lot more than that. My doctor called it advanced spatial reasoning—when he was writing notes he didn't know I could read. He said it was for 'application development in the areas of protein folding and interstellar-route finding.' Whatever that means. Do you like the drawing?"

Nya had no idea what to say to that, but Johanna, as always, saved her.

"It's beautiful," Johanna said, glancing back from her pilot's seat. "Nya, what do you say we hold off on calling the security folks, at least until we're out of this storm?"

They'd been aloft for an hour when Kester gave in to exhaustion and fell into a fitful sleep. Nya reached back and gently removed Kester's headset, then did her best to make her comfortable amid the pile of backpacks and fishing gear.

"She's out," she said.

"Good," Johanna said.

"So, now what?"

"I don't know. If she is what she says she is, Nya—if she was a beta tester at an Intertech drug discovery facility—it's a miracle she got away at all. I can't imagine how she did it."

"Me neither."

Nya leaned back in her copilot's seat, staring out the window, watching the rain sheeting off it, thinking about what Kester had shown her, what the girl evidently could do. "It's crazy timing," she said at last.

Johanna grunted. "The universe doesn't keep a schedule."

"True."

Just three days, she thought, and she would have been gone from Paradise, maybe forever. She never would have been back to that lake this weekend; never would have met Kester at all.

"You know," she said, "I could take her with me."

Johanna glanced pointedly at her watch, an old-fashioned chronometer she wore on her wrist. It had been a birthday present, something Nya had given her a couple of years before. "Took you long enough," she said.

"I'm a little slow sometimes," Nya admitted.

"That you are."

"Do you think it would work?"

"I don't see why not," Johanna said. "You said your orders authorized you to bring an assistant."

"I think they meant someone from the University."

"So, make her a student. You know what Admissions says. 'Find the best and the brightest . . .'"

"'Regardless of employment status or family of origin,'" Nya said, finishing the oft-given mantra. It was an old corporate policy whose stated purpose was to ensure anyone with sufficient ability had access to higher education on Paradise. It was also a sanctioned form of corporate espionage, a legal way to recruit from rival companies.

"If TransGalactic were a church, we'd call it offering sanctuary," Johanna said. "If it were an old-fashioned nation, we'd call it asylum."

"Instead, we call it free tuition," Nya agreed. "So, what? I order up a student ID for her?"

"You're a professor. You can take on graduate students. Your department would be thrilled."

"My failure to do so has been a common source of feedback during performance reviews," Nya said.

"Well, there you go. They'll be happy you're finally seeing the light. Even if it is on your last day."

Nya turned around in her seat and watched Kester for a time. She seemed to be sleeping more peacefully now. "It's crazy," she said. "This whole thing is crazy. What they're asking me to do. And now this. I'm going to take a perfect stranger with me?"

"Everyone else on that ship is going to be a stranger to you."

"I know," Nya said. She reached out and took Johanna's hand. "I don't want to think about that part right now. Just keep flying, okay?"

"Always do," Johanna said.

Together, they soared on through the unceasing rain.

CHAPTER 31

TransGalactic Vessel Carpathia

Inbound to Paradise

Mission Entry #35. Acting Captain's Log.

We are becoming old hands at the cloak-and-dagger business. This will be our second dark rendezvous in as many months. The first time, it netted us an Interlocutor and a sleeping madman.

This time, we are evidently bringing an ichthyologist on board. Dr. Nya Solarin, age thirty-eight in Earth years. Paradise-born, a lifetime employee, researcher, and instructor.

An academic who has never been into space.

What I still do not understand is why. The woman's record in drug discovery is unremarkable. She appears to be a taxonomist, a specialist in Paradisian evolutionary biology, but her work mostly seems to involve teaching undergraduates.

An undistinguished academic, native to Paradise, on a lifetime employment contract. Why go out of our way, risk the ship and mission, for someone whose skill set seems completely irrelevant?

There must be some explanation. Apparently, Dr. Solarin is also bringing a graduate assistant. Presumably, she wouldn't bother unless there were specific tasks with which she anticipated needing help.

At least their shuttle is on time. Remote sensing picked up the rapid interplanetary unit exactly where it was supposed to be. In a few moments, navigation will call and tell me we have matched velocities, at which point the AI driving the shuttle will nudge it the rest of the way to Carpathia. No need for umbilicals or spacewalks. We'll simply equalize the outer lock and open the door.

Just like before.

I used to look forward to planetfall. An approach to an inhabited system meant docking at a relay station, taking on crew, and refitting the ship. For some, it meant getting paid, or getting paid off. For others, it was a chance to see loved ones—but for me, it was simpler: the opportunity to walk different corridors for a while, find a bio-dome, stretch out, and surround myself with living things.

I am being childish. Here, on the mission of a lifetime, with an unprecedented opportunity at command, I'm pining for time in a park.

The next planet I will see up close and in person will be an albedo-locked holocaust world.

I doubt I'll ever set foot on it.

Ah! Navigation calls. Lieutenant el-Akinson; she is nothing if not punctual. Another young one with promise.

Another survivor.

I've asked the Interlocutor to join me when we board Dr. Solarin and her assistant. I fear I've grown too dependent, but her observations are invaluable. I want her first impressions and the comfort of her experience. As Piotre Raskovich has drifted into catatonia and become unresponsive these last few days, the Interlocutor has time to spare.

Duty calls. Time to take my aching spacer's body to the docking pod and see what this planet-born professor has to say for herself.

"It's not her fault, Captain."

Ian glanced sideways at the Interlocutor. She was staring straight ahead, all of her outward attention on the airlock door in front of them. She'd spoken the words quietly, unobtrusive as ever, yet still managed to name his thoughts exactly in five words.

Typical of her.

Of course, she was right. The mission, *Carpathia*, all of them were at risk, but Dr. Nya Solarin—whoever she was—could hardly be blamed.

The equalization seemed to take forever, though a glance at the docking pod's diagnostics told him all was well. It was just his own internal clock ticking away. He was anxious to be done with this, to go and run the race they might already have lost.

Not her fault. He repeated the words to himself as he repositioned his feet, nudging them deeper into their toeholds. Trying to maintain an attitude of indifference, to hide the tumult he felt inside.

The Interlocutor floated next to him, two Security personnel behind, presumably unnecessary but required by regulations. Otherwise, the corridor was empty.

Finally, the door spiraled open, the last few millibars of *Carpathia*'s slight overpressure equalizing with a gentle hiss.

Two women drifted in the airlock beyond.

Ian cleared his throat, hoping as ever that he sounded like a captain.

"Dr. Nya Solarin, I presume?" The older-looking of the pair nodded in response. "I'm Captain Ian McAllister. Welcome aboard *Carpathia*."

Nya Solarin looked uncomfortable in the zero gravity, both unsure how to move and seeming to be suffering physically. He could imagine what she felt. Swollen head and sinuses, nausea, a myriad of other pains and unpleasantness that came with being new to weightlessness. It would pass. And if it didn't, there were always drugs she could take.

At the same time, she appeared robust, healthy in a way he knew he was not, and he felt a pang of jealousy that surprised him. She had dark brown, sun-weathered skin, and long, jet-black hair which she wore pulled back. Her eyes were amber, flecked with gold. But mostly what he noticed was an obvious vitality he knew he no longer possessed. There were no broken vessels to mar the whites of her eyes, no excess fat or watery muscle. She was a planet-dwelling archetype, someone who looked like she could run up mountains if she wanted to—and probably did.

"Thank you," she said, interrupting his scrutiny. "And may I introduce Kester Aldan. She is my, ah, graduate assistant. My orders specified I could bring one additional employee if pertinent to my research."

"How do you do," he said, now studying the younger woman. She looked the more comfortable of the two. At least somewhat adept in space but with none of the physical signs of a lifetime's exposure. There was something wild about her, an intensity in her stare he found unnerving. "You've been out here before," he guessed.

"Once or twice," the young woman said. "Depending on how you count it." She kicked off the wall and sailed across the corridor toward him. For a moment, he thought they would collide, and he flinched more out of surprise than any sense of danger. He had the presence of mind to flash a hand signal to his Security team, bidding them to stay where they were. There was no threat there.

She pivoted neatly midair, snaked out an arm, grabbed a handhold, and came to a stop a scant meter in front of him. "Your eyes are black," she said.

"Yes."

"It's okay, Captain. I won't tell. I'm not quite human either."

"I see," he said, unsure what to make of any of this. This Kester Alden didn't strike him like a graduate assistant. "Well, you'll be wanting a toehold, Ms. Aldan. We are about to get underway."

The young woman shrugged and drifted away, though she never took her eyes from his face, studying him with that same disturbing intensity. It was as though she was memorizing every detail of him for some purpose he couldn't guess.

He glanced at the Interlocutor, who gave him a mild look that revealed nothing. Then he called the bridge. Lieutenant el-Akinson answered immediately, which was some comfort.

"They're aboard," Ian said, louder than was necessary. He could have subvocalized the whole thing. "Detach shuttle for return trip and resume our acceleration. One gee on a sixty-second ramp. Let's get our new arrivals' feet on the ground gently, please. And then take us to that transition point."

He heard an affirmative radiate through his jawbone to his inner ear. Satisfied, he shifted his attention back to Dr. Solarin, who was watching the exchange while clinging awkwardly to the wall. "As soon as your shuttle has departed, we'll be underway," he said. He pointed to the corridor's floor. "That direction will be down."

"Understood, Captain," she said.

The shuttle drifted free, and moments later, *Carpathia* shuddered to life, beginning a gentle acceleration. The floor, walls, and ceiling resolved into a frame of reference.

"I'm new at this," Nya Solarin said. "As I'm sure you can tell."

"You'll get the hang of it. You're traveling light," he added approvingly. The doctor and her assistant carried only a single bag between them.

"I assumed we could weave whatever we needed once we were onboard."

He nodded. "Exactly right. Many planet-dwellers have a hard time grasping that at first."

"Well. It's my first time, Captain. But I couldn't see the purpose in dragging a bunch of fishing nets with me."

He wasn't sure what to make of that, and it occurred to him that he didn't know what to do next. Get them settled? Summon this Nya Solarin immediately for a briefing? Offer them both something to eat?

How would Captain Marakan have handled this? Certainly, she would have thought beyond the docking and introductions.

"Doctor," he said, as the pause began to grow awkward, "we have a long journey ahead, but I'm afraid I can't let you rest just yet. We have a great deal to discuss. The Interlocutor," he added with a nod, "will show your research assistant to your quarters. We've given you a large cabin by shipboard standards. We're not short on room at the moment."

"Of course," Nya said. Kester said nothing, still staring at him with that all-consuming gaze. She was a strange one, he thought. There was something he didn't understand there.

"Yes, Captain," the Interlocutor said, speaking for the first time. "Please summon me to the briefing room if I am required."

Clever, he thought, watching as the Interlocutor turned to sweep Kester Aldan into her wake with a single gesture. She'd managed to find a subtle way to tell him not to use his own cabin for the conversation that lay ahead. Guessing, no doubt, that he would have chosen it because it was the only space on the ship that felt comfortable to him.

Of course, the command briefing room was far more appropriate. He'd almost forgotten there was such a thing. He hadn't had occasion to use it yet.

Gods, he thought. He was terrible at this.

"This way, Doctor," he said, turning to make his way down the corridor, hoping she couldn't see the uncertainty on his face.

They grew heavier as they went, *Carpathia* easing inexorably up the acceleration curve as micro-fusion bombs detonated behind the blast shield. The ship was stretching her legs now, even as Ian felt a dull ache begin in his.

Dr. Solarin might have been new in space, but under the increasing gravity, her natural strength shone through. Again he felt a spacer's pang of jealousy at the lightness of her step. He tried and failed to remember a time when his own body had been free of both drugs and pain.

"The first leg of this trip is going to be uncomfortable," he said. "One and a half gees at terminal acceleration, which we'll hold until we reach the transition point and depart this system."

Nya Solarin murmured assent but didn't respond further. They passed the remainder of the walk in silence. He didn't feel like playing tour guide, while for her part, the doctor seemed happy to hold her questions in reserve.

The command briefing room was a small module attached to the spine of the ship. The crew of *Carpathia* had kept it in immaculate condition in spite of its disuse. Ian hadn't set foot in the space since they'd begun the long return trip to Earth, when Captain Marakan had given him command of the *Sagittaria*, what felt like a lifetime ago.

The pod's furnishings were luxurious by shipboard standards. It held comfortable, well-padded chairs that doubled as acceleration couches, and sophisticated tactical displays tied into every system, weapon, sensory device, and remote on the ship. Two pieces of art adorned its walls. These weren't holographic projections or viewscreens but were instead paintings: old-fashioned acrylic on canvas, done by hand, commissioned fifteen years before in commemoration of *Carpathia*'s maiden voyage.

He noticed the doctor staring at them. The first of the pair depicted a nineteenth-century steamship surrounded by lifeboats: black ocean under black skies with icebergs in the water, everything about it giving the impression of freezing cold. The name *Carpathia* was visible on the steamer's hull.

The second painting showed *Carpathia* herself, their ship, approaching a strange-looking colony vessel: a mammoth construction shaped like an oversized onion.

"Kester would appreciate these," the doctor said.

"Is that so?"

"Yes. She's a bit of an artist herself. But tell me, Captain—what am I looking at, exactly?"

"Origin stories," he said, finding himself glad for the distraction. "The one on the left, the ancient steamship, is our namesake, shown at the height of her greatest fame. The one on the right depicts our maiden voyage. Both were rescue missions. Neither," he added grimly, "were particularly successful."

"I wondered about that," Nya said. "I looked up your ship when I got my orders. I assumed *Carpathia* wasn't named after a mountain range on Earth. But why name her for a vessel that was only noteworthy for rescuing survivors of a famous maritime disaster? It seems bleak."

He considered how to respond. Part of him wanted to tell her the tale—of *Carpathia*'s first mission and his own initial journey into deep space. It had been an ill-fated voyage from beginning to end, with a noble-enough purpose but an equally dark ending.

"It's a long story," he said at last. "I think I'd best save it for another time. For the moment, I'm afraid I have more pressing questions."

Nya nodded. "Of course, Captain. Where would you like me to begin?"

He indicated the acceleration chairs. She settled in; he did the same with a grunt of relief. "You can begin with your career, Doctor," he said. "I've read your corporate biography, scanned your lecture notes, and studied your papers to the limit of my ability. As far as I can tell, we've gone light-years out of our way to pick up an ichthyologist. Or maybe an evolutionary biologist? It's all a little unclear."

She laughed, but it sounded forced. "You'd get along well with my department chair," she said. "He has expressed similar sentiments in the past. Captain, I can tell you everything there is to know about me and my work; I'm happy to do so. But it might help me first to know where we are going and why. Because the truth is I have no more idea why I'm here than you do."

He considered. His orders were clear enough: Dr. Solarin was to be given full access. There was no particular reason he should force her to speak first.

"You're right," he said. "It's probably better if I tell you what I know. But you might want to get comfortable. It's a long story."

"Any chance of something to drink first?"

"Of course," he said, chagrined at having forgotten basic manners. "Do they drink coffee on Paradise?"

"We do. But I've always preferred tea."

"You and the Interlocutor will get along," he said. "Let's see what our mess steward can do." He subvocalized an order to the galley, and they settled into an awkward silence, the doctor still regarding the artwork on the wall while he tried to decide where to begin.

A few minutes later, a young officer arrived, delivered their drinks, and departed without a word. Nya took a sip of her tea, murmuring appreciatively. Ian left his untouched; he had little taste for the stuff.

He took a deep breath. "As near as I can tell," he said, "we are heading for a discovery without precedent in human history. And we are being guided there by a Chief Information Officer who seems to have lost his mind."

It took him an hour to lay it out for her. He told her about Piotre Raskovich, the Behavioral Conditioning that had failed, and his remarkable defection. He told her what the Interlocutor had reported, of decades worth of post-operant Conditioning, drugs, hypnotics, and the raw exploitation of childhood fears undone in an instant, the chains that shackled his mind to Magellanix's corporate goals snapping under the sheer surprise of the moment. He described what they knew of Ragnarock, the latest in the collection of holocaust worlds dotting the cosmos; the news of another species that had not survived the jump to sentience. And he told her about *Accipiter* and his own deepest fear, that they were behind, destined to lose a race where the stakes were life and death.

They grew heavier as he spoke, the acceleration building, pressing them into their padded chairs.

"It's an algebra problem," he concluded, finishing his description of their tactical position relative to *Accipiter*. Nya's tea was long since drunk; she was studying him with a thoughtful look on her face. "We move about at fractions of the speed of light when traveling as we are now. Then, when we reach a transition point, we jump light-years in no time—even slightly negative time, as best our instruments can determine. When we arrive at our destination, those jump events create energy signatures that cannot be missed or mistaken, both in the places we have left and the places we arrive. Those signatures radiate outward spherically at the speed of light, telling anyone who is listening that a ship has either entered or departed the region."

Nya Solarin nodded, seeming to understand. "So, a ship jumping first necessarily reveals its position to any ship that is following," she said "But it may not know if there is a ship behind it or not."

"Exactly," he said. "If *Accipiter* is out there and is far enough ahead of us, it might miss our arrival signature, completing its next jump before news of our presence reaches it. If they are two jumps ahead, neither of us will know the other is out here at all. Right now, we can only speculate, but if we're in a race, and we're close enough for them to hear us, well. In this business, second place is an awfully dangerous spot to be. If they reach Ragnarock before we do, they'll mine the terminal transition point—if it isn't already—deploying whatever weaponry they have brought. There won't be much we can do."

She held out her hands. "Captain, I'm sorry if I have put your ship at risk. I promise you this was not an assignment I asked for. The first I ever heard of *Carpathia* was when you arrived, and I was given just three days to respond. The offer was not," she added, "phrased in a way as to encourage saying no."

"Water under the bridge," he said. "You're a Carpathian now. As is your assistant."

"Is there a ceremony?"

He laughed. "Only if you want there to be. But it's your turn, Doctor. You've heard our story. You know as much as I can tell you of our mission. Now tell me: why does our Board of Directors think your work is so critical that they took such a risk?" He spread his arms outward in a helpless shrug. "I assume they believe we're potentially about to make first contact with an alien intelligence, and that if we do, you're the right person to do the talking." He looked at her; she had a half-smile on her face. "You have a guess," he said.

"In fact, I do. Not everything I've written has been published. I'm beginning to rethink some things about my career. Namely, how it was allowed to continue, given my lack of achievement. Maybe, as wildly speculative and unpopular as my research was, someone wanted it to proceed."

"The Board might think in greater time scales than we can imagine," he said. "They certainly live longer than we do. But what are these unpublished papers of yours? What do you do besides catch fish?"

"I pontificate," she said.

"About?"

"About the conditions under which sentience might be survived. Let me ask you a question, Captain. How many holocaust planets are there?"

"I don't actually know," he said. "Companies don't share that data. Take Ragnarock—if not for Piotre Raskovich, we wouldn't have learned about it for decades."

"Okay. Best guess?"

He thought about it. "Twenty? Maybe a few more."

"And no first contacts. Nothing out there alive."

"Not that I'm aware of."

"So, this is a first."

"It would be. Of course, no one has made contact with anything yet," he said. "What Piotre Raskovich described was an inert artifact."

"But the circumstances are highly unusual."

"Clearly." His lower back twinged; *Carpathia* was continuing up the acceleration curve. One-point-three gees, he thought. That was usually when he started to feel it. "Piotre believes that the artifact was placed on a volcano that hadn't yet formed by the time a nuclear exchange collapsed Ragnarock's ecosphere and eliminated all higher-order life on the planet. He is basing this on estimates of seafloor spreading rates. So, he speculates that the artifact must have been left there by someone who visited the planet after its demise. If not by us, then whom? Clearly not Magellanix. TransGalactic didn't do it, or we wouldn't be on this mission. So, either InterTech or some other corporation is in the business of leaving strange-looking hardware lying around on dormant volcanoes, or it was . . ."

"Someone Else," Nya finished for him. "Which is why I think I'm here. Not that I have any idea how I'm meant to help specifically, but I can at least see the logic."

"Explain?"

She sighed heavily. "Captain, I've spent the last decade speculating about the conditions under which a species might evolve into sentience and survive the experience. That and studying a very special fish. A fish that would seem, because of the habitat in which it lives, to have an evolutionary incentive to plan for the long term. And a fish that exhibits some peculiar behaviors in that direction."

"You think Piotre's artifact is an aquarium?"

She laughed. "That would be remarkable, wouldn't it? I haven't a clue. But I do know this: whoever or whatever built it, our human metaphors and ways of looking at things may be completely useless to us."

"How so?"

"Well . . . let me ask you this, Captain. What are your mission parameters? At their core?"

"They're straightforward enough, I suppose." He began ticking them off on his fingers. "One: find the artifact. Two: learn all that can be learned. Three: decide what to do with it."

She gave him a somber look. "And over what time scale do you expect this mission to play out? How long do you think we'll be on that planet?"

"Weeks," he said. "Maybe months. Possibly a year or two, I suppose, but it seems unlikely."

"So, to put it in a nutshell, it's your job to decide what to do with the artifact. And if it takes you a year to chart a particular course of action, that'll feel like a long time."

"Yes."

"And yet Piotre Raskovich believes, based on the data he has provided, that it could be over a million years old."

"Possibly. It could've been placed there very recently; it could have been much longer ago. There's no way to know."

"And this is my point, Captain. There's a basic incompatibility here that we might do well to consider. Assuming whoever put it there did so for a good reason, and supposing they did it a very long time ago, might we not then hypothesize that the time scales over which they think are vastly different from our own?"

"You're talking about a machine intelligence, not a biological one?"

She took a long, slow breath and exhaled softly. “Not necessarily,” she said.

“But how could anything biological ever learn to think over those kinds of time horizons?”

“That, Captain McAllister, is the question I have spent my career attempting to answer.”

CHAPTER 32

Their conversation lasted for hours, Ian mostly listening, fascinated, to Nya's stories of her research. The gravity grew steadily heavier, sinking them deeper into their chairs. The ship was performing well, he thought, accelerating smoothly in spite of the damage it had sustained. A small part of his brain consumed a stream of reports from *Carpathia*'s officers standing the watch, status updates piped via the grafts in his inner ear. They were on course and schedule to depart this region of space but, for the moment, still in safe-enough waters.

Most of his attention, however, was spent on this strange civilian sitting across from him. Dr. Solarin was unlike anyone he had met in his career. He hadn't wanted to like her, and he still resented the risk they'd taken from the detour required to come there. But she was an engaging speaker, at turns animated and sober, self-effacing while passionate about her work. She kept her explanations accessible even as they veered into topics of xeno-evolutionary biology, epigenetics, neurological development patterns in alien species, protein folding and convergent evolutionary trends, and a dozen other subjects besides, none of which were a serious part of his officer's curriculum back on Earth.

She was a natural. A born lecturer, he thought, someone who could command a room, would be comfortable in front of any audience. His own corporate finishing schools seemed dreary by comparison. He'd learned math, physics, tactics, economics, and history, all the hard way, in a no-holds-barred, up-or-out battle against a forced rating distribution. He'd graduated alongside a predetermined percentage of his classmates and matriculated into lifetime employment with quantitative skills as good as any, but he'd never enjoyed it and certainly never known anything of the life sciences beyond what drugs to take and his personal experience of accelerated physiological decay.

The doctor's stories of her fieldwork were particularly fascinating. He couldn't imagine such a life, where physical dangers took the form of rotten sinkholes and poisonous insects, where endurance was measured in kilometers hiked, not months of heavy gravity endured, and navigation meant orienteering instead of the mathematics of higher-dimensional space travel.

He had traveled thousands of light-years in a state-of-the-art starship. Nya Solarin flew a few hundred kilometers at a time in a solar-skinned lifter, but in her way, she was much more of an explorer than him.

At the moment, she'd veered into mathematical territory, explaining something called the Drake equation, which was an algebraic formula created in an early attempt to explain humanity's isolation in the cosmos. The mathematics seemed laughably simple and utterly hopeless at the same time.

"You teach this?" he asked finally.

Nya chuckled. "Not in the way you mean. The Drake equation hasn't been the subject of serious academic discussion for centuries. I discovered it by accident. I was writing an article on pre-spaceflight Earth history, trying to understand how people thought about the destruction of their ecosphere at a time when we knew nothing of life on other planets. I wondered whether that sense of uniqueness, the belief that Earth might be all there was, had led to any collective sense of stewardship over what was the only known viable habitat for humans in the galaxy."

"Did it?"

"Not so much, no," she said sadly.

"I'm from there, you know," he said.

"I didn't know you were Earthborn."

"Most officers are."

"Why?"

He shrugged. "A lot of reasons, I imagine. Damaged as it is, Earth is still our homeworld. Its billions outnumber the colony worlds combined. All the major corporations are still headquartered there, and because it was where space exploration began, Earth is still essentially in the middle of the information grid. Also," he added, "simple nativism. Anti-colonist bias. A presumption that anyone Earthborn has necessarily overcome more challenges, fought their way through a much bigger crowd to be selected and thus is more deserving of lifetime employment."

"Biggest fish from the biggest pond?"

"You would say that." He laughed. "Or maybe it's just that if you're born on a ruined world, you naturally look to the stars. But tell me more about this Drake equation of yours, Doctor. Explain to me the mathematics of cosmological isolation."

His voice sounded bitter in his ears. Why, we wondered, would that be? Some affection for Earth he'd not known he possessed? He hadn't set foot on it in a decade.

"There's not much more to tell," she said. "Mostly I use it to make a point, how information changes not just what we believe but how we formulate our frameworks for asking questions in the first place."

"That's awfully abstract."

Nya laughed again. "Well, it's a class for second-years," she replied. "I catch 'em at their most sophomoric. But the interesting part is the missing term in the equation. The inverse relationship between species-level life expectancy and technological sophistication, which you think would've been included."

"You're talking about holocaust worlds."

"I am," she said. "Like I said before, it's a matter of time scales. We humans are proud of the fact that we alone in the universe seem to have survived. But in spite of the capabilities of ships such as *Carpathia* here, for all that we've reached other worlds, humanity is still terribly young. We've been tool users for less than a hundred thousand years, whereas higher-order life has existed on Earth for half a billion, give or take. Our own sentience experiment, the lifespan of our species in its technologically accelerating state, is still just the blink of an eye."

"Wait," he said. "Do you think we haven't made it after all? That we still might wipe ourselves out?"

"That is precisely what I believe, Captain. Colonization solves nothing. Earth, all the planets we occupy, may themselves yet end as holocaust worlds."

He was about to respond to that when the door chimed. He waved it open, unsurprised when the Interlocutor stepped through.

She moved more slowly under the heavy gravity, but nothing in the shape of her stride had changed. Hers was no lurching, staggering gait. It was as though the viscosity of the air had increased around her and now her feet were more solidly on the ground.

The Interlocutor took a seat, saying nothing. Nya was still looking at him, waiting for a response, almost as though she hadn't noticed the Interlocutor's arrival.

"Well, given that, Doctor," he said, "I guess the question remains—why you? I think I understand the relevance of your research, but why would Corporate presume the artifact was created by something biological at all?

Isn't machine intelligence more likely? Why order us to pick up an evolutionary biologist but not, say, an academic focused on the Singularity?"

Her eyes glittered as though she had been expecting the question. "Are you a religious man, Captain?"

He shook his head, confused. "That's the second time I've been asked that question on this mission. Not particularly, no."

"So, you believe we achieved spaceflight on our own, with no help along the way?"

"I guess I've always assumed humans are calling the shots," he said. "If we aren't, then we can't tell the difference anyway, so what does it matter?"

"Aha! So, you're a pragmatist."

"It comes with the territory. What about you, Doctor?" he said. "Do you believe we created a machine intelligence in the heyday of AI research? That It gave us spaceflight, for reasons only It understands?" He forced a laugh. "Or maybe It is busy making Its progeny, hidden away from prying eyes?"

"In fact, I don't," she said. "I think we tried and failed—but as with so many things, the benefits of the effort were tremendous. Assistive technologies, the shuttle that flew me out here, all of our nanotechnology and weavers, and a thousand other bits of technological sophistication we take for granted. None of it would've been developed if we hadn't been chasing the Singularity."

"The mathematics of higher-dimensional travel came out of that research as well," he said.

She nodded. "Exactly. So, if we didn't create an actual machine god along the way, and if we never figured out how to copy and upload our consciousness, maybe it was for the best. Either way, now it seems to be more a matter of religious belief than active investigation."

"I suppose that's true," he said. "But then, I wouldn't have thought anyone was in your line of work, either. All we've ever found are planets with pre-sentient life or holocaust worlds, and yet here you are, working out a theory for how someone else might survive. So, maybe someone in a corporate lab somewhere is still trying to bring about the Singularity."

She shrugged. "You'd know better than me."

"Me? I'm just a lowly . . ." He stopped himself and glanced at the Interlocutor. He'd been about to say *lieutenant*. "I suppose we could ask Piotre," he said. "That might be interesting."

The Interlocutor chose that moment to speak for the first time. "Doctor," she said. "What do you suppose your young graduate assistant believes about these questions?"

She said it quietly, her voice mellifluous, peaceful as ever. Nya looked over at her, startled, almost as if noticing her for the first time.

"She's no research assistant," the Interlocutor added. It almost sounded like an apology.

"No," Nya sighed. "She isn't."

"Then what is she?" Ian asked, confused.

The Interlocutor held up a hand. "With your permission, Captain?"

"Of course."

"Let us not force the doctor to prevaricate, or to lie further by omission, or into any other discomfort. Dr. Solarin," she went on, "the remarkable young woman you have brought has been telling me her story, even as you and the captain have been in conversation here."

"She talked to you?"

"She did," the Interlocutor said. The words hung in the air for a moment. "If your plan was to deceive, you cannot have imagined to keep it up for long. Perhaps you thought you would wait until after the first jump event."

Nya exhaled, a defeated sound. "You're right," she said. "We wanted to get as far away as possible."

"It's understandable."

"Is she okay?"

"Kester is just fine, Doctor. She is resting in your quarters, building a three-dimensional model of the TransGalactic University campus on Paradise out of food paste she found in the galley. Some sort of dessert confection, I believe, that hardens in a way suited to her purpose. I might add that she is building her model from memory. It's stunning in its level of detail."

Ian saw the doctor wince. "Will someone kindly tell me what is going on here?" he asked.

"She's a beta tester, Captain," the Interlocutor said.

"I'm sorry?"

"She is a sport. Newly modified, drug-enhanced."

"TransGalactic sent us a beta tester?"

"No, Captain. The girl appears to have escaped from an InterTech lab."

Ian furrowed his brow, more confused than before. "How is that even possible?"

"Her tale is remarkable, but the crux of it is this: Kester Aldan appears to be the product of an extreme effort to extend the limits of human spatial reasoning."

"For what purpose?"

"Interstellar navigation and route finding, for one," the Interlocutor said. "Also drug discovery, as there are obvious protein-folding implications. Past that, who knows? What is certain is that the InterTech doctor in charge was tasked with creating a radically upgraded human mind."

"They told her all that?" He glanced over at Nya, who was sitting stock-still, avoiding both their gaze. "I thought beta testers were kept in the dark about the nature of their trials."

"They didn't tell her," the Interlocutor said. "But evidently, they succeeded in altering her beyond anyone's projections while simultaneously underestimating precisely what they had created. Kester was able to read everything her doctor wrote about her by the simple expedient of watching his fingers move and imagining where the virtual keys only he could see must have been positioned before him."

"Impossible."

"So I also thought. But there's more. She then used her newfound abilities to escape, overcoming her keeper in the process. There is, I might add, no reason to believe InterTech's security is any less capable than our own."

Ian regarded her but, as usual, could read nothing from her expression. His mind raced, trying to catch up to what he was hearing.

"How much of this did you know, Dr. Solarin?" he asked finally.

The scientist looked at him briefly, then away. "All of it," she said, her voice small, the animated lecturer now vanished. "We both knew."

"We?"

"Johanna and I. A friend of mine. My partner, at least some of the time. She was—is—a pilot. She flew me to my field sites. Kester found us in the jungle and asked for help."

"So, there's someone on Paradise who knows Kester's real story?"

"There is."

He gave her a long look. "Your friend might be in considerable danger, if I'm understanding the Interlocutor correctly."

Nya met his eye at last. "Johanna can take care of herself, Captain. We were on an unofficial flight. There are no records."

"Perhaps not, but if Kester is an escapee, InterTech Security will follow her trail," he said. "Conduct a full forensic sweep. TransGalactic would."

"I know. They won't have to work very hard; I left half my gear behind. But TransGalactic University will deny all knowledge. And by the time InterTech figures anything out . . ." She trailed off.

He nodded, considering. "True. Information lag is already increasing, and we are headed for parts unknown. And we won't be back this way, at least not for a very long time."

"Wait—we aren't coming back to Paradise?"

"My orders are to return to Earth when our mission is complete, Doctor. We cannot turn back nor delay further by going out of our way to hand a beta-testing escapee over to a TransGalactic authority. Nor can InterTech reach her where we are going. The girl is safe—as safe as any of us, at any rate. Though Magellanix," he added, "may of course succeed in killing us all."

BOOK FOUR

TRANSITIONS

CHAPTER 33

Ragnarock

Feyis cut his rations, then cut them again to a quarter food bar a day. Eleven hundred calories, well below subsistence level no matter how much energy he conserved.

It was a race: his baseline metabolic rate against the flight of a weather balloon, and all he could do was wait. How many times could it circumnavigate the planet before he starved to death? Would it drift through the right latitude and be found while there was still time?

Or maybe the race had ended before it began. Maybe the planet's unceasing equatorial storms had taken the balloon down hours after he launched it and all this was nothing more than the folly of hope.

Days turned into weeks, and then a month had passed. His body shed weight, consuming itself from the inside.

Air, water, shelter, food. He had three in abundance.

But not the fourth.

Some impulse drew him to move his camp to the edge of the sea. There was no reason to transport his gear; it was an irrational expenditure of effort, but he did it anyway. He found shelter in the form of a flat patch of crushed basalt under an overhang, protected from the wind but with a sweeping view of the water. He spent his waking hours staring at the vast expanse of ocean, reducing his exertions to a daily trek to the nearest snowfield, taking a hard, clamshell case one of the seismometers had been packed in to use as a bucket, hauling snow to melt for drinking water.

Other than that, he stayed put. Movement cost calories, and he had none to spare.

His thoughts were drawn over and again to the summit of the volcano upon which he was exiled. The weather balloon had tripped a memory, the billowing silvery sphere familiar somehow, but the details remained frustratingly out of reach.

So did the identity of his climbing companion.

As the weeks slid by, his ankle healed and his collarbone knit back together, and an idea began to form. He was fit enough; he could burn the last of his food stores, climb the mountain again, and see for himself what was up there. It would hasten his end, consuming calories he couldn't spare. But at least he'd know.

It was the last thing he would do, he decided. He did some rough math, then set aside six complete ration bars, one of each flavor, though even after all these weeks, he would've been hard pressed to tell them apart. He tucked them into the bottom of his pack.

He would wait three more weeks, and then he'd climb the mountain a second time. If he was going to die out there, he at least wanted a chance at knowing why.

To pass the time, he took to trying to predict the tides.

It was an impossible exercise, as Ragnarock had three moons. Funny, he thought; they named this planet after an apocalypse before ever setting foot on it, but as far as he knew, no one had ever bothered to name its satellites.

He decided he would call them the three sisters. All three had a reddish hue, but two were larger than the third. These he thought of as the twins, and the younger one the adopted daughter. Inventing Ragnarockian mythology on the fly, and why not? Someone should, and he had nothing better to do.

Their orbital periods were vastly different, the little one passing overhead twice as fast as her two elder siblings, who moved in a more stately fashion across the night sky. Their gravitational pulls interacted in strange ways, producing tides that were both erratic and extreme. The sea appeared to come and go at random, most often with no discernible pattern at all.

One day, some fluke of the sisters' alignment contrived to suck the ocean the farthest away from the land he had yet observed. The water level fell, and fell some more, exposing a hundred meters of long, low basalt shelf: an ancient lava flow that fanned out from the shore.

He retrieved a field scope from his kit and trained it on the newly exposed rock at the water's edge. Something was moving out there: a brown, filamentous mat, like strands of some primitive algae, bobbing in the water, evidently exposed only at this lowest of low tides. It was the first living thing he had seen; the first evidence that something multicellular had managed to survive the destruction of this planet's ecosphere.

Impulse struck.

He raced back to his shelter, moving faster than he had in weeks. He snatched up the seismograph case that served as a snow bucket, grabbed his climbing axe, and made his way down to the beach.

What he had in mind was absurdly dangerous. There was no telling how long this offshore tidal surge would last, and when it was over, he imagined the sea would return with a vengeance. But he went anyway, picking his way across the rock shelf, one eye on the ocean, the other on the uneven basalt beneath his feet. No matter how poor his chances of long-term survival, he had no desire to break an ankle out there.

Finally, he reached the waterline. The life form he'd seen really did look like some sort of algal mat, now plastered to the rock surface. He poked at it experimentally. It was stringy, rough to the touch, and irritating to his skin.

He grabbed a handful and tugged. It clung tight, but it came free easily enough when he brought the axe to bear, hacking at the holdfasts anchoring it to the rock. Once those were severed, he was able to peel the stuff away in long, thin strips.

Then he noticed something moving underneath: a dark green, segmented, insect-like creature about the size of his fist. It had at least a dozen legs and two pairs of long, thin antennae. He poked at it with the end of his axe. In response, the creature tucked itself into a crack in the rock and curled up in a little armored ball.

He marveled at it. Maybe, he thought, he was now looking at the most advanced life left on the planet. He wondered if he was observing an instinct that had survived millions of years, some ancient defense mechanism still present after millennia with no higher-order predators to fear.

He used the axe tip to pry it from its crevice, picked it up, and set it in his bucket.

He glanced up at the ocean. If the waves were about to come crashing back in, he couldn't tell.

He went looking for more of the creatures. He collected seven in all and then chopped as much of the algae as he could carry. He had pushed his luck far enough. He retreated the way he had come, looking over his shoulder the whole time, not relaxing until he was safely back on the trail to his camp.

A few minutes later, the sea returned. A wave built, then built higher still, reaching first ten meters, and then twenty, shoaling as it raced across the rock, a tidal bore that covered the beach in a running flood and smashed into the base of his cliff in a torrent of spray. He watched in awe at the sheer power on display, shaking his head at the risk he had just taken.

When the sea finally calmed, he got to work.

He unpacked his spare shelter and studied it for a time, trying his best to determine how to repurpose it as a drying rack. His thought was to spread the algae over the frame, with spare rope to tie the stuff into place. It would dry quickly enough, he thought, desiccated by the unceasing Ragnarockian wind.

And when it did, he would have a campfire.

His stomach rumbled. He took a tiny bite of a ration bar and turned his attention to the animals he'd found. They were still lying curled up, little armored balls with just antennae and eyes protruding.

They looked unappealing in the extreme.

Still. Other than his fast-dwindling rations, they represented the only potential source of protein available to him. They were as likely to kill as nourish him, but the little creatures were the only thing within thousands of kilometers that vaguely resembled food.

Would he have done it? Traded starvation for the potential of poisoning himself with untested fauna on an unknown planet? Eaten animals whose proteins might prove incompatible with his digestion, if not immediately fatal?

Or would he have taken what remained of his rations and climbed the volcano in one last fever pitch of energy, burning calories and shortening his life in exchange for the chance to know why he had come here in the first place?

He never found out, because Callie found him a week later, sitting by the remains of his fire.

At first, Feyis simply assumed he was hallucinating. He saw the wink of sun on metal and heard the faint drone of micro-blades but wrote it off to wish fulfillment, too much time spent contemplating his own end, some last surge of denial that hadn't quite let go.

Then a shadow passed over him: the tiny flier, wings dipping in greeting.

Feyis stumbled back to his tent. He'd left the suit's helmet and transmitter inside, an unforgivable lapse of discipline. Now it was squawking at him, leaving him feeling simultaneously euphoric and like a fool for losing focus, for giving up hope.

From inside he heard Callie's voice.

"Mission Generalist Feyis Sado," she was saying. "Calling Mission Generalist Feyis Sado. This is Materials Specialist Callandra diMarck. Are you receiving? Over." There was a ten-second pause, and she repeated the message.

He toggled the unit to Transmit, and said, "I read you! Thank the gods. I read you, I read you!" Over and over, unbelieving, all too much to take in.

"Copy that, Feyis. Anywhere to land down there?"

He rubbed his eyes, trying to clear his vision, to regain some control. "Yes," he managed to say. "There's a viable landing site approximately two kilometers northwest of this position."

"Copy. Do you require an immediate airdrop?"

"No," he said. "But I'm getting pretty hungry down here."

"Understood. I'll put down and rendezvous with you at your camp."

"Copy that. Nice to hear your voice, Callie," he managed to add. Then he stumbled out of his tent and back to the remains of his fire. He sat down heavily on the crude seat he'd made out of spare shelter parts and a few strategically placed boulders and settled in to wait just a little bit longer.

It took her an hour, and then there she was, picking her way confidently across the rocks with a heavy pack slung over her shoulders.

Also, he saw, not wearing an exposure suit of any kind.

She crossed the remaining snowfield to his campsite at a near-jog and dropped her pack.

"Feyis?"

"Callie!"

"My gods," she said. "It's really you. We thought you were dead."

And then she was hugging him and he her, full on, without reservation or hesitation. Human contact. He'd never expected to see anyone again. In the moment, it was overwhelming.

For a brief instant, he almost told her he loved her, but he stopped himself before the words could come out. Some inner caution told him it would be the wrong thing to say.

"How did you find me?" he asked instead.

"Your balloon," she said. "I've been on courier duty for the last three weeks. You were declared dead, and they needed extra pilots for the supply runs back and forth from the excavation to the main camp ever since."

"Wait—what? What excavation?"

"You remember—the nuclear-waste dump we found." She released him and stepped back, giving him a more careful look. "What happened to you out here, anyway?"

He shrugged helplessly. "I fell into a crevasse. Woke up on an ice shelf, twenty meters down, pretty hurt. I'm suffering from short-term memory loss. Which I keep hoping is going to be temporary, but it's not getting better. The truth is, Callie, I don't know why I'm here, who I was with, or why we came. I don't know how I wound up in that crevasse." He paused a moment, then added, "I remember you, though. But I'm not completely sure why."

She took a deep breath. "Maybe I better sit down," she said.

"Maybe so. Also—do you have something to eat?" He nodded over at the bucket, where his little intertidal creatures were hiding, half-concealed under some algae he'd added into what was now a crude aquarium constructed on their behalf. "Another week or two, and I was going to have to try the local cuisine."

Her face paled. "You haven't, have you?"

"No."

"Good. We found something similar. The team calls them 'hell beetles.' They're wildly toxic; if these are anything like the species we found, they would've killed you in a matter of hours. Painfully."

"Good to know."

She rummaged in her pack and came out with a full set of rations. "How about a food bar and a caffeine supplement instead?"

He reached out, took the packaging, and tore it open. "Don't mind if I do," he said around a first mouthful. "I can get the fire going again. I've got one algal mat left; been saving it for a special occasion. They stink when they burn, but there's not much else to do out here."

He ate as she talked, telling him the story from the beginning: their trip to the southern continent, their mission, the isotopic analysis of the gasses trapped in ice millions of years old. How they had confirmed that this planet had once been home to sentient life, that its inhabitants perished in a holocaust of their own making.

"We flew back to the main camp," she concluded. "There was no reason to build a field station at the South Pole. Our CIO ordered a planet-wide search for artifacts, looking for anything that might have survived the ice age that followed. Beginning with the usual suspects."

He swallowed a bite of his bar, thinking. Callie seemed to expect a response, but it was hard to concentrate. For one thing, she was the first human he'd seen in months, but it wasn't just that.

She was impossibly attractive. She had buzz-cut hair, a stubble of black fuzz poking out from olive skin, and jet-black spacer's eyes. It was hard to say how old she was, but clearly, she'd put her time in and was no stranger to space. She was short, maybe one point seven meters, and looked strong. She moved better in this gravity than he did, even after his ankle had healed. She had laugh lines around her eyes, her deeply tan, weathered face flushed from the sun and wind.

He was, he realized, completely, totally in love.

But it didn't seem to be mutual. She'd hugged him, but it felt chaste. Reunited colleagues, definitely; friends, maybe. Lovers, not so much, he thought.

"The usual suspects," he repeated slowly. "Meaning stable geologic formations."

"That's right." Her eyes shone at him, black surfaces mirror-bright in this light. "And we found something, Feyis. Our team discovered a mine shaft dug into mountains uplifted at least fifty million years ago. There was an enormous cavern, way down at the bottom, sealed tight. And inside, a dead species' lasting contribution to the universe: row after row of heavy plastic drums, a legacy written in nuclear shit, left behind for us to discover after all this time."

"Buried under all that rock and ice," he said. "Like I almost was." He was still hungry but decided not to eat anything more yet, not wanting to overwhelm his digestive system. "So, what happened next?"

"Apparently none other than Piotre Raskovich drop-shipped down from *Accipiter*."

That name! It was like he'd been struck. "Piotre Raskovich," he said. "Our Chief Information Officer! He was my climbing partner. But why?" It was like a key turning in a lock; the memories came flooding back. "He was cabin-bound, almost crippled. Why would he travel to the planet's surface? And why come all the way out here with me?"

"I don't know," Callie said. "He showed up right after we announced the discovery. He requisitioned a flier and a pilot—you. The assumption was that he was traveling to visit the nuclear dump we'd found. But I guess not. A few days later, he came back alone. The word was that you had been lost in some sort of accident, but no other details were ever given."

"And then what?"

"Then he was gone," Callie said. She stepped over to the remains of his fire, which had all but gone out, and set about rekindling it. "He returned to *Accipiter* on the same drop-ship that brought him down. We never knew what it was about. We just kept working on the dump site, and a week after his visit, *Accipiter* was gone."

"Gone where?"

"Back to Earth. Captain Johnston left a team of thirty to continue the work. We have a full field crew now, Feyis. With remotes in orbit. So, we've got satellite communication, though they're still limited."

"Earth," he said. He crumpled the empty ration packaging in his hand, then tossed it into the fire. Biodegradable, compostable, reweavable; also flammable. It curled, blackened, and began to smoke, and then disappeared abruptly in a tiny whoosh of flame.

"So, you and I are all alone out here," he said. "Does anyone else know I'm alive?"

"Not yet. Though I should call it in, obviously." She glanced at the device on her wrist. "We're out of satcom now, but there will be something overhead in a few minutes."

"Hang on. Before you do . . . Piotre Raskvoich and I never went to your dump site."

"Apparently not. This mountain isn't even in the same direction."

"We parked our flier at the base. I probably couldn't find a viable landing site anywhere higher. And then we must have climbed it together. I'm surprised he made it."

"He didn't look good in camp," she said. "Not from what I heard."

"But what the hell for? And how did I wind up in a crevasse? That's what's bothered me the whole time."

He took a deep breath, steeling himself. "There's another thing," he said. "My memory is a mess, so please don't take this the wrong way. But I remember you. I thought we might be—well—I'm not sure what. Not just fellow contractors, anyway."

She laughed. "Oh, Feyis," she said. "You don't remember, do you?"

"Remember what?"

"You imprinted," she said.

"I what?"

"You imprinted on me. Someone in Human Resources messed up and cycled us awake at the same time, back on *Accipiter*."

He winced, then put his face in his hands, unable to look up. "Oh, gods," he said. "I'm so sorry."

"Don't be!" She laughed again. "You didn't know I knew. You hid it really well, and no one else ever found out. Well, probably except for whoever was on shift that day in the hibernation hold."

"I bet they had a laugh."

"They probably did it on purpose."

He thought about that for a moment. "I've always believed that kind of stuff goes on sometimes," he said. "Having fun at our expense. But I am sorry. And I'm glad it was you that came for me."

She gave him a long look, then stood up abruptly, as though having made her mind up about something.

She stepped around the fire, grabbed him by his shoulders, and hauled him to his feet.

And kissed him, squarely on the mouth.

Sometime later, she let him go. He boggled at her and said, "What did you do that for?"

In response to this, she kissed him again. "Imprinted or not," she said, "someone has to welcome you back to the land of the living. Now tell me—isn't there something you want to do?"

He shook his head, confused. "What did you have in mind?"

"I think we should figure out what's up in that crater."

"You know," he said. "We really should."

CHAPTER 34

The plane climbed slowly. Callie had offered to let him do the flying, and now Feyis was fighting his way upward in a grudging spiral. At a thousand meters, the buffeting began, the flier battered around the sky by storms that grew worse the higher they ascended.

"Just like old times," he said, laughing.

"Pretty much," Callie agreed.

The sea was a white-capped gray foam far beneath them; the clouds thick overhead. Feyis doubted they'd find blue sky before they reached the crater rim, but he didn't mind. How could he? He was alive, flying into the unknown, and doing so with Callie. At that moment, knocked this way and that in his shoulder harness by an atmosphere that would never let them rest, exactly why he felt so strongly about her seemed unimportant.

Eventually, they drew even with the top of the volcano and then climbed above it. He banked the plane left, clearing the crater rim by a good hundred meters. There was no reason for heroics on this overflight. Their flier was built for endurance, not aerobatics, and a sudden downdraft could pluck them from the sky and smash them to pieces on the rocks and ice below before he had a chance to react.

And then, all at once, there it was: an enormous silver sphere, at least a hundred meters tall, bright as the sun on the sea. It glittered like a diamond even in the cloud-filtered light.

"Sweet absent gods," he said. "What is that thing?"

"No idea," Callie said. "I've never seen anything like it."

"It's so bright, you could see it from orbit."

"You could," Callie agreed. "I bet that's exactly what happened. Someone on *Accipiter* must have spotted it, once we had enough remotes deployed for a detailed survey."

"Not just someone," he said. "Piotre Raskovich."

His mind raced, trying to make sense of it all even as he eased into a counterclockwise circuit above the crater, keeping high enough that the turbulence posed no danger.

The object looked the same from all sides: a shining, infinitely faceted construct, resting in the bottom of the crater like some godchild had rolled a giant marble into a cup.

"Want to get a little closer?" he asked.

"Yeah, but be careful, okay?"

"Agreed. No reason to get killed over it. I feel like I'm speaking from experience here."

He pushed forward into a cautious dive. As they descended, he saw something flash on the crater floor.

Callie must have seen it too. "Looks like you left some gear behind," she said. "Let me get it on screen." She centered the flier's scopes on the crater, panning and zooming until she had a fix.

He glanced over. "That looks like a seismometer," he said.

"There's a couple of them. Other instruments, too. Wow. You guys hauled a lot of stuff up here."

"No wonder my back hurts all the time."

"I wonder if it's still operational," she said.

"My back?"

"The gear, Feyis."

"Probably," he said. "We would've downloaded the data, but we must have left our instruments behind. Maybe Piotre wanted long-term observations. Or maybe I was too tired to carry it all back to camp."

"You, tired?"

"Anything's possible."

They fell silent at that and continued to circle the crater. Feyis was simply awestruck by the sight of the artifact below. He imagined Callie felt the same. The artifact was overwhelming. It was huge, flawless, and in some undefinable way, completely alien.

"Now what?" he said at last.

"I don't know," she said. "But there's no way you'd ever land down there."

"Not in this flier, no." He thought it over, considering. "Let's go back to camp," he said. "I think we should talk this over before we do anything more. Including," he added, "reporting me alive."

They flew the return trip in silence, then made the short trek to the remains of their fire, where they sat down to rations, water, and electrolytes.

To Feyis, the whole thing felt weirdly familiar, like this had been home for so long, he had forgotten anything else.

"It's not from here," Callie finally said, when they had eaten and drunk their fill.

He swallowed his last mouthful of a food bar. "I think you're right, but talk me through it."

"Well, for starters," she said, "the artifacts we've found elsewhere on this planet don't look anywhere near that tech level. We're talking plastic containers of nuclear waste and fission by-products. Nasty, primitive stuff. Nothing to suggest a civilization that could construct something that could survive a million years without a scratch."

"Agreed," he said. "Extreme long time horizon construction is difficult. Also, there are seafloor spreading and subsidence rates to consider. This volcano might not have formed at all until after the nuclear exchange that killed the world."

"Okay. Suppose that's true," Callie said. "If the original inhabitants of Ragnarock didn't put it here, then who did?"

"What about InterTech or TransGalactic? Could it be anthropogenic?"

"You think that thing's a remote of some kind?" She laughed. "If it is, we're playing for the wrong team."

"I'm starting to think that's true in any case." He got to his feet and made his way to his drying racks, then set about gathering more algae for the fire.

"Maybe we're thinking about this wrong," he said. "What if Piotre Raskovich himself is the key?"

"How so?"

"I'm not sure. But imagine our Chief Information Officer up there in orbit on *Accipiter*. What's his job, when you get down to it?"

"Mountain climbing?"

"Besides that."

"Processing data," she said.

"Right. So, suppose he has his remotes in orbit, and he's sitting in his cabin, watching the data streaming back. Imagery, ground scans, atmospheric temperature profiles, wind shear measurements, whatever. And then all of a sudden, he sees this."

"It'd be hard to miss."

"It would've stood out like a sore thumb to anyone looking, which probably no one else would have been, because we know how protective Piotre Raskovich is with his data."

"It is his job."

"Exactly. But even the most basic signal processing would have noticed a bright, shining, perfectly spherical object sitting in a volcanic crater. So, then what does Piotre do?"

"He reports it to Captain Johnston," Callie said.

"And how would she respond?"

Callie hesitated. "She'd send a team to the surface to investigate," she said. "She'd want instruments on site, detailed readings, all the analytics Raskovich could dream up."

"Right again. But why would she send Piotre himself? Why would our captain order him, of all people, to the surface? He's not qualified for this kind of work. But she did it anyway. She waited until you found the nuclear site, which she used as an excuse to drop-shop him down. Allegedly to inspect your find, but actually to come out here . . ." He trailed off, thinking. "It doesn't make any sense. And not to take this personally, but why kill me over it?"

Callie nodded. "You're right. Why wouldn't Captain Johnston want her crew to know what they'd found?"

"Yeah," he said. "I know we're just contractors, and life feels a little cheap sometimes, but doesn't it strike you as absurdly risky? Dispatch your cabin-bound, physically incapacitated CIO to a heavy-gravity planet? To climb a mountain?"

"And push a highly professional, seasoned, very experienced guide down a crevasse?" Callie added. Feyis felt himself blush. "You're right," she went on. "There's no logic to it. Because then what? Raskovich reports you missing, packs up, returns to *Accipiter*, and they all just head back to Earth?"

They both fell silent at that. Clouds drifted by. Scattered snowflakes fell, but the air was still.

Feyis trained the miniature laser that had saved him in the crevasse on a corner of unburnt algae, which caught, blackened, and curled. He poked at it until it rekindled, then turned his attention to the sea, still considering.

The ocean looked as vast and mysterious as ever but sorrowful, too. Like it was missing whatever leviathans once graced its waves. *Something ought to be breaching*, he thought, *cresting the surface; there should be ripples to be seen from above, hinting at secrets hidden below.*

He looked back to the fire, thinking of the ghosts of alien whales, vanished spirits of unknown beings. All that remained were marine cockroaches they couldn't eat and filamentous algae for them to warm themselves by.

"It doesn't add up," he said finally.

"No," Callie agreed. "It doesn't. Even if the captain was planning to murder you to keep the secret, there had to be better ways to do it."

"Yeah, like a hibernation accident. It wouldn't be the first time something went wrong."

Callie laughed at that and got to her feet, stepping around the fire to stand before him. She held out her hands and hauled him to his feet. "Accidents do happen," she said.

He stood. They remained like that for a time, still holding hands.

It was absurd. He'd nearly died, the archaeological find of all time was resting in a crater a kilometer overhead, and all he wanted to do was look into this woman's eyes and the hell with all of it.

The fire climbed higher, sending smoke curling against the late afternoon sky.

"You're right," he said at last, dragging his mind back to the problem at hand. "Captain Johnston has the authority to do whatever she likes. She could return to Earth and quarantine the whole crew back at the relay station for as long as she wanted. She could keep us at Occipitus Prime forever. Or in hibernation, for that matter."

Callie nodded, looked away, past him, and out to sea. "And why risk our CIO's life?" Her eyes narrowed, as though an idea had occurred. "There is another possibility," she said. "What if it was all Piotre's doing?"

"How could it be? He's conditioned. All the officers are. He might've been weird, but no one ever said he was bad at his job."

"But just suppose," Callie said. She let go of his hands and took a step back. "He's a data man, maybe the best in the fleet. And suddenly, he finds himself in possession of information unique in all of human history."

"And?"

"What if— I don't know. What if his Conditioning failed?"

"That's impossible, Callie," Feyis said. "I mean, I'm just a contractor. I don't know much about Behavioral Conditioning, but I've been at this a long time and I've never heard a single case of it breaking."

"But we wouldn't hear about it, would we?" she persisted. "We'd be the last to know. And what if it did fail? What if he decided to do something rash?"

"Like what?"

"Maybe he decided to steal it," Callie said.

"How? It can't exactly be stolen. It's— Well. Big."

"But the data could be. Knowledge of it could be stolen. Just suppose, Feyis. Imagine our CIO, suddenly free to act, decided on impulse to conceal satellite imagery. To hoard the knowledge he'd just gained."

Feyis considered. "You think he reprogrammed the orbital remotes?"

"Maybe. Just follow it through with me, okay? Say he hides the images. Then what's his next move? He's the Chief Information Officer. He'd want more data. Orbital photography wouldn't be enough. It's trivial to fake."

"So, he invents a reason to come down here?"

"Exactly," Callie said. "And maybe I gave him one—the nuclear-waste dump. He could come to the planet's surface under the guise of wanting to see it for himself."

"If you're right, I bet Captain Johnston was surprised when he offered."

"Probably, but she'd never suspect him of anything. Like you said—he's conditioned. Betrayal would literally have been unthinkable."

"Okay," he said. "Say Raskovich comes to the surface and requisitions a flier and a pilot but no other support crew, because he's already planning . . ." He trailed off. "Son of a bitch," he muttered.

"Yeah," Callie said. "He would have already been planning to murder you, report an accident, take his data back to *Accipiter*, and sell it when he gets back to Earth."

"But sell it to whom?"

"It'd have to be InterTech or TransGalactic, I'd think," Callie said. "A company with enough resources to mount an expedition fast, before Magellanix could send more assets this way."

He looked at her, considering. "But what could he possibly sell it for? What possible trade would be worth it? Money?"

Callie shrugged. "I have no idea. Why do officers ever think about anything the way they do? Maybe he didn't know himself. But suppose he succeeds. What would that mean?"

"It would mean that in about a year," Feyis said slowly, "an enemy corporation will be sending a ship out here."

"Or maybe a fleet," Callie said.

He thought it over. "I don't know," he said, after a time. "It seems pretty farfetched."

"It is," she agreed. "I mean, you're right—I've never heard of Conditioning failing, either. Maybe Captain Johnston had some other reason to do what she did. But if Raskovich was just following orders, then Magellanix itself will be back, sooner or later."

"Having already left me for dead," he agreed. "Me being the only person on this planet who knew about this place."

"Right."

"So, what in the world do we do?" he asked.

"I have no idea."

"Me either. But until we think of something, I'm probably better off staying dead."

Callie took his hands again but this time pulled him close.

"You probably are," she agreed.

They talked it through for another hour. In the end, the plan was simple. He would remain on the island and learn all he could about the artifact in the crater. Callie would provide field support as best she could.

"I'll be back with a hot meal," she promised. "And coffee."

"How about a change of clothes?"

She smiled. "That, too."

"And something with vertical landing capability would be nice."

"I'll see what I can do, but I doubt any of our long-range craft are getting down safely in that crater," she said. "You're going to have to climb."

"I could parachute in."

"In that crosswind? Now you're just getting lazy."

"True. One last thing, Callie: what about your flier? Lieutenant Farrow is going to know where you've been as soon as you dump your inertial recorders back at the main camp."

She considered. "I could run it out of power," she said. "Put it into the ocean and wait for a rescue."

"Too risky. And besides, we can't crash a plane every time you come out here to visit. You'll have to find a way to erase the data."

"I'll work on it."

"Okay."

"You know you're going to be out here for a long time," Callie said.

"That," Feyis sighed, "is true. And I gotta tell you—I'm in no hurry to see you leave."

"I'm in no hurry to go," she said. She gave him a long look. Then she stood, crossed the campsite, and made her way to his shelter without a backward glance.

He got to his feet and followed.

❧

They made love slowly, just discovering each other like two old friends reintroducing themselves after years apart. When it was over, she rolled over and kissed him in what was obviously a goodbye. There was nothing more to say and no reason to delay her departure any longer.

A few minutes later, he was watching her go, the plane drifting skyward, heading west, until a storm cell swept in, obscuring it from further sight.

Leaving him marooned again, with nothing but the unceasing winds of an eons-old nuclear winter for company.

It was too close to nightfall to begin what would come next; there was nothing left for now but sleep. Still, he missed her already and wasn't looking forward to spending the night alone.

When he awoke, the dawn was still hours away. Two of Ragnarock's moons, the sisters, were shining through gaps in the cloudy sky.

At least his mind was clear. Feyis knew what he had to do. It was what he trained for, why he'd been hired, the type of thing Mission Generalists were good at.

He assembled his gear. When everything was ready, he hefted his ice axe, cinched the straps tighter on his pack, and began once more to climb.

CHAPTER 35

It was a grinding, miserable slog of a climb. One foot in front of the other, short on technical drama but long on suffering. If he'd had a proper medical facility at which to recover, Feyis thought, it all would have been a bit easier. Stem cells, platelet injections, enhanced gene therapies to regrow bones and restitch traumatized nerves—any modern tech would have made the aftermath of a twenty-meter tumble into a crevasse a minor inconvenience.

Instead, the ankle and collarbone which hadn't bothered him during his inactivity ached the entirety of the limping, drawn-out affair. Fortunately, he was good at suffering. It came with the territory.

When at last he crested the crater rim, the air was bitingly cold, the wind whipping around him at what had to be seventy kilometers an hour.

Then the mist parted, and there was the artifact, just as he and Callie had seen it from above: a great, spherical, glittering thing that shone and sparkled even under the heavy clouds.

He clambered from the ridge, half-scrambling, half-sliding down the scree slope. The going was difficult, and he chided himself not to hurry. He had months on his hands to study it. Maybe years, as long as Callie could keep him resupplied.

He wished she were with him now, and wondered what she was doing. Likely, she was back at base camp, figuring out how to overwrite the inertial flight logs. Or maybe trying to liberate a food processor for him without being noticed.

Conspiring with him to conceal his survival had put her in danger. Feyis knew he should feel guilty, but mostly, he just missed her. Selfishly, he looked forward to the day they could explore this place together or, better, sit in the mouth of his tiny shelter after making love, stare at the water, and do nothing at all.

It took him the better part of another hour, but he reached the crater floor without incident. Up close, the artifact's geometry seemed even more perfect, its facets flawless. It was something not of this world, he thought, all out of space and time.

Who had placed it there on this volcano? And for what possible purpose?

He didn't know, nor could he guess how any of this insanity would play out. Maybe *Accipiter* would return. Perhaps Piotre Raskovich had found a way to sell out to a competitor, and some other company would be the next to send a ship this far into deep space. Either way, he had been swept up in events beyond his imagination and control. Here he was, standing at the base of an unprecedented archaeological discovery—and for the moment, it was his and his alone.

His first task was to determine which of their instruments had been left behind. He picked his way across the crater floor slowly, taking inventory. It was an impressive collection. He found a pair of seismometers, a miniaturized weather station, a Geiger counter, and an isotopic analyzer for rock and ice samples, much like the one he and Callie had used on Ragnarock's southern continent, what felt like years before.

There was also, intriguingly, a subsurface radar imaging system, and a shortwave transmitter with enough power to talk to a ship in far orbit.

"Well, huh," he said, to no one in particular. The radar unit's emitter was shaped like an upside-down mushroom and had been positioned on a level, ice-free rock surface. Someone—presumably he—had cleared the smaller gravel away, making a tidy site from which to operate it.

The unit came with embedded diagnostics and an imaging screen. There was also an empty clamshell case that would have contained several hundred miniaturized receivers, tiny spherical devices that had presumably been scattered around the crater floor. Once deployed, they would have listened for echoes from the unit's ground-pulse radar and relayed what they heard back to the main processor, which would in turn have stitched everything into three-dimensional images of whatever lay below the surface.

Curious, he powered the unit to life. Its memory was blank. It had been deployed and was still set for use, but its records had been wiped clean.

The unit's power meter indicated it was mostly charged. "Well, why not?" he muttered.

Then he triggered the device.

There were no warning hums, no deep subsonic resonance to jar his bones and jangle sympathetic nerves, no indication that the machine was doing anything at all aside from plain text that appeared on the screen.

Transmitting, the unit said. And then, *Imaging*.

And, finally, *Ready*.

Feyis poked at an icon that appeared. The screen responded promptly, giving him a detailed view of what lay beneath his feet.

The artifact was positioned atop an enormous shaft that plunged downward three kilometers into solid rock.

"Holy shit," he muttered.

What was he looking at? Maybe it was a power source, he thought. Could the artifact be tapping into geothermal energy, some magma pocket deep beneath the volcano?

He poked at the screen again, thinking he had read it wrong, but no. The ground imaging showed a bright white column stabbing straight down. It was impossible to tell what it was made of: the subsurface radar simply bounced off it.

It occurred to him that he might be seeing a weapon of some kind. A sphere sitting on top of a kilometers-long cylinder, with a shaft approximately as wide as the artifact itself? It reminded him of a mortar shell resting on top of a launching tube.

He flipped the unit off and considered. There was no context for this, no reference manual, training instructions, operator's handbook, or procedure to follow.

So, for lack of any better plan, he decided to get on with the job.

The rest of the instruments were straightforward enough. He didn't need the weather station to tell him it was freezing cold and didn't really want to know how hard the wind was blowing.

He saved the transmitter for last. This was a two-meter dish, woven from a light mesh, a nanofiber construct that was both incredibly strong and lightweight.

He knelt in front of it and he turned it on, only to discover that the user interface was secured, requiring authentication codes he didn't possess. He grunted in disappointment. Without those, the unit was of no use, except maybe as a drying rack for his algae back at camp, and he had no desire to lug it down the mountain.

Feyis got back to his feet, considering all that he had found. Instruments still deployed, a transmitter with enough range to talk to a ship in orbit but requiring secure access to use. And of course, the artifact itself, whose purpose he could not guess. It could be a ship, a probe, a biodome, or a long-range communicator. A weapon, a monument, or maybe an exotic gravestone.

Or any combination thereof.

He wished Callie were there.

He spent the night in the crater, awakening to find his tent buried under half a meter of snow. He fought back the momentary panic, chiding himself for behaving like it was his first time in the field, and methodically dug his way free.

Eventually, he poked his head clear of the new-fallen snow, like an old Earth marmot crawling from its cave to regard the coming spring. He was unsurprised to see the artifact exactly as it had been. Not a flake clung to its surface.

He made his way to its base, reached out, and touched it for the first time.

It felt slick under his fingers. Its temperature was the same as the air around him.

On impulse, he packed a snowball and hurled it at the sphere. He wasn't sure what he expected to happen, but there was no flashing emitter fire, no point-defense systems triggering in response. The projectile hit the artifact without a sound, slid down the surface as though it were frictionless, and joined the snowdrift piled at the artifact's base.

He activated the ground radar again.

Nothing had changed.

"Hello," he said. He raised his hands to his mouth, shouting this time. "Hello!"

Nothing happened. He felt slightly foolish, but that was all.

Now what?

Food, he thought. *Attend to the basics.* Breakfast was indistinguishable from dinner the night before, save for the flavor. He chose chocolate and drank water to wash it down.

What more could he accomplish? He'd seen the artifact up close. Learned something at least, but was no closer to divining its purpose or unraveling Piotre's goals than he had been before climbing the volcano.

He'd brought food for several days. He decided he would remain, if for no other reason than the scrambling, five-hundred-meter ascent back to the crater rim seeming unappealing at the moment, to say nothing of the long slog to base camp that would follow.

But in truth, he had little idea what to do. Maybe the artifact would never respond to anything at all. People might die over it; he had the sense that someone would before all was said and done.

In the meantime, he was left to wander up and down this volcano, maybe for years, Sisyphus making a pilgrimage to a boulder someone else had already lifted.

He sighed heavily and decided he might as well survey the crater again. Maybe the fresh-fallen snow would offer some clue.

He apologized to his ankle and got to his feet, wondering again how long it would be before Callie returned.

CHAPTER 36

Carpathia

During her first week on the ship, Kester found a small, seldom-used observation pod slung under *Carpathia*'s bow. Unique among all the modules she had explored, this one was perfectly transparent, a nubby little protrusion that had been woven from material with enough structural integrity to survive the endless stream of micrometeors she had learned were endemic to space travel, while also offering its occupants an uninterrupted view of the stars.

She wondered what it was for. It served no practical purpose she could see. It wasn't armed and held no instrumentation, not even an interface screen. But mass, as she understood it, was expensive to haul around, so it must have some purpose.

She'd asked Nya, who didn't know either. The captain had been in earshot at that moment, conversing with Dr. Solarin about the planet they were bound for and the strange artifact that had been found there. He'd given her a funny look but hadn't said anything.

Whatever its intended purpose, the pod had become her personal space. She would sit there for hours, feet dangling over infinity, with no one to bother her. She could count as many stars as she wanted and draw patterns in the unending night forever.

But something in her had changed. Slowly, she was developing a measure of control. The headaches were less common now, and the trance state was a little less all-consuming. Occasionally, she would come to with no idea how much time had passed, be forced to reference a chronometer, to reground herself in the present as she rode out aching waves of pain. But increasingly, she found she could control her strange powers. She could turn the patterning off and on; count and snapshot and memorize; draw constellations of infinite complexity in her mind and then close her eyes and let them go.

It was a comfort but a small one.

Per was still lost.

She missed him terribly, and the guilt made it even worse. She had seen the darts coming and knew where they would fly. She had chosen to duck in the critical moment, sacrificing him to save herself.

She could lie on her back and stare at the stars forever, but the reality of what she had done never changed.

And she was always alone.

Late evening, shipboard time. Kester had consumed her dinner calories without noticing what she was eating, sitting quietly in Nya's company, the doctor lost in thoughts of her own. Now she pushed her dessert away, uninterested. She hadn't touched the sweet paste these Carpathians seemed to favor, a substance she'd encountered her first day on the ship and used as modeling clay for reasons she no longer remembered.

She murmured goodbye to Nya and left the galley the way she had come in, clumping along slowly in the heavy gravity. They were three jumps into their journey. She had learned that the ship's acceleration profile varied slightly from transit to transit, depending on the specific trajectory they needed to make the higher-dimensional mathematics work. In relative terms, this particular subspace slog wasn't bad—probably ten percent above what she had grown up with on Aldan's World. It didn't bother her. Her upbringing had made her strong, and she'd long since recovered physically from whatever Dr. Herecic had done to her back on Paradise.

She'd never really be a part of this ship's crew, she thought, but in this one regard, she felt like a proper Carpathian, stamping through the corridors without complaint.

It was three-tenths of a kilometer from the galley to the forward observation pod, a few minutes of exercise in the form of an after-dinner walk. The passageway was empty of traffic as usual. She reached the bow and irised the door open with a touch.

In the dark of the pod beyond she saw the silhouetted shape of a man, standing facing away from her, backlit by the stars.

He turned to regard her with dead black spacer's eyes, which seemed to make holes in his skull in the dark shadows of the room. He was, she now saw, impossibly thin, with receding hair. His flesh looked soft, and when he moved, it shifted about like he was made of water tissue, like one of the deepwater fish Nya had told her about.

The flash of anger at seeing her hideout occupied vanished. This man before her was repulsive, and yet she felt a moment of kinship.

Not just a man, she thought. *A broken man.*

"I'm sorry to disturb you," she said. "I didn't know anyone else came here."

"You aren't disturbing me." His voice came out as a mechanical rasp, a sort of dying wheeze.

"I'm Kester," she said.

"Ah. So, you're the doctor's assistant. My name is Piotre Raskovich."

"So, you're the Chief Information Officer."

He laughed but did it in such a way as not to smile. He hardly seemed to open his mouth at all.

"Guilty as charged," he said.

"Are you? What crime did you commit?"

"Many. I am a thief and worse." He gestured at the empty seats around him. "You can join me if you like."

She stepped into the pod. Up close, she could see the man was wearing some sort of ocular interface, the type of unit she had seen a few of the crew use. It was a data reader, a high-speed design that worked by projecting light directly onto the eyeball.

She'd tried one on once but removed it immediately. The last thing she needed was an even higher-density way to stream information into her brain. Her own eyes were quite enough.

Piotre Raskovich regarded her another moment, then, seeming content to leave her to her own devices, turned back to the stars. As he did, she noticed his hands began to move, independently of the rest of his body.

They were tracing subtle, fluid patterns in the air.

She watched for a time, feeling a little wincing pain in her temple that faded as quickly as it had come. Whatever he was working at, she could make no sense of it. Nor would she, she supposed, without knowing the shape of the interface he used, without being able to guess what he saw.

"What are you writing?" she asked.

He looked back at her, startled, as though he'd forgotten she was there.

"I like the way your fingers move," she said. "They're like water. And they trace complicated things, but I can't tell what you're trying to say."

"You have good eyes," he said.

She shrugged. "Not especially. It's just that I'm good at processing information."

He regarded her for a long moment.

"Math," he said finally.

"What?"

"You asked what I was writing. I'm not. I'm doing math."

"Oh," she said. "I like math. Topology, anyway. I like shapes. And folding things."

"As it happens," he said, "that's exactly what I'm trying to do."

"Really? How come?"

"I'm trying to find a new route between the stars."

"Yeah? Want some help?"

He laughed again, that same rasping sound. *All these spacers*, she thought. *They all sound like they're about to die.*

"Do you know how route-finding works?" he asked.

"No," she said. "But I know we're going somewhere that only a few ships in the Magellanix fleet have explored, somewhere TransGalactic has never been at all."

"You're well informed."

"Am I? It doesn't feel like it." She thought for a moment, then added, "How did you manage to steal it, anyway?"

He winced and shook his head. "Don't ask. But it's true that we're going to use Magellanix's own data to get where we're going."

"What kind of data?"

He regarded her a moment, then seemed to come to a decision. "All kinds," he said. "Extensive observations of the local gravitational topology. Background field distortions. Cosmic-radiation signatures. It's hard to explain."

She gave him a wintry look. "Try me."

He shrugged. "Okay, Kester," he said. "It's sort of like this. Imagine a flat sheet of some flexible material: a rubbery synthetic that you can poke and bend and twist any way you want, but it will never tear."

"I'm pretty sure I can imagine that," she said.

He didn't seem to notice her sarcasm. "Okay. Now further imagine the sheet isn't smooth. It has all these bumps and dimples, nobs and protrusions. It's very rough. Like a topographical map."

"Okay." He sounded a lot like Dr. Herecic, she thought. She supposed she shouldn't be surprised. "Let me guess," she said. "Now you want me to imagine your bumpy map has been crumpled into a ball."

He gave her an odd look. "Well, yes."

"And now you're going to tell me we can't see this map of yours directly, but instead, we have its shadow, or rather a series of pictures of its shadow, taken with the light positioned in different places."

He was staring at her even harder now. "That's it exactly."

"And you're trying to draw a picture of the map."

"Not quite," he said. "I'm trying to decide where to poke a hole in it."

"Show me," she said.

So he did.

CHAPTER 37

The Interlocutor turned away from the video feed and eyed her captain. He was still studying Kester and Piotre Raskovich, listening carefully as the former Magellanix CIO explained the mathematics of higher-dimensional travel, route finding, and transition events.

"We could have just asked her," he said.

"She has to choose it, Captain. Consider what her experience has been."

"And if Piotre betrays us? Tells her this whole thing is a setup?"

"He won't."

"Does Dr. Solarin know?"

"That I engineered this meeting? No. But she will certainly know they have met. She saved the girl's life; they talk. Even as strange as her brain has become, that still counts for something."

"Hmm."

"You are troubled."

"Captain Marakan would have no qualms," he said.

The Interlocutor gave him a soft smile. "Then perhaps, Captain McAllister, in this regard, you may surpass her."

He nodded, seeming satisfied. As she knew he would be. After all, it was what he needed to hear.

She returned her attention to the screen, watching as Kester and Piotre continued their discussion, diving further and further into mathematics that were incomprehensible to her but on which all their lives might depend.

CHAPTER 38

According to *Carpathia*'s shipboard chronometers, it was eight in the morning, though Nya had already been awake for hours, the heavy gravity imparted by their current acceleration having again left her unable to sleep. In a few minutes, she was scheduled to meet with Piotre Raskovich and would finally have the opportunity to hear his story firsthand.

She had passed the early morning alone in her cabin, skimming technical journals but unable to focus on the content they contained. At times like these, when day should have been dawning, she found herself at her loneliest, the ache for Johanna's missing company the most acute. On Paradise, they had become so comfortable with each other. Weeks would pass with no expectations and hardly any contact, each lost in their own work and professional worlds. Then, without warning, their romance would rekindle. Like a storm blowing in from the sea: a flurry of early breakfasts and shared sunrises, steaming cups of something hot Johanna had learned to brew, and plates of some exotic fruit Nya had found, sequenced, and declared likely not to kill them. It was forever a running joke between the two, whether Johanna's piloting or Nya's botany would doom them first.

Full-time friends and occasional lovers, and Nya missed it all. The physical connection, Johanna's quick wit, her sense of the absurd, her utter fearlessness in moments of truth.

Now she found herself surrounded by these Carpathians. She wondered about them, out there in deep space for so long, so physically miserable. It had only been a month and she was already sick of the food, the gravity, and her tiny cabin. The uncomfortably narrow corridors, forever feeling stuck inside, while the Carpathians, their senses deprived, seemed to retreat more and more into virtual realities when they weren't on duty. Such things held no fascination for her. She hadn't been raised with them, couldn't understand the appeal.

She tried to imagine having a relationship out there but couldn't see how it could ever work.

The crew were still human, though. They must have needs. She had almost asked the Interlocutor about it. *Does the crew ever date? Or at least have sex, if for no better reason than to pass the time?*

In the end, she'd been too embarrassed to bring it up.

This life couldn't be good for anyone. Wondering, jump after jump, what acceleration profile the captain would require, how much gravity they would have to endure. And all the while, the slow, creeping claustrophobia, the walls that felt a little closer every day.

They're all mad, she thought. *Every single one of them—they must be.*

As much as she missed Johanna, a part of her was glad she was being spared this. She would've hated it.

Then again, at least she'd be safe.

That was the other thought she could never quite shake. The InterTech Security team that had been hunting Kester would find their campsite and determine in an instant a TransGalactic research team had been there. They would never have guessed why, wouldn't have known what to make of her fishing nets, the rest of the gear she'd left behind. But that was beside the point. What they would do next was obvious. They would activate a security operative on the TransGalactic University campus and begin asking questions. Every company maintained its agents, students in deep cover, embedded moles angling for any bits of information about competitive research activities they could glean.

Her and Johanna's flight to that lake had been off the record. Technically, no one knew where they were. But it wouldn't take long to determine who the only academic was who might have been interested in the site.

And then what? She and Kester were long gone, light-years from Paradise itself, well beyond InterTech's reach.

But they would find Johanna.

The two of them had argued about it in the brief time before she left. The good news was that while corporate espionage was commonplace, on Paradise physical violence was comparatively rare. It was a by-product of near-ubiquitous surveillance. Paradise was Earth's oldest colony, well established as an information-dense society. It had a data grid that rivaled Earth's. Neighborhoods, cities, universities—for as much as the vast majority of the planet's surface was wilderness, their world was bound together in a shared information architecture. And university employees were expected to keep their whereabouts known.

In the end, Johanna had agreed she would set her status tracking to the highest level of reporting. TransGalactic University would know where she was at all times. That would keep her safer than anything else they could imagine.

Johanna hadn't been thrilled by the idea. But there wasn't a third seat on the high-speed shuttle that had brought Nya and Kester to *Carpathia*—and in any case, Johanna would never have come.

Which left Nya worried and guilty. She wondered if she would ever get to make this up to Johanna somehow or at least tell her the story one day.

Maybe, she thought. *Or maybe I'll never set foot on Paradise again.*

The cabin's screen warbled at her. It was time. Finally, she would have her opportunity to hear about Ragnarock and the artifact directly, from the one person who was there.

The summons directed her to the same briefing room she had seen her first day on the ship. As before, she found herself captivated by those strange paintings on the walls, a maritime disaster in one, and in the other, *Carpathia*—this ship—approaching a primitive monster of a vessel, an enormous, bulbous, onion-shaped thing.

Captain McAllister and another man waited for her.

"Dr. Nya Solarin, meet Mr. Piotre Raskovich," the captain said, by way of introduction.

Good gods, she thought. If the Carpathians were an unhealthy lot, this man Piotre was a walking corpse. He looked like he could barely stand, but he found his feet somehow and gripped her hand delicately. It felt like his muscles were made of water, like she was being caressed by a sessile squid, one of the weird, inter-tidal creatures she had studied early in her career that lived in the shallows of Paradise's inland tropical seas.

And his eyes—those could have belonged to some creature from the deep as well. They were jet black, liquid obsidian pools, little more than holes in his head.

She fought back a shudder as she returned his handshake.

"Hi-how-are-you?" she said automatically, wincing at her inanity.

"How am I?" Piotre Raskovich twisted his mouth in an attempt at a smile, his lips moving as though they weren't accustomed to the shape. "That's the kind of question I would expect from your Interlocutor."

She released his hand and took a step back.

"Would you?" She attempted a smile of her own. "I get the impression she doesn't usually need to ask."

Piotre's smile disappeared. "That is true," he said. "To answer your question, Doctor, I am fine. Better now that I am awake. I have no desire to dream through another jump event. And speaking of your Interlocutor—here she is now."

"I apologize for being late," the Interlocutor said. She made a self-deprecating gesture. "I find it difficult to move quickly in all this gravity."

Nya had been thinking the opposite, watching her glide through the door. Thinking she moved like she was completely unaffected by it, like she was born out there.

Captain McAllister cleared his throat. "Please, all of you—be comfortable. We have much to discuss. Mr. Raskovich has agreed to tell his story again." He gave the man a curt nod. "It won't be the first time he has shared this narration, and I appreciate his indulging in repetition. I believe it will be useful for the doctor to hear."

"Of course, Captain." Piotre Raskovich sat heavily. Nya followed suit. The Interlocutor, she noticed, continued to stand, finding a corner beneath the paintings where she seemed to disappear under her hood.

She was like a chameleon, Nya thought. The Interlocutor would have made a fantastic jungle predator.

"How are your memories these days, Mr. Raskovich?" the captain asked. He sounded solicitous, like he was handling something dangerous—or maybe a child.

Or both.

"Filled with gaps, Captain, as usual. I recall the find with great clarity, but mundane matters, including the tactical situation at Ragnarock and the defenses we may have left behind—most of our voyage from back to Earth—have vanished from my mind."

"Understood. Well, for Dr. Solarin's benefit, please—tell us what you can."

"As you wish."

Nya listened as the former CIO laid it out. It was much as the captain had described. The artifact, the find, and also Piotre's Conditioning, the nightmarish control mechanism to which he had been subjected since his youth. A tropical, old-Earth centipede for a metaphorical companion?

Hell of a spirit guide, she thought.

Then he described the failure of that Conditioning, the one thing his corporate masters couldn't prepare him for. The completely unexpected. She wondered what sort of changes were already being envisioned somewhere in the Magellanix Human Resources department, by whatever scientists were in charge of such things.

She decided she was glad she didn't know.

Raskovich spoke for over an hour, the captain interjecting occasionally with this or that point of clarification but by and large letting the man tell his story as he saw fit. Nya remained silent the whole time, trying to take it all in, to understand.

In truth, Captain McAllister had already relayed the details to her accurately enough. What more did he hope she would learn by going straight to the source? Something he had missed?

Or did he have some other purpose in mind?

When at last the former CIO was finished, he was visibly tired. The captain dismissed him. Piotre looked happy enough to depart, moving across the floor in a lurching, halting gait, his body with little left to give.

The door sealed shut behind him. Silence filled the room, broken at last by the captain's quiet voice.

"What do you think, Doctor?"

She considered. "The story is as you related it, Captain. His memories of the find are highly detailed. Though there is a glaring omission."

Out of the corner of her eye, she saw the Interlocutor incline her head in silent agreement.

"What specifically?" the captain asked.

She took a breath. "He couldn't have made that climb by himself."

"What makes you say that?"

"His physical condition. He can barely walk. Ragnarock is a high-gravity world. And climbing mountains, I can tell you from personal experience, is still a matter of heart, legs, and lungs."

"Do you have a hypothesis?"

"Someone must have helped him."

"There was a contractor," the Interlocutor said, speaking for the first time.

"There was," Captain McAllister agreed. "His name was Feyis Sado. Piotre Raskovich enlisted his aid, though I doubt he told him why."

"What happened?" Nya asked.

"Raskovich left him for dead in a crevasse on their way down."

"So, he's a murderer as well as a traitor?"

"Yes," the captain said mildly.

"Why didn't you tell me before?"

"It wasn't relevant at the time, Doctor."

Nya thought for a moment, feeling abruptly out of her depth. What game were they playing at? How could murder on a mountainside not be relevant?

The Interlocutor shifted toward her, giving a glimpse of her face, half-concealed under her hood. "The captain is correct. But tell me, Nya—what else struck you about his tale?"

Nya shook her head at the abrupt change of subject. She considered. There had been something else—an assumption out of place. "It hadn't occurred to me until just now," she said slowly. "But we have been presuming something that may not be true."

"Explain," the Interlocutor said.

"Well . . . Piotre Raskovich assumes that whoever built that thing possesses technology far beyond our own."

"Correct."

"But why?"

"Because it's probably been there at least a million years," the captain said.

"True," Nya agreed. "Let's take it as given that it is tremendously old. Still—what do we really know about the technology involved? All we know for sure is there is a great big silvery multifaceted spherical object parked in a volcanic crater. Couldn't TransGalactic build something like that?"

Ian opened his mouth to respond, hesitated, then said, "I doubt that anyone has ever thought about it."

"Exactly, Captain! But suppose you had. How would you go about it?"

He rested his chin in his long fingers, as though stroking a beard that wasn't there. "Weavers," he said finally. "Weavers to build weavers. We would set up a regenerating system, where every physical component would cycle out and replace itself as it aged. And use woven composites that would last a very long time."

"What about power? What would you use for an energy source?"

The captain shrugged. "Probably solar. Maybe geothermal, at least while that volcano was still reasonably active. Not fusion. Building a reactor capable of repairing itself for millions of years without direct oversight would be beyond us. But the kind of limited AI you'd need to oversee the continual reconstruction of a geothermal engine or a solar array—that could possibly be done."

"So, it's conceivable?"

"Conceivable, yes."

"But no one has ever invested deeply in the technical problems involved," she said.

"Not to my knowledge."

She smiled and discovered she was enjoying this. "And why not?"

"It's as you've already said, Doctor. What good are time scales like that to us? What problem do they solve?"

"Right. Not quarterly shareholder statements, that's for sure," she said, with just a touch of bitterness, thinking of all her funding debacles throughout her career. She shook her head, putting the thought aside. "All I'm saying is we shouldn't just assume they're radically advanced technologically. Maybe they are—but maybe not. But in other ways, in the time scales of their planning, they may have exceeded us tremendously."

"If true, what would that mean, Doctor?" the Interlocutor asked.

Nya laughed. "I have no idea! Just that we should be careful to differentiate between that which we cannot comprehend intellectually and that which we cannot relate to philosophically."

"That," the captain said after another moment's thought, "is a very abstract concept, Doctor."

"Well maybe that's why your Board decided to include an academic, Captain," she said.

From her corner, the Interlocutor smiled quietly in approval.

Kester was waiting for Nya back in her cabin. She hadn't seen the girl in days. She had no idea where she'd disappeared to and hadn't wanted to intrude, content to leave her to her own devices.

"What did you think of Piotre?" the young woman asked, as soon as she had set foot inside.

Nya blinked, startled. "How did you know?"

"He told me."

"I didn't know you'd met."

"I've been working with him. He's nice, in his way."

"I'm not sure that's the word I'd use. He's a murderer, Kester."

"So am I. Though that's not the word you'd use in my case, either. But I shouldn't say *nice*. That's not exactly it. I think he's badly broken. They hypnotized him into believing there was a centipede living inside his brain telling him what to do. And then he fell in love with it."

"Fell in love with it?" Nya said, not sure she'd heard correctly.

"Sounds weird, right? But I'm not sure it's any stranger than what I was raised to believe. Anyway, he gave me an interesting problem to solve."

"Oh?"

"Yeah. I think this is what Dr. Herecic intended for me all along. The questions he used to ask, the exercises he had me do. It's too much to be coincidence."

"What exactly are you working on, Kester?"

"Route-finding," the girl said calmly, as though it were the most natural thing in the world. "Interstellar navigation. Piotre stole all of Magellanix's data about the region of space where we're headed. I think the captain's worried there's another ship out there that's going to try to kill us. Piotre's old ship, maybe. Anyway, Piotre asked me if there was another solution."

"Another solution?" Nya repeated.

"Yeah. A different route. Same data, new answer."

She stared at the girl, mind racing, trying to keep up. "Is there?"

"Almost certainly," Kester said. "Probably more than one. Maybe a lot more." She gave her a serious look, all laughter gone. "I'm telling you, I think this is what they made me for, Nya. Why they did this to me."

Nya thought about that for a time. "I suppose it makes sense," she said. "And if so, it's terrible."

"Yeah. Then again, it might keep us alive. It already saved my life once, you know. But not Per's."

Nya crossed the room and found a seat on her bunk, close to Kester but not quite touching her. "You know you don't have to do it if you don't want to."

Kester stared at her, that old uncanny look, which Nya knew meant she was memorizing everything she saw. "That's nice to say," the young woman said. "But you'll think differently when the time comes. If there's another ship out there, they'll ask you to make me help if I say no. And you will, too."

Then she did something strange. She held out a finger to Nya's lips. It was a curious gesture, the first time Kester had made physical contact with her of any kind that she could remember.

"Shh," Kester said. "You don't need to worry. I'll help. If it comes down to it, I'll want to live too."

CHAPTER 39

Eight jumps and three months out of Paradise, Ian got the bad news.

They'd long since left shared space behind. They were in Magellanix territory now, navigating from the data Piotre Raskovich had stolen, going where no TransGalactic ship had ever been. From there, the path they were heading "down" led to Ragnarock and nowhere else.

By definition, any other vessel out there was an enemy. A very specific enemy—because if there were a ship ahead of them, it would mean their side trip to Paradise had cost them dearly. That they were losing their race.

And then, without warning, there it was.

"Signature event, Captain," his remote sensing officer reported.

"Goddammit," Ian said. He had chosen to stand watch on the bridge that particular rotation, hoping to reassure the crew with his presence. The young woman who had just delivered the update glanced over her shoulder, looking at him in dismay.

He winced, shamed at the break in protocol. A captain was supposed to be stoic.

"Very well," he added quickly. "Run the numbers. Will they have detected us before they jumped away?"

"Calculating," the woman said. She called up a tactical display, causing a holographic projection to hover over her console in reds and blues, rendered large enough for him to see.

It was possible they'd gotten lucky. Emission signatures traveled at the speed of light, while ships moving between jump points traveled at fractions of that. Still, it was conceivable for the timing to work out just right, such that a ship jumping into an area would detect the back-propagating signature of a second ship jumping away, but the departing ship would be gone before the arriving ship's transition signature reached it. Elementary geometry, played out over hundreds of millions of kilometers at relativistic velocities.

"Sorry, sir," the officer said. "Our arrival jump was in their detection window. Unless they weren't looking, of course," she added hopefully.

If only it were true. But he could think of no reason why anyone else out there wouldn't be doing exactly what they were doing: using every resource at their disposal, every sensor array, radio telescope, and onboard AI to scan the skies for enemies.

"Very well," he said. "That'll be all."

"Aye, sir."

Which left him standing there, wondering how long to wait before he could leave the bridge with his dignity intact. Feeling as always the uncomfortable scrutiny of his crew, hard at work at their tasks, studiously ignoring him but no doubt aware of every nuance of his movement.

He gave it a few minutes, then decided he had delayed long enough. He left the bridge as quietly as he could, all too aware of the sets of eyes even younger than his watching him go.

He retreated to his briefing room and summoned what he had come to think of as his council of war. Captain Marakan's staff had been senior officers, shaped and molded by a TransGalactic corporate academy that had spent centuries perfecting its craft. Whereas he had a band of misfits at his disposal. A Human Resources officer, a theoretical xeno-evolutionary biologist, a madman who had once been an enemy intelligence officer, and, today, the daughter of a machine-god cult as well.

Nya Solarin arrived first, her body language suggesting she was hating every step. Given the choice, he doubted she'd ever set foot on a starship again.

The Interlocutor followed shortly after. She no longer moved with the same fluid indifference she had once shown in the heavy gravity, though in her case, he suspected the real toll was on her mind. The strange effects of the jumps on her psyche had continued, something about the hyperdimensional displacement of traveling between the stars interacting badly with all her buried memories. She wasn't quite so inscrutable as she once had been. No one as old as she was, who had been asked to hold so much, should be subject to such uninvited recall.

She too would probably never take to the stars again, he thought. Not if given the choice.

Piotre Raskovich arrived third. He appeared physically weak as ever, but something in his countenance suggested an uptick in his mood. Maybe he'd never expected to make it this far. Or maybe it was just that he'd been given something to do. According to the Interlocutor, he was enjoying teaching

Kester the mathematics of higher-dimensional travel, showing her how to use her strange abilities to find new solutions to old problems.

Kester arrived last. She stepped into the room, took one look at the tactical display he had rendered in midair—the same one his remote-sensing officer had just shown him—and said, "Well, we're fucked."

"Have a seat," Ian said quietly.

The four of them did. He sighed and settled heavily into an acceleration chair of his own.

"The tactical situation is as you see it," he said, indicating *Carpathia*'s position and velocity, the jump point they'd arrived at, the one they were headed for, and the propagation rates of their emission signature. "Kester has given us her opinion. I would hear from the rest of you as well."

Piotre Raskovich was the first to speak. "That has to be *Accipiter*," he said, indicating the telltale signature of the ship that had just jumped away.

"One would assume."

"With Captain Johnston in command."

"You would know better than I, Mr. Raskovich, what sort of rotation schedule Magellanix uses with its senior officers."

Piotre made as if to respond, but the words didn't come out. Some residual bit of Behavioral Conditioning perhaps preventing him from relating that particular detail? His mind, too, was so badly broken by what he had experienced.

"Hypothetically?" the Interlocutor suggested.

"Hypothetically," the former CIO repeated gratefully. "Commander Anne Johnston is no fool. She will have heard our arrival into this region of space, and yet she still jumped away, thus betraying her own position. She could have decelerated and ambushed us at the jump point. But she didn't."

"It would seem not," Ian agreed. "The question is: why?"

"Hypothetically, again, Captain?"

"Of course."

"Perhaps she's in a hurry. It may be that my betrayal has been discovered and that she cannot afford to wait here, because for all she knows, she is herself running a race and losing."

Ian cocked his head in surprise. It was obvious, but he hadn't thought of it. "You're saying that, as far as she knows, we might not be the only ship TransGalactic has sent."

"Correct, Captain. We might ourselves be reinforcements. She may be forced to assume she is behind some third ship."

"So, instead of wasting time to take us unaware, she what? Leaves remotes at the jump point? Or mines the far side, deploys weapon pods to ambush us when we arrive?"

"All of those things are possible, Captain," Piotre said. "Any of them might prove fatal to us. Perhaps she'll race all the way to Ragnarock, conserve whatever weaponry she has onboard, and engage us there when she finds she's first to arrive. She'll have the advantage of time and a planetary system to hide in. She could conceal herself behind one of Ragnarock's moons. Deploy remotes all along our route. Anything she likes."

"Thank you, Mr. Raskovich," Ian said, raising a hand. The former CIO fell silent. Ian looked around the room. "Does anyone else have any comment?"

After a moment, Nya Solarin cleared her throat and said, "I'm not a tactician, Captain."

"Speak your mind, Doctor."

"Well—what choice is there? We can't turn around, can we?"

"In fact, we could," he said. "It is within my purview to declare the situation tactically hopeless and retreat."

"But you won't."

"I'm unlikely to," he agreed. "Interlocutor? Do you have a thought?"

The Interlocutor shook her head and remained silent, those monk eyes boring through him as they had done so many times before. Seeming to say *It's your decision, Captain. Get on with it already.*

"Kester?" he asked.

"I think we'd better go a different way," the girl said.

"I'm sorry?"

"Piotre's original solutions were— Well." She had a faraway look in her eyes. "I'm sure everyone did the best they could. But there are alternatives."

"So, you've found something."

"Yes."

"Mr. Raskovich?"

The man gave a mirthless laugh. "What can I say, Captain? Her mathematics are strange." He made a deprecatory gesture. "Forgive me, Kester. Your mind does things mine cannot. It is difficult to comprehend your solutions. Ordinarily, we would model things in terms of five-dimensional manifolds, that is, three-dimensional space twisted on itself in a fourth dimension, and then twisted again through a fifth. But you are able to work in much higher dimensions. For you, it's like . . ." He trailed off, as though struggling to explain.

"It's like this, Captain," Kester said. "Imagine a hallway. One of *Carpathia*'s corridors, with a hatch at one end and another at the opposite."

"Go on," Ian said.

"We're at one end and *Accipiter* was at the other, and they just now walked through the far door. And beyond that, there's another hallway, and another door, and so on. The doors being the jump points, and the hallways being what we pass through in regular space."

"I'm with you, Kester. What's your point?"

She laughed. "My point is we should go through the wall."

He gave her a long look. "And what would we find on the other side of the wall, in this analogy?"

"Ragnarock."

"Explain."

"We should start turning now." She smiled slightly. "The current solution is still approximate, Captain, but I have enough to at least inform an initial course deflection."

"How much more time do you need?"

"Not long. Maybe another day or two."

The young woman's words hung in the air. Could he really consider such a thing? Attempt a jump using untested mathematics, invented on the fly by a beta tester from a rival company?

What, he wondered, would Captain Marakan have done?

She would have preserved option value, that's what: kept all her possibilities alive while deferring the decision. "Very well," he said. "Give me an initial minimal course-deflection estimate and then get back to work. Mr. Raskovich will assist you as best he is able."

"Aye, aye, sir." She gave him a mock salute, turned, and left the briefing room. Piotre Raskovich offered him a curt nod of his own and followed after.

Their small module fell quiet again. "Will you make this bet, Captain?" Nya asked him at last.

"You understand the tactical situation, Doctor. We are found out. *Accipiter*, speaking frankly, can choose how to destroy us now that she knows we're here. You know Kester as well as anyone. Do you believe her? Can she do what she says?"

The doctor was silent for a long moment before answering. "I don't know, Captain. She's different. It's like she knew this was coming. I wouldn't doubt her abilities. She's enhanced, modified, broken down, and rebuilt—

I don't have the words for it. But from the moment I met her when she came running out of the jungle, it was obvious her capabilities were far beyond our own."

He nodded. "Interlocutor?"

"I concur with the doctor, Captain," the ancient woman said. "InterTech appears to have succeeded in creating a mind capable of solving old problems in new ways. Setting aside the damage they've done in the process, it's a remarkable achievement."

"Very well," he said. "We will begin the course deflection Kester recommended while she finalizes her solution. If the girl thinks it's viable, we may very well attempt this sideways jump of hers. If not, we will revert to our original course. And fight it out as best we can."

"And in the meantime?" Nya asked.

He sighed heavily. "We do what starship crews do best. We wait."

It took Kester another eighteen hours to finish her work. Ian was in his cabin when he got the word. He had taken the unusual step of ingesting soporifics, forcing his body into badly needed sleep—but he'd left instructions with his bridge crew to wake him as soon as Kester was ready.

Now it was decision time. Kester had resolved the exact location of their new jump point and declared it stable enough for their purposes. It would work—or so she said.

He activated a device implanted under the skin of his left wrist, causing it to diffuse yet more pharmaceuticals into his bloodstream. Drugs to counter drugs. His mind came awake first, but his body momentarily refused to respond, creating a momentary panic: that old claustrophobic feeling, part of why he hated doing things this way.

When he felt ready, he vocalized another command, causing a holographic projection of Kester to appear floating in the center of his room.

If she noticed his discomfort or thought it odd that he was lying partially immobile in bed, she didn't comment.

"It's doable, Captain," was all she said.

He grunted. Piotre Raskovich stepped into the frame alongside her. Behind them, he saw nothing but stars. The two were working in the forward observatory again. They had taken to frequenting the place, which called to mind the reason for the room's construction, the story he had yet to tell.

He shook his head, trying to focus.

"The girl's right, Captain," Piotre was saying. "We'll have to accelerate the deflection and pull three gees, but we can reach her transition point. It should take us directly to Ragnarock."

Piotre's image loomed large as he leaned in and fiddled with a set of controls, and then he and Kester were replaced by a tactical display showing *Carpathia*'s current position and velocity, along with the new jump point, and the course change that would be required to reach it.

They were, Ian saw, practically on top of it.

"Can that be right?" he said, voice raspy in his own ears, trying to make sense of it all.

Kester evidently misunderstood. "I'm sorry, Captain—did you want something closer? There might be another answer. I thought this was good enough."

"It's close enough," he assured her. "Far closer than I would have thought. Mr. Raskovich?" he asked, still struggling to believe what he was seeing.

How could there be another jump point so near? What were the odds?

"It is as the girl says, Captain. Her way of solving the simultaneous equations involved." He waved his arm weakly in the air, making a dismissive gesture. "No, no—do not worry. I won't bore you. I don't understand myself. But clearly, there is a density of solutions we have never before anticipated."

"Just how dense are we talking here?"

"This new solution space may change everything, Captain. Much of what we thought we understood about interstellar navigation may have just been rendered obsolete. If that is, jump points identified this way are stable enough to use."

"Meaning *if we survive*."

Piotre shrugged. "Yes."

"Your opinion?"

The former CIO shrugged again. "Who knows? This was all a gamble from the beginning, was it not?"

It was for you, Ian thought, and at that moment, he wanted to ask him why. Why do it? Even if he somehow pulled it off, why put himself through this? What possible prize could be worth it?

Because his mind didn't know how to do anything else. That was what the Interlocutor had said. Piotre's brain was a machine programmed to monetize information. All this, the theft, defection, murder, betrayal, the insane errand he had set them on, was a sort of default action taken by a mind operating without guardrails, trying to interpret a lifetime's training the only way it knew how.

Ian shook his head again. His body was fully awake now. He climbed slowly from his bunk. Kester and Piotre were watching him, clearly waiting for a decision.

He found himself wanting to solicit a final opinion. To ask again, seek a more formal consensus. He wanted Captain Marakan to tell him what to do.

Quit stalling, he thought. *And decide.*

"Very well," he said. "Kester, pass your coordinates to Navigation. We'll begin the course deflection immediately. The two of you will please join me in the briefing room. It seems that we have a few more hours to kill, and we're all going to be a little uncomfortable. I owe the doctor a story about Carpathia's origin. As this may be her end, this seems as good a time as any to tell it."

CHAPTER 40

In response to his summons, Ian's strange council of war gathered again. This time, there was nothing to do but settle into their acceleration couches, endure the heavy gravity, and wait.

"You all understand what we're about to attempt," he said when they were as comfortable as they could be. "We'll follow Kester's mathematics. Her solution should jump us around *Accipiter* and take us directly to Ragnarock. The system is defended. Piotre tells us that Captain Johnston left weapons remotes behind. He also now tells us he has memorized the authentication codes that will disarm them."

Ian paused, looking first to Piotre Raskovich and then the Interlocutor. How she had managed to pull those memories from him, he had no idea, but he was grateful. If true, it gave them a much better chance at survival.

Piotre nodded acknowledgement. "Yes, Captain," the former CIO said. "My memories may be incomplete, but I am clear on this point."

"Very well. So: we will attempt to pass *Carpathia* off as a Magellanix vessel when we reach our destination. The remotes deployed there should take us for *Accipiter* and let us through. There are risks involved; that goes without saying."

He saw Nya nod thoughtfully. Kester looked indifferent; the Interlocutor was equally impassive.

"For the moment," he went on, "there is little more to do. But I've promised Dr. Solarin a tale about the origin of this ship, and the strange paintings on our walls. I think I'll tell it now, in the event that we have no further opportunity."

He wondered why he was doing this. Truth was, he'd never told the story to anyone. Maybe it was just that if he were to die out there, flicker into nonexistence in a fit of abstract mathematics gone awry, he didn't want to carry it with him.

To whatever lay ahead.

"I'd like to hear it," Nya said.

"As would I," the Interlocutor added.

He took a deep breath. "Very well," he said. "The first thing you should know is that *Carpathia* was conceived as a marketing stunt. This ship was designed and built in pursuit of what was supposed to be the greatest public-relations coup of all time.

"The steamship you see in the first painting is our namesake. The reference is obscure. The original *Carpathia* was a nineteenth-century vessel that briefly became famous for rescuing the survivors of what was then the greatest maritime disaster in history: the sinking of a passenger vessel called the *Titanic*." He made a quick circle with his left hand, a spacer's tic, warding off the bad luck of naming a dead ship aloud. He hoped the Interlocutor hadn't noticed. Though doubtless she had.

"Like the *Titanic*, that *Carpathia* also came to a bad end," he went on. "I hesitate to mention it. The crew of this ship never would. We TransGalactic spacers are a superstitious lot."

He looked in Piotre's direction. "Magellanix may have solved this problem," he added.

"In fact, we have not, Captain," the former CIO said. "Magellanix crews suffer from similar inefficiencies."

"Well, there you go. In any event, *Carpathia* the steamship was sunk by a submarine in a war that broke out a few years later. Our Marketing department went with the name anyway."

He paused again, contemplating the artwork on the wall as he had so many times before. "This ship," he said, "the *Carpathia* we call home, made her maiden voyage just fifteen years ago. We were under Captain Marakan's command, and it was my first trip into deep space. I was the most junior officer onboard, assigned to the navigation department. I was happy to leave Earth. The TransGalactic Officer Training Academy was, to put it mildly, stressful."

He shook his head at the memory. Those had been dark days. He'd almost quit. Fully half of the candidates washed out, returning to their homes to lead anonymous lives, never spoken of in the fleet again.

"Like the original *Carpathia*," he went on, "our mission was to rescue a ship. In our case, a colony ship two centuries old. You see it there, depicted in the second painting." He glanced over at Kester, who was staring transfixed, no doubt memorizing every detail. "Unlike your people's, Kester," he said, "the colony ship you see here was built before the mathematics of higher-dimensional travel were invented. It was a sub-light-speed vessel, a multigenerational seed ship that had been launched a hundred years before any of us were born."

"I know its name," Kester said. She brought her hands to her mouth, talking through her fingers as if trying not to let the words escape. "The *Santa Maria*. We were told stories about it. They were heretics. At least, that's what the Prophet said."

Ian nodded. "I can see why you would've thought so, given your Singlist upbringing. Certainly, they were highly committed to their particular belief system."

"aSingularism," Kester said.

"Yes," Ian agreed. "They were anti-Singularists. Highly devout ones. I'm not a student of such things, but we were given background material for the mission, so I can tell you something about their beliefs. Foremost of which was there had been and would be no Singularity. We humans had failed at inventing our own god and would never create a machine intelligence to guide us.

"They also believed we would forever fail to achieve immortality. Then as now, no one had found a way to upload consciousness and live forever in some distributed computational system. The difference," he continued, "was back then, that fact was a profound disappointment. Vast resources were still being spent on the effort. The aSingularists believed, perhaps rightly, that any such attempt was futile.

"And finally, they thought—incorrectly, as it turned out—that the stars could never be reached in a single lifetime. Jump points and interstellar travel had yet to be discovered, and of course, when they were, they were the most unexpected technological advancement of all time. When *Santa Maria* was conceived and built, humans had the technology to construct colony ships, but they could only travel at sub-light speeds. Nor had cryogenics yet been made viable. Do you see? Any journey to another world would take generations, and anyone attempting such a trip would have to be awake the entire time. Even if they trusted their automated systems to run the ship for them, the years couldn't just be slept away."

He paused again, looking around the room. He felt abruptly foolish. What did he think he would accomplish, lecturing this cast of characters this way?

"So, why did they do it?" he asked rhetorically.

Dr. Solarin surprised him by responding. "The Earth was dying," she said. "This was about two centuries ago, correct?"

"Yes."

She gave him a sober look. "That was before the recovery began," she said. "A time when wholesale ecosystem collapse was still the norm. Global carbon dioxide was too high, oceanic pH slow to recover. The race was on to reinvent agriculture and reforest the world. The atmospheric drawdown had begun centuries before, but . . ." She trailed off, shaking her head. "People generally do not appreciate how close we came, Captain, nor how much was lost. Acidification. Desertification. Ninety-nine percent of all species on Earth were gone forever. Most of what remained was only in the form of sequenced DNA, stored against some future date when their reconstruction might be possible. And, of course," she concluded with a sort of helpless shrug, "billions had died. There was plague, famine, and war on continental scales. All the sins of the past, the debts accrued, paid back in full."

"Yes," he agreed. "The mission planners spelled it out in us for some detail. So, that was the backdrop: the world against which *Santa Maria* was conceived. And perhaps it explains why a twelve-generation trip, which today sounds absurd, was something they were willing to contemplate.

"But more importantly, it was a matter of faith. That crew knew their children, grandchildren, and great-grandchildren after that would be born only to die in service of their mission. Their descendants would never be given a choice, just expected to endure, to live their entire lives on a journey which for them would have no end."

He paused, again surveying the room. The Interlocutor looked thoughtful, like she was considering something that had never occurred to her before.

Or maybe remembering something else she had forgotten.

"So, you see," Ian went on, "those that built *Santa Maria* believed humanity had to atone for its sins. They called themselves aSingularists for a reason. They sought to define themselves in opposition to those who had pursued a machine intelligence, virtual realities, even immortality—all of which they considered mortal sins. They believed that Earth was the price humanity would have to pay and that the suffering of a multi-generational trek through space was an act of contrition. The completion of which would be proof that humanity required no gods, invented or otherwise, to secure its future."

He was about to go on when Piotre Raskovich spoke for the first time. "Where'd they get the money?" he said.

Ian almost laughed; trust the former CIO to ask that particular question. "It was old money," he said. "Very old. American and European money, left over from aristocracies that dated back at least a millennium."

"So, they were already rich."

"Yes."

"They were hypocrites," Kester put in. "Blaming others for wasting their resources on a fool's dream. Then using their own on the same."

"I don't know if we can judge," Ian said. "It was a different time."

"Oh, I can," Kester said, eyes flashing in his direction. "I can definitely judge."

He held up his hands. "Be that as it may, the aSingularists' ethical framework wasn't as much of a concern to our Marketing department as the route the *Santa Maria* had taken. I don't know who figured it out, but someone ran the numbers and determined that the *Santa Maria* might be passing close enough to a newly discovered jump point for an intercept to be possible. Do you see? She was still out there somewhere, and we were going to bring her home. And when we did, Corporate believed the brand value that would accrue to TransGalactic would be incalculable.

"Like I said, it was a marketing stunt from the beginning. Even if it sounded straightforward enough." He let out a heavy sigh, remembering. "Except for one thing: no one had heard from that ship in almost two hundred years. Their leader made an unexpected decision shortly after they launched: he cut off all contact with Earth."

"Why?" Nya asked.

"To stabilize his crew's environment," the Interlocutor said.

Ian blinked, looking at her in surprise. "Interlocutor?"

"I know the story, Captain. I had forgotten, but it has come back to me. One of the many gifts of this trip. The strange way in which my mind seems to interact with these jump events of yours." She smiled a mirthless smile. "Wouldn't that be interesting, if everyone responded thus? If all this flitting around between the stars came at the cost of confronting one's own past? In any event, he was a reverend, Captain," she continued. "That's what his people called him. Did you know that? I imagine he was a charismatic man. But as much as he might have held his people in thrall, the prospect of their having contact with an outside world they would never rejoin must have terrified him. So, he turned off his communication systems to keep his crew focused on the task ahead."

"Like a modern-day Cortez?" Nya Solarin asked. "Just another colonist burning his ships on the beach to motivate his men?"

Ian bowed his head and sighed heavily. "You're both right. Though certainly, no one in our Marketing department would have described him thusly." He shrugged. "Bad for the brand, they would've said. In any case, I was focused on the technical problem, which was that we didn't know where the *Santa Maria* was.

"She'd been out there almost two hundred years. Our calculations suggested she should have reached about two percent the speed of light, chugging along on an ion drive that was a modern marvel at the time but would be a hopeless antique today. No one knew exactly what acceleration profiles her engines could sustain. And, most importantly, she would have made minor course corrections along the way, as her crew gathered better and better data on the system to which they were headed.

"Or, to put it in Marketing-speak, it was as if someone fired a needle at relativistic velocities through an infinitely large haystack, and it was our job to go find it and bring it home." He stopped, grimacing. "Their words," he said apologetically. "Not mine."

He raised a hand in silent salute to the pictures on the wall and pressed on.

"*Carpathia* launched to no fanfare at all. We were what was known as a high beta endeavor. High risk, high reward. Our mission planners were realistic enough to know we would probably fail. After so much time, the search volume was enormous.

"Our jump would bring us close to *Santa Maria*'s most likely location, matching our best guess of her velocity. Then we would begin looking for her with telescopes and transmitters, EM scanning pods, and all the other instrumentation with which *Carpathia* was equipped."

He looked at each of his audience members in turn. "Imagine our surprise," he said, "when we didn't have to search hardly at all. We found *Santa Maria* exactly where she was most likely to be, in the dead center of our estimates. It was as if since her original launch, she hadn't altered her course a single iota, like she'd been set on autopilot and left to her own devices, with no human intervention at all.

"We'd done it. We'd found her, exceeding our best-case scenarios. But once the celebration ended, the crew began to whisper, wondering how such a thing was possible. Some thought we'd gotten lucky. Others that this was itself a form of divine intervention. Then as now, many faiths were represented among the crew of the *Carpathia*. Some believed our finding *Santa Maria* so easily was the work of some patron machine intelligence, its invisible hand guiding us in an act of beneficence. Forgiveness of the *Santa Maria*ns, an absolution of their heresy.

"I am not a religious man. I was cynical: I believed Marketing had more data than they let on. That the mission would never have been funded without someone, somewhere, knowing more than we were told. I'm fairly certain Captain Marakan shared this line of thinking, though she never said as much."

He flicked a glance at the Interlocutor, but she seemed lost in thought and didn't meet his eye.

"In any event," he went on, "we were all wrong. No one had altered the *Santa Maria*'s course, updated her acceleration profile, or made any change to her planned route for the simple reason that no one had been alive on that ship for almost the entirety of her flight."

He paused again, looking around the room. "Of course, we didn't know it at the time," he said. "Docking with that ship was the strangest experience of my career. *Carpathia* is not a small ship; *Santa Maria* was even larger. We were dwarfed by it, this gargantuan obsolescence, this self-contained world they had built to keep a population of a hundred people alive and reproducing for generations in space.

"In its way, ours was a first-contact mission. The situation was surreal. All of the original crew would of course be long dead by then. We were there to undo their legacy, to tell an entire generation of crew that the purpose to which they had been born was null and void. Looking back, I suppose the ethics of it were debatable, whether we had any right to do such a thing at all." He shrugged. "Saving the children from the sins of the parents and all. But as it turned out, it didn't matter.

"Our first set of messages were carefully constructed lies. *Carpathia*, we told them, was a second seed ship, launched after theirs and equipped with better engines. Faster but still multi-generational, with orders to share our tech and upgrade their ship. We told them we were there to shave years off their voyage. The idea was to proceed by degrees and ease them into their new reality. I would be curious, Interlocutor, your opinion of our approach."

The ancient woman did something surprising: she removed her hood and smiled. "Then as now, Captain," she said, "I approved."

He cocked his head. "I'm sorry?"

She smiled. "I wrote those messages, Captain. I would've told you earlier, but I had forgotten."

"You were consulted on the project," he said in disbelief.

She smiled again and arched an eyebrow as if to say *Of course I was.*

"Then you must know that no one answered."

"Yes," she said.

"You never cease to amaze, Interlocutor. In any case: their ship had reached the halfway point of its mission some years before, and an automated system had flipped it on its axis, just as we do, to begin the long deceleration burn.

"Day after day ticked by without any response to our calls. Finally, Captain Marakan gave the order to board.

"I was on the first mission team, along with a dozen contractor specialists: engineers who understood *Santa Maria*'s obsolete technology. We also brought a handful of security personnel disguised as scientists. Operating procedures demanded an officer be included, and now that we had found our quarry, since I worked in the navigation department, I was considered expendable.

"The painting is a bit of artistic license. We never got that close; Captain Marakan kept station several thousand kilometers away. She sent us in a shuttle instead. The trip took hours. The team around me seemed calm enough, but I felt like I was about to throw up the entire time. But if anyone wondered at their sweating and nervous junior lieutenant, they had the grace not to comment, for which I was grateful.

"We reached *Santa Maria* and docked without incident: their airlocks had power and conformed to the specs we had been given. The air inside was breathable according to the instruments in our suits. Though we kept our helmets on, for obvious reasons."

He paused and looked around the room again. Nya Solarin, Piotre Raskovich, Kester, even the Interlocutor—all were staring at him, engrossed. It occurred to him to wonder that he felt no nervousness, no shame at admitting his fear. He had for the moment dropped the pretense of being a captain and was simply telling them a story.

He closed his eyes, remembering. Took a deep breath, exhaled slowly, and came to the point at last.

"As I said, the reason no one answered our hails was that no one was left alive to do so. The *Santa Maria*," he said, "was a death ship. Five years into their mission, her crew had committed a mass murder-suicide by the simple expedient of locking themselves in their outer cargo bay—the one that held all the vehicles, mechanicals, primitive weavers, and everything else they had meant to use to build their new home—and opening the door.

"It's ironic. Their engineers succeeded beyond all expectations. Their ship still functioned with no human supervision at all. Their autopilots even corrected the slight perturbation to their course that would have resulted from evacuating their cargo bay, so even the moment of their death was quietly erased from the ship's passing.

"As you might imagine, the results of our expedition were never broadcast. Our PR coup never came to pass. Perhaps other ships have since returned. Or maybe TransGalactic sent some vessel to blot *Santa Maria* from the stars with a single fusion-tipped missile.

"Or maybe that ship is still on its way, carrying the ghosts of its dead."

He made the spacer's ward again and looked at the painting, lost now in the memory.

"Where were they going?"

The doctor's voice. He turned and regarded her.

"You never told us," Nya said, "what planet they were bound for. All you said was they had been out there a long time."

"You're quite right, Doctor. I didn't say. Though I think Kester knows." He looked at the girl. She inclined her head briefly but said nothing.

"They were bound for Epsilon Eridani IV," he said. "The closest presumed habitable planet known to humanity at the time. Of course, we call it by a different name now.

"You grew up there, Doctor. They were headed for Paradise."

The tale was finished. No one spoke for a time. Then the transmitter in Ian's ear chirped to life, subvocalizing a message from his young navigation officer. They were in position.

"I'm needed on the bridge," Ian said. "You all are welcome to join."

"Of course, Captain," the Interlocutor said.

The others nodded assent. Together they made their way slowly to the bridge. When everyone was settled into acceleration couches, he took a last look around at his strange crew.

If this worked, they would arrive at a transition point near Ragnarock, sailing into the teeth of whatever planetary defenses or weapons remotes Captain Johnston had left behind. That would be Piotre's job. He had the codes that would authenticate *Carpathia* as one of Magellanix's own.

But at the moment, the mechanics of deep-space combat seemed too abstract to matter. First, they had to survive. Kester's math had to work, her strange brain had to have produced a solution that would skip the jumps that lay ahead, bringing them exactly where they wanted to be.

If she was wrong, he supposed he'd never know.

Navigation began the final countdown.

It was time.

CHAPTER 41

Kester

"Three."

Kester listened calmly as the navigation officer counted down from the bridge.

"Two."

He had a nice voice, she thought. It reminded her of Per's.

"Jumping on my mark."

She closed her eyes. She wasn't nervous. It would probably be the safest jump *Carpathia* had ever done, at least judging from what Piotre had shown her, how they usually solved topology problems around there.

"Jump."

It began with an itch on the back of the right foot. That's what the victims reported: the skin over the Achilles tendon scratching and peeling. Just an annoyance at first, but then the thin red line appeared. Running up the back of the calf, the blood responding angrily to the foreign invasion, the fungal spores of Aldan's World taking hold.

Every morning, they checked themselves. Ship-born, native-born, it made no difference. It was colony law, a requirement to provide a complete description of anything unusual to the surviving medical officers. Kester took the routine for granted. She'd never known anything different in her twelve years.

Most of what they reported amounted to nothing. Aldan's World was a swampy, itchy place, full of native organics that produced allergic reactions, to say nothing of the hundreds of species of benign Terran fungi that had managed to hitch a ride with them in spite of their decontamination procedures back on Earth.

Death sentence or athlete's foot? That was how their mornings began, somewhere between neurosis and ritual as they tried to will their skin to remain clean.

And then, one morning, hers wasn't.

She'd slept that night in the common shelter, crammed into a crude building woven from strips of native bark, something the kesters wouldn't eat. Stuffed in there with twenty other preteens: her generation, the chosen ones that were supposed to inherit their world. She'd always been a deep sleeper. A loud snorer, too. It was part of how she'd gotten her nickname, her peers claiming that was what she sounded like, sawing away, making enough noise to raise the dead.

She woke late that morning. The other children were gone, probably off doing their chores or maybe shirking them. Such things had grown more frequent of late.

She performed her morning ritual, the waking self-inspection—and found the angry red line running up the back of her right leg.

She hadn't felt an itch at all. No flaking, no peeling, no warning.

It didn't even hurt. But still, there it was.

She ran from the shelter, desperate to find Per. Her best friend, nothing more, not yet, though everyone knew they were bred for each other, would fall in love when the time came.

If they lived that long.

The other kids were standing outside the shelter, waiting. It was a clever trick. One of the boys—she could see his face but couldn't remember his name—had ground up a handful of scarlet berries from one of the iridescent floating plants that grew deep in the swamps. He'd made a paste the color of blood and painted her leg with it while she slept. Then waited until it was almost morning and flaked the dry bits away, leaving a stain that looked like the real thing.

Simple childhood cruelty. He liked her, obviously. And was jealous too, of Per.

She didn't sleep so well after that. Even when the nameless boy died a couple of years later.

He was one of the first of her generation to go.

When the Prophet got sick, the remaining elders tried to hide that red line, but there was no concealing his condition for long.

She was fifteen. She could tell by the way he moved that the fungus had come for him at last. He wobbled when he walked, trying to keep his balance, the infection already deep in his body, working its way into his brain.

A few days later, he gave up all pretense and disappeared inside the governor's mansion. The best of the remaining habitat modules, capital building of the colony that never was.

She hadn't thought she'd see him again. But then the proclamation came.

Tending him was to be everyone's duty.

She almost ran away then. There were few left who would've complained. But morbid curiosity made her stay.

Before long, her turn came to lance the boils and bathe him, place wet rags on his forehead, sit with him until their dwindling supply of narcotics took hold and he slipped back into drug-induced sleep. Their last remaining biologist said it was safe enough. The fungus didn't pass directly from human to human. It didn't work that way.

She wondered about that, but when her turn came, she took the needles anyway and stepped inside the sick room.

The stench was overpowering.

The clinical term for the Prophet's condition was *advanced progression.* All she saw was a dying man covered in boils.

She'd thought she needed this, needed to see him, do her part and make his inevitable passing real. But in the moment, no pity moved her hand. No compassion welled in her, to tend this Prophet who had brought them to this place. All she could think about was the pus. The sheer, bloody, awful abscesses, the red-white cream smear that would squirt out when she lanced him, staining her hands, getting in her eyes. To hell with duty. She ran outside and threw the needles into the mud. They stuck like darts, lancing little bubbles of methane gas instead. *Pop, pop, pop.* Nothing to fear there, nothing that could harm, no infection, just a simple, flammable organic compound. That was fuel, fire, CH_4, nothing less and nothing more.

And in that moment, she knew. The instantaneous, irretrievable, irreversible desertion of faith, more profound in its sudden absence than it ever had been as the defining backdrop, the canvas onto which her preplanned life had been so carefully painted.

There was no Machine God. There was no god at all, just this planet, her home, her world where she had been born and would certainly die.

She ran out of needles before she ran out of mud.

Then she heard a voice calling her.

"Kester!"

It was Per. Running to her, and she to him, away from that awful, awful place. They cleared the mud and bogs and fought their way through prickle-vines and runners until they reached drier upland slopes.

They knelt together on the hillside, side by side, and looked down on their broken colony. So young, and so old, and all out of time. All alone at the end of the world.

There was no salvation in their youth. The children of Aldan's World wouldn't prove to be immune. It just took a little longer.

She and Per didn't return to the colony until after the Prophet was dead. No one particularly seemed to care. As long as they did their chores and brought food and water, all was forgiven.

Six months after that, they were bound for Paradise. The surviving adults had brokered a deal with a company called InterTech that would trade passage for work of some kind. In fact, the adults had made their deal long before and were only waiting for the Prophet to die. Hanging on, letting the nature of the world they'd named for him run its course.

Hoping some of them would outlive him and would last long enough to be clear of this place. That was their one last act of faith.

Or maybe simply desperation.

The Interlocutor

"Three."

The Interlocutor wondered if it would be any different this time.

"Two."

Would Kester's new mathematics change the visions that were sure to come? Or was she destined for more of the same, random recollections of all she had forgotten?

"Jumping on my mark."

Who knew? Her brain responded so strangely to this way of getting around between the stars. All she could do was open herself to it and accept whatever was to follow.

"Jump."

One thing was obviously different.

This time, it was her head in the jar.

The glass was gray, imposing a monochromatic filter on the world as she bobbed down the river, the world spinning this way and that, given motion by the vagaries of the current.

It was curious not to have a body.

After a time, the shoreline began to drift by more slowly. She seemed to be drifting into the shallows.

Then the jar bumped the bottom and ground to a halt, stuck in the mud.

A cloaked figure appeared, bent down, plucked her from the river, and carried her to shore. She was clunked heavily onto a desk. There came a loud grinding noise as the top of her jar was unscrewed.

She felt a brief thrill of pain as fingers hooked into her eye sockets, worked her head free.

The world restored itself to full color. She looked up to see an older version of herself placing her head on the desk by the river.

For a moment, neither of them spoke. She listened to the sounds of the birds all around and the softly babbling stream behind her. Thought about the gentle current that would soon gather speed and rush away in a crashing cascade over the causeway that was actually a bridge that was also a dam . . .

"How do you feel?" her older self asked.

"Disappointed," she said.

"Oh?" The monk that was and would be her pursed her lips. "In what?"

She tried to shrug and failed, forgetting for a moment that she was only a head on a desk. "It's just a little heavy-handed, is all."

Her older monk self did shrug, making the gesture she could not. She felt missing nerve ends twitch in sympathetic vibration.

"The subconscious does what the subconscious does," the Interlocutor she would become said. "There's no reason to be professionally offended. And whether you appreciate it or not, there is opportunity here. So, I'll ask you again. How do you feel?"

"I'm still disappointed."

"In what?"

She tried to deflect her own line of questioning. "I thought I'd like being a girl more," she said.

"That's what bothering you?"

She sighed a breathless sigh. She had no lungs; there was no air to come out. The truth was it had been a little bit of a letdown at first. So, she'd switched back, discovered she liked being male no better after all, become a biological female again, and decided to call it good. In the grand scheme, she'd mostly been left with indifference.

"That's not really it," she admitted.

"Mmm."

"I should never have taken the job."

"Ah."

She watched herself nod gravely and felt a pang of envy. She'd tip over if she tried and wind up nose-first on the desk.

"You'd be dead by now," the old monk reminded her. "You could never have afforded all of this," the figure added with a little deprecatory gesture at herself. "Nor would you have been granted the opportunity even if you had the money."

"Even so."

"Pish."

"The work meant something!" she said in protest. "And I was good at it."

"You're better at this."

"Debriefing executives? Reviewing promotions? Terminating contractors and handling HR complaints?"

Her older self sighed and leaned fractionally across the desk, deepening their eye contact. "You were a grief counselor," she reminded her. "Working with an endless stream of environmental refugees. You had neither financial nor emotional currency left to spend, and if you think this was bad"—and here she waved at the river, no doubt meaning all those other heads in all those other jars presumably sliding quietly past, which she couldn't see since she couldn't turn to look—"it is nothing compared to the torrent that was going to drown you. Be glad you were snatched from the waters. Metaphorically speaking."

"I know from metaphors," the Interlocutor said, annoyed. "So, you can stop torturing yours."

"Interesting word choice."

"Does it bother you?" she asked, feeling perhaps she had scored a point at last.

"That isn't what we do, as well you know."

"Well. Magellanix is going to put us all out of business, anyway," she said. "This Piotre Raskovich of yours. He is the end of your—our—profession."

"Hardly." The old monk laughed. "Were TransGalactic to condition its officers the way Magellanix does, we'd need ten times as many Interlocutors just to keep track of the damage we'd done. Piotre Raskovich is proof of that. Top-down control always fails. But," the old woman added, offering a little admission the Interlocutor knew was only to make the rest of it easier to swallow, "it's fortunate they've had a setback. The work of Conditioning would certainly be different."

"The opposite of empathy," she agreed.

"More like its twisted cousin."

She thought for a moment. "I still wish I'd said no to the job," she said.

"You shouldn't. It was the right thing to do," the older monk said. "This was your path. Don't live in regret of it."

Then she stood, took the Interlocutor's young head gently in two hands, and placed her back into the jar, pushing on her head until she popped through like a too-small cork shoved through the top of a bottle of wine.

The old her waded slowly into the current and set the younger her adrift. "We chose the river," the woman said, her voice already fading. "Which goes on forever but only for those fortunate enough to sit next to it. We're still alive. Consider that. Whereas that way . . . lies only the sea."

She watched the shoreline bobbing by, gathering speed, the current growing faster as it must, and then all at once, she was sucked over the dam, cascading down, down, down, pulled under, until there was only dark water all around.

Ian McAllister

"Three."

Ian settled in, trying to relax.

"Two."

Thinking *Breathe. Just breathe.*

"Jumping on my mark."

His last thought was that Captain Marakan would never have let it come to this. She would have found some other way.

"Mark."

"If you are viewing this," the woman in the recording said, "perhaps there is a God. Machine or otherwise; I wouldn't care to guess. But perhaps we were wrong about that, too. Certainly, we were about everything else."

His first thought, inanely, was she was pretty. His second thought was that he was a complete idiot. There, given charge of this boarding party, their mission of glory run to ruin, the *Santa Maria* nothing more than a flying tomb, and his simple dumb animal brain thinks, *Hey, she's kind of cute*?

In fact, she was beautiful. Fatigued, stressed, but still vibrant in an unmistakable way. Dark skin, dark hair, and a brutal intelligence in her eyes. His overwhelming impression was of someone clearly, desperately alive.

"My name is Dr. Sumanti nel-Askaran," the recording went on. "I am a systems specialist by training. It's my job to know more about *Santa Maria*'s inner workings than any human alive. Which is why"—and there she actually winked like she was teasing a child with a secret, and later he would think it was the single most human thing he had ever seen—"I know how to hide recordings like this one and set them to play forever."

The moment of lightness passed, and he saw again the strain in her face. Her dark brown skin seemed to lose some of its color, the stress taking hold as the moment of levity passed. He saw how gaunt she was, the look of someone who had recently lost a lot of weight.

"If you have found us, we are no doubt in permanent orbit in the Epsilon Eridani system, our automated drives having finished our journey at last. If my math is right—and it usually is—we should be there in another three hundred twenty years or so.

"And if you are watching, not only will we all be long dead, but we will have left no descendants to remember us. So, this recording will have to serve as both obituary and epitaph."

She paused a moment, as though considering. "On second thought," she said, "the hell with that. I have no appetite to eulogize. You'll have to settle for an indictment instead."

She took a breath and cleared her throat. "Here goes. The Reverend is a breeding-rights thief and a madman. He is a serial rapist and worse. It isn't just that he wants to fuck us all; it's that he wants the kids. All the kids, for his own."

She paused again and shook her head wearily. "I imagine you doubting me, hypothetical future viewer. *Maybe*, Ms. Askaran, you are thinking, *you're being a bit melodramatic*?

"Or perhaps, you wonder, if it's as bad as all that, why don't you do something about it? After all, isn't the crew fifty percent women?"

She stared hard at the camera. "It's closer to eighty percent now. The men who disagreed are dead, executed for heresy. And the remaining few, the Reverend and his faithful, have all the guns. As for doing something about it, we're about to. Because I think I speak for all of us when I say I'd rather put myself out an airlock than damn my children to this place."

She snorted. "I find my faith lacking these days, but here is a final prayer. I pray no one receives this. But if someone does, I pray the Singularity happened after all and you are some machine intelligence, not a human child of a cult like mine.

"Are you? Are you a machine? Is it possible after all?"

She gave a last, helpless shrug.

"I certainly have no idea. But the others are calling. I have to go."

She fiddled with an interface for a moment and then added, simply, "Goodbye."

Nya Solarin

"Three."

Here we go, she thought.

"Two."

All our fates, cast to the roll of the dice. She was glad it was Kester who had thrown them.

"Jumping on my mark."

Johanna would have approved.

"Mark."

Nya breathed deeply. It was a warm summer night, one of the rare cloudless ones in these latitudes, the stars bright and the air clear. The day's work was done. The lake was perfectly still. All was quiet save for an ever-present soft hooting from the forest: one of the deadlier species of leapers, moving in packs through the jungle.

Fortunately, they had the extra security of a point-defense system Johanna insisted they bring, image recognition combined with a focused microwave emitter that would discourage the creatures from leaving the safe confines of their trees. There was no reason to sleep in the tent tonight.

She smelled the rich, damp peat of the jungle mixed with the pungent sweat of their lovemaking. Johanna lay next to her, beads of perspiration softening her face, staring dreamily at the stars.

Nya fished a reader from her pack and called its screen to life. For whatever reason, she wasn't tired yet. She rolled away from her partner and began scrolling text, looking over a list of scholarly publications on which she was hopelessly behind.

"Seriously?" Johanna muttered next to her.

"Didn't know you were awake," she apologized.

"At least tell me you're reading a romance novel."

"Um . . ."

Johanna put a hand on her shoulder. "Give it here," she said.

She fought back in mock protest before surrendering and handing the tablet over. Johanna made a show of reading the title of the article she'd selected, narrowing her eyes, and pronouncing the words slowly in an affected drawl.

"Fault tolerance and neuronal pathway redundancy in *novacoelentara Herecicii*," she intoned. Then she sighed. "Am I that boring?"

"Anything but, my dear," Nya replied with a soft laugh. "You're too exciting, and now I have all this energy. I can't sleep."

"And this will help?"

"It might."

"Huh." Johanna handed the tablet back, then said, "Can I ask you something?"

"Sure."

"How many articles like this have you read?"

"Well . . . I did do the math once," she admitted.

"I'm sure you did."

"Ten a day, five days a week, sixty weeks a year, fifteen years . . ."

"Never mind," Johanna said. "I don't know want to know. What's this one about? What's a *novacoelentara Herecicii*?"

She laughed, embarrassed. "It's a jellyfish," she said. "Of sorts."

"You're serious?"

"It's all the rage right now. In certain academic circles, anyway."

"How can a jellyfish rage?"

"No, I mean . . ."

"I know what you meant," Johanna said. "Tell you what. Read it to me. You can put me to sleep with dreams of planktonic predators."

She laughed, delighted. "So sexy, with the technical talk!"

"I pay attention. Now shut up and read."

"Your wish is my command, dear, but I'm not sure I can do both at once."

"Nya . . ."

She laughed again. "You asked for it." She skimmed over the introductory materials. "Let me just skip ahead to the interesting part— Hang on . . ."

The paper had originally been published by the InterTech researcher for whom the jellyfish was named. The fact that it had been shared openly meant it was of only academic interest, deemed to have no drug-discovery or other commercial applications. This, in turn, meant the introduction would run a little long, with excessive citations of all the relevant fieldwork for the last fifty years, with which she was more than familiar.

"Ah," she said. "Here we go. This is the good bit."

"I doubt it," Johanna muttered.

She ignored that and dove in. "To outward appearances," she read aloud, "*novacoelentrara Herecicii* resembles an overly large Terran jellyfish, although the similarities are only superficial. The organism and its congeners are remarkably intelligent, capable of advanced levels of electromagnetically based three-dimensional image formation. In effect, its tentacles act as a distributed neural processing net, capable of differentiating suitable prey items from other organisms in the water column."

She fell quiet, considering for a moment. That was interesting—three-dimensional pattern recognition in an otherwise unremarkable invertebrate?

She shrugged and read on. "In other words, the animal's appendages form a decentralized but highly capable brain whose robustness is enhanced by the organism's ability to swiftly regenerate any damaged or missing pieces . . ."

She glanced over at Johanna to see if she was following this, but her lover, partner, pilot, and friend was already snoring peacefully, fast asleep in the warm summer night.

Piotre Raskovich

"Three."

"Two.

"Jumping on my mark."

"Mark."

A metallic gong accompanied a flashing icon, lighting up at shoulder height in his feed, just right of his central vision. Command priority override, interrupting his work again, stabbing directly into the sweet spot of his data stream.

Captain Anne Johnston was calling. She wanted something, and he felt certain he should know what that something was but found he couldn't recall.

He grunted, shifting awkwardly under the heavy acceleration. Ragnarock was two long, painful weeks in the past, fading behind them as kilometers ticked by in the hundreds of thousands per hour.

He wished he were asleep. He would have preferred to hibernate the whole way back to Earth, but he had duties to perform.

If only he knew what they were! His brain was not what it had once been. A painful, too-obvious consequence of the centipede's absence.

"Yes, Captain?" he said, flicking the alert into its own window with a deft nudge of his thumb. He gave fully twenty percent of his holographic real estate to Captain Johnston's image, resenting every pixel. "How may I assist?"

"I need final coordinates for the mines, Mr. Raskovich, and I needed them five minutes ago. Why the delay?"

Her tone rankled. He felt a momentary burst of pure annoyance. Another gift of the centipede's absence: he, Piotre Raskovich, free agent and mercenary, self-interested human being, was perfectly capable of admitting to himself how he felt about his superior officer.

"Sorry, Captain. Just working through the final checksums now." In fact, he hadn't started, had forgotten she'd asked. "Time horizon?"

She gave him an odd look. "The standard deployment, Mr. Raskovich. As we've discussed. Six remotes with a ten-year active horizon."

"Yes, sir." The memory returned as she said the words. Of course, that was what she wanted. His captain intended to position six weapon pods in this region of space for the next decade, on the off chance someone not from Magellanix reached this system before they returned. It was his job to produce the deployment coordinates, optimized for the modest expected drift in the jump point itself in the years ahead. She was doing the logical thing, leaving enough firepower behind to reduce an intruding ship to a diffuse ball of drifting gas.

Better safe than sorry.

The work was trivial; he finished it in a matter of minutes and signaled back to the bridge. "Sending the trajectories through now," he said.

Captain Johnston's face reappeared in his feed. "Confirmed," she said. "And, Mr. Raskovich?"

"Yes, sir?"

"Are you quite well?"

"Sir?"

"I'd like you to report to Medical, Piotre. Full bio-scan. Let's make sure you didn't pick up anything on your surface expedition."

Did she suspect him, he wondered? Had he been acting too strangely? She couldn't help but notice that his behavioral patterns had drifted substantially from baseline norms.

"I've been through decontamination, sir," he said.

"I am well aware of this ship's procedures for officers returning from planetary expeditions, Mr. Raskovich. Get yourself to Medical by the end of the day. That's an order."

"Aye, sir."

He put it off for an hour, wanting to watch the remotes first, focusing *Accipiter*'s telescopes on their departing forms. They drifted away, picking up speed under the gentle thrust of their modest engines as they headed for their respective stations. They were shaped like bells, with fusion piles at the fat end and thrusters out the back. Nubby black little engines of death. Half were emitters with enough power in their microwave lasers to cause an enemy ship to superheat from within and detonate like a miniature sun going critical. The rest were old-fashioned fusion warheads mounted on high-speed missiles. Either would make a nasty surprise to anyone who might chance by without the proper codes to deactivate them, tell them they were friend, not foe.

He would need to steal those codes along with everything else. Otherwise, whatever ship his buyer sent wouldn't live to reach Ragnarock.

The thought produced the barest tickle in his mind. What was this? Some vestiges of the centipede? Was it still there after all?

He missed it so much. Missed its mandibles, sharp and poisonous. Its hundred tiny feet that would caress his medulla oblongata just so in moments of truth like this one. And tell him what to do.

The codes, he thought. He had to steal them. Memorize them. Give them to his buyer.

No, the memory of the centipede seemed to say, running one of its delicate appendages across a nerve, playing him just so, sending a sharp little thrill of pain down his spine.

The secrets of Ragnarock might belong to you, the last remaining vestiges of the centipede said, *but the weapon remotes will never be yours to give.*

BOOK FIVE

EXOGENEITY

CHAPTER 42

Ragnarock

Feyis Sado celebrated the first anniversary of his exile by putting off work for the day. His schedule called for him to return to the crater, to once again ascend the route he now knew by heart. It would be his seventeenth trip in the last year.

But this particular expedition was nothing more than routine monitoring, with no particular urgency. The artifact never changed.

He decided it could wait a day. Instead, he made himself a fire and got quietly drunk.

He loosely referred to the stuff as vodka, though it wasn't. He'd learned to distill the substance, fermenting the intertidal algae that was his only source of organic material. The liquid left a tongue-numbing taint that took some getting used to, a by-product of an exotic organic that never quite boiled away. Still, making his own alcohol appealed to him, more than simply drinking what Callie left behind. It gave him something to do.

If it had a reason, he told himself more than once, *it wouldn't be a hobby.*

One Ragnarockian year. He put his flask to his lips, took a sip in salute to no one, winced, and swallowed the liquid down.

One year. Two hundred and eleven days and nights, each twenty hours in length. Once around the unassuming M-class star that had in a far distant past been a source of energy, light, and life for the sentient beings that dwelled on this planet.

Or, said differently, a little over half an Earth standard year alone on an ice-bound, albedo-locked, forever-frozen wasteland. The planet he now called home.

He poked at his dried-algae fire and took another drink.

He'd changed. Physically, for the better: he'd healed well and seldom thought about his collarbone and ankle anymore. He'd lost weight and added muscle mass, almost getting used to the heavy gravity as his body adapted to its new environment. He'd practically worn grooves into the glacier, walking up and down the mountain that had once tried so hard to kill him.

Callie had brought him a year's worth of rations the last time she'd visited, and he'd grown adept at harvesting the algae reachable when the planet's moons conspired to produce extremely low tides. But it was hardly an abundant life. Most of his planning centered on calories consumed and expended, how much fuel he needed to take in for a day's work.

The isolation, the cold, the relentless wind—those things were working on him on a deeper level, in ways he could feel but didn't quite understand. He had spent day after day in the crater, taking readings that never varied, monitoring the near-space transmitter Piotre Raskovich had left behind. All the while, time ticked slowly by, with no hint that someone was out there, that some corporation, Magellanix or one of its competitors, had returned.

And then back to base camp, to restock, rest, and recover, and then ascend the mountain once more.

But for all the work, hauling gear up and down, harvesting algae, and counting calories, for all that he kept himself busy, the defining fact of his existence was solitude. This was isolation in the extreme. He had experienced human contact exactly three times in the last year. First when Callie had rescued him, and again when she had returned, bringing him stolen rations and a handful of other gifts to keep him alive. And then a final time, when they'd agreed upon the plan, the approach they would take, and how they might survive.

Part of that plan was a decision that she wouldn't return again until the end. Someone would send a ship to this place eventually. Until then, he would stay dead.

He took another sip of his drink. Then he thought, *To hell with it*, squeezed his eyes shut, and gulped the rest of it down.

The real issue, what they debated so intently on Callie's second visit, was satellite coverage. Captain Johnston had left remotes in orbit when she and *Accipiter* departed the system. There were a handful of them up there, slowly going about the business of imaging Ragnarock's surface. Despite the omnipresent cloud cover at equatorial latitudes, it was only a matter of time before one of them would overfly his volcano on a clear day and discover the artifact. It might happen even sooner, depending on what sort of active scanning those satellites were doing and whether the artifact would even show up to anything other than visible light. Eventually, though, signal-processing alarms would trip, and Lieutenant Farrow and her officers back at base camp would be alerted to the hundred-meter silver alien sphere resting in the crater.

The remotes would be retasked and more images taken. His camp would be seen. Teams would be sent to investigate.

The jig would be up. Something had to be done.

They'd decided Callie would volunteer for the assignment of monitoring the remotes' diagnostics and output. She would look for an opportunity to reprogram them, retasking them to leave a hole in their coverage such that they would never scan this place. Barring that, she would try to find a way to delete any offending images they captured or override any alarms the signal-processing AI was sure to trip.

If she couldn't get access, they decided, they would be forced to expand their conspiracy of two to include a third. There were thirty human souls on Ragnarock, including the two of them, five officers, and two Security personnel. Neither officers nor Security would ever help them; they were Conditioned, incapable of such an act.

They would have to look to their twenty-one fellow contractors for help. Ten were mission generalists like Feyis: jacks of all trades, survivalists, explorers, field-tech experts. There were three other materials specialists like Callie, experts with weavers, those who could synthesize anything and operate everything. The rest were a mix of life scientists.

They had friends among them. It came with the territory, the shared physical effort, and the suffering of working together under extreme conditions. By now, the crew *Accipiter* had left behind had built a permanent base camp together, with wind for power and hydroponic gardens for food.

It would be her call, they agreed. Callie knew these people and was in a better position to judge whether someone could keep their secrets.

That had been the plan. But when she'd returned a month later for her third and final visit, she'd brought with her a bit of unexpected good news.

"There aren't any images," she said. "I didn't find a single one."

"How is that possible?" he asked sleepily. They'd made love shortly after her arrival, and he was deeply tired, more than content to hold her close and drift into accompanied sleep for the first time in months.

"Wake up, Feyis!" She poked him in the ribs. "This is important."

"Mmm?" He rolled over and stared at her, struck as usual by the beauty in her weathered face, the depth of her eyes that had seen as much or more than his own. His accidental imprinting had long since faded. This was something different now.

Maybe it was love.

Or maybe it was just the loneliness, the simple fact that she was the only one in the universe who knew he was alive.

Did it matter?

He wasn't convinced that it did.

"Feyis!"

"What?"

"The remotes! I'm trying to tell you—there aren't any satellites overflying this specific part of the planet. Or if there are, none of them are taking high-resolution images when they do."

He propped himself up on an elbow, abruptly awake. "Someone left a hole in the coverage?"

"Nothing else makes sense," she said.

He'd thought for a moment, listening as the wind whipped outside. "You're telling me someone reprogrammed the satellites so no one in the field team would discover this place?"

"Yeah," she agreed. "Maybe all this was Raskovich's doing the whole time. Maybe he did defect somehow and that transmitter up in the crater isn't for *Accipiter* at all."

"Could he have been a plant?" he wondered. "Some sort of sleeper agent, planted decades ago?"

"More likely than his Conditioning failing," Callie agreed.

"Either way, I guess there's no reason to expand our conspiracy."

"No," she said. "It's just us."

"I wonder how long until I get to come in from the cold."

"A year, maybe?"

"Maybe two."

She curled her body against him. "We're all cold, Feyis."

"I know."

He'd wrapped his arms around her then, and together they'd drifted off to sleep.

He woke the first morning of his second year in exile with a raging headache. He debated drugging it into nonexistence but decided to save his remaining painkillers. He might need them for something more exotic than a hangover before all was said and done.

He crawled from his shelter and surveyed the sky. It was a rare clear day, nothing above him but blue, and beyond that the cold vacuum of space. *No satellites up there*, he thought. No remotes to peer down at him from orbit.

Nor would there be any inbound flying craft. No Callie, come to visit him from main camp. No respite from the loneliness. That was the final thing they'd agreed upon when last she visited. He had what he needed to survive. Food for a year, a power source, and a radio. Barring an emergency, she wouldn't come again. The risk was too great: changing inertial flight recorders, inventing excuses. Lieutenant Farrow might be as bored and tired as everyone else, but protocols were protocols, officer Conditioning hardwired—and Security never rested.

Callie's job, like his, was mostly to wait. He would monitor that transmitter. When and if someone returned to this system, only then would she have a decision to make.

If a Magellanix ship appeared, they would tell all and hope for the best. They'd claim they'd detected a conspiracy within the company and, not knowing the extent of it, acted the only way they knew how to protect company assets.

He didn't much like their odds in that case.

But if some other corporation sent a ship, TransGalactic, InterTech, or one of Magellanix's other rivals, Callie would return to his island, they'd offer up what they knew to the new arrivals, and they'd attempt to switch employers as fast as they could.

In the meantime, he missed her. The logic of it didn't help that part at all. Theirs was the strangest relationship he'd ever been part of. The longest, too, but did it count? Three visits in a year, with no hibernation involved.

Was it a relationship? A friendship?

A conspiracy with benefits?

Or maybe it was just expediency. Maybe whatever he felt was as one-sided as it had ever been, whether the imprinting had faded or not.

Maybe she just pitied him, he thought morosely.

He sighed heavily, trying to will himself not to give in to fatalism. Some days, he felt like part of himself had never left that crevasse. He'd fallen inside this mountain, been swallowed whole, his bones to be spat out thousands of years from now. Extruded at the glacier's terminus for some other company, some other crew, maybe some other species to find.

Maybe someday, some alien archaeologist would come to this godsforsaken place, look at his broken ape skeleton and cracked teeth, and wonder at the hairline fracture in his clavicle.

Maybe they'd think he was sacrificed to some angry god.

Then again, maybe he had been.

He shook his head and winced, regretting it immediately. He should take the painkillers after all. This was no way to start his second year in this place.

Enough self-pity, he told himself sternly. However long it took, whatever he thought about it, his job was simple. He needed to survive, endure the ever-present creeping cold, and keep listening. In the absence of hope, work would have to suffice.

Time to climb again, he thought to himself.

In the end, maybe that was all there was.

The climb.

CHAPTER 43

Carpathia

For the Interlocutor, the nightmare vision vanished as abruptly as it had come. One moment, that awful tumbling cascade, the world seen through gray-tinted glass, her stomach lurching as she went over the falls—which made no sense; she had no stomach, she was only a head in a jar, and was this some phantom pain, some vestigial memory of nerves long severed? And then down, down, into the dark waters from which she knew she would never return.

The river or the sea? She had made the wrong choice. Consigned herself to oblivion, too afraid to face the endless, too much the coward to begin each day anew. And then it was over. She was awake and gasping, back on *Carpathia*, cradled by the restraints securing her in the acceleration chair. Her stomach was the only continuity between two realities. She was still nauseated, but it was just the butterflies of zero gravity now.

She was in freefall. The jump was over. Evidently, they had come out the other side.

She twisted around, surveying the scene. All was quiet on the bridge. She seemed to be the first to wake.

A brief moment of horror overtook her then as she recalled stories of hyper-jumps gone wrong.

What if she was the only one left alive?

She tossed the thought away, angered by her own foolishness, and fixed her gaze on *Carpathia*'s central display, the readouts and diagnostics and streaming updates projected in the open space at the front of the bridge for the crew to see.

The projection was dominated by a tactical map with *Carpathia* positioned at its center, surrounded by a star field slowly resolving into focus as the ship's automated systems scanned nearby stars, measuring distances and referencing internal data, trying to determine where they were. To one side of the map was a pair of chronometers, neon digits incrementing steadily. One tracked mission time. It was omnipresent; she'd seen it the first day she'd set foot on the bridge and had come to regard it as a source of comfort: an unending, steady heartbeat rhythm of all the seconds, minutes, hours, and days since they had departed Occipitus Prime six months earlier.

The second timer was a countdown to the jump event itself. It showed four minutes and forty-eight seconds to go.

Four forty-seven. Forty-six. Forty-five . . .

It made no sense. It should be tracking the passage of time since they arrived in this new quadrant of space, incrementing upward now that the jump was done.

Had they jumped? Or hadn't they?

Something nagged at her. She took a closer look at the first chronometer, the one tracking total mission time. She was a Human Resources officer, not a mathematician; gods knew *Carpathia* had enough of those. But she could read a clock and had looked directly at it before the jump. Unless she was misremembering that, the timestamp had been five minutes later than the one she was now seeing.

Which simply could not be right.

Or could it? Was it possible? Ships had been known to go backward in time when jumping, but only when measured in Planck units at the absolute limits of detection.

Never on the order of minutes, not to her knowledge.

What would it mean if they had? That there were two of her, two of all of them for the next few minutes? Were *Carpathia* and its crew now in two places at once?

The thought was interrupted by an alarm that flashed in angry shades of red in one corner of the display. A hibernation chamber was reporting a malfunction, followed by another, and a third.

Their occupants were waking up.

The Interlocutor released her restraints, navigating the zero gravity in her usual clumsy fashion until she positioned herself next to the nearest member of the bridge: a young communications officer staring blankly at the ceiling, eyes wide open. Little globules of spittle drifted lazily above the man's mouth, perfect spheres of saliva that spread out to form a tiny halo above his head.

She pressed two fingers to his neck. His pulse was weak and erratic, jumping like a terrified bird. Cardiac arrest, she thought—or something near to it.

She pivoted and kicked her way again through free fall, this time sailing inexpertly across the bridge toward Captain McAllister's acceleration chair. His body was rigid, taut against the restraints, and he was muttering "No!" in a kind of strangled cry, over and over again. The muscles of his face seemed to work, but the rest of his body was still asleep, his nervous system unable to give voice to the shout.

Trapped in a waking nightmare. She could empathize—but this wasn't the time for an abundance of compassion.

Carpathia needed its captain, and it needed him now.

The crew called her a monk. She approved of the word, had encouraged it subtly, knowing the ancient archetype buried in their collective subconscious would allow them to relate to her better. She wore the robe and hood for a reason. It gave others a frame of reference.

But it wasn't entirely fiction. She possessed no religiosity of her own, but hers was an order of ascetics. And like certain monks of old, and ancient as she was, she was still not without her own physical training.

She backhanded her captain across the face, one time, hard.

His eyes snapped open. She pressed her forehead close to his, dominating his field of vision. She'd spent the last six months slowly preparing him for a moment like this. Just in case he ever truly lost his way and fell victim to the insecurities that were his constant companion, both his source of strength and greatest weakness.

"You are needed," she said savagely. "Now."

His eyes focused. She held his gaze, keeping his attention until some coherence returned to his underlying patterns of thought.

"Understood," he rasped. "Situation?"

"We have jumped, but I don't know where," she said. "The onboard chronometers are behaving strangely. A high percentage of the crew has likely experienced psychological stress from the event, and several hibernation chambers are malfunctioning."

The captain nodded once, then released his restraints. He turned his attention to the central display, taking it in. "Sweet missing gods," he muttered. And then he was off with a kick and a twist, sailing neatly across the bridge to an empty command station, flipping through incoming diagnostics, screening, filtering, processing, uttering orders.

Taking charge.

She allowed herself a smile, knowing he couldn't see.

"We've got trouble," he said. "There's a remote weapons system out there, demanding an authentication signature. Wake Raskovich. We need him now."

"Yes, sir!" she said.

Piotre Raskovich's acceleration chair was halfway across the bridge. The Interlocutor eyed the distance, performed a quick mental calculation, and pushed off. She underestimated her strength and found herself sailing past him, forced to reach out at the last minute and grab him awkwardly, her momentum snapping her around until she wound up in a sort of awkward embrace with the former CIO.

At least he was alive. His eyes were open and he had a curious look on his face, almost bemused, as though something interesting had just occurred to him.

"Interlocutor," he said calmly. "How may I help?"

"Authentication codes," she said.

"Ah." Without another comment, he released himself and launched himself neatly across the empty space, leaving her to follow awkwardly behind. "Captain?"

Ian McAllister didn't turn from the display console as he said, "We are where Kester said we'd be, Mr. Raskovich." His voice, the Interlocutor was pleased to hear, was now perfectly calm. "We performed the girl's skip-jump and arrived within sub-lightspeed range of Ragnarock. Your former captain has behaved predictably. We are being interrogated by what I assume is a Magellanix jump-point defense system. It's unclear how much time we have to respond, but I'm guessing not much, so if you would be so kind?"

"Of course, Captain. It's what you brought me for."

The Interlocutor watched as the former CIO leaned forward, studying a stream of data now flowing past, a string of simple alphanumerics that meant nothing to her but presumably held a great deal of significance for him. He positioned his hands over a virtual interface as if to enter a response.

Then she saw something pass through his face: an expression first of surprise and then of pain.

His fingers twitched. His mouth opened, but no sound came out.

He frowned, screwed his face up tight, and reached again for the interface, trying once more to key in the commands, the authentication signatures only he knew, the response that would tell the remote weapons *Accipiter*'s captain had left behind to stand down.

Then he turned abruptly, jackknifing his body around, lost his grip on the console, and vomited, a spray of bile spewing into the open space of the bridge.

"I—I can't," he gasped.

"Mr. Raskovich," Captain McAllister said, voice still calm. "This is not the time for a change of heart."

"It's the centipede, Captain." His fingers twitched again, spasmodically. "It won't let me."

The Interlocutor felt the flash of an idea, but then it was gone. Her mind wasn't working right either. Leftover damage, collateral hangover residue from the jump and the visions it had produced.

"Captain," she said, just to keep him talking, give him a focus. "How much time do we have here?"

"Unknown. We have range and bearing on the remote. There is no way to tell how many others it's communicating with. It could be alone, could be tight-beaming orders to a dozen just like it." He shrugged. "A TransGalactic ship would have left a standard deployment of eight. Mr. Raskovich told us previously he remembered six."

"Options?" she asked.

"No good ones. If we go to an active search, the AI on those remotes will interpret us as an enemy and respond. It's the same old problem. They know where we are; the reverse isn't true. They could kill us in a hundred ways. A near-ship detonation, a beam weapon, some sort of focused EM emitter."

She frowned, considering. "Understood," she said. She looked again at Piotre Raskovich, still locked in a battle with himself, his body contorted now, his mouth frozen in a rictus grin. Only his fingers were still moving, twitching spastically, unable to let the information free that part of his mind so desperately wanted to impart.

Then, in an instant, she understood.

"Kester!" she said. "She would know."

Before the captain could respond, she turned and launched herself once again through the zero gravity. She made a better show of it this time, reaching Kester's acceleration chair more or less as she intended. The young woman was still in her restraints but scratching frantically at the back of her calf, hard enough to draw blood in a little pink cloud.

"Kester. Kester!"

Kester opened her eyes, stared vacantly at her, and muttered, "No! I won't do it. He's disgusting."

"Wake up, Kester." The Interlocutor eased Kester's hand away from her leg. "Wake up," she said again, a little more forcefully.

And then Kester was awake, some switch flipping inside, back to her old self.

"Interlocutor," she said.

"Come with me."

The young woman stared curiously at the damage she had done to her leg.

"Okay," she said.

The Interlocutor led her back to the central console. "Captain," she said. "I believe Kester can help us one more time."

Ian gave her a brief look, then returned his attention to the information scrawl in front of him. "You misunderstand, Interlocutor," he said. "This isn't a math problem. These aren't codes that can be broken. This is one-time work, memorized response sequences. We either know what to say or we don't."

"But Piotre does know," she said. "He's simply blocked by the remains of his Conditioning. Kester? Would you mind having a look at his fingers and telling us what he's trying to say?"

Kester frowned and stared at the man's hands. Then she looked over to the interface projected in the air in front of him, her uncanny gaze consuming all.

Her focus returned to his hands. She furrowed her brow. Her eyes took on a dreamy, faraway look.

Then she shook her head. "It's gibberish," she said.

"One-time codes would appear that way," Ian said, apparently grasping what the Interlocutor intended. "These are Magellanix authentication protocols."

"How long would it be, Captain?"

"I don't know. Hundreds of digits, probably."

"But no matter its length," the Interlocutor said, "if Piotre is stuck trying to get it out, he'll likely repeat it, over and over again."

"I understand," Kester said quietly. She frowned and again focused that piercing gaze. Seconds ticked by. The Interlocutor watched the ship's chronometers out of the corner of her eye. She wondered how much time they had.

Wondered too whether, if the end did come, they would feel it at all.

"There's something," Kester said. "He's definitely repeating a pattern."

"Can you read it? Tell us what characters he is trying to enter?" the captain asked.

"I don't know."

"Kester—please!"

"Maybe. Maybe! It's a lot," Kester said. "And he's twitchy. Let me watch. Maybe I can stitch it together somehow."

Kester fell quiet again. More time passed. The Interlocutor felt Ian growing increasingly uncomfortable. She understood why. He was compelled to act. He couldn't let them die for lack of making a choice, even if there were no good options left.

She shifted her position subtly, interposing her body between Kester and the captain, not wanting him to distract her further.

"Okay!" Kester said abruptly. "I think I have something."

"Enter it here," Ian said immediately. "I'll transmit the signal when you're done."

The Interlocutor watched, fascinated, as the young colonist entered a string hundreds of characters long. The sequence was completely random to her eyes. As the captain had said, this was a one-time code, unguessable and therefore unbreakable.

Unless a Chief Information Officer lost his mind and decided to give it away.

When Kester was finished, Ian swiped a large red icon whose significance was obvious enough.

Send.

A moment passed, and another. She imagined the situation as the captain would see it: an interrogation, and now a response, both moving at the speed of light, the latency measured in transit time over hundreds of thousands, maybe a few million kilometers.

They were right or they were wrong.

They would live, or they would die.

And then they had their answer.

"There," Ian said, pointing at the console. "Signal incoming. Mr. Raskovich?"

The CIO's face relaxed, all tension gone from his body. Whatever hold his Conditioning had reclaimed had vanished again.

"It's a confirmation, Captain. We're clear."

"Very well," Ian said.

Except they weren't.

Not at all.

CHAPTER 44

Nya Solarin drifted in the space between sleeping and wakefulness. The memory of Johanna lingered, her physical presence like a pool of quicksilver sand from the beaches of a subterranean Paradisian shore, draining slowly through her fingers while she tried to resist the temptation to clench her fist.

Don't try to hold on, her half-awake self thought. *Just let the moment last as long as it might.*

Then she heard a voice. A man's voice, sounding in unpleasant, clipped tones. She couldn't process the words but the fear was unmistakable.

A second man answered. That voice she knew: the young man who was her captain.

The first voice spoke again, and this time she recognized it as belonging to Piotre Raskovich.

"What for? We're fucking dead, Captain," he said.

She opened her eyes.

She was on the bridge of *Carpathia*, held weightless in her acceleration chair by a gentle set of restraints. Her fellow Carpathians—the Interlocutor, Captain McAllister, Piotre Raskovich, Kester—all were clustered at the central command center such that when she lifted her head, she found herself sighting down her nose at the entire group.

"That will do, Mr. Raskovich," the captain said. His voice was icy calm. "Kester, give me a bearing to the inbound remote, please?"

"Okay," the young woman said.

Nya released the magnetic locks holding her in place, sat up, and then, once her head stopped spinning, pushed herself into a standing position. She hooked a toe on the lip of the acceleration couch, getting just enough of a grip with her foot to keep from drifting away. She took a longer look around the bridge. A half dozen other figures seemed to be in a similar state: *Carpathia*'s bridge crew, now stirring, waking up groggy and disoriented.

"Got 'em," Kester said. She began to recite a series of what sounded like spherical coordinates that Johanna probably would have understood immediately but which meant little to Nya.

"Very well," the captain said. "Listen up, everyone. We've got an inbound weapons remote that has gone supercritical. We're going to point our blast shield at it and try to ride out what's coming. To do that, we have to pivot the ship. This is going to be a hard burn, so find something to hang onto. Burn commencing in five. Four. Three . . ."

Nya saw the four of them grab for handholds and toeholds, and it occurred to her that no one had noticed her, that she should probably get back into her acceleration chair before the captain finished his countdown. But her brain was still too groggy, and before she could respond, *Carpathia*'s attitude thrusters fired. The centripetal acceleration of the abrupt maneuver sent her careening across the bridge and into a far bulkhead. She bounced away, dazed and flailing through open space, grasping for a handhold, the whole thing playing out like some farcical physical comedy. Except this was no joke; she could wind up with a broken neck this way.

Then she heard the captain say, "Reversing burn on my mark. Mark. Full stop."

Which sent her back the way she had come, this time smashing into one of the acceleration chairs. It clipped her knees out from under her, and then she smacked headfirst into some other obstruction she never saw. Returned to unconsciousness, she knew no more.

She awoke a second time and cried out in pain as a sharp stabbing sensation knifed through her ribs. She squeezed her eyes shut and, when she felt she could, poked at herself gingerly, the professional biologist in her trying to assess the damage.

Something was definitely broken.

Then she heard a voice from behind her.

"Lay still."

Kester stepped into view, holding a damp sponge. She placed it on Nya's forehead and swabbed gently.

There were traces of blood, reminding her of that window in the rain, long before, the day they'd fled to Paradise City. She wondered for a moment what patterns Kester saw as she tended to her.

"What happened?" she asked.

"Shh," Kester said. "Don't talk. You'll just make it hurt more."

Which was true.

Kester made another pass with the sponge. Her hair was longer now; she'd refused to cut it the entirety of their journey, and it made a sort of halo around her face, waving gently in the few tenths of a gee they were currently under. Not for the first time, Nya was struck by how young Kester really was.

"Please. I have to know."

"You were out of your chair when the captain pivoted the ship," Kester said. "It was a pretty violent acceleration. The rest of us were holding on to something. You hit your head. Twice, actually. You sort of—bounced."

"Right. But why did the captain reposition the ship?"

"Ah. Of course. Sorry, Nya—I forgot you didn't know. *Accipiter* mined the jump point, just like we thought. Piotre Raskovich had the codes, but his Conditioning wouldn't let him tell us. He was trying to type them out with his fingers, so I read his hands and guessed what he was attempting to say. It was only a hundred and fifty-three digits, so once he repeated it a couple of times, it wasn't hard. The captain transmitted the codes and the remotes shut down, but one of them was a fusion device that had already gone critical and was going to detonate anyway. Fortunately, it was nice enough to tell us where it was, so the captain repositioned the ship such that we'd take the explosion on the blast shield. Except the shield is designed to surf on tiny little bombs, not great big ones. So, now it's in pretty bad shape. There's a remote inspecting it. I saw the images. It's got micro-fissures, big pits, a web of cracks, whole cavities gaping open, you name it. It's a mess. Although actually very pretty."

"Huh." Nya thought for a moment, attempting to process the torrent of words. She breathed in gently, hoping to get enough air to ask the next question without inviting too much more pain into her ribs. "Where are we now?" she said.

"Heading for Ragnarock. Well, sort of. The explosion launched us just thirty degrees off the direction we wanted to go. Which was lucky. Most of the other possible outcomes were a lot worse."

"How bad is the damage?" Nya asked, still wincing in pain.

"I don't think *Carpathia* can jump anymore. Oh, here. I almost forgot. The Interlocutor said to give you these."

Kester held out a pair of pastel turquoise lozenges. Nya took them gratefully and let them dissolve under her tongue, feeling immediate relief as the systemic painkillers spread through her bloodstream.

"Better?" Kester asked.

She took a deep breath. "Much," she said. "I'm sure others have it worse."

"Yeah. There were casualties."

"So, now what do we do?"

"We stay out of the way," Kester said, "while the crew sees how much of the ship still works. The captain said he'd address us later." A shadow crossed her face. "Address us," she repeated. "He sounds like the Prophet sometimes."

Then the darkness was gone, and she was just Kester again. "Except nicer, I think," she added. "I'll see you in a bit. I'm going to help one of the engineers inspect the blast shield if she'll let me."

Captain McAllister briefed them the following day. For Nya, this time, the paintings on the walls held no fascination. *Funny*, she thought, *how the simple need to survive can focus the mind.*

"Our initial inspections are complete," he began. "The good news is our fusion emitters still work, and the blast shield can sustain enough force to provide modest course corrections. We have begun what will amount to a long, looping trajectory in-system, using the initial acceleration imparted by the detonation of *Accipiter*'s remote. It's going to take a while. We'll be passing around the system's single gas giant, bending and turning and braking the whole way, arriving in orbit around Ragnarock about a month from now. Kester performed the calculations. Admirably, I should note."

The girl shrugged. "It was easy."

"What we cannot do," he went on, "is stop, go back, and spend time carefully positioning remotes to cover our rear. And of course, our own weapons systems were badly depleted a year ago, and we never resupplied when we returned to the Sol system. So, we are armed but not heavily, and since we cannot maneuver, we cannot deploy what we have effectively.

"The good news is that Kester's skip-jump worked. If indeed that was the *Accipiter* we detected, we are ahead of it now. Unfortunately, we will be forced to squander much of the lead we gained, limping the rest of the way to Ragnarock itself. We should arrive at the planet before *Accipiter* transitions in-system, but probably not by much. Which leaves us a very narrow window in which to act."

"Can we repair the ship?" Nya asked.

"We can, but it will take months. Fortunately, *Carpathia*'s particle accelerator is unbroken. We can still project singularities, but we won't be able to achieve the acceleration profiles required to cross them with enough velocity to pass through the event horizon.

"We can open the door, but we can't walk through before it closes again," Kester added helpfully.

"So, we're stranded," Ian went on, "Until we can capture an asteroid and use it for raw materials to weave a new blast shield. We're about to become a mining operation, one which will last for months. In the meantime, we will proceed with our mission."

"The Magellanix personnel left behind on Ragnarock will have heard us coming, Captain," Piotre Raskovich said. "The remotes would have alerted them if nothing else."

"Yes," Ian agreed. "And there is also the possibility of additional weapons remotes positioned in-system. Further layers of defense."

The former CIO shrugged helplessly. "I don't think there are," he said. "Though I'm not sure I could say for certain."

"No, I imagine not." The captain gave him a long look. "We'll just have to hope we can respond in time with the authentication codes if it comes to it."

Piotre Raskovich said nothing to that.

"And then there's this," Ian went on. "We received a plain-text transmission three hours ago from the planet's surface. I invite all of you to read it for yourselves."

He waved a hand and six short sentences appeared, projected in midair. Nya leaned in closer and read:

—

Calling ship inbound third planet this system
Presume you are non-Magellanix in origin
Hello
We know why you are here
We stand ready to assist
Do not respond to this message

—

The room fell quiet. Nya scanned the message a second time.

"Someone else found the artifact," she said.

"Perhaps," Ian said. "It was always a possibility. There was never any way of knowing how detailed their planetary surveys would be over the course of six months."

"But how could they know we aren't a Magellanix ship? And why would someone offer to help us, even if they knew that we weren't one of their own?"

"Those are the correct questions," the captain agreed. "And I would welcome any opinions on the matter. Interlocutor?"

The ageless woman raised an eyebrow fractionally, a gesture that Nya had come to interpret as an expressive shrug. "The simplest explanation is the most likely, Captain," the old monk said. "It's a trick. Because of the confusion with the remotes we encountered, while the Magellanix field crew on Ragnarock must know there is a ship in-system, they may not be sure exactly what has happened out here. So, perhaps they have done the logical thing and sent a cryptic message in the hope that we will respond and reveal something of ourselves."

The captain nodded. "Telling us not to respond, in an attempt to solicit a response?"

"It's a possibility," the Interlocutor said.

"But not the only one," Kester said. "Maybe someone else had the same idea as Piotre. Maybe they found the artifact and are trying to— What was the word you used, Piotre? Monetize it?"

"The team there is mostly contract field workers," Piotre Raskovich replied. "Aside from their officers, they are unconditioned. As we have seen, command-and-control structures can fail."

"So, what do we do?" Nya asked.

"Another good question," Ian said. "Whoever is down there, we will honor their wishes by not responding to their message. As for the rest, *Carpathia* is badly damaged but our shuttles are not. They are not jumpships, but they are still perfectly capable of sustaining high-gee acceleration for an extended period of time. A team will go ahead, including all four of you. Kester, I would happily give you control over the drone swarm that will mine an asteroid and reweave our blast shield, but as we travel to visit something unprecedented in human history, your unique mind may be better used there before all is said and done."

"There is an argument, Captain, that all minds are unique," Kester said.

"Be that as it may. I will be adding two additional members to your team as well. The first is a security agent, for obvious reasons. Her name is Agent Quinque, and she is highly capable. The second will be a military commander, the officer in charge."

"Who?" Nya asked.

He gave her a wan smile. "Me."

"I— Uh— Isn't that a bit unusual?" She gestured at the painting on the wall of *Carpathia* approaching the ancient colony ship. "I thought mission teams were led by lieutenants."

The young captain sighed. "Yes. Should *Accipiter* arrive and discover us, it would ideally fall to me to decide whether to fight or to negotiate a surrender if no other options remained. Worse, I have no one to whom the job of command can fairly be entrusted. *Carpathia* is woefully short on senior officers." He gave a small, self-deprecating laugh. "Unfortunately, a decision larger than the fate of *Carpathia* falls to me alone."

"I don't understand," Nya said.

"The artifact," the captain said calmly.

"What about it?"

"He has to decide whether or not to blow it up," Kester said.

"It is not an outcome anyone wants," Ian said, "but Kester is right. My orders on this point are clear. The artifact, if it exists, will not be allowed to remain in Magellanix's hands."

Nya stared at him in disbelief as the implications suddenly became clear. "You cannot possibly be serious," she said.

"Unfortunately, I am."

"The artifact could be millions of years old."

"Yes."

"It is literally without precedent in human history."

"All the more reason our competitors cannot be allowed to possess it. But for now, Doctor," he went on, holding up a hand to forestall further objection, "I suggest we focus on the task at hand. What I need from you is a gear list. We'd planned to have the luxury of *Carpathia* herself as a platform from which to work. That will no longer be possible. You'll have the shuttle's cargo space at your disposal. I suggest you assemble an inventory of what you need immediately. We'll leave as soon as you are ready."

She stared at him, disbelieving, opened her mouth to respond, but no words came out. She looked to the Interlocutor for help, but the Human Resources officer seemed unwilling to look at her directly.

Which left Kester to get to her feet, cross the room, and take her by the hand.

"Come on, Nya," she said. "I'll help you get packed."

CHAPTER 45

Once again, weeks slid into months, Feyis keeping track of the passage of what he thought of as his second exile more by glimpses snatched of Ragnarock's three moons than the chronometer he wore on his wrist. Night after night, they danced overhead, each with an orbital period all its own. And so, he passed his days playing at ancient astronomy, attempting to decipher Ragnarock's lunar calendar, telling time and tide with little else to do beyond his treks to and from the crater.

Then, one day, his phone rang.

Callie had left him the device on her last visit. It was a field transmitter, a tiny thing that fit in his palm, with a case woven from the same smooth black composite as the rest of his gear. Weatherproof, radiation-proof, foolproof, and capable of sending a signal via one of the handful of remotes now stationed at Ragnarock's Lagrange points.

There was just one problem: the communication was not and could not be secure. Any signal they sent would surely be noticed by Lieutenant Farrow's personnel at the main camp.

They'd debated for hours before she left that last time, trying to think of a way to communicate without risk of discovery. Callie had even proposed building shortwave radios, suggesting they might bounce messages off the upper ionosphere, doing things the really old-fashioned way. But in the end, they'd discarded that idea—and other, even more archaic modes of communication—as impractical. Instead, she stole the transmitter and left it with him, along with the agreement that they wouldn't use it unless the consequences of detection were less than the risk of inaction.

Which meant no sleepy, dreamy, goodnight-my-dears.

For the first month, he'd carried it with him everywhere, checking it obsessively, looking in vain for some indication that she'd called. But she never did, and as time passed, he grew so used to his isolation, he'd almost forgotten about it.

Then it rang. In fact, it shrieked like a banshee: he'd configured its alarm to sound like it was warning him about an incoming missile, not wanting to miss it if she called.

"Gods!" It was the first word he'd spoken aloud in a week. He dropped the flask of algae distillate he'd just begun to sip. As near as he could tell, today was the solstice, the onset of Ragnarockian summer, and he figured he should celebrate. It was shaping up to be a warm day, the temperature flirting with freezing levels, and the sun was out. He'd taken his shirt off and built a fire, planning to get drunk on fermented native biomass with a subdural painkiller he'd been saving for use as a kicker afterward.

The transmitter was in the pocket of his synthetic over-layer, which he'd tossed on one of his drying racks. He fumbled around, retrieved it, and stabbed at the control surface, which showed a single green icon labeled *RESPOND*.

"Callie!" he said.

"Feyis!"

"What's going on?"

"Listen carefully," she said. "We don't have much time. There's a ship." Her voice was calm, the transmission flawless. It was disorienting, like she was standing right next to him on the ice. "I don't know whose it is or what exactly happened. We're outside any possibility we considered. So, I decided to call."

"Tell me," he said, algal intoxicants abruptly forgotten.

"We're in lockdown here. This call will be reported and traced in a matter of minutes. Either I make a break for it now, steal a flier, and we roll the dice together, or we give ourselves up."

"What happened?"

"All I know for certain is that a ship entered the system," she said. "It authenticated itself to a remote defense system Captain Johnston left behind at the transition point."

"*Accipiter*?"

"I'm not sure. The officers are being tight-lipped. Whoever is out there didn't authenticate themselves in time to prevent one of the remotes from triggering. There was some sort of delay; the closest weapons pod was on run-up and went critical before a shutdown signal came. It was a fusion warhead, and the word is that it detonated early, but no one knows how close it got."

"Then what?" he asked breathlessly.

"Management hasn't said a word. I only know this because Mikaela was on watch when one of the other remotes called back to Ragnarock and reported its status. You haven't met her. She was cycled active after your mission. But she's good people; told a bunch of us what happened before Lieutenant Farrow classified everything. The point is," Callie went on, "there could be a TransGalactic or InterTech ship inbound to Ragnarock right now. Or maybe there was one but it was destroyed. It's even possible there was a Magellanix ship out there and someone didn't get the authorization codes out in time. *Accipiter*'s remotes might have killed it by accident, in which case we're still all alone out here, and no one is talking while the full-timers above our pay grade sort through the mess."

"Well, shit," he said after a moment, trying to sort through all he had just heard.

"Yeah."

"So, what do we do?"

"Two choices," Callie said. "Either I make a run for your island right now, or we admit you've been alive this whole time and face the consequences. Whatever they might be," she added.

He thought for a long moment. "It's your call," he said finally.

"Like hell. It's both our necks."

"Then go get the flier," he said.

"I'm standing next to it right now," she said. "I'll be there by sundown."

He put his algal vodka away, donned his shirt, and got to work, thinking he might as well clean house before Callie arrived.

And then, after all those months apart, she was there, back-winging the tiny flier to a perfect landing, somehow managing to take the steps that unfurled from the cockpit door two at a time, enfolding him in her arms, he hugging her back. Eventually, she released him, just enough to put one hand on the back of his neck, bending him toward her, forehead to forehead. They stood like that, as if they could will the last four months of unshared experience directly into each other's minds.

Gods, how he had missed her! The sense of longing was so profound; how much he had missed simple human contact, and in a staggering moment of incomprehensible relief, he started to cry. On some level, he'd never expected to see her again, thought he might never see anyone again, and as the sun set and the temperature dropped and the wind began to blow, he came face to face with just how profoundly sad that was.

She kissed him for a time, which was its own sweet wonder, the simple thrill not the least of it, but they stopped there. This wasn't summer camp.

There would be time to sneak off to the tent later, in the spirit of mission contractors and field personnel since time immemorial, but first, they had to talk.

"Hi," he said when they both finally came up for air.

"Hi, yourself." She smiled, and he spent a moment or ten or maybe an hour in that smile, studying the deepening lines around her eyes that it made, the places in her cheeks that almost but didn't quite dimple.

"You cut your hair," he said inanely, because it was true.

"Better for rappelling in high winds."

"Logical." He ran his hands over it, a single centimeter of rough black stubble. "It suits you."

She smiled and kissed him again.

"Now what?" he said, after this had gone on for a time.

She laughed. "You got anything to eat?"

"Not really. I was hoping you brought dinner."

"You're in luck. I'll cook. We have a lot to talk about."

Twenty minutes later, he was shoveling a third helping of some form of pasta into his face, his belly already beginning to knot in protest; it was the most food he'd had in months. It tasted delicious beyond all sense and reason, the noodles falling apart in his mouth like someone had designed a delivery system for salt and carbohydrates with the same attention to detail as a weapons engineer manufacturing a planetary defense system.

Eventually, he stopped himself and pushed the plate away, aware that Callie was watching in amusement. "I gotta quit," he said, "or I'm not going to be of any use to anyone. But damn."

"Can I cook, or can't I?"

"I'm what you call an easy mark."

"Hey, if you don't like it . . ."

"No!" He held up his hands in mock surrender. "I didn't say that."

They got to their feet and spent three minutes doing the dishes together, by the simple expedient of scraping nanotech-woven synthetic flatware clean with Ragnarockian snow.

At which point they could avoid it no longer.

"So," he ventured.

"Yeah."

"We've kind of made our bed here."

"Certainly, we've placed our bets," she agreed.

"You want to go over it again? You've had more time to process this than I have."

She nodded. "Here's what we know. Seventy-two hours ago, a ship entered this system. *Accipiter's* remote defense modules interrogated it and received an authentication signal to shut down. Which is exactly what we would expect were *Accipiter* herself or any other Magellanix ship transitioning in-system."

"And the timing is right for a round trip to Earth."

"Correct. *Accipiter* has been gone over a year."

"Don't I know it."

"So, a ship arriving now," she went on, "is consistent with Corporate sending a resupply mission more or less immediately after *Accipiter* returned to Earth. That by itself doesn't mean much. Maybe Corporate Headquarters knows about the artifact. Or maybe they think this is a holocaust world and simply decided to send an immediate resupply mission."

"Except that one of the remotes detonated," he said.

"Correct. And rumor has it there was some sort of delay between the remotes interrogating whatever ship had just jumped in and their receiving an authentication signal in return."

"Which means?"

She shrugged. "I can see three possibilities. First, whatever ship was out there authenticated too late, took a supercritical fusion pile in the side, and is now irrevocably dead."

"In which case we're also dead."

"A little bit, yeah. My theft of the flier will be noticed, Lieutenant Farrow will find us, and the subsequent penalties leveraged from on high within Corporate will be . . . severe, one imagines."

"Not good," he said. "What's the second possibility?"

"A Magellanix ship but one that had some issue post-jump and took a little extra time to get the authentication signature out. Such that by the time it did, one of the remotes was already spun up and gone critical but detonated harmlessly out of range."

"In which case we are also out of luck."

"Yes, but I don't think it's likely. If a Magellanix ship was out there intact and operational, the incident would have been followed up by a transmission to Ragnarock reporting its status, and now everyone would be talking about how a resupply ship was on the way. I can't see why our management team would withhold that information. No harm, no foul, so to speak."

"Okay. So, what's possibility three?"

"What we're now betting on," she said. "It wasn't a Magellanix ship at all, and they managed to survive and are headed this way. They might be damaged, but they're definitely running quiet and not calling ahead, and our leadership isn't saying anything, because they don't know anything."

"A ship not belonging to Magellanix but with the right authentication codes to turn off a remote system defense pod," he mused. "You could see how there could be some delays."

"Right. And there's only one way an enemy ship could get its hands on those codes."

He took a deep breath. "Piotre Raskovich," he said.

"The very same."

"So, now what?"

"We do what you're best at," Callie said.

"And what might that be?"

She smiled at him. "We wait."

"Ah."

"But first we make another phone call."

He nodded slowly. "About that," he said.

"Yes?"

"The long-range transmitter Piotre Raskovich left behind is still in the crater."

"I realize that," she said.

"I'm pretty tired of hiking up to that particular crater."

"One imagines."

"And it really isn't any fun doing it at night."

She smiled again. "It can probably wait until morning. It's a two-week slog from the transition point to Ragnarock."

"Tomorrow, then?"

"Yeah."

"So, we have about ten hours to kill."

"Something like that," she agreed.

"I'll put the dishes away," he said. "But past that, I have to tell you, there isn't much to do around here. Unless you're into analog tidal prediction and the classic three-body problem."

"Sounds like one too many," she said.

He laughed.

"Agreed."

~

True to their word, they reached the crater the following afternoon. It was snowing sideways, one of the worst storms Feyis had endured. He considered turning around, but the weather didn't get truly nasty until they were three-quarters of the way there, at which point the right thing seemed to be to try for the relative shelter of the crater itself as opposed to a beating a long retreat down the glacier.

Classic escalation of commitment, he thought, as they trudged bleakly onward into the near whiteout. Callie didn't complain. She had settled in on the rope behind him, seeming content to put her mind to the task.

One foot in front of the other.

They made a harrowing crossing of the bergschrund. He glanced briefly over the snow bridge at its thinnest spot, contemplating the dark blue hole falling away beneath them. He wondered if it would ever stop bothering him, if mountaineering would ever feel the same.

And then they were on the upper slope and cresting the rim, three solid points of contact at all times. The wind managed to get even worse until it felt like they were about to be kited off into the sky like his old weather balloon, never to come down again.

He eyeballed the way down into the crater, the cruddy loose scree at the top and firmer footing below. How many times had he done this? He honestly couldn't say.

"You ready?" he said.

"Suppose so."

"Let's go make the call."

They picked their way down slowly. He knew the route by heart, but this was a new thing, doing it with someone else, and as the wind eased back and his spirits lifted, he couldn't help but narrate the descent like he was some sort of tour guide.

"Here's where I sprained my ankle for the third time," he said. And then, later: "This boulder field up here isn't as bad as it looks." And: "I sometimes stop here for a bio-break."

"Gods, Feyis," Callie said finally. "Enough already."

They walked the rest of the way in silence.

He had grown so used to the artifact, he scarcely noticed it anymore. It was an inert, static thing. Possibly the most important find in human history, yes, sitting on top of a kilometers-long tube bored straight down into what at least at one time had been an active magma vein, certainly, but mostly useful now as a way to stay out of the wind.

But it was only the second time Callie had seen it.

"Damn," she said contemplatively. She stood in the ripping wind, seeming oblivious to all else, just staring at it, the unassailable fact of its existence defying sense and reason.

When she'd had her fill of the view, they made their way across the crater floor to the shelter he'd constructed. He'd cached food over the intervening months, and deployed and positioned the rest of the monitoring equipment as well. Seismometers, ground-scan sonars, and radiometers were now stationed strategically around the artifact.

Most importantly, there was the deep-space transmitter Piotre Raskovich had left behind. It was far more impressive than the handheld device he and Callie had used, equipped as it was with its own dish antenna and a heavy-duty power source.

He wondered for a moment how Raskovich had managed to procure it from the *Accipiter*'s inventory without being caught. A minor trick, he supposed, compared to the whole of what they presumed the man had done, and for an instant, he was struck again by the sheer implausibility of it all.

Maybe this whole thing was some delusion. Maybe he hadn't been pushed at all, and this conspiracy-murder-plot theory of theirs was some mad fantasy. Maybe he'd just slipped and was lying at the bottom of that crevasse even now . . . For just an instant, it was as though reality fell away, and he was stumbling, falling, with nothing to cling to, nothing to believe in, and he found himself reaching out to take Callie's hand, squeezing it, searching for some connection, something that was real.

She squeezed back. Maybe she understood somehow, or maybe it was a simple reflex, but either way, it grounded him, leaving him shaking his head, the disorientation gone as abruptly as it began.

He released her and they knelt in unison and went quietly to work, unpacking, activating, and powering up the transmitter Piotre had left behind. The interface was still locked, so they couldn't actually use the device. Fortunately, Callie had stolen another control unit from camp. It was a simple matter to swap them out, and the rest of the device's components, the satellite dish, and power supply were simple hardware, ruggedized field units designed for interoperability and ease of repair. They performed their tasks in quiet harmony, professionals doing a job now, no different from so long ago, when they were drilling ice cores trying to determine what had killed this world.

Fifteen minutes later, he stood up slowly, stepping back and out of the way, leaving her to run the final diagnostics.

"Ready," she pronounced.

"Okay."

Callie stared at the communicator for a moment. "Uh, Feyis?"

"Yeah?"

"What exactly do we want to say here?"

He'd been wondering the same thing. "I guess we tell them we know why they're here," he said. "And see if they want to offer us a job."

CHAPTER 46

The shuttle detached from *Carpathia* with a slight shudder. Nya stared through a viewport, grateful for the rare chance to see the great ship from the outside. The rough, dark shape seemed to go on forever. *Carpathia* was just so massive, with its elongated hull housing the particle accelerator that was its beating heart. All up and down its spine, she saw nubby protrusions and modules and remotes, form following function, all that was required to turn a flying singularity engine into something more.

Carpathia was a technological marvel she had come to appreciate. It was even beautiful, in its own way, but on a deeper level, she was just so tired of life onboard a starship. The endless physical strain, the claustrophobia, the way these Carpathians played so casually with their consciousness, slipping in and out of hibernation, spending weeks drugged in acceleration couches, here one moment and asleep the next, with a never-ending stream of pharmaceuticals and neurotransmitter suppressing cocktails and virtual realities to ease their passage between the stars.

It came with a price, that much was certain. The blackened eyes, gaunt frames, and watery muscle tissue, all by-products of the parade of drugs fighting their daily battle against the sheer alien brutality of a life in deep space. Only Agent Quinque, the Security team member now accompanying them, seemed unaffected. Quinque was a physical marvel, statuesque and feminine, like some ancient Olympian ideal of the female form, chiseled in marble and brought to life. Who knew what level of training and augmentation she had been subjected to? She hadn't said much when she joined their expedition team, just shook hands with everyone and gave her word she would keep them safe.

For her part, Nya had no desire ever to return to this life. She longed for Paradise. For gravity that was the same day after day, a stream from which to drink, the first ripple of her salmon breaking the surface of the water at dawn, and the touch of Johanna's hand . . .

And then they were away, the shuttle's engines kicking in with a jolt that interrupted her reverie. *Carpathia* receded quickly into the distance until it was just a silhouette, and then a hole in the stars, and then gone.

The shuttlecraft was similar to the one she had taken from Paradise, what felt like a lifetime ago. The same basic principles of high-speed transport applied to it as they did to all interplanetary travel: a blast shield and a series of fusion bombs whose detonations would be converted to kinetic energy, surfing on a wave of exploding artificial miniature stars.

It still struck her as a strange way to get around.

Five days. That's how long this would take, gel-packed in acceleration couches and breathing fluid under heavy gees the whole way. Now she had a decision to make. Should she endure the time awake or take the soporific that was standard-issue for a trip like this? Should she ease herself back into unconsciousness and fast-forward to the next interesting part?

She decided on wakefulness. She had a lot to think about.

The old familiar elephant weight settled onto her chest as the shuttle accelerated in earnest, and then the couch began to squeeze gel into her. It tasted vaguely of mint. She wondered idly if there were alternatives, if she could have asked for coffee or tea. Then she exhaled for the last time, the way she'd been taught, and the viscous, oxygenated fluid penetrated her lungs. She experienced a moment of pure panic as her body fought millions of years of its evolutionary history, a wave of claustrophobia and drowning and regret—she should have opted for the drugs!—and then it was over, and she wasn't breathing but still alive, taking oxygen from the liquid, and the gravity was tolerable again.

They'd turned her into her own kind of fish.

There were six of them on this mission, four awake and two asleep. Kester was slumbering in the next chamber over. Piotre Raskovich, the former CIO, had also taken the easy way out.

Captain McAllister was of course awake; he had to pilot the ship. The Interlocutor had also chosen to remain conscious, as, perhaps unsurprisingly, had Agent Quinque.

Quinque. Her thoughts drifted back to the enigmatic figure. She had met security personnel before; Paradise University had its share, but not like this. Her name was Latin for *five*. Nya had asked the Interlocutor if she knew why and also the reasons for her physical appearance.

"*Five* denotes her rank," the Interlocutor had said. "They usually work in teams. The fives command the fours, and the fours the threes, and so on."

"So, they all have the same names?"

The Interlocutor almost laughed. "Not at all. She told you that for your convenience, since it is easy to remember and understand. Her real name isn't *something she would share so readily.*"

"But why does she . . ." And there Nya had hesitated, not sure how to phrase the question.

"Look the way she does? Objectively beautiful as defined by the majority of humans in our society?"

"Well, yeah."

"It's for psychological purposes," the Interlocutor had said. "There are three morphs, as you've certainly noticed: one hyper-feminine, one hyper-masculine, one gender-neutral. Agent Quinque is, obviously, the former."

"How do they choose? Do they even get to choose?"

"All the usual ways. And yes," the Interlocutor had said.

"Are they ever subjects of yours?"

"More often than you might imagine. The mental makeup required is unique. Absolute adherence to a rigid chain of command, the ability to follow orders to the point of self-annihilation while retaining individuality, creativity, and the freedom to act and improvise. Suffice it to say the company has spent a great deal of resources producing these people."

"You admire them."

The Interlocutor smiled sadly. "They were among my first subjects," she said. "It was a very long time ago."

The journey passed in relative silence, save for the occasional status updates provided by the captain, and there was little for him to report. *We're accelerating. Still accelerating.* And on and on, into the endless night.

Nya's thoughts drifted away from Agent Quinque to more-pressing matters. First among which was simply this: what the hell did they expect her to do?

They were heading for a find without precedent in human history, bound for an icy volcano in the middle of an equatorial ocean on an otherwise albedo-locked planet. Maybe they would be alone; maybe there would be hostiles waiting for them. Maybe they could make it to the planet undetected; maybe they'd be picked off by a surface-to-air projectile on their descent and die without so much as a moment's notice.

But suppose everything went well, she thought. Suppose they reached the volcano and found the artifact exactly as Piotre described—unguarded, untended, just waiting for them?

Then what?

Was she supposed to find a way to talk to the artifact? To activate it somehow, unlock its presumed hidden alien purpose, and set it in motion to who knew what end?

No one had any idea. They were all just making it up as they went along.

Which hadn't stopped the captain from telling her to prepare a field kit, as though Nya had some idea what to bring.

In the end, she'd kept things basic, in part because she didn't have much room. The shuttle itself was large enough, but the drop-ship attached to it—the bit of hardware that would get them to the surface of Ragnarock and back again—was tiny. They'd packed exposure suits needed to survive down there. Wearing one would be a new experience for her, as her cold-weather mountaineering history was limited to a handful of snow camping trips a decade before. That had been early in her career, back when she was performing surveys in the high latitudes of Paradise, chasing after a colonial worm that slept under the ice through the winter and then hatched out in the spring in great swarms.

She smiled at the memory, which made her face feel funny in the gel.

As for the rest of her gear, she'd decided on a full-spectrum EM emitter, an acoustic projector, and a holographic rendering engine with a library of content she hoped summarized human history in as favorable light as was reasonable. For lack of a better plan, she figured she'd start by trying simply to communicate in all the different ways she could conceive. She could send it signals across the electromagnetic spectrum, play it music, create olfactory cues with the chem lab she'd brought in case it had a sense of smell.

Whether any of that would produce a response was anyone's guess. The artifact might be nothing more than a statue, some inert bit of artwork, or even a cast-off husk of broken equipment.

She'd used her remaining volume allotment on a pair of nanotech weavers. The captain hadn't seen the point. They wouldn't have much time, he'd said; *Accipiter* itself was likely only a few weeks away. What did she expect to manufacture down there that they hadn't already thought of?

To which she'd replied that since she'd been given neither mission parameters nor definitive success criteria, she was opting for flexibility. They'd brought her along because, since she'd spent her career pondering the evolutionary conditions that might lead to survivable sentience, she might have some insight as to how Someone Else might think.

Well, she didn't. The only thing she seemed more aware of than anyone else was the depth of humanity's ignorance.

It had been a moment of peevishness, and she regretted it later, but the captain acquiesced and she got her weavers.

For whatever good they might do.

And then there was this, the bit of despair creeping just below the surface of her thoughts: it was all probably a moot point anyway. This was a scientific expedition, but it might not remain one for long. If they ran into opposition Agent Quinque couldn't handle, or if *Accipiter* reached the system and discovered their presence, that would be that.

She'd asked the captain how he'd do the deed if it came down to it.

The shuttle, he'd said mildly. It had taken her a minute, and then she'd understood. Fusion bombs weren't just useful for getting around between planets. He could point the shuttle's emitters at the surface of Ragnarock itself. There was no way to know what material properties the artifact possessed, but it would hardly matter when the shuttle was capable of vaporizing the volcano altogether.

There was a reason, he said, that corporations made war on each other with their ships, far from relay stations, colonies, or habitable worlds.

Gods, she thought. *How in all the universe were we humans the ones that managed to survive?*

Or had they? In geologic time, the whole human experiment was still just the blink of an eye.

This was going badly. She needed to quiet her mind. It was going to be a long five days otherwise.

But she couldn't. Her thoughts spun and spun some more, and the claustrophobia was threatening to overcome her. She couldn't relax. She tried to shake her head, to toss the thoughts aside, but failed. In the gel-packed acceleration couch, she could barely move.

She checked the chronometer. How long had it been so far, and how much more of this did she have to endure?

They'd been underway for twelve minutes.

Hell with this, Nya decided. She subvocalized the command she'd been given to memorize. The acceleration couch eased a soporific into the gel crammed into her body, and she knew no more.

In a blink, she was awake, with no memory of time passing. The couch had helpfully evacuated her lungs prior to rousing her from drug-induced sleep, so her experience of waking was a long, clean breath, a gentle humming sound in her ears, and a lightness in her bones and body that was a welcome relief.

They were coasting in free fall. Nya released her restraints and joined the others in the crowded space that passed for the shuttle's bridge. Captain McAllister had told them they would traverse the last few million klicks under constant velocity, his way of sneaking up on the planet. There would be no more smashing hydrogen atoms together in fusion fury this close to Ragnarock. This approach would take longer, but they wouldn't be telling everyone they were coming.

In the meantime, Nya finally had her first look at the planet itself. Ragnarock shone pearly white on the shuttle's monitors, a world of ice and clouds, with only the occasional glimpse of a still-liquid equatorial surface ocean, mostly hidden beneath an unending series of storms.

Ragnarock. A planet trapped in a multi-million-year ice age, forever stuck in the aftermath. Doomed by the foolishness of its former inhabitants, dead via old-fashioned nuclear war. She mulled the name in her mind, wondering whether that made them the great wolf Fenris from the story. After all, they were returning with the same class of weapons that killed this place so long ago, just modernized a bit.

But for all the darkness of its past, the planet was still beautiful.

As they approached, the shuttle's automated scanning systems picked out a handful of satellites silhouetted against the white backdrop.

"Comm-sats," Nya heard Piotre Raskovich grunt from his acceleration bed, where he too was just waking up. "And imaging remotes. I reprogrammed them before we left. There should be a hole in the coverage, but there's no way to know whether the artifact itself has been detected."

"Understood," Ian said.

There was no sign they had been noticed. No remotes hailed them; no weapons systems were activated. Nor were there any more mysterious transmissions from the planet's surface. If someone down there already knew they were coming, they said nothing more.

Hours ticked by. She watched the planet grow larger until it dominated the viewscreen. Finally, the captain announced they had achieved geosynchronous orbit.

"We're about forty thousand kilometers above the surface," he said. "Piotre's volcano is directly below us. Kester, any luck yet? You see anything down there?"

"Just clouds, Captain," Kester said. She was working with the shuttle's high-resolution imagers. "A lot of clouds. Patterns. Eddies and gyres, swirling and whorling. It's all very pretty. But no alien artifacts."

"It's as I remember it," Piotre Raskovich said. "You will recall it was some time before our initial survey got its first glimpse of the artifact."

"Very well," Ian said. "I see no reason to delay. Agent Quinque, is the drop-ship ready?"

"Yes, sir," she replied. Her voice was deep, resonant, with an accent Nya couldn't place.

"Then if you would be so kind as to lead the way," the captain said.

"Yes, sir," Agent Quinque replied. "You all will come with me, please."

The five Carpathians passed from handhold to handhold, Raskovich following Quinque, then Kester, then Nya herself, with the Interlocutor last. When they reached the rear of the shuttle, they lowered themselves through a hole in the floor, easing through a narrow mating coupling and then settling into the drop-ship itself.

The vehicle that would take them down from orbit was teardrop-shaped, a bit like an ancient deep-sea research submersible. Seen from outside, it would have looked like the shuttle was laying a dark gray egg.

The drop-ship had eight seats. They would only be occupying five of them.

"Good luck to all of you," Ian's voice sounded in the space around them. Of course, he wasn't coming with them, Nya thought with some bitterness. He'd remain in orbit, where he'd decide whether to destroy the artifact if the time came. "Agent Quinque, the drop-ship is yours."

"Acknowledged, Captain," she said. "Sealing the hatch now. Seats, please, everyone. And strap in."

They did as instructed. Nya found herself sitting directly across from the Interlocutor. The woman appeared to her suddenly, unaccountably old.

"We'll put down at the base of the volcano," Agent Quinque said. "Piotre tells us there is no suitable place any higher, and we will not attempt a landing in the crater."

That latter had been Nya's recommendation. A drop-ship coming in hot, she thought, might be easily misinterpreted as an aggressive act. Better to have to climb the mountain than start off on the wrong foot. Piotre had accepted the logic of her decision without comment. Whatever he thought about resuming his mountaineering career he'd kept to himself.

"You may find the descent a bit rough," Agent Quinque continued. "This planet's atmosphere appears to be highly energetic."

Quinque paused a moment, running final checks, prepping the ship for detachment. Then, apparently satisfied, she said, "Dropping in five. Four. Three. Two. Drop."

Then the bottom fell out, taking Nya's stomach with it, and the planet rushed up to pluck them from the sky.

CHAPTER 47

They heard it before they saw it. It wasn't thunder, Feyis thought immediately: he had a sense for such things now. There was another storm brewing, but this wasn't thunder-snow weather.

That was a sonic boom shaking their shelter.

It was midafternoon, snowing hard enough that he and Callie had retreated inside. Their only illumination was a tiny dome light that made the inside of their tent glow a pale blue.

"Drop-ship," he said.

Callie nodded. "Whoever they are, they're here."

"I just hope they don't land on us."

"No kidding. Want to go have a look?"

It suddenly felt so surreal, he almost laughed. He'd waited all this time, hoping and dreading, knowing someone would come eventually, but with no way to know who. Now they were there, and he was about to find out.

"I guess we might as well," he said. "I'll get the binoculars."

"I'll bring the hot chocolate."

"Good idea."

They stepped outside together. There was only one decent landing spot on this entire island; the long, nearly flat snowfield about a kilometer away. Snow swirled in their eyes as they took off at a slow, crunching jog, the closest thing they could manage to high-speed travel in Ragnarock's gravity.

It was less than a minute before they saw the drop-ship punch through the clouds on a tongue of flame. They fetched up against an outcropping of rock jutting through the snowfield and watched the ship come down.

"No school like the old school!" Feyis said. He had to shout to be heard above the roar.

"Glad we're not any closer."

"Copy that."

The craft slipped sideways, its attitudinal jets firing as it fought the crosswind.

"They'll be having a rough time of it in there," Callie said.

"I don't envy them." He watched another moment as the tear-drop-shaped craft hammered its way to the ground. It was braking hard, causing a blast of superheated snow to explode into steam.

"There has got to be a better way to do that," he said.

"There are lots," Callie said. "But no good ones if you want to get back into orbit without any facilities on the ground to help you."

"Fair point."

At last, the roaring subsided, and then there was only the wind. The drop-ship had burnt a deep pit as it came to a rest, the top half of it visible above the ice.

"Binos?" she said.

He produced the pair of high-powered binoculars from under his jacket and handed them over. Callie studied the craft and said, "It's not one of ours."

"How can you tell? They all pretty much look the same."

"It's got the TransGalactic logo painted on top."

"Ah," he said. "Marketing."

"Marketing," she agreed.

She handed back the binoculars and he had a look for himself. There it was, the iconic silhouetted rocketship emblem. Also the word *CARPATHIA*—DS1. *Carpathia*, Drop-Ship One, or so he presumed.

"This is weird," he said. All these months, all this strategizing and plotting and scheming and wondering if he'd even survive, and suddenly there they were, literally falling out of the sky, an enemy drop-ship from a company that might turn out to be their new employer.

Or maybe they'd be gunned down on sight as soon as they showed themselves.

"Very weird," Callie agreed.

"You want to go over the plan again?"

"Not sure it rates as a plan. We have no weapons and no leverage other than what we know. We show ourselves and hope for the best."

"Hell of a job interview," he said.

"You're not wrong. Want to go see who's in there?"

"Definitely."

He tucked the binoculars away. They joined hands and resumed their trek across the snow.

CHAPTER 48

The drop-ship sank into the snow, finally coming to rest in the neat circular pit it had excavated with its exhaust. A short time after that, Piotre Raskovich succeeded in unclenching his body.

At least that part was over. He wasn't certain he'd survive the trip back to orbit, should any of them make it that far.

First things first. He knew what Captain McAllister intended: he would have done the same thing if their roles were reversed. The captain was prepared to sacrifice them all, and the artifact too, rather than let the find remain in Magellanix's hands. Whatever marketing value a defecting former CIO might hold paled against the cost of letting a rival possess what was in that crater.

His broken mind shrank from the thought of how little his life now mattered.

He had come to realize, or perhaps, if he was being honest, the Interlocutor had helped him realize, that his greed, his theft, all of these things were as defined by the abrupt absence of his Conditioning as his actions had been during the long decades when the centipede was in control. He was a machine optimized to extract value from information. In the absence of ethical guardrails, he'd simply carried on with that programming, but with one critical difference.

He had decided to perform that extraction for his own benefit.

Well. He'd come a long way, but he hadn't gotten paid yet. Damned sure TransGalactic owed him, but first, he had to live.

The Security Agent—Quinque, she'd said her name was, which he took to mean she was part of some sort of detail, or team, or perhaps was the fifth of a series of clones; who knew how TransGalactic did such things?—said, "Systems nominal. You may free yourselves from your restraints whenever you feel ready. Running postflight checks and status now."

He released the harness that had held his body intact during the descent and found his feet, reminded immediately of that other unenjoyable feature of this planet: its gravity. That unrelenting extra ten percent tug, no different from a transit passed under mild acceleration, but painful nonetheless.

Particularly when moving about, and especially when climbing mountains. How well he remembered.

Agent Quinque brought the cameras online, giving them a panoramic view across the snowfield into which the drop-ship had dug its crater. They had landed in the wide, flat terminus of a valley. They were below the cloud deck, but it was snowing and visibility was poor. The valley sloped away between a pair of cliffs and out of sight. Somewhere farther on lay the sea, for the moment not visible in the driving snow.

An alarm squawked in the cabin. Automated imaging-processing and motion-detection systems had just detected two figures standing on the snowfield, less than a klick away.

"We have visitors," Agent Quinque said. "Magellanix personnel, presumably."

She zoomed in, revealing a pair of hooded individuals wrapped tight against the wind and cold. "No obvious weapons," she said. "Threat level appears minimal, but recommend we monitor for intent. Bringing point-defense systems online."

Piotre thought they looked like a pair of field generalists, judging from their clothing. Definitely contractors. Officers would have been in more formal attire, even in a snowstorm.

One of the figures removed their hood, a sort of balaclava that had covered the head, neck, and face.

He felt Nya Solarin lean in closer beside him. "What are they doing?" she asked.

And in that moment, he understood.

He turned away from the screen and caught her eye. "They're saying hello," he said.

She gave him a quizzical look.

"I know that man," he said. He shrugged helplessly. "I tried to kill him. His name is Feyis Sado."

At which precise moment the centipede awoke.

Later, he would compare it to the physiology of addiction, like a gambler losing a bet, the same endorphin release in defeat as in victory. But in the moment, it was pure ecstasy, followed by pain so overwhelming, it threatened his hold on sanity. The centipede was stirring, looking around, poking through the bits and pieces of the wreckage of his mind.

It was alive, awake, and cataloging his crimes.

It could have killed him then and there. His was an accumulated backlog of sins, any of which could rightly have been deemed mortal. Stolen coordinates, stolen shuttles, stolen authentication codes: all unforgivable. The attempted murder of a contractor was nothing in comparison to the sheer incalculable value of his data theft.

The centipede sent another jangle of pain flashing through his medulla oblongata, but it was almost friendly this time. He experienced it as a thrill in his testicles, a wave of sexual pleasure he hadn't felt in years. He wanted to reach down and grab his crotch but recalled the company he was in. He was, after all, standing in a crowd of the enemy, all of whom were staring directly at him.

"What did you just say?" Nya Solarin asked.

The pain faded, the centipede granting him the freedom to act. It too understood the situation, the importance of the next few moments.

"That's the contractor," he stammered. "Who helped me climb the mountain."

"She says this twice, the second time says it's the first time she says something." the Interlocutor said. She sounded calm as ever, as though she were commenting on the weather.

Prevaricate! Lie!

The centipede's commands came clearly, bringing concomitant relief. He knew what to do.

"His name is Feyis Sado," Piotre said. "He's the one I tried to kill on the descent."

Feign remorse!

The centipede commanded and he obeyed, giving his head a slow, sad shake. "There was a crevasse. A large one, near the bottom of the glacier. The last one we would have to cross before we returned to camp."

"What exactly did you do?" Nya Solarin demanded. "You left out the details before."

"I am only just recalling them," he lied. "I crossed the snow bridge first. Mr. Sado had the trail position on the rope, so he anchored me from behind, belaying me over the crevasse. When I reached the far side, I was supposed to anchor myself in, in case he fell. Instead, I waited until he was in the middle, and then I jumped."

He gave what he hoped was a piteous grimace. The centipede chittered in his mind, pleased. "I slid down the snowfield," he went on. "My weight pulled him off the snow bridge and into the crevasse."

"And then?" Nya said.

"I turned my helmet transmitter off and cut the rope." He shrugged helplessly. "I never went back to look. I didn't see how anyone could have survived the fall."

"The implications are clear," the Interlocutor said. "These two must have sent the signal when we first entered the system. That man out there knew what you had done and why. He guessed what you would do next and enlisted help."

Play along, the centipede commanded. It calmed him, stroking his mind. *Remain helpful.*

Of course, it was right. The problem wasn't the TransGalactic employees there in the drop-ship with him. It was the shuttle forty thousand kilometers overhead, and the superheated deuterium spheres it could use to wipe this volcano clean from the map.

But meantime, *Accipiter* was on the way, he thought. It had to be. Help was coming.

He shrugged, imagining he was the Interlocutor, mimicking her favorite mannerism, wondering if someday she would get the joke.

"So it would seem," he said.

Playing along.

CHAPTER 49

"Now what?" Feyis said. The cold was beginning to bite his face in earnest. He felt foolish, standing there exposed.

"We wait," Callie said.

"Yeah, but for how long?"

"However long it takes, I guess."

He shifted awkwardly, squinting his eyes. "*Carpathia,*" he read the name of the ship aloud. "You ever heard of it?"

"Can't say I have. You?"

"Think so, but I can't place it." He tried to assume a nonchalant look, which was difficult with snow blowing in his face, and also while knowing they were both being scrutinized by whoever was inside that drop-ship.

Mercifully, it only took a few minutes for the ship's occupants to make up their minds. A small, dark opening appeared near the nose and an articulated ramp unfurled, maneuvering and repositioning itself, seeking purchase on the far side of the pit that had been blasted in the snow.

Two figures appeared, making their way slowly down the ramp. The one in front was the larger of the pair and moved with a steady, sure gait, seemingly unperturbed by the act of crossing a catwalk over a deep hole in the ice whilst being buffeted by a crosswind.

The second wasn't doing nearly as well.

"They aren't wearing biohazard suits," Callie said. "Just cold-weather gear."

"Meaning they have some good information about this place."

"I think their presence here pretty much indicates that much."

"Fair point."

The two figures reached their side of the bridge and made their way across the snow.

"I bet one of them is security," he said.

"I think you're right. Remember to smile."

"I'll try."

The larger of the pair hung back, presumably to provide immediate and lethal support if needed. The smaller of the two crossed the remaining distance toward them without any sign of hesitation. The new arrival stopped ten meters away and removed their head covering, revealing black hair, startlingly clear eyes for a spacer, and deep, bronzed skin.

"Feyis Sado?" she said. "My name is Dr. Nya Solarin. It's a pleasure to make your acquaintance."

"Uh, hi," he said, taking the proffered hand. "Nice to meet you. This is Field Specialist Callandra diMarck."

Dr. Solarin shook Callie's hand as well. "You're also a Magellanix contractor?"

"I am," Callie said. "But hopefully not for much longer."

"Well, isn't that interesting," the woman said. "My Human Resources department tells me we're hiring."

"Wonderful!" Callie laughed, sounding genuinely delighted. "What's the job?"

Nya Solarin pointed vaguely in the direction of the volcano's summit, though it couldn't be seen, hidden as it was by the cloud deck a few hundred meters overhead.

"We need to get up there," she said. "And we have a lot of gear."

"Scientific expeditions often do," Feyis said. "I assume that's what yours is? A scientific mission?"

The doctor regarded him appraisingly, then smiled. "I'm sure you have a lot of questions."

"I do."

"About Piotre Raskovich in particular."

"Well, yeah," he agreed. "There are some things I'd like to know. But as my colleague said, we'd be more than happy to talk with you about an employment contract."

CHAPTER 50

The Interlocutor had taken up a position on Piotre's right shoulder, disconcertingly close in the cramped drop-ship. Kester flanked him on the other side. Together, the three watched on the drop-ship's main viewscreen as Dr. Solarin and Agent Quinque made their way across the ramp, over the snow pit, and onto the ice field.

He breathed deeply, trying to hide his discomfort.

Quinque and the doctor were about to meet with the two Magellanix contractors, and he had no idea how the drama would unfold.

Relax, the centipede told him, bringing his beta waves under control. He felt his heart rate slow. *Stay calm.*

Nya Solarin reached the Magellanix contractors. The Security agent hung back, the better to provide supporting violence if any were required.

He heard the doctor introduce herself. Noise-canceling algorithms struggled to keep up with the whipping wind outside, resulting in a slight distortion in the voices that were projected into the tiny passenger compartment around him. He couldn't make out the contractors' response, but then he heard Feyis Sado say his name.

That part came through perfectly clear.

"What do you know about him?" Kester asked abruptly. "Other than you tried to kill him, obviously."

Play along, the centipede hissed.

"Not much," Piotre said. "He is a Mission Generalist. The other one"—and there he paused, searching his memory, pleased to discover data previously missing was readily accessible again—"is a Materials Specialist—Callandra diMarck. There was an incident in their post-hibernation cycling. The male imprinted on the female, which perhaps explains why they are together here."

"Your recall has improved," the Interlocutor remarked mildly.

Too much! He tried not to wince. *Play along, but don't be too helpful.* He braced for the centipede's disapproval, but it lay quiet, seeming content to let him correct his own mistake.

"It comes and goes," he said.

"Hmm," the Interlocutor said, returning her attention to the screen.

"Let me see if I understand," Feyis was now saying. "My former Chief Information Officer, upon discovering that there was an alien artifact in this crater, went insane? And decided to steal it and kill me in the process?"

"More or less," Dr. Solarin said.

"And you're asking me to work with him?"

"As part of the terms of your employment with TransGalactic, yes."

"Oh, you sweet absent gods that never were," Feyis said, which Piotre understood to be the darkest curse the man was capable of.

"For what it's worth, Piotre Raskovich says he wishes to apologize," Dr. Solarin added.

Piotre winced. He had said no such thing.

Feyis barked out a harsh laugh. "Send him out, then," the man said. "Let him apologize to my face."

Piotre glanced over at the Interlocutor, who was now, disconcertingly, staring directly at him.

"It seems you have your opportunity, Mr. Raskovich," she said. "If amends are what you seek, here is that rarest of chances. You get to make them."

Play along!

"You're right," he said. "This is better than I could have hoped."

He got to his feet and cycled the hatch open. A blast of cold air struck him in the face, stinging his eyes and making his nose run.

He ducked his head and stepped through the hatch, onto the waiting ramp. The articulated construct stretching out in front of him looked absurdly fragile. He glanced down and wished he hadn't; the pit carved by the drop-ship's thrusters reminded him uncomfortably of a crevasse.

Gods, how he hated this place. The gravity. The wind. The snow.

The prospect of falling.

It is no longer your choice to hate it, the centipede hissed in impatience, with the faint promise of pain. *There is only your duty now.*

He grunted assent and began to pick his way across.

Height and exposure and crosswinds notwithstanding, Piotre reached the other side without incident and clambered awkwardly over the lip of ice and onto the snow. The group stood a hundred meters away, waiting for him. Agent Quinque had joined the rest, which he took as her way of signaling that the threat level had diminished.

If only that were true.

Shame and regret, he thought. Those would be his tools, and he had plenty of both. His actions, his betrayal, the infinite mistake he almost had made that he must now set to rights.

Yes! Shame! The centipede agreed. *Now use it, and make it good.*

He walked slowly toward the small group. When he reached them, before anyone else could speak, he tore the covering from his face, exposing his gaunt, pallid skin to the biting wind.

"Feyis Sado," he said.

Then he collapsed forward onto both knees, letting the gravity drag him down.

"I have failed you comprehensively," he said. The wind seemed to pull the words from his mouth, out and away into the never-ceasing storm. "What I did was unforgivable. In ancient times, a corporate officer in my position would offer their lives in atonement. I can only offer an apology."

He stared hard at the ice, willing himself to project remorse. Seconds ticked by in silence.

"Convenient time for it," the man grunted. "You're still looking to get rich from all this."

Grovel!

But Piotre needed no urging. His and the centipede's desires were as one now, and he could've torn at the snow and ice with his bare hands until they bled, and felt only delight.

"Yes," he said. "That was my aim. It no longer matters. I will never be paid for what I have done. I understand that now. I only want to know what lies in that crater, the same as the rest of you."

The wind whipped and howled. His knees began to ache. He'd chosen an uncomfortable position, kneeling as if in prayer.

The centipede responded by suppressing the offending nerves. The pain eased immediately.

How could he have forgotten? He'd never be alone again.

"Oh, for fuck's sake," the man finally said. "Is this an apology or a proposal? Here. Get up."

Piotre raised himself to a sitting position. Feyis Sado's hand clasped around his like a vice. The contractor hauled him to his feet and clapped him roughly on the shoulder. The shock of it almost knocked Piotre back to his knees.

"Forgiven and forgotten," Feyis said. "Now come on. We've got work to do."

The centipede wriggled in pleasure.

This is why, it reminded him. *The conditioned are always stronger.*

Which was true. The need for human connection was no longer a malady with which he was afflicted. That weakness had been excised, and he could not have been more grateful.

They regathered in the drop-ship. It was big enough for all of them and provided better shelter than the contractors' field tent. Also, their rations were evidently better, or at least novel for Feyis and Callie, who seemed to value having variety in what they ate.

Piotre couldn't have cared less what they had for dinner. But it gave Feyis and Callie a chance to tell their tale, and that interested him greatly.

It was remarkable and mundane at the same time. They'd managed to perform an act of betrayal that in some ways rivaled his own. Yet they'd learned almost nothing useful about the artifact itself, save for one critical detail he had until this moment forgotten.

The artifact was sitting on top of a shaft, a tunnel bored kilometers deep into the heart of the volcano. He'd known this, learned of it at the end of his survey before he and Feyis had left the crater. A key fact he'd lost track of in all that followed.

What did it mean? None of them could say. Dr. Solarin looked thoughtful, but if she had an opinion, she was keeping it to herself.

Interesting as that was, it was the smallest detail of their story that was the most important of all. The pair were in possession of a surface-to-surface communicator. Callie had stolen a sat-link, though they had only dared use it the one time.

The Materials Specialist even went so far as to produce it from under her jacket, setting it on the console that was serving as their dinner table. It was all he could do not to grab for it then and there. He knew Ian McAllister was standing by in geosynchronous orbit, with the shuttle's deuterium emitters pointed at the volcano. Soon enough, *Accipiter* would reach this system, and when it did, McAllister's hand would be forced. Captain Johnston could not know she had been beaten there. There was no way she could guess that *Carpathia* had done the impossible.

When *Accipiter* arrived, even a crippled *Carpathia* would hear. In the shuttle, Ian McAllister would have all the advance warnings he needed to wipe this volcano from the surface of Ragnarock.

But not if Piotre could find just a few minutes alone with the field contractor's transmitter! All he needed was enough time to call the officer in charge at their main camp. Lieutenant Farrow. The woman's name came to him. She was competent, would know what to do.

But how? How was he going to get his hands on their radio without being caught?

Do what you do best, the centipede chided him. *When the moment arises, steal it. Just remember,* it added with a little shiver of its metaphoric mandibles, *to put it back where you found it when you're done.*

The meal was over, the tale told. They recycled their spent food containers, grist for Dr. Solarin's weavers to repurpose in the future. It was late afternoon, and their instruments indicated a brief break in the wind.

"Now or never, then," Dr. Solarin said. "We should get started."

Feyis held up a hand. "If you're looking at the wind gauge," the man said, "believe me when I tell you it can be deceptive. The storms bait you, and just when you relax, they come at you from behind."

This with a glance in Piotre's direction.

"But is it possible to climb it now?" Dr. Solarin said.

"Possible, yes. But I wouldn't advise it. Best to leave in the morning," Feyis said. "Trust me. I've done this enough times."

"No," the doctor said. "There's no time to waste. If it can be done, we start right away."

Which was surprising, Piotre thought. Dr. Solarin was in scientific command only. He hadn't expected her to start giving orders.

But Feyis just shrugged and said, "So be it."

"Any other objections?" Dr. Solarin asked the room.

Piotre could think of several but remained silent. He, too, had little time to waste.

"Good. It's settled then."

He felt the flurry of excitement build around him as preparations began in earnest. Climbing teams were discussed, gear unloaded and sorted, decisions made about what to bring on the ascent.

It occurred to him that this time he had no synth-suit to aid him. Whatever happened out there, physically, he'd have to do this on his own. But even that now felt like a minor concern. He had one job to do, one duty to perform. A single imperative, and if he had to climb this volcano again, he would.

Only one thing mattered. He had to find a way to steal that radio. One simple call and all would be put to right.

CHAPTER 51

Captain Marakan had warned Ian about the loneliness of command, but even she couldn't have anticipated this: drifting in zero gravity, alone in a shuttle, locked in geosynchronous orbit around a dead world while time ticked past. He had no one to talk to, no safe way to communicate with either his ship or his field team, leaving him wondering what the hell was happening while he stared at the endless band of clouds wrapping Ragnarock's equator like some sort of puffy white blanket, concealing all.

His crew was down there somewhere, but they were under strict orders not to contact him for fear of detection by the Magellanix remotes in orbit. Scientific judgment belonged to Nya Solarin now. Agent Quinque was responsible for their safety, but Nya was in command.

There was little enough he could do from there. Except, of course, for the one thing which he feared most would be required of him.

As for his ship, by now *Carpathia* should be squatting on an asteroid while a swarm of drones sought out veins of heavy metals for harvest. They would weave the ore into a replacement blast shield, and *Carpathia* would be whole once more. He hoped the repairs were proceeding well, hoped the young lieutenant he had left in charge would prove equal to the task of command. But there was no way to be sure. *Accipiter*'s weapons remotes were still out there, and the shuttle lacked the equipment required to tightbeam a message halfway across the solar system in a way he could be certain wouldn't be overheard.

There would be little point in receiving status updates anyway; it was mere curiosity that made him want to know. Even under the most optimistic of projections, long before *Carpathia* could fly and fight again, *Accipiter* would arrive. When it did, he would be out of options at last.

He could see it in his mind's eye. *Accipiter* would gate into the system with an electromagnetic howl, the characteristic signature of its arrival spreading out into space. *Carpathia* would detect it, her web of sensory arrays ever vigilant, even in her crippled state. Then the young lieutenant he had left in charge would contact him. That was one signal they'd have to risk, that single bit of information.

They're here.

One data point, which would mean everything to Ian.

Accipiter would certainly call ahead as well. Her captain would send a directed pulse of EM to the field team she had left behind. The question was, what would *Accipiter*'s captain say?

What did Magellanix really know?

That Piotre Raskovich had betrayed them, certainly. But would they have discovered why? Did *Accipiter*'s captain know about the artifact, or merely that their former CIO's Conditioning had broken? A holocaust world had intrinsic interest, and maybe that was all they thought Raskovich had stolen: route coordinates, jump points, and the knowledge of a new world where a sentient species had once lived and died.

Then again, maybe Piotre hadn't covered his tracks well, and *Accipiter*'s captain already knew everything, down to the coordinates of the volcano and the details of the find.

Either way, *Accipiter*'s captain couldn't know *Carpathia* had found a way to get there first. They'd have some time to act. He'd give his field crew as much time as possible to learn all they could about the artifact, and then he'd call them back to the shuttle, regardless of what they'd discovered. They'd retreat to the drop-ship, return to orbit, and to hell with who overheard.

Which would leave him to do his job and consign the island, artifact and all, to oblivion.

Except.

How could he possibly?

He'd reconfigured the fusion emitter almost as soon as he dispatched his team to the surface. It would be his job to attack a planet from space, a violation of every treaty, convention, charter, and basic principle of civilized behavior of which he was aware.

To say nothing of what he meant to destroy.

Maybe he'd spent too many hours talking with Nya Solarin. Although he was no academic, her research fascinated him. Could sentience ever be survived by the species with which it was afflicted? Or was apocalypse inevitable?

What did that say about humanity? And its own missing gods, machine or otherwise?

He didn't want to destroy what was down there. No one would. How could a single human just make the decision to . . . blow it up? In service of what?

Preventing it from falling into another corporation's hands?

Maybe all this was just the loneliness of command. Maybe his doubts were nothing more than the pain any captain felt, faced with an impossible decision that was theirs alone.

It was almost enough to make him envy Piotre Raskovich's Behavioral Conditioning.

Ian knew he was young and inexperienced. Hopelessly insecure and probably, on some level, simply naive.

When the moment came, could he pull the trigger?

He honestly had no idea.

Sometime later, the clouds parted briefly, and for the first time, Ian could see his team directly, trudging up a glacier in two ragged groups.

He thought about the heavy gravity, thin air, and raging cold.

He still envied them.

Then the clouds reconvened and his brief view was gone, leaving him alone with his thoughts once more.

It just wasn't fair. What could they learn in just a few days? The discovery deserved a lifetime of study. Multiple lifetimes, really.

One thing was certain: when *Accipiter* arrived, he would order them down off that mountain in plenty of time to bring them home. He might become responsible for ending humanity's best chance to learn something about its place in the universe, but he'd be damned if he was going to get his people killed in the process.

He was certain Captain Marakan would have approved of that much.

Past that, he couldn't say.

CHAPTER 52

The climb was brutal, lasting all through the night. Nya wondered if she'd done the right thing, giving the order to leave immediately despite Feyis's warnings about the weather. Hours dragged by, her uncertainty growing with every step. By the time dawn finally broke, she almost didn't notice, experiencing it more as a lessening of the darkness than anything resembling daylight.

Hard as it was for her, she didn't want to think about the strain on Piotre Raskovich. Somehow, he kept moving, Agent Quinque at his side, not letting him fall.

As for the Interlocutor, she climbed without comment, as indefatigable as she was ageless.

By the time they reached the volcano's rim, the wind was blowing so hard, it threatened to toss them into the sky like kites with their strings cut. Feyis Sado described this as "typical." She gritted her teeth and kept going, her eagerness to reach the crater floor and see the artifact in person overcoming her fear and exhaustion.

They picked their way down on a slow, stumbling descent that seemed certain to break someone's leg.

"This is the easy part," Feyis said.

"Shut up, Feyis," she heard Callie reply.

No one else said much of anything.

And then at last, they were down off the crater wall, and there it was.

The artifact.

It was massive, surpassingly, obviously alien: a shimmering, glittering sphere, everything about it suggesting Otherness in a way that Nya felt more than understood.

There had been no word from Captain McAllister. No terse coded warnings; no messages from on high. Presumably, she had time, and space, and freedom to act—at least for now.

"Let's set up camp," she said to Feyis and Callie, even as she saw Piotre Raskovich sit down heavily on a flat slab of rock, looking like he would never move again. "I'd like to walk the perimeter immediately. Agent Quinque? Any objections?"

"You're in command now, Doctor," the agent said. "The rest of us will unpack the gear and make this place habitable. By all means, you should get to work."

"Agreed. Kester? Want to come?"

"Definitely," the young woman said.

Nya made her way across the crater floor, Kester trailing behind. The artifact was simply beautiful in a way she couldn't describe. Up close, there was something in the precision with which each individual facet seemed to have been shaped . . . Humans, she thought, might make an enormous starship or a relay station kilometers across. Equally, they might machine a finely detailed bit of jewelry.

The artifact seemed to be a mix of both.

But this was no time to wax poetic or luxuriate in emotional reactions. Someday, her work there would be scrutinized at a level of detail she didn't want to contemplate, and she knew she didn't have much time.

She began a long, slow ambit, forcing herself back to logical patterns of thinking. *Begin by cataloging the possibilities*, she told herself. That seemed as good an approach as any.

First, this: either the artifact was inert, or it was in some sense active. If the former, perhaps it had once been capable of activity but lost its abilities over time. If so, why? It could have broken down. Its power source might have failed. Maybe it was sabotaged or damaged. Or it could have been programmed to shut itself down. Perhaps indefinitely, or perhaps just for a period of time.

Equally, it might never have done anything more than it was doing right now, which, according to Feyis and Callie, was basically just sitting there. In which case it could be a message of some kind, an exotic form of interstellar note. Or maybe it was a warning, or a surveyor's stone, or a flag meant to lay claim to this place.

Perhaps it was simply intended as a work of art.

But if, on the other hand, it was in some sense active, if it had some agency of its own, then the question became: was she staring at a mechanical agent or a biological entity?

The odds seemed to suggest the former. Nya had an active imagination, but even she struggled to conceive of a closed biological system persisting for millions of years. Possible? Yes. But probably not.

Follow it through, she thought, as she continued her ambit. If the artifact was inert, this was all for naught anyway. She would run out of time, Captain McAllister would destroy it, and that would be that. She doubted she would divine its purpose if it couldn't be coaxed into some kind of response.

Certainly, there was no way she could think of to bring it home with them. It was simply too big for that.

But what if it was capable of activity? Then the question became whether it was already aware of their presence and simply choosing not to respond.

This was her best hope and the reason she had brought with her every mechanism she could conceive to attempt to communicate with it. There were approaches that Feyis Sado and Callandra diMarck, clever as they were, simply hadn't had the resources to attempt.

Finally, there was the matter of the great vertical shaft underneath it, which itself suggested several possibilities. Was there some protected, hidden chamber down there? Was it a launching system of some kind? A storage vault?

Or maybe it was an energy source. The artifact could have been geothermally powered. There might still be magma trapped that deep, that even now it was tapping for power.

A thought tickled at the back of her mind. The geology of this place . . . was it relevant somehow? She thought about the volcano, how it would have drifted away from the hot spot on the seafloor where it formed, slowly going dormant over the long passage of years.

The thought, whatever it was, flitted away and was lost.

She walked on.

As best she could summarize, her job was to find a way to communicate with this thing. She'd come all this way to try to figure out how to say hello, and success could look like just one thing: for the artifact to say hi back.

Whatever the artifact was, even if it was aware enough to have detected their presence, it couldn't have any way of knowing what humans were or what they wanted. In which case it might choose to stay quiet and play dumb. Why not gather as much information as it could?

She completed her circumnavigation. There was no more reason to wait. If it was information the artifact wanted, Nya was ready to provide. She had spent weeks on *Carpathia* debating what to include in what she had taken to calling her History Lesson. She'd decided to keep the focus on technological achievements, hoping to put her species' best foot forward with things like the wheel, electricity, life-extending pharmaceuticals, and Singularity creation.

If she was guilty of a certain editorial heavy-handedness, who could blame her? Most of the lenses through which humanity's progress could be viewed weren't so attractive. Famine, environmental collapse, war.

Genocide.

The rest of the team had done a credible job of constructing a field camp in the hour she'd been gone. She found Feyis and Callie sitting together, sipping water, watching her approach in what looked like companionable silence.

"Hey, guys," she said. "Anyone want to help me play a holo?"

"I'm in," Callie responded. "The projector is in the main shelter. I'll grab it."

"Thanks."

With Feyis and Callie's help, Nya positioned the gear to display her History Lesson in holographic images next to the surface of the artifact. The Interlocutor joined the three of them, and together they watched as scenes from the great apes to the ancient pyramids to the dawn of interstellar travel played out in images twenty meters high.

The recording lasted half an hour. The artifact, unsurprisingly, didn't respond, so they repositioned the projector a sixth of the way around its base and tried it again. Six times in all, until they had made their way back to where they started.

Then, at Nya's direction, Feyis and Callie hauled the projector halfway up the crater wall, set the brightness of the display to maximum, and played the content over again, this time directly above the top of the artifact. The distance and distortion caused her summary of human history to waver and shimmy and dance like some strange ghost of all things past.

There was still no response.

Not that Nya had particularly expected one.

"Let's go back to basics," she said.

Feyis was standing closest to her, having watched the proceedings with great interest. "What did you have in mind?" he said.

"Math. And this time, we're going to set the spectrum a bit broader."

"I wondered about that."

"Yeah. Visible light is a laughably narrow set of frequencies to work with, but I figured it might communicate something about how we humans see the world."

"Ah. Clever," he said approvingly.

"Maybe not. We'll keep it simpler this time."

She configured her projector to work its way up and down the entirety of the electromagnetic spectrum. Essentially, she shot the thing with a modulated EM emitter, using a series of binary pulses to try and demonstrate how humans approached the language of mathematics.

She kept the power levels deliberately low. If the artifact was able to detect what she was doing at all, the last thing she wanted was for it to interpret her actions as acts of aggression.

The artifact remained as it had been. If it felt threatened on some level, it certainly didn't show it. Nor did it betray any sign of interest in her activities.

Eventually, evening descended, a darkening of skies already heavy with clouds and snow.

One day had come and gone, with nothing to show for it.

Well. No one said this would be easy. Fortunately, history books and math lessons weren't the only tricks Nya had up her sleeve.

Nya slept fitfully for two hours, awakening in the thick, oppressive darkness that came just before dawn.

Time, she thought, *to give chemical forms of communication a try.*

She had brought a machine designed to aerosolize and release aromatic hydrocarbons of her choosing. Unable to think of a better approach, she simply walked up to the artifact and held the device aloft. *We humans are carbon-based,* she hoped to say. *This is benzene; this is toluene; we know about these things. Here are complex sugars, combusting.*

She worked her way through a series of esters, feeling like a pagan witch of old. Burning sage, she thought, in an effort to talk to a spirit.

There was no response.

Feyis was next to wake, crawling forth bleary-eyed from the shelter. She asked him to build a fire. He gave her a look that spoke volumes about having been required to haul algae up the hill but did it anyway.

Still, the artifact did nothing.

Nya spent additional hours repeating the same exercise against a silicon base, just in case there were some crust-dwelling fire-eaters in there.

If there were, they sat unmoved.

She soldiered on. She already regretted the hours of sleep she'd allowed herself the first night; had no intention of sleeping again for the duration of her time here.

Fortunately, there was no shortage of chemical stimulants at her disposal. Caffeine gave way to heavier drugs, her physical energy levels undiminished even as lack of sleep combined with a failure to achieve any result led to a slow but growing despair.

At the end of their third day in the crater, mental fatigue was beginning to get the better of her. She collapsed heavily onto one of the cases in which her weavers were packed and watched dully as Kester flew a remote—a little propeller-driven drone that could just stay aloft in the winds that whipped through even the bottom of the crater. The strange young woman had been at it for the last two days, having announced her intentions to scan the surface of the artifact through the drone's instruments. Nya had seen no reason to object. She'd looked over the images Kester was capturing. To her, the surface of the artifact looked the same everywhere, and if Kester thought differently, she wasn't saying. But she kept at it, whatever her reasons.

And as for Nya's weavers, so far, Captain McAllister had proven right. The polished carbon cases they came packed in made useful chairs to sit on, but otherwise, they'd been no help at all. She could think of nothing she might create that she hadn't brought with her already.

As she watched Kester at her task, a darker thought began to take shape.

She, Dr. Nya Solarin, tenured lifetime faculty at TransGalactic's prestigious University of Paradise, sole active practitioner in the study of xeno-evolutionary trends and the great Sentience Problem, was blowing it.

Badly.

The consequences were too great to contemplate.

She got to her feet in frustration, only to see the Interlocutor making her way across the crater toward her, bearing two cups of hot, steaming liquid.

"You need to sleep," the old woman said.

"There's no time."

"Even so."

"I'll sleep after I've failed and the captain blows this place to hell."

"Mmm." The woman took a sip, infuriatingly calm as ever. Nya sighed heavily, then accepted the second cup and took a drink of her own. The liquid was pungent, perking her up immediately. She wondered what she'd been given and decided not to ask. It couldn't be worse than the stimulants already raging through her bloodstream.

"What haven't you tried?" the Interlocutor asked.

Nya shrugged. "Brute force, I guess. I've got the EM emitter. I could always dial up the wattage."

"And what do you suppose might happen if you did?"

"Who knows? I could try to cut that thing open, but something tells me it would be impervious to anything we've got on hand. Still, maybe the captain was right. I should've spent my weight allowance on weapons-grade munitions. As opposed to these weavers." She gave the crate a disgusted kick.

"Perhaps," the Interlocutor said.

"I don't suppose people in your profession are actual telepaths? It would be nice if that wasn't just a myth."

The Interlocutor smiled at that. "Would you like me to lay hands on it?"

"If you thought it would help."

"Alas," the Interlocutor said. "My abilities are limited to that to which I can relate. An impervious, unresponsive, inert mass doesn't give me much of a starting place."

"Yeah, me either. Maybe we should have brought a priest instead. We could be staring at the first direct evidence of a Machine God and not know it."

"You could ask Kester for her perspective. She has experience with such things."

Nya glanced over at the girl, still enraptured with the images from her drone. "I'm not sure anyone understands Kester's perspectives," she said.

"That is probably true," the Interlocutor said.

"At least Piotre is happy."

"Oh? What makes you say that?"

"He seems different somehow. More at peace. Like he's let go of whatever expectations he had, maybe. What did he think he was going to get out of all this, anyway?"

"The usual," the Interlocutor said. "Immortality. A world of his own. A military to defend it."

"Not very imaginative," Nya said. And then: "Would it really have happened?"

"It's possible. I don't know what the Board planned for him."

"But why? Why would they ever pay him off, once they had whatever knowledge he had to sell?"

"Marketing." The Interlocutor half-smiled. "What else? Piotre's idea was they could make a cult hero out of him. An example for others to follow."

"Huh." Nya thought that over. "Dream big, I guess."

"Mmm."

"Well. He seems over it. Like the thrill of the discovery is enough for him now. He's doing his best, telling us everything that he knows."

"That's good to hear," the Interlocutor said. Her tone was perfectly flat, but Nya got the sense she was missing something.

She decided not to ask. She had enough on her mind already.

"So, you've no advice for me, then?" she said instead.

"Just refreshment, I'm afraid. And the most banal of thoughts. Trust your instincts, and assume it was the right thing for you to be here. Ask the questions only you would think to ask. If that fails, put all your instruments and notebooks and ideas away, and get up and go for a walk."

Nya laughed, a grim, humorless chuckle. "That was the first thing I tried," she said.

"Even so," the Interlocutor said. "You can always try again."

CHAPTER 53

Piotre's opportunity came during their fourth day in the crater.

Patience, the centipede had hissed at him, over and over again, sensing his desire to force the endgame, to make amends.

Patience.

And then, there it was: a single, perfect moment in which to act.

Dr. Solarin was absorbed in her work, still attempting to communicate with the artifact, now digging deeper into her content library, rendering ever-more-obscure imagery from humanity's past. She'd crack soon, he thought. She'd gotten nowhere and was clearly beginning to despair.

Kester was engrossed with her survey drone. She'd been flying it for two days nonstop, as obsessed as the doctor in her work. There was no threat from that quarter.

The Interlocutor had wandered to the far side of the artifact, somewhere out of sight. She'd been carrying a thermos of tea. He knew from experience she'd take her time with it. A creature of rituals, that one. Incomprehensible rituals to him, but the patterns were obvious and predictable.

Agent Quinque, the one he truly feared, had left hours before on the long trek back to the crater rim, hauling heavy equipment, probably to scan the skies for enemies. There wasn't anyone as capable in the Magellanix field crew Captain Johnston had left at the base camp, and Piotre hoped for their sake they didn't happen to send a survey craft this way.

With luck, he wouldn't have to deal with the security agent until *Accipiter* arrived with overwhelming force, its hibernation hold full of Quinque equivalents waiting to be unpacked and set into motion. But for the moment, she wasn't in camp, which was the important thing.

That just left the contractors Feyis and Callie. The pair had left camp for a long, trudging survey of the seismographs still placed around the edge of the crater, giving him the moment he had been waiting for. Everyone had lost track of him, as the centipede said they must. Because they trusted him. Because they all wanted to believe in him, for him to find redemption and be their friend.

Such weakness. They needed to believe the Magellanix way was inferior, that Conditioning was a mistake when the opposite was so clearly true.

He made his way back to the team's shelter and slipped casually through the front door. Most of their equipment was stored neatly in the outer vestibule, safe from the cold and snow, but still outside the warmer, inner compartment where they all slept.

There, just as he hoped, was a gear bag, boldly emblazoned with the Magellanix company logo.

Callie's things.

It unsealed at a touch, the smart fabric detecting the heat of his finger. The bag was waterproof, weatherproof, radiation-proof, pathogen-proof, and light to carry, and could have been sealed under layers of bio-authentication which she had left disabled. Callie hadn't bothered to lock it down, and why should she?

They were all friends there.

He rummaged through her gear quickly. Just as he expected, there was Callie's transmitter, a ruggedized clamshell device that fit in the palm of his hand.

He pocketed it and grabbed a food bar for good measure. He unwrapped it and stepped back outside, chewing ostentatiously.

He needn't have bothered. No one was watching; no one cared what he did.

Piotre wandered casually back across the crater floor, making for a large rock outcropping, where he concealed himself from sight of the shelter just in case anyone returned. He found a rock flatter than the rest and squatted down on its edge. In a fit of inspiration, he pulled his outer layers down around his ankles. They had ways to recycle bodily waste, of course, but if someone saw him from a distance, the extra level of deception couldn't hurt.

He was instantly, miserably cold.

The centipede assured him he didn't mind.

He flipped the radio open and powered it to life.

He'd thought this part over carefully. Captain McAllister had done the logical thing. The man was up there in orbit with the power to destroy this place at the touch of a button and must therefore be taken unawares. The shuttle's sensory capabilities were limited, but somewhere out in deep space, *Carpathia* would have her remotes deployed and would be listening for *Accipiter*'s arrival. Even unable to fight, her sensory capabilities were state-of-the-art.

When *Accipiter* arrived, Ian's people on *Carpathia* would signal him. That couldn't be helped. Ian would know how much time he had before he had to order his field team back to the drop-ship, destroy this place, and then make a run for it in the shuttle.

At which point the prize would be lost.

This meant Piotre couldn't simply order the contractors and officers staffing the main Magellanix camp to come there and fight some bloody battle on the side of the volcano. Even if they overcame Agent Quinque, which was unlikely, there was still the problem of the captain and his shuttle—and his fusion bombs.

That in turn meant Captain Ian McAllister had to die. Moreover, it needed to happen with no advance notice.

The solution was straightforward.

It would take *Accipiter* some time to reach Ragnarock from the transition point, but Captain Johnston could send a weapons remote ahead at a much higher speed. Such a device need not be limited to a human-survivable acceleration profile and would be all but undetectable.

If only Captain Johnston knew to do so, she could simply blot Ian McAllister and his shuttle from the sky.

And that was where Piotre could help.

There was also the question of whether the *Carpathia*'s shuttle was capable of picking up transmissions not aimed directly at it. He thought not but couldn't be sure. Everything would be encrypted, but he would prefer McAllister not know there was a call coming from the volcano at all.

No choice, the centipede said.

At least the weather was as bad as ever. There was no way he'd be seen from above by something as mundane as a camera. He was sure Captain McAllister would be watching, but equally, he couldn't be scanning actively, imaging this crater in one of the hundred ways otherwise available to him, for fear of detection by the Magellanix team on the planet's surface.

Do it now.

He turned on the transmitter.

It took a few moments, and then a male voice he didn't recognize answered his call.

"Callie?" the man on the other end said. He sounded out of breath. "Is that you?"

Piotre felt a surge of annoyance at the breach of protocol. "This is Chief Information Officer Piotre Raskovich, and I will remind you to follow standard comms procedures. One-time authentication code follows. Do not respond until you have it confirmed, Mister. Do it now." And with that, he spat out a sequence of digits, a command code only he knew, one that he couldn't have revealed under duress even if he had wanted to.

The young man, whoever he was—probably field crew, judging from his lack of professionalism—went quiet. There was a long pause. Seconds ticked by, and then the voice came back.

"Confirmed," the man said. "Go ahead, sir. I copy."

"That's better." Now, to say this as succinctly as he could. "Relay following to your commander. 'Enemy ship TransGalactic deep-space scout *Carpathia* in-system. Damaged at jump point by *Accipiter*'s remote defenses. *Carpathia* is currently effecting repairs via asteroid mining; location and timing unknown. Enemy shuttle in geosynchronous orbit over following coordinates. Latitude: eight point five three six one degrees north. Longitude: one hundred seventeen point five two five degrees west.

"'Enemy field team on surface at said location, investigating archaeological find of extreme importance. Do not approach. I repeat: do not approach.'"

He took a breath and plunged ahead. "'Magellanix vessel *Accipiter* or similar expected inbound this system immediately. Message vessel captain on arrival. Dispatch high-stealth predator-class remotes or equivalent and kill enemy shuttle. Imperative this attack take place without warning or shuttle will destroy site of extreme repeat extreme value on planet's surface.'

"Now confirm it, Mister," he finished.

"I, uh, confirmed, sir. But I don't understand. According to your call signature, you're using Callie's—I mean Field Generalist diMarck's—radio. Is she with you? Is she okay? And how are you still on the planet? Sir?"

"I said maintain to comms protocol, dammit! Your Field Generalist has betrayed the company and will be dealt with in time. Now confirm my instructions. Do you understand me?"

"Yes, sir. I mean, no, sir, I don't understand, but, yes, sir, your instructions are clear. I'll inform Lieutenant Farrow. Sir."

"Good. Do it now, and do not contact this device under any circumstances. I may or may not communicate again. In the meantime"—and here he broke discipline himself, just for a moment, so great was his urgency —"you tell your lieutenant to send my message to *Accipiter* when it gets here and to kill that fucking shuttle dead. You got that?"

"Yes, sir!"

"Very well. Get to it."

He shut the radio's case with a satisfying *click*. Now the only trick that remained was easing it back into Callie's backpack without being noticed.

But first, deception becoming reality, or maybe his own body pleased to be back in the centipede's fold, he shoved his remaining thermal underlayers down around his ankles, and, grunting in satisfaction, took a long, rattling shit on the crater floor.

Pants comfortably restored, he stepped back around the rock outcropping to find Agent Quinque waiting for him. She held Feyis's transmitter in her left hand and a small, black sidearm in her right.

"Sit down," she said. Her voice, he noticed immediately, was quite different from before. It was a man's voice. The same man, he realized in a moment of mandible-chittering, spine-chilling despair, that he had just been talking to on the radio.

The Interlocutor, he realized.

She'd known all along.

"Neat trick," he said, too stunned for the moment to know how else to respond. "But why the deception? Why bother? If you knew, why wait for me to steal it?"

"Data," Agent Quinque said. Now her voice was female again, the same as it had been the few times she'd spoken in their days together. "Corporate will want all the details of your Conditioning lapse. If indeed you ever suffered one and this hasn't been a hoax from the beginning."

"Oh, I suffered one," he said.

Then he paused, wondering. How had he admitted even that much? He shouldn't have been able to say anything at all.

"That part is true," he added, mostly just to see if he could.

Where was the centipede? It couldn't be gone again. But it was! What was going on?

"They will also be interested in every detail of the actions you chose to take when you returned to Corporate control," Agent Quinque continued.

"Ah."

Impossible! The centipede—his companion—the moment of surprise . . . it had happened again.

"Is there anything more you'd like to say for the record?" Agent Quinque asked. "Because I'm afraid we can't afford to have an enemy agent running around in this camp, and I haven't got time to babysit you."

"Not really, no," he said.

He had a pretty good idea what was coming next, even without the centipede to advise him.

She nodded, her face still expressionless. "Fair enough," she said.

It was almost a mercy when she pulled the trigger. A tiny dart hit him in the side of the neck, and he crumpled to the ground, saved from cracking his head on the hard rocks of the crater floor by Agent Quinque's impossibly strong arms.

As if from afar, he watched, bemused, as his vision faded to black.

CHAPTER 54

Kester was losing herself again. She knew it, but she didn't care.

She was trancing, phasing, falling deep as the snow that drifted in piles outside the shelter Callie and Feyis had rigged for her. It was dangerous and stupid and might even prove fatal if she wasn't careful, and she had no intention of stopping.

It was like old times, like her room in the InterTech lab, staring at the ceiling, counting stars, and drawing constellations in her mind. Like hunting for drop bears to make the trees fall, or watching raindrops on windows as Nya and Johanna sped her through the skies of Paradise.

Or folding singularities and jumping sideways and backward through space and time.

It was like all those things but more. The artifact! The puzzle of puzzles, the mystery of all mysteries, and maybe—just maybe—she was beginning to understand.

The others couldn't see it. Each of them had stated the obvious, but they had all managed to miss the critical point at the same time.

It shimmers, they said. *It glitters, glistens, refracts.* They called it a sphere, this millions-faceted, tessellated construction. They marveled how it caught the diffuse light filtering through the clouds of Ragnarock, how it scattered and reflected that pale ambiance in ways that were strange and complex and beautiful. They stood overwhelmed by its magnificence and the sheer scale of it, the sense and presence of the Other.

They saw what they came to see. Dr. Solarin wanted to talk to it. Piotre Raskovich wanted to profit from it. The captain was peering down at them from orbit, deciding whether or not to destroy it.

Only she knew its secret.

Each of the facets was different.

It was subtle. And it had nothing to do with their size or shape.

It was their reflectivity. The facets were only a few centimeters across, but each was unique. That was why the artifact shimmered and glittered and made the light dance the way it did.

So, she'd decided to map it. To memorize it. She'd taken the little drone flier, one of Nya's toys, and used its high-resolution recording equipment and laser rangefinders to measure the albedo of each facet individually.

What did it matter to her how many millions of them there were?

The flier was easy enough to control. The device had enough onboard AI to know how to compensate for crosswinds, to hover while its optical stabilizers provided her a steady stream of data, surveying the artifact's mirrored surface in the minutest detail.

As was typical, she lost track of the passage of time. Occasionally, the snow and wind howled in the crater so hard, she was forced to ground the tiny drone, but not often. At some point, Callie offered to build her a separate shelter so she could labor in peace, protected from the storms. The materials specialist was a kind soul and probably worried that Kester might freeze to death otherwise.

She hadn't eaten since they'd arrived there, though she observed this fact with a detached, intellectual awareness. She ought to be hungry. She wasn't, and that was all.

The only thing that forced her to take breaks was the battery power of the drone itself. It was a primitive device mechanically, unable to recharge from a beam of focused current while still aloft, and it was too small to be equipped with a photovoltaic skin of its own. It reminded her of a childhood toy Per used to play with back on Aldan's world—before the kesters ate it. Every few hours, she was forced to bring it to ground, swap out one battery for another, replace the spent one in the charging port connected to her private solar array, a flexible set of mats she'd rolled out around her shelter like so many swaths of magic carpet. She'd take care of her body's few biological requirements, and then she was back and flying again. Continuing her survey, recording every detail, both in the drone's memory and her mind.

As time passed, what had begun as a vague idea was turning into a conviction. There was a pattern in the reflectivity of the artifact's millions of facets. They weren't random.

And what better variable than albedo could anyone choose to encode information on a dead planet, locked in an ice age forever? What else would be, as the doctor liked to say, top of mind?

It was, when she thought about it, actually kind of obvious.

But if it was a message, what were its authors trying to say?

She was beginning to think maybe she had an idea about that as well.

Back on *Carpathia*, Nya had told her a story about a pair of interstellar probes constructed in ancient times. They were the first objects humanity managed to hurl out of its solar system, little more than flying antennae equipped with radioisotope thermoelectric generators and instrument packages that even a child raised on Aldan's World would have considered primitive. Nya said they'd been launched in an effort to get the best pictures of Earth's neighboring planets that had yet been taken, and then set on courses that would carry them into the infinite void forever.

But even in those days, some enterprising, forward-thinking humans had wondered whether Someone Else might find them someday.

Those folks had planned accordingly. They'd included audio recordings etched in gold, of whales and children and language and music, all sensible if slightly romantic choices. Not so different in spirit, Kester thought, from the History Lesson Nya had created.

Those long-dead visionaries also thought to include a map, a route back to humanity's home system encoded in the emission signatures of a set of pulsars observable from Earth.

There had been some, Nya said, that thought this was a bad idea. This was before humanity's soul-crushing loneliness had come to be understood, when some still feared the unknown and wondered whether aliens with hostile intent might roam between the stars.

Eventually, it came to light that the map was badly wrong anyway, at least past certain time scales. When technology made such things possible, InterTech sent a ship to collect the probes, housed them in a museum, and made money selling tickets.

The story had stayed with Kester. And she'd started to wonder.

What if whoever put the artifact there had had the same idea? Except instead of a golden record, maybe they encoded information by using the reflectivity of individual facets of their sphere. A hundred million continuous variables, each with a value slightly less than one.

Floating-point variables.

Variable points that floated.

Points in transition.

Transition points.

And that was the thought she didn't dare voice aloud.

What if the artifact itself was a map?

Was it possible?

She thought maybe it was. But time was running out. Even lost in her work as she was, she knew they couldn't stay there forever.

So, she decided to memorize it. She could spend the rest of her life studying it if that was what it took.

A sudden movement broke her focus. She saw Agent Quinque in the peripheral vision of the drone as she repositioned it to record the next sector of facets in her survey.

Ordinarily, she would have given the agent no mind, but at that moment, Quinque was carrying a limp, unmoving Piotre Raskovich. Kester watched as she hauled him bodily back to the shelter, where the Interlocutor stepped into view, carrying a thermos of tea.

Curiosity piqued, she repositioned the drone's camera, focusing on the pair in order to read their lips.

"So, he made the attempt?" the Interlocutor said.

"Yes. You were right," Agent Quinque replied.

"And he suspected nothing?"

"No. The ruse was successful. He believed his call was received by the Magellanix camp. He had no idea Feyis and Callie had configured the transmitter for local communication and found a way to fake the signal."

"Field contractors," the Interlocutor said.

Kester smiled to herself. The Interlocutor was funny sometimes, once you understood her sense of humor.

"Is he hurt?" the Interlocutor added.

"No. He'll sleep for a while. Then we'll have to decide what to do with him."

"That will be your decision, of course. You're in charge of operational security."

"Yes. Still—do you have a recommendation, Interlocutor?"

"I'd say we should keep him on ice, at least for now."

Kester smiled again. It was almost as if the Interlocutor was enjoying this.

"That should be easy enough to manage. Should we call the captain?"

"I think not," the Interlocutor said. "He knew this was possible, and it changes nothing as far as the decisions that lie ahead."

"Understood. And, Interlocutor?"

"Agent?"

"Thank you."

"You are most welcome."

Kester watched another moment as Agent Quinque followed the Interlocutor inside the main shelter.

So, she thought. Piotre Raskovich had betrayed them.

She wasn't surprised.

Everyone always betrayed each other.

Just ask Per.

She refocused the camera, and the drone obligingly fired its sighting laser once more. Accumulating data, helping her build a map in her mind of the artifact's surface and the strange, subtle variations each of its facets contained.

CHAPTER 55

When Ian finally received the message he'd been dreading, it was less than a kilobyte in length. The sum total transmission from *Carpathia*, all he needed to know, encapsulated in just two data points. A location and a time.

Accipiter was there.

He did some quick math in his head and then grunted in acceptance. *Accipiter*'s arrival was within a few hours of what his navigation officers predicted a month before, back when they'd been losing a race he'd thought there was no way to win. That had been before Kester's jump, before her mathematical heroics and feats of spatiotemporal reasoning had given them this brief window to act.

A window that was now about to slam shut.

There'd been no word from his crew on the planet's surface. He knew only that they'd reached the crater, having seen them during those rare moments when the cloud cover cooperated. The doctor appeared to be doing what she had planned, rigging her gear and performing the series of experiments she'd brought.

But the communication protocols he'd established with the team meant all he knew was what he could glean from the occasional glimpse through his scopes. There would be no unnecessary surface-to-orbit chatter. Instead, they were operating with a pair of failsafes, a simple system intended to communicate by the absence of a message, which would be triggered only if something went horribly wrong.

Agent Quinque had configured a personal implant, a device wired directly to her nervous system, controllable with a thought. In essence, she had programmed herself to call for help every six hours unless she overrode the signal. Should she fail to trigger the override—either because they needed help or she was incapacitated or dead—it would activate and ping his shuttle, risking betraying them in exchange for letting him know things had gone badly awry.

As a backup, he'd sent his crew to the surface with a second device, a bit of equipment as primitive as Agent Quinque's cybernetics were advanced.

This was a simple handheld device, a field-portable piece of hardware he'd entrusted to the Interlocutor's possession. It, too, was set to act as a failsafe, to ping him four times a day unless it was specifically told not to.

The Interlocutor had assured him the interval was more than enough time for any sleep she required. He'd accepted her at her word. As far as he could tell, she subsisted on meditation and unending cups of tea.

Those were his security precautions. As for what he could do in case of an emergency, his options were limited. The shuttle didn't have a second drop-ship. If something went wrong, he could reduce the volcano to incandescent gas, retreat to *Carpathia*, and determine what to do from there.

But there was one other signal they had agreed upon as well.

Progress.

Should the doctor make any material advancement in their understanding of the artifact, should she learn or discover something that would change the decisions facing them, she would contact him.

Thus far, there had been nothing.

As for outbound communication, there was only one signal he would send to his people in the field: come home. And there was only one reason to send it: the arrival of *Accipiter*.

Now *Accipiter* was there. The only question that remained was how much more time he should give his team to work.

He'd been over it again and again: there was little else to think about. If *Accipiter* were capable of the same acceleration profile as *Carpathia*, and if she came crashing in-system at all possible speed, she could be there, he estimated, in just over seven days.

Assuming, however, she was equipped with the same class of high-speed interplanetary shuttle he was currently piloting, she could get a team there in five. Shuttles were faster than starships, owing to their specialized design and reduced mass. There was no obvious reason why *Accipiter*'s captain would send a team ahead, but he couldn't afford to take that chance.

He decided to give his team four more days: three in the crater to finish whatever work might still be done, and then one additional day to descend the mountain, reach the drop-ship, and return safely to orbit again.

At which point he'd have one job left to do.

Destroy the artifact.

Or perhaps not.

Because what if he didn't? What if he decided to commit treason, to betray his corporate masters and leave the find intact, to flee from this place with the prize allowed to remain in enemy hands?

What then? What would the Interlocutor do?

What, for that matter, would Agent Quinque do?

He didn't know. Quinque might break his neck with a subtle twist of her wrist, fire the shuttle's fusion engine, incinerate the artifact, level the volcano, and then fly them back to *Carpathia* in the time it took everyone else to realize what had just happened.

Or she might follow his orders blindly.

Or anything in between.

He sighed, frustrated and exasperated with himself, awash once again in his ever-present impostor's syndrome. Captain Marakan would never have . . .

He shook his head in irritation. He was there; she was not. His immediate task was straightforward.

He activated the comm unit and sent a signal to Agent Quinque's implant.

"Accipiter is here," he said. "Return to orbit in four days."

"Understood," she responded immediately.

Four days, he thought.

And then he would have to decide.

CHAPTER 56

In the end, Nya was simply forced to rest. First her ability to concentrate started to go, her mind wandering further and further afield as sleep deprivation set in. Then the hallucinations began. By her fifth day, she was imagining that the boulders littering the crater floor were snow shelters, fliers, or storage vans. She'd catch herself looking over her shoulder, thinking that an entire village had sprung up behind her when she wasn't paying attention, only to whirl and stare and realize, *No, those are just rocks; all is as it was.*

She began to confuse the Carpathians with one another or with individuals from her past. She spent half a day thinking that Agent Quinque was Johanna, that somehow her lover had traveled all those thousands of light-years to be by her side. She mistook the Interlocutor for a professor from twenty years before, a merciless woman who had drilled her endlessly on plate tectonics and marine geology and all those other long-cycle processes whose mathematics and chemistry she had been required to know in the minutest detail.

She was so tired. Too tired to think, to create, to imagine some new path forward. Too tired to run through her battery of tests and holos again, knowing the exercise would prove futile. When she learned of it, she accepted Piotre Raskovich's betrayal with a dull sense of inevitability, feeling no remorse.

What she felt was despair dancing at the edges of her vision like a little swarm of black butterflies, pressing ever closer to her eyes, her mind, her heart.

It was the drugs, she realized at last. This wasn't normal fatigue. She ought to be tired, but because she hadn't let herself sleep, she was passing into someplace beyond exhaustion. Some sort of accumulated response to the stresses of the journey, the constant trips back and forth between enforced unconsciousness and waking restfulness, the steady parade of pharmaceuticals waging war with her body's endogenous rhythms and natural processes.

This is what failure feels like, she thought. *On an epic, unprecedented scale.*

No. Not failure.

Collapse.

It was Agent Quinque who finally offered her some relief, in the form, inevitably, of yet more drugs. Maybe the agent had some compassion in her own way. Or maybe her deterioration was so obvious, the agent was afraid she would wander away and fall off a cliff unobserved.

"Dr. Solarin?" Quinque said softly, having made a point—Nya processed dimly—of approaching her slowly, arms spread wide, doing all she could not to surprise her or appear a threat.

"Yes?" she managed to say.

"Please take this." Quinque held out her hand and uncurled a gloved fist, revealing a device Nya recognized as a subdural implant.

"What is it?"

"For you, it is rest. Which you desperately need."

"Yeah? How much rest are you offering?"

"One REM cycle. Please, Doctor. I insist."

Something in that last word stopped Nya's protests before they began. Agent Quinque was right, of course. And even compromised as she was, Nya had no desire to learn what a security agent was capable of if she were forced to insist further.

"Okay," she acquiesced. Without another word, she turned and shuffled off to the shelter, thinking she'd better get comfortable first. Quinque padded behind her, footfalls soft as one of the predators of the high karst country Nya had once called home.

She unsealed the door and stepped inside. When she shut it behind her, the sound of the wind died immediately. These tents were amazing, her addled mind thought. If they built a big-enough one, they could live forever up there. Why, they could build an entire city! And study the artifact for the rest of their lives.

She stripped off her outer layers, down to just a thin undershirt, and rolled up her left sleeve. The implant was shaped like a lozenge and pulsed a soft electric blue. She pressed it to the inside of her elbow, squeezed it, and felt the tiniest pinprick, the device's way of telling her it was working.

Then she fell into an unconsciousness as deep as any she had ever known.

She awoke four hours later to a crowd.

Feyis, Callie, Agent Quinque, and the Interlocutor were all sitting quietly, taking a modest meal. Even Piotre Raskovich was there. His body, at any rate; whatever the Quinque had done to him, he had yet to return to consciousness. *Stacking us in here like cordwood*, she thought. The tent was turning into a storage facility.

Only Kester was absent. Why didn't Quinque knock her out, she wondered? *Why does she get to keep playing with her flier when I have to be made to sleep like a child?*

The answer, of course, was that she, Nya Solarin, was mission-critical. Kester was never supposed to have been there at all.

The Interlocutor saw her watching them and gave her a slight smile. "How do you feel, Doctor?" she said.

How did she feel, anyway? She performed a brief mental self-examination. "Better," she admitted. She caught Quinque's eye. The woman's gaze, roving, flitting from place to place, her unending vigilance some base state of her programming. *When does security get to relax*, Nya wondered? Maybe never.

"Thank you, Agent," she said.

The statuesque woman nodded gravely. "It's good to see you refreshed. Unfortunately, there is news from the captain."

Which could only mean one thing. "*Accipiter* is here?"

"Affirmative."

"How much time do we have?"

"Three days. And then we must be gone from this place before the enemy arrives."

With that, Agent Quinque nodded once, turned, and ducked her way out of the shelter.

"If you need anything from us, just let us know," Callie added. She and Feyis followed Quinque out, leaving Nya alone with the Interlocutor and Piotre Raskovich's unmoving form.

"That was nicely choreographed," she said.

The Interlocutor looked back at her, impassive. "Cup of tea?" she asked mildly.

"No! I don't want a cup of tea!" She was out of bed and on her feet almost before she knew she had stood. There was no time to wonder whether she was feeling some aftereffect of the sleep drug or if the Interlocutor was provoking her deliberately.

"Gods damn it!" she cried. "Three days? What's three days? I could spend three years and get nowhere. I've tried everything. I've used up all my tricks, all my clever ideas. What I need is time. I can't innovate on demand. I can't schedule breakthroughs. Gods!" she said again. "Why bring me in the first place? They should have sent a team of materials scientists. Or Machine God priests. What am I possibly supposed to know that others don't?"

She collapsed back on her bunk, shaking her head, feeling a mixture of relief at finally giving voice to the frustrations of the last week coupled with a note of shame, disgusted with herself for her outburst and her lack of control.

And a tinge of resentment. The Interlocutor must have seen this coming.

"How long have you known?" she asked abruptly.

"I'm not sure I understand," the Interlocutor said.

"The captain's message. He didn't call when I was asleep, did he? I bet he called hours ago. You staged this. To manipulate me, control me. Get me to sleep, then shock me awake, to provoke me into some sudden insight? Admit it! You planned this."

The Interlocutor was resting in a synth-woven chair, having folded her bed into a sitting configuration. She seemed to settle deeper into its depths with a sigh.

"I admit nothing, Doctor. But only because I am not forced to. You needed sleep. Agent Quinque and I discussed it and decided it was time to intervene. In point of fact, news of *Accipiter*'s arrival did reach us in the four-hour window in which your body and mind were in a forced state of recovery. That part is a simple coincidence. But if it makes you feel any better, I certainly would have considered the tactic you proposed, had it been advantageous to do so."

"Do you know," Nya said, "at times, I simply despise you?"

"It comes with the territory," the Interlocutor said. "But how you may feel about me personally is irrelevant. My job is to help you. And whatever you may believe, I do understand—far better than anyone else here, and better than you probably imagine—the pressure you are under."

"The pressure I'm under." She laughed. "What do you know about pressure? What does anyone?"

She trailed off. A glimmer of thought danced at the edges of her mind. An earlier idea, from days before, when they'd first arrived.

"Pressure," she repeated.

She cocked her head sideways as if to alter her vision and focus, to peer at some distant unknown place.

"Pressure," she said a third time.

And then she knew.

"Oh," she said. She stood up and stepped to the shelter's door. She ran her finger along the seam. The smart fabric unsealed under her touch. She listened to the faint hiss as it equalized with Ragnarock's atmosphere outside. The shelter was heated and flexible. It was warmer inside than out. It obeyed the ancient imperatives of Boyle's law. Pressure times volume equals temperature, with some constants thrown in to trip up young students taking chemistry exams.

A millennium's worth of advances in organic chemistry, protein folding, and drug synthesis, but the physical universe they lived in was organized in the same fashion it had always been.

Pressure. Volume. Temperature.

All things that described a planet's atmosphere.

She resealed the tent and turned to regard the Interlocutor, who was staring back at her with a twinkle in her eye. "Do you know?" she said. "What I think we might do?"

"Of course not," the Interlocutor said. "But I recognize an epiphany when I see it. Would you like to tell me?"

"In fact, I would," Nya said. "We are going to weave a tent. A really big one. And then we'll pressurize it like a giant balloon."

"Why would we do that?"

"Because we're going to emulate what the atmospheric conditions in this crater will be a few million years from now when this volcano subsides back to the sea."

"You think the artifact has some sort of pressure lock on it?"

"No," Nya said. "I think that if someone or something is aware in there, the one way we can tell them we understand them is to communicate that we think on the same time scales they do. Even if, of course, we do not."

The Interlocutor nodded once. "Then you have work to do," she said gravely.

"We all do," Nya said. "And there's no time to waste."

Once she had her mind around the problem, Callie claimed that it would take two of their three remaining days to weave Nya's tent. She seemed thrilled at the assignment, though Nya suspected this had more to do with the sheer challenge of it than any belief the experiment would produce some result. Still, Callie's enthusiasm was infectious: she was almost childlike with delight. The former Magellanix employee spent the next few hours familiarizing herself with the design differences between Magellanix and TransGalactic weavers—there weren't many—clucking over her newfound toys like a mother hen with a nest full of chicks.

Then Callie got to work, and Nya could finally take a break, sitting back and watching as the woman calculated tensile strengths, computed the necessary fabric thickness and the raw square meters of the stuff were going to need. They'd be turning volcanic rock into something resembling spun glass, an ultra-strong, flexible material that had to cover the enormity of the artifact while not being ripped to shreds in the wind.

Good thing Callie was a materials specialist, Nya thought. They were going to need a lot of material.

The weavers themselves were deceptively simple devices, cubical in shape, with an upper chamber into which raw material was placed, and a lower chamber where power, programming, and a fast-replicating swarm of nanobots came together to do the real work. There was also an output chute, which began extruding spun silver thread as though they were some fantastical pair of mechanical spiders.

They were remarkably fast. The biggest challenge was figuring out how to collect the sheets and knit them together without their being blown away. Even at the bottom of the crater, the wind could dip down, threatening to lift the thousands of square meters of fabric the project required, tear it free, and send it flapping into the sky like an enormous wounded bird.

Feyis, ever the pragmatist, suggested they pile rocks on the stuff.

There was no shortage of those.

The hard part would come at the end. How in the world would they get the tent into position? The artifact was massive. They could weave enough fabric to cover it, but they couldn't just toss it up there like a magician throwing a scarf over a crystal ball. Nor could they lower their tent from the drop-ship; the craft wasn't built to hover, and the exhaust it emitted taking off and landing would incinerate the material in an instant.

Nor did the little imaging drone that so captured Kester's imagination possess anywhere near the lifting power.

In the end, Feyis rolled his eyes, sighed heavily, and admitted there was another weather balloon packed away at camp, back at the base of the volcano. The kit included several helium canisters and, he added grudgingly, was something he could probably manage to haul up there, given enough time.

Nya thanked him profusely and didn't ask for any details of his progress as he trudged in and out of camp over the next two and a half days.

He didn't look like he wanted to talk about it.

~

Just half a day remained before the captain's order to begin the descent when, at last, they were ready. The Carpathians gathered around Nya to watch. Even Kester, her flier grounded now, joined the group to observe the final touches with interest. Nya had apologized for interrupting Kester's work some hours before; obviously, the drone wouldn't be able to record any more images once the tent was in place.

But the strange young woman had just said, "That's okay. I have what I need."

Nya didn't know what exactly Kester meant by that. For the moment, it didn't seem to matter, as she had plenty else to occupy her mind.

Callie had woven a dozen pouches into the tent. These were spaced at thirty-degree intervals around the top and would be inflated with the helium from Feyis's balloon. Feyis and Callie had also attached half a dozen guide lines, one for each of the six of them. Even the Interlocutor would be needed to help haul the tent into position, though the old monk seemed unconcerned, assuring them she was stronger than she looked.

Per Feyis's suggestion, they waited for evening, when the wind subsided as much as it ever did. Nya fretted; they had so little time left. They'd come all this way, only to be rushed at the end.

Fieldwork, she thought. There was never enough time.

The sun fell, the wind picked up and then calmed back down, and when it remained gentle for half an hour, a very tired Feyis opined this was as good a time as any. Nya had no reason to doubt his word. He'd logged more hours in this crater than any human alive.

She took a deep breath and exhaled noisily.

"Let's do it," she said.

"Copy that," Callie said. "Here we go."

They eased the valves on the helium tanks open, releasing a trickle of gas through lines Feyis had rigged, slowly inflating the pouches. A cheer rose up as the tent achieved lift, rising from the ground like a great shadowy ghost. It spread out and was caught by a gust of wind. For a moment, Nya thought they'd lost it; the entire assembly billowed like a sail, but then the wind subsided again, and the fabric luffed and fell slack.

Callie gave it more helium and the tent drifted higher into the sky. The guide lines snaked away, the group fanning out in all directions. Nya had positioned Agent Quinque and Feyis at the farthest lines. The two took off at a jog, circumnavigating the base of the artifact. The others followed more slowly with less distance to cover.

The tent was bell-shaped, so seen from afar, it must have looked as though some enormous predatory jellyfish had crept up on the artifact, slid up its side, and now, as it cleared the top, was preparing to drop down from above.

They reached the critical point, the bulk of the tent cresting the top of the artifact. One bad gust of wind and they'd lose it for sure. The substance was tough—it probably wouldn't tear, but if it blew free and fouled on a cliffside, they'd have to find a way to retrieve it and start the whole process again.

"Vent the gas!" Nya shouted. Callie dumped the pouches in response. Their luck held just long enough. The wind stayed calm, and as if by magic, the sides of the tent slid down, draping over the artifact, until they were in position to close the ring at the base like a giant sphincter muscle contracting.

She realized she was holding her breath. In spite of the week's disappointments, she couldn't help but hope for some reaction from the artifact. Maybe their makeshift tent would burst into flames or disappear in a flash. But nothing happened. The strange alien construction remained inert as ever.

The question now was how to affix the tent to the ground. This, too, Feyis and Callie had solved with piles of rocks, strategically prepositioned around the artifact's perimeter. Agent Quinque chose to reveal something of her hidden strength. The woman was a blur of motion, the level of physical capability on display staggering as she weighted the edge of the fabric with stones.

And then, at last, the tent was in place. They would continue to improve the seal over time, further weighting it down and burying the edges, but it wasn't going anywhere. It would hold.

Callie had woven the fabric such that one side of the tent had a small vestibule, which formed a nubby protrusion at the base. This was to provide them a place where they could work, safe from the elements but next to the artifact's surface, so they could observe it directly should anything change.

There was a brief clearing in the clouds. Nya imagined the captain up there in orbit, gazing down on them through high-definition imaging equipment, wondering what the hell they were doing. She'd wanted to send status reports, but his orders were clear. Critical information only.

She'd say something when she knew something.

The six of them gathered in the vestibule, and Nya asked the only question that mattered.

"Can anyone think of a reason not to proceed?"

"It's your call, Doctor," Agent Quinque said.

"Okay, then," she said. "Let's raise the temperature and see if anything happens."

Feyis nodded. He and Callie stepped back outside, returning moments later with the environmental unit from their shelter.

"It'll take a little while," he said. "You've built a considerably larger tent than this heater was designed for."

"How long?" Nya asked, embarrassed that she hadn't thought that part through.

"Figure at sea level, we'd be at just under a thousand millibars. Ragnarock's atmosphere is a bit thinner than Earth-standard but nothing crazy. We're about seven hundred up here, so—let's see . . ."

Callie had bent over the environmental unit's control panel, hard at work overriding its settings such that it would spend its stored power at maximum rate, generating heat faster than its manufacturers likely imagined would ever be required.

"Three hours," she said, not looking up.

"Well, there you go," Feyis said. "Then what do you think happens, Doctor?"

"Gods only know," Nya said. "We've got about twelve hours left before we have to leave this place forever. Maybe we'll at least get an A for effort and whatever is in there will come out and say hello."

CHAPTER 57

Ian had three minutes to live.

His first thought was that he'd gotten lucky. It was only by chance that he had any warning at all.

By virtue of a simple fluke of geometry, a chance scanning of the sky with his shuttle's telescopes had picked out the incoming missile silhouetted against one of Ragnarock's moons. The weapon system that had come to kill him was running dark, all EM emissions silenced, no longer under acceleration but still unable to prevent detection in that most old-fashioned of ways: it was backlit perfectly. It was, Ian thought, as though it had been staged for a photo, its twenty-meter, snub-nosed, fusiform body silhouetted black on white.

It was picturesque. But also lethal.

The visual had triggered a geometric anomaly in the shuttle's image-processing systems. Not unlike, he supposed, the alerts that had captured Piotre Raskovich's attention a year before, starting all this madness in the first place. Automated tracking systems engaged, providing him an image feed now displayed on his main screen along with a range, bearing, and estimated intercept time helpfully annotated underneath.

A hundred eighty seconds with which to work.

He recognized the missile's design from his officer's training years before. It was, unsurprisingly, a Magellanix weapon.

His next thought was to wonder about the identity of the ship that was now in the process of killing him. Was it really *Accipiter* out there? With Captain Anne Johnston in command?

Probably, he thought. Whoever it was, they were smarter than him. Or, at least, less prone to foolish mistakes. He had overlooked the obvious. His inexperience had caught up with him at last, and this time, it was going to cost him his life.

"The remotes."

He muttered the words aloud, the first human voice to sound in the shuttle since his brief conversation with Agent Quinque.

The gods-damned weapons remotes.

With the benefit of hindsight, it made perfect sense. The first thing *Accipiter* would have done upon arrival in-system was to interrogate her remotes, out at the transition point. She would have authenticated herself, and the remaining weaponry she'd left behind would have given her a status update, which would of course have included an incident report of their encounter with *Carpathia*. It must have been confusing at first.

Another ship in this system, ahead of her?

She'd never know how *Carpathia* managed the feat. Likely, she assumed there was a third ship all along.

It didn't matter now. Either way, he was dead because he was an idiot. Whoever the enemy commander was, she hadn't brought her ship to Ragnarock on some crash-acceleration profile. Nor had she sent a high-speed shuttle ahead.

She'd done the expedient thing and simply sent a missile instead. Probably several. He'd just gotten lucky and seen one of them.

He could see it all play out in his mind's eye. She'd known Piotre Raskvoich for a traitor, had known there was an enemy ship behind her, and had transitioned into Ragnarock's system, only to learn someone had beaten her there. Someone with the right authentication codes to shut down the weapons remotes she left behind.

So, she'd fired a volley of missiles, unencumbered by constraints on their acceleration profiles—no onboard humans to keep alive!—with what were probably some pretty basic instructions.

Kill anything you find.

But it wouldn't be quite as simple as that, would it? He felt a brief glimmer of hope. The missile he'd just seen—it would at least interrogate him first, wouldn't it?

Maybe not. He'd only seen it because it had been backlit by a moon, but his shuttle was parked in orbit above Ragnarock, lit up by a pearly sphere of blue and white behind him.

There was no way it had missed him. It would even now be imaging his craft in every detail, right down to the TransGalactic logo boldly emblazoned on its side.

Hope faded as quickly as it had arisen and was replaced by something more like acceptance.

Now he only had two minutes to live and a decision to make.

The shuttle couldn't maneuver in any meaningful way, nor was it equipped with any sort of point-defense system that would be useful against what was coming for him. He couldn't fight, and he couldn't flee. He could, he supposed, dip his nose toward the planet, fire his maneuvering thrusters, and burn himself up in the atmosphere, saving the incoming missile the trouble.

Not a particularly attractive option.

Or he could use the time that remained to destroy the artifact, thereby completing his mission the last way he knew how.

Which would of course doom his field team in the process. He'd told them they had four days. The missile had gotten there faster than that. They'd still be in the crater, nowhere near their drop-ship, with minutes instead of hours to get clear.

It would be easy enough to do. He'd left a command window open, with a large red icon labeled fire in the lower right corner. All he had to do was poke a finger at it and the shuttle would take care of the rest, engaging its fusion core, sending a string of miniature deuterium spheres toward the volcano, lasering them into criticality on the way down . . .

Or he could not.

That was a choice too.

Ninety seconds.

He could send his team a message instead. He composed it quickly in his mind: *Run and hide! Get yourselves the hell off that mountain, back to the drop-ship, and into space as quickly as you can.* Maybe they could make for a crater on one of Ragnarock's moons, hunker down, and wait this thing out.

Not pleasant, but better than the alternative.

Sixty seconds.

It would be a horrible dereliction of duty. He'd be no better than Piotre Raskovich in his own way. A traitor to his cause, a betrayer of his corporation, a weakling of a captain who, faced with the first difficult command decision of his career, couldn't get the job done.

Was that how he'd be remembered?

He thought about it for a few precious seconds and discovered that he didn't care.

He knew what he was going to do.

Was he preserving knowledge? Saving the archaeological find of all finds for future generations? Giving humanity a chance to understand something about its place in the universe?

Mostly, he just couldn't bear to condemn his people to death. They were his responsibility. They'd served under him, worked for him, had believed in him despite his naiveté and inexperience. Or at least suspended their disbelief, which amounted to the same thing.

Either way, they'd followed him this far.

He'd be damned if his incompetence would cost them their lives.

He waved the command window away, dismissing the launch button from the screen. Easing his finger from the trigger, putting down the metaphorical gun.

He wrote the message and sent it in plain text, not trusting himself to use his own voice. Agent Quinque responded with an immediate confirmation of receipt, acknowledging the contents. Then he flicked his communication system silent, not having the heart to hear anything more she might have to say.

With that done, he sat back and watched the missile track toward him, the lethal, dark shape passing in front of an infinite backdrop of stars.

He wondered what it would look like when the missile detonated. It was nighttime down below. His team would see the explosion. It should make quite a display of fireworks, the flashing heat of a second sun burning briefly through the night and clouds.

But it wouldn't last. He'd spend a few brief moments as a burning cloud of plasma, which would cool quickly, reduced to a ball of gently diffusing gas.

Something Captain Marakan had said came to him then. A rumination of hers on the nature of things, words she'd uttered in the aftermath of *Carpathia*'s disastrous maiden voyage, their failed effort to save the *Santa Maria.* A spacer's reflection on the inevitable, the destiny of all complex systems, even the universe itself.

"*Entropy, entropy, Ian,*" she had said. "*In the end, all winds down.*"

CHAPTER 58

Night had fallen, dark, heavy, and cold, bringing drifts of fresh snow and the slow annihilation of what for Nya had briefly felt like optimism. The six of them were clustered inside the tent's vestibule, where the temperature was a balmy thirty degrees centigrade. This was the equilibrium value they'd reached two hours before, the warmth required to balance the math and create enough overpressure around the artifact's surface to simulate a descent to sea level that would not play out for tens of millions of years, as continental drift, subsidence, and erosion did the slow work of eons.

Winding the clock forward. It seemed like an appropriate solution for a Carpathian.

Except once again, nothing had happened.

Nothing at all.

They would be forced to leave the following morning. Half a day remained to do the work of a lifetime. Exhaustion was a welcome friend now. It took Nya's mind away from self-recrimination.

From ruminating on her failure.

The artifact wasn't going to open. It wasn't going to wake up, look up, rise up, power up, do anything at all. Maybe in the end, it was just some exotic alien work of art or had died from natural causes a million years before.

Or maybe it simply wanted nothing to do with them, in spite of her cleverness and monkey-brain tricks.

There were a million explanations. None of them mattered.

She had failed.

She felt a pressure on her elbow and jumped, startled to see Agent Quinque standing beside her. "Step outside with me, Doctor," the Agent said. "I need a moment of your time."

Quinque's voice brooked no debate. Her grip on Nya's arm was soft but insistent, all that strength and power barely hidden beneath the surface of her touch.

The team around her didn't seem to notice. Feyis and Callie were huddled in quiet conversation. The Interlocutor had slid into some sort of trancelike state, Raskovich was still drugged, and Kester was passed out on a rough pile of discarded thermal gear in the corner, unmoving.

"Okay," Nya said.

Without another word, Quinque led her out of the vestibule and into the dark. It was snowing hard. They walked for no more than a minute, the Agent taking long strides that Nya found difficult to match.

They paused behind a rock outcropping. Alone, just the two of them—but why?

"Look up," the agent said.

Her voice was as powerful as her touch, leaving no room to argue. Nya squinted, looked upward, and saw nothing. Not even the clouds, just a black backdrop from which small flakes fell in great clumps, stinging her eyes.

Then the sky turned bright orange.

It happened without sound or warning. The darkness around her vanished in an instant as the cloud layer was backlit from above by a second sun. The clouds burned, pulsing, seeming to glow from within with a diffuse glare that was sourceless but still impossibly bright.

"What the f—!" She bit off her curse, squeezing her eyes shut. Explosion, some part of her brain said. "Are we under attack?"

"It was the captain," Agent Quinque said.

"What?"

"He sent me a message ninety seconds ago. His shuttle was being targeted by an inbound weapons remote. A high-speed missile, a hunter-killer device fired from whatever ship gated in three days ago. He was lucky; his imagers caught a glimpse of it passing in front of one of this planet's moons. Such that he had a narrow window of time in which to act."

Nya opened her eyes again and stared upward at the still-burning sky.

"What happened?"

"He died, Doctor. But that is the wrong question."

"Then what's the right one?"

"If Captain McAllister knew he was about to die," the agent said, "then why are we still alive?"

"I don't understand."

"Think, Doctor." Agent Quinque jogged her arm minutely, and she felt a shock run up her arm and into her neck. "The captain had a task to complete," Quinque went on. "He had a duty and chose not to do it. He didn't use the shuttle's engines to destroy this place. But he should have."

"He spared us? Is that what you're suggesting?"

"I'm not suggesting anything, Doctor. For the moment, I'm simply stating facts."

The agent released Nya's elbow. Nya fingered the joint carefully, relieved to find it intact.

"There is an enemy ship in this system," Agent Quinque continued. "And it has done exactly what Piotre Raskovich was trying to advise it to do when we foiled his attempt. It dispatched a high-speed interplanetary weapons system, which found and destroyed *Carpathia*'s shuttle. Though presumably not *Carpathia* herself."

"But how?" Nya said. "You intercepted Piotre's transmission. You and the Interlocutor fooled him. How could they know?"

"The captain suspected they figured it out on their own," Quinque said with what sounded like genuine remorse. "They queried their remaining remotes when they arrived. It's my fault. I'm Security. I should've made certain the captain had considered that possibility. I didn't think to ask him, and I didn't double-check his math. He calculated how much time we had left on the assumption *Accipiter* would come here herself or, at worst, dispatch a high-speed shuttle. Not that she would deploy a weapons system immediately."

Nya's brain was almost working again, her mind catching up to what had happened even as the burning sky began slowly to fade to black.

In the distance, she heard shouting. It sounded like Feyis, wondering where she and the Agent had gone.

"Ian's dead." She spoke the words aloud, giving voice to them to see if they sounded real.

"Yes," Agent Quinque said.

"And he didn't finish the job. He spared us."

The agent stared back at her, saying nothing to that. Watching her, letting her think it through.

"And now it falls to us," Nya said at last. "That's what you're thinking, isn't it? That the captain failed. That he should've killed us to finish the mission, and since he didn't destroy the artifact . . . we have to."

Still, Agent Quinque said nothing, just held her with her impassive stare, waiting like the Interlocutor would have done. *Gods*, Nya thought. *Human Resources. Security. No wonder they're in the same department.*

It's the same damned discipline.

She heard Feyis shout again but still couldn't make out what he was saying, the man's words snatched away by the never-ceasing wind.

"We have no way to destroy it," she said at last.

"Are you sure about that?"

"How could we possibly?"

"To begin with," the agent said, "there's the fuel in the drop-ship."

"It can't fly up here!"

"That is inaccurate. It can't land up here."

"But it's our only way to escape this place."

"That much is true," Agent Quinque agreed. "But where would we go? It's a drop-ship, not a shuttle."

Nya thought about it for a moment. "One of Ragnarock's moons," she said.

The Agent gave a terse nod. "That was the captain's final suggestion. Though, obviously, we must discount it, given his strangely emotional decision-making when facing his own demise. You are nevertheless correct. The drop-ship could take us to a moon. It's built to escape higher-gravity worlds than this one, and it has the range. But then what, Doctor? What would we do?"

"Wait and hope, I guess," she said. "For *Carpathia* to rescue us."

"That, too, is conceivable," Agent Quinque said. "We might remain hidden for months, years even. We have food, air and water recyclers, and power. Most importantly, we have the weavers you saw fit to include on this mission. *Carpathia* might repair herself. She might fight or sneak her way through to retrieve us. We might escape with our lives."

"But?"

"But our primary duty is no longer to survive, Dr. Solarin. Other mission parameters must take precedence."

Understanding dawned at last.

"You're talking to me out here alone because it's my call. Is that it? I'm in command now. And you want to know what I'm going to do."

"You are in scientific command, Doctor. I'm in charge of security. And this is a security concern now, at least in part," Agent Quinque said. "To be candid, it's not entirely clear whose decision this is. It would be better for everyone if you and I came to a consensus."

"Ah." Nya considered. Above her, the sky was growing darker by the moment, the brief evidence of Ian McAllister's death already fading away.

Not much of an epitaph, she thought.

"Nya! Agent Quinque!" She heard Feyis shout again, close enough now that his words were distinguishable.

"We're right here," she called back. She stepped out from behind the rock, suddenly aware that she wanted his company. She had no desire to have this conversation with Agent Quinque alone. Not yet, at least. She wasn't ready.

"What the hell is going on?" Feyis said, spotting her at last.

"Our captain is dead," Nya said. "He was attacked. Probably by *Accipiter*. We need to go tell the others."

CHAPTER 59

When Nya returned to the vestibule, the others were already awake—save for Piotre Raskovich, whom Quinque now roused by jamming a stimulant-loaded needle into his arm.

Then the agent laid it out for them, recounting the story she had given to Nya about Captain McAllister's final actions.

Her words were met with silence. Agent Quinque turned to Nya, seeming to indicate it was her turn to speak. But no words came. Nya looked away, fixing her attention on the wall of the artifact behind them. She knew she ought to set some direction, to give a speech about their next moves, but at that moment didn't know what to say.

The Interlocutor saved her. "This is a lot for all of us to process," she said mildly. "May I recommend, Doctor, that we reconvene in half an hour to discuss our options?"

Nya exhaled in relief. "Of course," she said. "I'm sure that with a little time . . ."

She trailed off abruptly and felt her jaw drop. She pointed numbly.

The artifact had opened at last.

Nya had imagined it in so many different ways. How could she not? On some level, she had always expected the thing to reveal itself. So much surface area enclosing all that volume; there had to be something in there. Something that would come out or invite them in if only they could figure out the secret knock.

But what would it be like if it actually happened?

Maybe, she'd thought, a dot would appear, a pinprick with light pouring forth, which would stretch into a crack, then widen into a door. Or maybe the surface of the artifact would start to ripple, turn from a solid to a liquid, and then flow apart like mercury to reveal a passage inside.

Maybe there would be some slow, grinding noise as of mighty, creaking doors. Or a perfectly circular aperture would widen like a muscle unclenching.

Or there would come a blast of sulfur like a gate to hell.

But what Nya saw instead was simply an opening where there hadn't been one before. Without any transition of any kind, in no time at all, the artifact abruptly had a rectangular hole in its side, perhaps two and a half meters high and a meter and a half wide. The bottom was almost even with the crater floor, such that anyone who wanted to enter would have to step over a small lip, like a doorsill.

The opening was pitch-black. It was impossible to see anything inside.

It had been pure chance that Nya was the one facing the wall and so had noticed it first. Now the others turned and saw what she was seeing. For a moment, no one spoke.

Then Feyis bent down, rummaged through a pile of their gear, and offered her a high-powered, handheld torch without a word.

Nya flicked it to life. The beam stabbed through the modest illumination provided by the vestibule's lighting, reached the gaping opening in the side of the artifact, and—stopped.

It didn't reflect. It didn't illuminate. Where the torchlight touched the hole, it just ceased to be.

"Albedo zero," Kester said.

Nya looked at her. "What was that?"

"Perfect darkness. Null information. No data."

"No data," Nya repeated. "That's a curious way of describing it."

Kester shook her head. "Not really."

"Okaaay," Nya said slowly. "Feyis, you have that climbing axe you're always lugging around?"

"It's outside. Hang on." He stepped out, returned a moment later, and handed her the ice tool like he was presenting her with some medieval weapon.

She hefted it. *Lights and sticks,* she thought. The basics of all fieldwork.

She stepped toward the artifact, reaching out with the axe carefully, not sure what to expect. Maybe it would meet some rigid surface, or maybe it would feel like stabbing honey, like poking it into a viscous fluid.

Instead, there was only a void. Like the flashlight beam, the end of Feyis's ice axe disappeared from sight as it entered the hole. Nya felt nothing, no resistance of any kind.

She withdrew the climbing tool. It appeared unchanged by her experiment.

At least it wasn't a smoldering, smoking stump, she thought. *Or been rendered into nonexistence.*

"We should be recording this," she said.

"I already am," Callie said with a nod of her head. She had donned a hood with imagers woven through it, one they had frequently used for surveying the crater and perimeter of the artifact.

"Thanks," Nya said. "Okay. For the benefit of whoever views this someday, we must assume we are now in a First Contact situation. We have observed a clear state change in the artifact, though whether in response to the sea-level pressure conditions we are simulating or some other stimulus, we cannot say. We also note an obvious coincidence in timing with the loss of Captain McAllister's shuttle . . ."

She trailed off, thinking.

A coincidence in timing, indeed.

An idea was beginning to form, but she knew enough not to try to force it. She resumed her narration; that at least was comfortable ground. "There are a number of options for how we might proceed," she went on. "We might attempt to fly the drone inside, though it should be noted that intrusive explorations must consequently carry an increased level of personal risk . . ."

But before she could continue, a second extraordinary event occurred.

Numbers appeared directly above the newly formed door—if a door was what they were seeing.

08:00:00

The characters were dark purple at first, almost invisible, then growing brighter even as they began to change color, marching up the visible spectrum. Purple turned blue and then green, giving way to yellow, orange, and red, and then disappearing entirely, only to return moments later and finally settle into a kind of aquamarine color. It was as though, Nya thought, whatever controlled them had some idea of what the human eye could perceive, but was coloring over the edges of the lines a little bit, just in case.

She turned and looked at each of her fellow Carpathians. Their faces glowed at her in the illumination from the artifact's display.

"You all seeing this?" she said, breaking the hush that had fallen over the group.

"That's affirmative," Callie replied.

Then the numbers began to decrease.

07:59:59

07:59:58

07:59:57

"Um, Nya?" Kester said. "It's the same font you used. Remember? When you were trying to teach it the development of human language?"

"That," Nya said after a moment, "is a pretty emphatic demonstration of comprehension."

"There's something else," Kester said. "The eight hours. It's the captain's original timing."

"Kester is right," Agent Quinque said. "We were supposed to leave the crater exactly eight hours from now."

"Someone is trying to tell us something," Feyis said.

"Or warn us," Quinque said.

"I think you're both right," Nya said. "And that what's going on here is, whoever they are, we have confused the hell out of them."

"Care to explain, Doctor?" the Interlocutor said, speaking for the first time since they had all reentered the vestibule. She had, Nya noted, positioned herself next to Piotre. Agent Quinque was flanking him on the other side, although he wasn't moving at all, just staring wide-eyed at the artifact behind her.

Nya took a breath, gathering her thoughts, wondering if it made sense. "I think our plan with the tent worked. That we demonstrated to whoever or whatever is in control of the artifact that we understood the critical point: they were planning to be here a long time. At the same time, all of our actions along the way—including what happened to Ian—have communicated the exact opposite. We've been telling it we understand but showing it there's no possible way that can be true."

"I'm not sure I follow," Feyis said.

"It's a matter of time scales," she said. "It always has been. Think about it this way. Assume we are looking at a construct built by a spacefaring race. Assume further that their experience of the cosmos is the same as ours: wherever they go, they find holocaust worlds like this one. But suppose they think over much longer time horizons than we do. Enough to put a long-term outpost on a dormant volcano, located on a holocaust world locked in an ice age.

"Why? Why go to all that trouble? The only answer I can think of is to see what happens next."

"What could possibly happen?" Feyis said. "The inhabitants of this place are dead. Their cities are buried under kilometers of ice. Trust me—Callie and I ought to know."

"You're right," Nya agreed. "In the short term, not much is going to change here. But think over longer horizons," she went on, feeling herself warming to the idea, the explanation, her thoughts becoming clearer in her head as she spoke them aloud. "Maybe they wanted to know if this planet's ecosphere would recover. Maybe they're not interested in the former inhabitants of this place at all. Suppose they're ecologists, not anthropologists, and they're collecting ultra-long observations on the recovery of worlds that have died. There's still life here, isn't there?"

"Nothing you'd want to eat," Feyis said.

"Well, right! But there's a liquid equatorial sea, an algal community pumping oxygen into the atmosphere. The ocean lives. The land is dead, but life begins and ends in the sea."

"What are you saying—that they're using this place like some sort of natural lab?" Callie asked.

"If you're accustomed to thinking in very long time scales, why not? It makes perfect sense. You put your observation post on a dormant volcano, estimate the subsidence rate, and now you have some idea how long your outpost is going to have a nice, stable platform."

"And then we come along," Kester said quietly.

"Exactly. And then we come along. Assume they have been observing us from the very beginning. What've we done? We've blown their mission parameters all to hell, the same way their presence here snapped Piotre's mind a year ago. We're the anomaly, the unplanned event. So, they sit, and wait, and watch, while I dance around like an idiot, teaching Human History 101.

"And then look what happens: we find a way to tell them that, on some level, we get it. Even though nothing in the history records I shared would suggest anything of the kind! Everything I communicated could only have been taken to mean that we are ourselves a pre-holocaust race, ticking away on a breakneck tech-adoption curve, racing to our doom. I made a record practically celebrating just how fast we achieved our current technology.

"So, what do you think they do, whoever they are? They stay quiet because they're confused. The only thing that makes sense is that we're some sort of pre-holocaust race that just happened to make it this far, and what are the odds of that?"

"So the tent, and your trick with the pressure change," the Interlocutor said. "To put it in my language, you found a way to empathize. To say we understand you despite all evidence to the contrary."

"Exactly," Nya said. "And then look what happens! We confuse things even further because we start a war up in orbit. You have to figure they noticed the thermonuclear explosion fifty thousand kilometers overhead. How do you suppose they might interpret that? What would they do?

"I think they're going to leave. And, just in case it isn't clear enough, they set a clock ticking in a wavelength we can see, in a language we understand, with the very timing that we ourselves have been discussing.

"But before they go, they've left us with a decision." She nodded to the pitch-black aperture in the artifact's side.

"Whether we go with them? Is that what you're saying?" Feyis asked.

"That's exactly what I'm saying."

"So, we're to be emissaries?"

"Or research cadavers," Kester said darkly.

Nya paused. "You're right, of course," she said after a moment. "We might even be killed by accident. There's no guarantee we wouldn't drop dead in ten steps due to a simple misunderstanding."

"But why?" Feyis demanded. "Why leave any potential for misunderstanding? What you're saying makes as much sense as anything else in the last year, but why be so bloody vague about all this? If they know enough to understand everything we've said, to use our numerical system and communicate in our symbology, to open a door we won't even have to duck to get through—then why not let us see inside?"

"It's a leap of faith," Kester said. "Maybe it really is the Machine God."

Nya gave the girl a long look. "Null data. Those were your words," she said.

"Exactly," Kester said. "Maybe they want to see us proceed in the complete absence of information. To find out how we grapple with the unknown."

"Your upbringing speaking?"

Kester nodded. "The Prophet always said we'd be tested."

"Is that what you believe?" Nya asked.

Kester laughed, but it sounded hollow. "Of course not. I don't believe in anything. You should know that by now."

"Well, you might still be right," she said. "It could be a test of faith. Or maybe they're trying to give us maximal choice with the least possible information because they're running an experiment and they don't want to bias the outcomes any further.

"If I'm right, we've badly exceeded their mission parameters. Imagine they were expecting to wake up a couple of million years from now and see if this planet's ecosphere had repaired itself, and instead, they blundered into a First Contact mission themselves." She almost laughed at the irony.

"I mean, what if on some level they're just a bunch of bloody ichthyologists too?"

"Your point is made, Doctor," the Interlocutor said. "But there's a broader issue here. A moral one. You are in scientific command. Agent Quinque is in charge of security. But I would assert that the choice to enter the artifact is an individual decision that each of us must make."

"I agree," Agent Quinque said. "We appear to be far beyond operational concerns. For the moment, at least," she added.

Nya took a deep breath and let it out in a long, slow exhale. "So, how about it?" she said. "Anyone want to be our species' ambassadors to the stars?"

Feyis looked at Callie. "What do you think? The adventure of a lifetime? The ultimate in fieldwork?"

"You cannot possibly be serious," Callie said.

"The alternative isn't great. No telling what Magellanix will do."

"I'll take my chances with the drop-ship." She took Feyis's hands in hers. "I've got too much to live for here."

"There's your answer, Doctor," Feyis said. "We're staying."

"I understand." In another time, another place, Nya would have felt genuine happiness for the two of them. *How odd*, she thought, *that here are the only two humans I have seen in a year that might be in love.* "Kester, how about you?"

"I'm not going in there," Kester said.

She nodded. "Agent Quinque?"

"I still have a job to do, Doctor. The safety of those who remain will be my responsibility. Also, I'm the only one that knows how to fly the drop-ship."

"A few minutes ago, you were willing to wield it like a blowtorch for the sake of destroying everything in this crater."

"Yes," Agent Quinque said. "But now our mission parameters have changed."

"What about him?" Feyis asked suddenly, nodding to Piotre Raskovich, who was now awake but had neither moved nor spoken. "Does he get a choice too?"

"I think he should," Nya said.

"There are security concerns," Agent Quinque said.

Nya gave the agent a look. "How so?"

"Because, Doctor, it is still my responsibility to preserve our option to end his life rather than let him return to Magellanix control with what he knows."

"Well, that's blunt," Piotre Raskovich said, speaking for the first time. "I don't suppose you'd care to at least ask me if I want to go before you decide whether to terminate me on the spot?"

Agent Quinque gave him a chilling look. "Would you?" she said.

"My Conditioning would compel me to stay," he said. "If it were still in charge. In fact, I no longer know exactly what is guiding my decisions." He grimaced. "I too am well beyond my mission parameters."

"We can't just hand you over to Magellanix," Agent Quinque said. "No matter what state your behavioral control mechanisms are in."

"No, you cannot. If it came to that, you would be forced to kill me, and my only consolation is that you are professional enough that it would be painless. And so, I find myself compelled to go. Though I will make a terrible emissary," he went on, smiling sickly. "My mind is badly broken. My body is equally ruined by the life I have led. What could they possibly learn from me?"

"I imagine quite a lot," the Interlocutor said. "Anyway, I think I'll go with you."

"Seriously?" Nya said. She couldn't imagine it; had never even considered the possibility.

"Yes, Doctor. There is balance in it. Piotre and I have been together in this almost from the beginning. We are two logical endpoints, two solutions to humanity's greatest problem. How should we organize, to build collectives that can accomplish more than individuals? And, of course, we are perfect examples of the price individuals have paid for that pursuit."

She paused, then gave her trademark minutest of shrugs.

"But what about you, Doctor?"

"Do you know, I think for the first time, I have hope," Nya said. "That it can be done. That sentience can be survived. Whether the artifact is, whether its builders evolved or were themselves manufactured, it's given me a reason to believe. If another species made it this far, maybe we can too. But as for what I want to do?"

She blinked, willing herself not to cry. "I want to go home."

CHAPTER 60

In the end, they were faced with the most trivial of decisions. What, exactly, should they pack? They were making it up as they went, Nya thought, without precedent or protocol.

The consensus was to keep things simple. Piotre and the Interlocutor would bring enough food and water to sustain themselves for two weeks, and—they hoped—provide the artifact examples to copy, presuming the artifact's builders possessed the technology to do so.

They would wear the clothes on their back and bring a spare set. This was to demonstrate the custom of washing and changing.

Nya tried to insist that they take one of the weavers, but the Interlocutor refused. "You'll need them where you're going," she said. "You could wind up on one of Ragnarock's moons for years."

Agent Quinque had agreed. "Redundancy would improve our odds of survival."

"Exactly," the Interlocutor said. "It's difficult to imagine it will make much difference for us. Besides, Feyis isn't coming, and neither Piotre nor I want to lug the thing around."

So, Nya had given up the argument, but she did persuade them to take along a copy of her History Lesson, encoded on a tiny solid-state memory device. A symbolic offering, if nothing else.

At this point, the countdown showed just over seven hours to go.

"I believe it's time, Dr. Solarin," the Interlocutor said.

"I suppose you're right. I wish I knew the right words to say for an occasion such as this."

"Well," the Interlocutor said, "there is the very real possibility we will be right back. For all we know, they merely want to see if we will step through, and plan to deposit us unceremoniously on the ground immediately after."

Nya forced a laugh. "You're right, of course," she said. "It's possible. But I don't believe it."

"Neither do I. But please—be at peace, Doctor. Neither fear for us, nor mourn us, nor celebrate us as ambassadors of our species. As different as we are, Piotre and I are both behaving perfectly selfishly in this. There is no altruism here. Humans take actions that meet their needs, whether they know it or not, and this is no different. Which is as it should be, for what we are going to do."

"Humans take actions that meet their needs," Nya repeated. "Is that what you learned in your time as a Human Resources officer?"

The Interlocutor smiled. "That and the value of physical contact," she said. She stepped across the vestibule, surprising Nya by giving her a hug.

Nya returned it full-force, once again forced to blink back tears.

The opening in the artifact was just wide enough for two to walk abreast. The Interlocutor and Piotre carried a single bag between them, which the Interlocutor slung over her shoulder.

"What about you, Piotre?" Feyis asked. "Any last words?"

"Only that I tend to agree with the Interlocutor," Piotre Raskvoich said. "More often than not."

Then the two of them joined hands, stepped through the door, and vanished.

Seconds ticked by, then minutes, with the artifact as usual not changing at all.

Then the door disappeared. It was there one moment and gone the next, faster than the human eye could follow. Much later, they would review Callie's recording, dissect it moment by moment, frame by frame, and see that there was, in fact, a transition phase, that the door disappeared from the outside in, diminishing to a single albedo-zero point in the center which then winked away, returning the entire surface to the silvery substance of the artifact itself as though it had never been.

But in the moment, the door appeared simply to vanish.

And in the next, the ground began to shake.

It began as a low-frequency tremor, so subtle it caused Nya to sit down at first, thinking it was a wave of dizziness or even simple nausea. Then the vibration increased in intensity. The others around her were reacting to it as well, struggling to keep their feet.

There followed a deep rumbling sound like a distant sonic boom, except that it came from beneath them.

"The shaft," Feyis said.

Nya nodded. "I get the idea that we are beginning to run out of time here," she said.

"I agree," Agent Quinque said. "A recommendation, Doctor?"

"By all means."

"We should get away from here. Out of the crater and off the mountain, while we still have time."

"I second that," Callie said.

"Third," Feyis added.

So they did.

They left cameras behind, remote monitoring that would relay measurements to the drop-ship. Then the five of them began the long trek out of the crater.

When they reached the rim, the swirling snow had concealed the artifact once more. They paused for a brief rest, looking back at where they had been, but there was nothing to see.

They formed into a single rope team and began the descent. Feyis led; Nya followed, with Callie and Kester behind and Agent Quinque anchoring the rear. They stepped across the gaping bergschrund and got down to work, settling into a rhythm for their descent.

Nya tried not to think about the timer ticking down and how many hours remained to them.

They'd make it, Feyis assured her. Trust him; he ought to know.

He was right. Six hours later, they stepped across the last of the crevasses, the one where Feyis had almost died. Nya thought she heard him mutter something, but whatever he said was lost to the wind.

Then they were hiking down a snowfield, and then crossing more rocks, and at last they found themselves trudging across the long, flat stretch of ground to their landing site.

The drop-ship was as they had left it. At Agent Quinque's command, it extended its landing ramp, re-forming a bridge over the gaping pit blasted when they'd landed.

"A thought," Feyis said. "Before we go?"

"What's that?" Nya said.

"The plan is to hide on a moon, correct?"

"Pretty much, yeah."

"And this ship has an unused weight allowance? More than enough thrust for the five of us, given that we left gear and people behind?"

"There is extra lift capacity, yes," Agent Quinque said. "What's your point, Mr. Sado?"

"We should bring some ice with us," Feyis said. "It might be useful, where we're going."

The agent nodded once and unslung her pack. She removed a laser cutter from her gear and got to work without a word, chopping ice into blocks they would have to haul across the ramp.

Nya suspected the agent was embarrassed that she hadn't thought of it. What could be more critical to their long-term security than enough fresh water to drink?

Well. The woman had been proven human after all. There was a certain charm to it.

When their preparations were complete, they strapped in, ready to launch.

"We have a decision to make," Agent Quinque said, appearing satisfied when they all had found their positions and their ice was safely stowed. "We have twenty minutes left. Trust Mr. Sado at his word; our descent consumed exactly as much time as he said it would. We can leave. Equally, we might choose to remain."

"You're going to have to explain that," Feyis said. "Seven hours and a few thousand vertical meters ago, I thought you said you wanted to get away from here."

"I should've been more precise. In the emotion of the moment"—and there, Agent Quinque actually grimaced—"I misspoke. More correctly, I wanted us to retain optionality on departure, which required an immediate exfiltration from the crater."

"The difference being?"

"*Accipiter,*" Kester said. The young woman had been staring at the dropship's cabin floor, seeming lost in thought.

"Correct," Quique said. "There is the chance that *Accipiter* dispatched more than one weapons remote in-system. There may be an active missile overhead."

"Ah," Feyis said. "And you think if the artifact is about to leave, its departure could provide a distraction?"

"Yes. But it is a matter of balancing risk. Dr. Solarin, your opinion?"

Nya thought it over. "It's impossible to know," she finally said. "I mean, the volcano is dormant. It's unlikely that the shaft beneath the artifact is somehow plugging a magma core. Callie, you're the materials scientist; what do you think?"

Callie considered. “If we had built the artifact, and the shaft is a launching mechanism of some kind, we wouldn’t waste energy on anything other than thrust. It’s inefficient. A launch might destabilize the volcano by accident in the process, but in that case, you’d think we’d have enough warning to get clear. Of course,” she added, “this is all conjecture. I really have no idea.”

“Welcome to my career,” Nya said grimly. “I think this one is your decision, Agent Quinque.”

Quinque said nothing immediately, instead panning and zooming through the images still streaming from the crater, paging through data and readouts from the monitoring equipment they had left behind.

Nothing had changed.

“Very well,” Quinque said finally. “We will hold the launch for the moment. At the first sign of geologic instability, we go. If the artifact is built like one of our ships and there’s some blast shield under it we can’t see, and a fusion device under that to provide the shockwave to pop the artifact out of that crater like a cork from a bottle—to use one of the Interlocutor’s metaphors—there’s no telling if we’ll have time to get clear or not. If the issue is geologic instability, yes. A sudden nuclear detonation, no.”

“Fair enough,” Nya said. “We wait—for now.”

The last few minutes seemed to pass with agonizing slowness. Then, with just under ten minutes remaining, the artifact began to sink. With cameras they had positioned at the base, they could see the rock surrounding the artifact vaporize, billowing away in great roiling clouds of smoke. Whether this was from heat, chemical or biological dissolution, or some other molecular process, Nya couldn’t tell.

When it was halfway below the surface of the crater, the artifact settled to a halt.

“Picking up deep seismic activity,” Feyis said. “I’m seeing temperature anomalies in the crater as well,” he added. “It’s getting hot up there.”

“Twenty seconds to go,” Agent Quinque said.

“Really hot,” Feyis added.

“Ten.”

“Surface earthquake,” Feyis said. “Sides of the crater are starting to shake.”

“Five. Four. Three. Two. One. Zero.”

And then it was gone.

They had no way to track it, no cameras to follow its passing, and no active remotes to ping it as it went. The artifact was simply there one moment and gone the next. They couldn't even guess the acceleration profile, how many gees it had pulled. Maybe the Interlocutor and Piotre were dead already, Nya thought, smashed flat, pulped in an instant.

Or maybe they'd been pickled and preserved.

Or . . . perhaps the makers of the artifact had transcended such mundane things as gravity and kept their internal environment however they liked.

There was no way to know.

"The crater is collapsing!" Callie said. "Half the wall is giving way."

"Seismic activity still increasing," Feyis said. "This is going to get worse before it gets better."

"Right," Agent Quinque said. "Launching now. Settle in, people. We are departing in fifteen seconds."

The drop-ship's engines roared to life, hydrazine under extreme pressure, doing things the truly old-fashioned way, with a shock of noise and an unpleasant, innards-rattling vibration.

Nya breathed in, exhaled, heard Quinque say, "Launching now," and then felt a hammerblow to the chest as they were up, away, and gone.

If there had been a second missile, they never knew. Maybe there never was, or maybe everything *Accipiter* sent had already been spent to end Ian McAllister's life in some algorithmic desire for absolute certainty. Or perhaps there had been an entire arsenal waiting for them but it had been drawn away by the artifact's departure.

Whatever the case, no orbiting weapons remote detonated, terminating their journey before they ever knew they were in danger. Instead, they simply flew to the moon Quinque had chosen—the little sister, Feyis called it—keeping cameras trained aft the whole time, watching Ragnarock recede behind them.

Two days later, they found a crater in which to hide. There they settled in for what might be, as far as any of them knew, the balance of their lives.

CHAPTER 61

Kester had returned to her beginning, the child daughter of a doomed colony once more. Counting her, five remained: the indefatigable Agent Quinque, the contractors Feyis and Callie, and an increasingly morose Nya Solarin.

They'd tucked the drop-ship under an overhang at the bottom of a crater, hung their solar arrays from its walls, and tunneled inward. They made poor troglodytes. They built themselves five rooms in total, crude chambers where they could find solitude and sleep when their bodies allowed.

Like Aldan's world, life on Ragnarock's smallest moon was limited by a lack of physical resources, but in this case, it wasn't a shortage of building materials that was the problem. After all, there were no kesters to tear their home asunder. Their weavers functioned perfectly. Drawing their power from the sun, they could spin rock into habitat forever. They were even capable of reweaving themselves should the need arise and their magical inner workings begin to fail.

But they were badly short on ice. They had what they brought with them and no more. Their moon was a dead rock, with no snow banks frozen in the shade, no crystallized water laced through its dust and dirt, and no trapped veins buried deep for which they might drill.

They couldn't make fuel or oxygen. They must recycle everything and build a perfectly enclosed ecosystem, forever constrained by simple, life-giving water.

They deployed the drop-ship's radio telescope on the moon's surface, waiting and hoping for the day when *Carpathia* would call. Agent Quinque said when the ship was repaired, *Carpathia* would launch a remote to burst a transmission in-system that couldn't be back-traced to its position. In anticipation, they hard-lined their own miniature observatory to the drop-ship on weaver-spun cabling, and then Feyis and Callie camouflaged the whole thing with woven strands of netting and chunks of lunar rock.

After that, they settled in to wait.

Days turned to weeks, and weeks into months, but Kester didn't mind. She still had a puzzle to solve. There was no miracle this time, no blinding flash of insight, no sudden turning of a cryptological key in a hyperdimensional lock. Instead, the work was a steady grind, her brain worrying away at the endless patterns and combinations like the ocean eroding the land, digging channels and canals until, gradually, understanding came. She began to see how the facets related, the meaning of the alien geometry. Order crystallized from disorder as she chased and traced and followed it down and through and out until she finally knew where the artifact had gone.

Its builders hadn't just encoded a single jump point. Whoever they were, they'd left instructions for thirteen in sequence, nested together in a set of concentric spheres like a child's toy, an egg within an egg within an egg, and she knew them all.

She told no one.

Partly this was simple pragmatism. What good were interstellar navigational instructions when their ship was incapable of a jump? How could some feat of cosmic decryption aid them when the only crypt that mattered was the rock one in which they lived?

But it was more than that.

Knowledge, she now knew, was—decidedly—power. Piotre Raskovich had taught her that much. Information held value, and she had no desire to tell anyone how valuable she had just become.

Kester had done her share of extravehicular work during their initial excavation phase. Agent Quinque taught her how to use a suit, to stay safe in the killing environment of hard vacuum. But Kester had remained inside ever since. There was little enough outside work to do, nothing Quinque, Feyis, and Callie couldn't handle.

But now that she had deciphered the meaning of the artifact's strange surface, she found herself bored, growing as restless as the others had been all along. One day, she decided to take a trip outside their tiny lair, for no other reason than to walk on the surface of the moon.

She made it halfway up the crater wall, paused to rest on a ledge, lay back, and lost herself in the stars.

The temptation was so strong, the pull irresistible. She had come full circle and returned to making constellations in her mind.

Except Ragnarock's smallest moon was no bio-lab on Paradise. To lose track of herself out there was death measured in falling kilopascals as her suit's emergency reserves ticked away.

Hours passed. The suit chirped, then squawked, then outright screamed at her when her oxygen was almost gone.

Kester couldn't quite bring herself to care.

In the end, it was Nya Solarin who came for her, retrieving her without a word and returning her to their caves and their life-giving air.

They never spoke about it.

Kester stowed her suit and didn't go outside again.

She needed a new pastime, so she took to watching Ragnarock with their tiny observatory. Its primary mission was to listen for *Carpathia*, but they'd also left a telescope on the surface, so she worked out the geometry of Ragnarock's rotation relative to their own. Their moon was tidally locked. They had debated hiding on its dark side but, in the end, decided the advantages of observing Ragnarock directly exceeded the risk of discovery.

Kester watched the planet turn, capturing images, hoping for a glimpse of their volcano, wanting to know what had become of the crater where the artifact had rested for so long. As always, there was the cloud cover to contend with, but she had plenty of time.

Eventually, the weather cooperated, and she got a look.

The volcano was gone.

She called the doctor to share what she had found.

"So, they left no trace," Nya said. She didn't seem all that surprised. "I bet they used the same power source that launched them into space. They could have hollowed out the volcano from underneath and sunk it beneath the waves."

"I wonder if anyone will ever go back there," Kester said.

"Probably Magellanix will. They'll put down submersibles, survey whatever is left."

"That will be a lot of fieldwork."

"Don't tell Feyis and Callie," Nya replied.

"I doubt they'd be interested."

"I don't know," Nya said. "Anything might be better than this. If they wanted to switch employers again, you could hardly blame them."

Kester doubted that but said nothing more.

They decided they'd give it six months, and then use the drop-ship's broadcast capability, go active, ping away, and to hell with who might be listening. If *Accipiter* was out there somewhere, so be it.

But it never came to that. Fate had something different in store, as it so often had in Kester's short existence. Three months into their exile, they received a message at last. *Carpathia*'s repairs were complete, and if the captain or anyone else from the field crew that had been dispatched to Ragnarock was listening, they were to acknowledge the signal and help would be on the way.

Kester wondered about the veracity of the message, but whatever procedures Quinque used to validate it, the agent didn't ask for her opinion. And of course, Kester thought, Quinque might not even care if it was fake or real. Maybe even a security officer could get tired of life in exile and conclude anything was better than this.

But the message was genuine. Two weeks after they sent their response, a Carpathian shuttle arrived at their moon to take them home.

Except, of course, Kester had no home to which to return.

Carpathia was now commanded by the young lieutenant Ian McAllister had left in charge, his former navigation officer elevated to acting captain. The story the woman told them explained much. *Accipiter* had gone chasing after the artifact. *Carpathia* had watched her go on passive remotes but been unable to engage, as she was still latched onto her asteroid, her blast shield not yet functional. She had been reduced to little more than a mining colony, with dreams of one day becoming a starship again.

But *Accipiter* hadn't returned. There were no known transition points along the route she had traveled. To the newly acting captain and her remaining crew, this had made no sense at the time, but it was clear enough now. *Accipiter*'s captain had seen the artifact leave Ragnarock and had decided to go chasing after.

Sometime later, *Carpathia*'s crew had detected an emissions signature. It appeared to be a single transition event.

And that had been that. Where *Accipiter* had gone since, they had no idea. Perhaps it was still out there, surveying the terrain, conducting gravity-anomaly scans, and performing the topological computations required to search for a new jump point. Or perhaps it had returned to their system—but if so, they'd detected no sign.

The real question was simply this: what should *Carpathia* do? They'd never fight their way through whatever weapons remotes remained at the system's edge, nor could they pretend to be *Accipiter* a second time.

They were stuck between two impossible choices. Should they follow *Accipiter*, possibly still prowling around out there somewhere, with no destination in mind? Or try the impossible, turn themselves into blockade runners, try to get back out of Ragnarock's system the way they had come in?

Meanwhile, Kester was trapped between impossible choices of her own.

Per might still be alive. InterTech had a state-of-the-art bio-lab just kilometers from where he'd been shot. They might have saved him.

Maybe that's why they hadn't caught up to her in the jungle. Her captors might have assumed they could track her later at their leisure and had focused on retrieving Per first. They would have been right, too, if Nya and Johanna hadn't been nearby.

Had Per saved her twice? Once by almost dying, and again by resuming something that could hardly count as life?

She needed to return to Paradise. Needed to find out.

On the other hand, Kester alone knew where the artifact had gone. She could tell the others. But if she did, she suspected her life would never be her own again.

What should she do?

Follow after what might be the Machine God she had been raised to believe in?

Or chase a lost love who might be dead already?

Either way, she couldn't let the Carpathians kill themselves trying to run a blockade that had defeated them before. Suicide by *Accipiter* weapons remote was no answer, and Kester had no desire to spend the rest of her life hiding on a moon. She'd been raised into a cult and was free of it now. Maybe there was a Machine God, and maybe there wasn't, but for her part, she could no longer see what difference it could possibly make.

So, if they couldn't run the blockade, and she had no desire to go chasing the artifact, she'd have to give them a third way: a side door out of this system.

Kester knew she could find another transition point. But if she did, she'd turn herself into an even more valuable asset. In the end, she now understood, TransGalactic would tear her mind apart if that was what it took to figure out what InterTech had done.

It occurred to her to wonder what Piotre Raskovich would do. After all, she knew things that no one else did. She was the cipher, the answer to the riddle, the key. She could make ships jump sideways, take them through dimensions and folding conformations no other human could find.

Actually, she thought, she knew exactly what Piotre would do. And when that answer came to her, she called on the acting captain, Dr. Solarin, Agent Quinque, Feyis, and Callie because it seemed like they all ought to hear from her at the same time.

She, Kester, child of Aldan's World, scheduled a meeting, in a moment of corporate understanding that would have made the Interlocutor proud.

"I know where the artifact went," she said to them. "I can tell you how to find it. But first, I want to make a deal."

EPILOGUE

The Interlocutor smiled at Piotre Raskovich and sipped her tea. Sitting across the desk from her, the former CIO offered a slight smile in return.

The desk was positioned in a field, at the edge of a river that babbled softly past. To her profound relief, there were no heads in jars bobbing along in the current. It was just a river.

"I hated places like this," Piotre said. "I feared them endlessly. Unbound nature and open spaces. Rotten logs, and holes in the dirt where vermin scurry and crawl."

"Your employers used it against you," she said.

Piotre shrugged. "No different than you would."

"Indeed."

"So, where are we now?" he asked. "Some shared delusion? Is this a group hallucination? Have we been uploaded? Am I dreaming of you, or are you dreaming of me?"

"Well," she said, "we're in my metaphor."

"So I assumed," he said. "But if I walked up the trail into these woods behind us, found a nurse log, and kicked it apart, do you think there'd be a centipede waiting inside?"

"Care to find out?"

He laughed. "Not really."

A goblet of wine had appeared on the desk. She hadn't noticed, but there it was. Piotre reached for it.

"Cheers," he said.

"To health."

Piotre took a swallow. "Martian," he said, wincing. "Horrible stuff. I stopped drinking it decades ago."

"Well. All metaphors are imperfect," she said.

"Indeed," he said, mimicking her. He took another drink and got up from the desk. He walked heavily to the shore and cast the contents of the goblet into the water in a cascading spatter of red.

"What happens now, I wonder?" he said, his back turned to her as he regarded the river rolling past.

"I don't know."

He returned to the desk and sat back down. "Not for us," he said. "I mean for the world. It seems no one is going to profit from any of this. Except perhaps InterTech, given what Kester can do. If they can reproduce the result with others."

"True," she said. "Kester's abilities should prove more valuable than something as esoteric as knowledge of the existence of alien life."

"You equivocate," Piotre said. "Why? I see the key to the universe in her. New routes, new jump points—those things mean new systems to reach, new colonies to build, wealth to extract. InterTech found a way to make the human mind open doors that will take them places no one has ever been."

"Yes," the Interlocutor said. "But there is a problem."

"Oh?"

"Your fugue state reacted badly with your broken Conditioning."

"I recall," Piotre said drily.

"I experienced something similar," she said. "In my case, I suffered from the return of lost memories. My mind, damaged in its own ways, interacted as poorly with hyperdimensional travel as yours."

"And?"

"I assumed it was just me. Isn't that funny for one in my profession? But then the process accelerated with Kester's jump, and it wasn't just you and me, with our extremely altered cognition. Half the crew was impacted. I interviewed a few of them afterward in the brief time before we departed in the shuttle for Ragnarock. They reported remarkably similar experiences. Demons from their past, hidden memories, old psychological wounds torn anew. And there was something else as well."

"Tell me," he said. A new drink had appeared in his hand, a clear glass with a smoky, amber-colored liquid. He sniffed it carefully.

"The ship's chronometer," she said. "We went backward in time, and not at the time scales usually observed. This wasn't a matter of the moment it takes for photons to transit atomic nuclei. We traveled backward for almost five full minutes. That jump Kester managed—it wasn't just a new twist, so to speak, on an old hyperdimensional puzzle. It was something different altogether."

"Forgive me," Piotre said. "But—so what? What difference do a few minutes make, over the scales of time and distance in question?"

"I'll tell you what I think," the Interlocutor said, taking another sip of her tea. "And you'll have to forgive me if this sounds foolish. It may be that I spent too much time with Dr. Solarin. But what if InterTech stumbled on the answer that Nya has been seeking? What if they accidentally created a method of travel, through remarkably horrific methods, inhumane, immoral, ethically indefensible means—"

"The kind of stuff any of our companies would do," he interrupted.

"Well, yes. But in spite of their process, what if by accident, they created a system of travel that requires us to confront our own demons in order to use it? What if all the wealth of the universe can only be reached by individuals self-actualized enough not to be crippled in the process?"

Piotre took a long, slow drink.

"You did spend too much time around the doctor," he said at last. "But if you're right, it doesn't sound like the kind of thing that happens by accident."

"Don't tell me you're a religious man after all this."

"Not particularly, no."

She shrugged. "Well, I don't suppose we'll ever find out. I have a feeling that wherever we're going, what happens next will play out on very different time scales than even you and I are accustomed to."

It was Piotre's turn to shrug. He mimicked her so perfectly, it almost seemed as though she was talking to herself.

"You never know," he said.

"That is true," she agreed. "Even after all this time, for all we humans have built and said and done, individually and together, that remains true. You never really know."

ACKNOWLEDGMENTS

Carpathians began a long time ago as a very different novel and has been helped immeasurably by many people along the way. Some of the core ideas were conceived in the time during and following my years studying oceanography, which seems a lifetime ago. A lot of friends over the years patiently listened to me talk through the ideas for this book, read early drafts, and offered their thoughts, kind advice, and—most importantly—encouragement.

You all know who you are. I thank each and every one of you.

A very special thank you to Susan McDougall and David Biek for revisions, editing (lots of editing!), and feedback all along the way.

The cover art is by the amazing Chris Era. You can find him at Fiverr.com/chris_era.

And speaking of art, a final thank-you to Molly, for helping me never forget the importance of it in our lives.

ABOUT THE AUTHOR

Paul A. Dixon is an award-winning science fiction and fantasy author as well as a proud father, long-distance runner, climate technologist, and driftwood artist. Dixon is deeply convinced that the pun is the highest form of humor. Dixon resides in Washington.